D0387647

Women I've Known

Women I've Known

New and Selected Stories

Greg Johnson

Ontario Review Press ✦ Princeton, NJ

Ontario Review Press
9 Honey Brook Drive
Princeton, NJ 08540

Distributed by W. W. Norton & Co.
500 Fifth Avenue
New York, NY 10110

Library of Congress Cataloging-in-Publication Data

Johnson, Greg, 1953–
    Women I've known : new and selected stories / Greg Johnson.—
1st ed.
        p. cm.
        ISBN 0-86538-119-4
        I. Title.

    PS3560.O3775W66 2007
    813'.6—dc22
    [B]
                                                    2006053271

First Edition

ACKNOWLEDGMENTS

I would like to acknowledge my editors at Ontario Review Press, Raymond Smith and Joyce Carol Oates, for their help in bringing this project to fruition. Their generosity and discernment have been most appreciated. I would also like to acknowledge my former editor at Johns Hopkins University Press, John Irwin, for his help in ushering three of my previous collections into print. Finally, many thanks are due to the editors of the following magazines and anthologies, where these stories originally appeared, usually in slightly different form:

"Crazy Ladies": *Southern Humanities Review* and *Prize Stories: The O. Henry Awards*
"Leavings": *Kansas Quarterly*
"Wildfires": *Cimarron Review*
"The Metamorphosis": *Ontario Review*
"The Boarder": *Southern Review* and *New Stories from the South: The Year's Best*
"Fever": The PEN Syndicated Fiction Project
"A Dry Season": *Missouri Review*
"Escalators": *Carolina Quarterly*
"Hemingway's Cats": *South Carolina Review*
"Evening at Home": *Prairie Schooner*
"Scene of the Crime": *Southern Review*
"Alliances of Youth": *Kansas Quarterly*
"Last Encounter with the Enemy": *Chattahoochee Review*
"To the Madhouse": *Ontario Review*
"Double Exposure": *Ontario Review*
"First Surmise": *Michigan Quarterly Review*
"Women I've Known": *Blithe House Quarterly*
"Shameless": *Ontario Review*
"Who, What, When, Where": *Southeast Review*
"His Parents, Naked": *TriQuarterly*

—*for* Dedrick Burch

CONTENTS

V: New Stories

I

from *Distant Friends*

Crazy Ladies

Every Southern town had one, and ours was no exception. One year, my sister and I had an after-school routine that included watching the Mouseketeers on TV, holding court in the neighborhood treehouse we'd built, along with several other kids, in a vacant lot down the street, and finally, as dusk began and we knew our mother would soon be calling us to supper, visiting the big ramshackle house where the crazy lady lived. Often she'd be eating her own supper of tuna fish and bean salad, sitting silently across from her bachelor son, John Ray, who was about the same age as our parents. Becky would slither along through the hydrangea bushes, then scrunch down so I could stand on her shoulders and get my eyes and forehead—just barely—over the sill of the Longworths' dining-room window. After a few minutes I'd get down and serve as a footstool for Becky. More often than not we dissolved into a laughter so uncontrollable that we had to race back through the bushes, snapping branches as we went, and then dart around the corner of the house to avoid being caught by John Ray, who sometimes heard us and would jump up from the table, then come fuming out the back door. He never did catch us, and to my knowledge was never quick enough even to discover who we were. Naturally his mother didn't know, and didn't care. But there came a time—that summer afternoon, the year Becky was thirteen and I was eleven—when the crazy lady took her obscene revenge.

For me, that entire summer was puzzling. Our father, the town druggist, had begun keeping unusual hours. We could no longer count on his kindly, slump-shouldered presence at the supper table, and when he did join us there was a crackling energy in him, a playfulness toward Becky and me that he'd never shown when we were younger. And while our father, a balding and slightly overweight man in his forties, had taken on this sudden, nervous gaiety, our mother underwent an alarming change of her own. Her normally delicate features, framed by fine, wavy auburn hair, had paled to the point of haggardness. There was a new brusqueness in her manner—she scrubbed the house with a grim ferocity, she made loud clattering noises when she worked in the kitchen—and also a certain inattention toward her children, a tendency to focus elsewhere when she talked to us, or to fall into sudden reveries. This bothered me more than it did Becky, for it seemed that even she was changing. In the fall she'd be starting junior high, and she'd begun calling me "Little Brother" (with a slight wrinkling of her nose) and spending long hours alone in her bedroom. All through childhood we'd been inseparable, and Becky had always been called a tomboy by the neighborhood kids, even by our parents; but now she'd started curling her hair and painting her stubby nails, gingerly paging through movie magazines while they dried. What was wrong with everyone? I wanted to ask—but when you're eleven, of course, you can't translate your puzzlement into words. For a long while I stayed bewildered, feeling that the others had received a new set of instructions on how to live, but had forgotten to pass them along to me.

One humid afternoon in August, the telephone rang; from the living room, we could hear our mother snatch up the kitchen extension.

"What?" she said loudly, irritated. "Slow down, Mother, I can't make out—"

At that point she called to us to turn down the TV; from my place on the floor I reached quickly and switched the volume completely off, earning a little groan from Becky. She sat cross-legged on the couch with a towel wrapped tightly around her head, like a turban. We'd been watching *American Bandstand.*

"*You* turn it up," I said, with the same defiant smirk she'd begun using on me.

"Hush," Becky whispered, leaning forward. "I think something's wrong with Grandma."

We sat quietly, listening. Our mother's voice had become shrill, incredulous.

"Why did you let her in?" she cried. "You know she's not supposed to—"

A long silence. Whenever our mother was interrupted, Becky and I exchanged a puzzled look.

"Listen, just call John Ray down at the bank. The operator, Mother—she'll give you the number. Oh, I know you're nervous, but— Yes, you can if you try. Call John Ray, then go back in the living room and be nice to her. Give her something to eat. Or some coffee."

Silently, Becky mouthed the words to me: *the crazy lady.*

I nodded, straining to hear our mother's voice. She sounded weary.

"All right, I'll call Bert," she said, sighing. "We'll get there as soon as we can."

When she stopped talking, Becky and I raced into the kitchen.

"What is it, Mama?" Becky asked, excited. "Is it—"

"It's Mrs. Longworth," Mother said. Absent-mindedly, she fiddled with my shirt collar, then looked over at Becky. "She's gotten out of the house again, and somehow ended up in your grandmother's living room." Briefly, she laughed. She shook her head. "Anyway, I've got to call your father. We'll meet him over there."

But what had the crazy lady done? we asked. *Why was Grandma so frightened? Why were we all going over there?* Mother ignored our questions. Calmly she dialed the pharmacy, setting her jaw as though preparing to do something distasteful.

Within five minutes we were in the car, making the two-mile drive to Grandma Howell's. Dad was already there when we arrived, but he hadn't gone inside.

"Well, what's going on?" Mother asked him. She sounded angry, as if Dad were to blame for all this.

He looked sheepish, apprehensive. He always perspired heavily, and I noticed the film covering his balding forehead, the large damp circles at his armpits. He wore the pale blue, regulation shirt, with *Denson Pharmacy—Bert Denson, Mgr.* stitched above the pocket, but he'd removed his little black bow tie and opened his collar.

"I just got here," Dad said, helplessly. "I was waiting for you."

Mother made a little *tsk*ing noise, then turned in her precise, determined way and climbed the small grassy hill up to Grandma's porch. Dad followed, looking depressed, and Becky and I scampered alongside, performing our typical duet of questions. *Do you know what's wrong?* Becky asked him. *Why did you wait for us?* I asked. *Is Mother mad at you?* Becky asked. *Are you scared of the crazy lady?* I asked. *Scared to go inside?*

I asked this, of course, because *I* was scared.

Dad only had time to say, uneasily, that Grandma's St. Augustine was getting high again, and I'd have to mow it next Saturday. It was just his way of stalling; he'd begun evading a lot of our questions lately.

The front door was already open, and as we mounted the porch steps I could see Grandma Howell's dim outline from just inside the screen. Then the screen opened and I heard her say, vaguely, "Why, it's Kathy and Bert, and the kids..." From inside the room I heard a high, twittering sound, like the cries of a bird.

In the summertime Grandma Howell kept all the shades drawn in her living room; she had an attic fan, and the room was always wonderfully cool. It was furnished modestly, decorated with colorful doilies Grandma knitted for the backs of chairs and the sofa, and with dozens of little knickknacks—gifts from her grandchildren, mostly—set along the mantel of the small fireplace and cluttering the little, spindly-leg tables, and with several uninspired, studiously executed paintings (still lifes, mostly) done by my grandfather, who had died several years before I was born. A typical grandmother's house, I suppose, and through the years it had represented to us kids a sanctuary, a place of quiet wonder and privilege, where we were fed ginger cookies and Kool-Aid, and where Grandma regaled us with stories of her childhood down in Mobile, where her family had been among the most prominent citizens, or of her courtship by that rapscallion, Jacob Howell, who'd brought her northward (that is, to our town—which skirted the northern edge of Alabama) and kept her there. Grandma liked to roll her china-blue eyes, picturing herself as a victim of kidnapping or worse; through the years she refined and elaborated her act to rouse both herself and us to helpless laughter, ending the story by insisting tongue-in-cheek that she'd met, and adjusted to, a fate worse than death. (Grandfather Howell was a postal clerk, later the postmaster, and by all accounts a gentle, kind, rather whimsical figure in the town; it was always clear that Grandma had adored him.) Now, at sixty-one, she looked twenty years younger, the blue eyes still clear as dawn, her figure neat, trim, and erect, her only grandmotherly affectation being the silvery blue hair she wore in a tidy bun. On that day I decided she'd always seemed brave, too, even valorous in her quiet, bustling self-sufficiency, for that afternoon I saw in her eyes for the first time a look of unmitigated fear.

"Yes, come in, come in," she said, still in that vague, airy way, trying to pretend that our visit was a surprise. Then she turned back to the room's dim interior—her head moving stiffly, I thought, as if her neck ached—and said in a polite, tense, hostessy voice: "Why look, Mrs. Longworth, it's my daughter and her family. We were just talking about them."

Grandma Howell nodded, as though agreeing with herself, or encouraging Mrs. Longworth's agreement. The twittering birdlike sound came again.

By now we were all inside, standing awkwardly near the screen. Slowly, our eyes adjusted. On the opposite side of the room, and in the far corner of Grandma's dainty, pale-blue sofa, sat Mrs. Longworth: a tiny, white-haired woman in a pink dress, a brilliant green shawl, and soiled white sneakers, one of whose laces had come untied. The five of us stared, not feeling our rudeness, I suppose, because for the moment Mrs. Longworth seemed unaware of our presence. She kept brushing wispy strands of the bone-white hair from her forehead, though it immediately fell back again; and she would pat her knees briskly with open palms, as if coaxing some invisible child to her lap. It was the first time I had encountered the crazy lady up close, and my wide-eyed scrutiny confirmed certain rumors that had circulated in the town for years—that she wore boys' sneakers, for instance, along with white athletic socks; that her tongue often protruded from her mouth, like a communicant's (as it did now, quivering with a sort of nervous expectancy); and that, most distasteful of all, the woman was unbelievably dirty. Even across the dimmed room I detected a rank, animal odor, and there was a dark smear—it looked like grease—along one of her fragile cheekbones. The palms and even the backs of her hands were filthy, the tiny nails crusted with grime. Like me, the rest of my family had been stunned into silence at the very sight of her; it was only when her tongue popped back inside her mouth, and she cocked her head to begin that eerie, high-pitched trilling once again, that my mother jerked awake and abruptly stepped forward.

"Mrs. Longworth?" she said loudly, trying to compete with the woman's shrill birdsong. "We haven't met before, but I'm—"

She gave it up. Mrs. Longworth's head moved delicately as she trilled, cocking from side to side as if adjudging the intricate nuances of her melody—which was no melody at all, of course, but only a high, sweet, patternless frenzy of singing. (For it was clear that Mrs. Longworth thought she was singing; her face and eyes, which she still had not turned to us, had the vapid, self-satisfied look of the amateur performer.) She would stop when she was ready to stop. My mother stepped back, then drew Grandma closer. They began a whispered conference.

"How did she get in?" my mother said hoarsely. "Why did you—"

"It happened so fast," Grandma interrupted. Her face had puckered, in an uncharacteristic look of chagrin. "I was outside, watering the shrubs, and suddenly there she was, standing in the grass. Right away I knew who she was, but she looked so—so frail and helpless, just standing there. Then she asked for a glass of iced tea. She asked in a real sweet way, and it was so hot out, and she didn't *act* crazy. But once we got inside…"

Grandma's voice trailed away. I saw that her hands were shaking.

"You *know* what happened the last time she got loose," Mother said. She was almost hissing. "Wandered down to the courthouse and started screeching all kinds of things, crazy things, and then started taking off her clothes! In broad daylight! It took four men to restrain her before John Ray finally got there."

Becky whispered, excitedly, "But doesn't he keep her locked up? At school the girls all say—"

"Yes, yes," Mother said impatiently, with a little shushing motion of her hand. "But she managed to get out, somehow. I've never understood why John Ray can't hire someone to stay with her in the daytime, or else have her committed. My Lord," she said, whirling back upon Grandma, "just imagine what could have happened. People like her can get violent, you know."

"Ssh. Kathy, please," Grandma said anxiously. She glanced back at the crazy lady, who had continued trilling to herself, though more softly now. "She isn't like that, really. I don't think she'd hurt anyone. In fact, if you'd heard what she told me—"

"Mother, the woman's crazy!" my mother whispered, hard put to keep her voice down. "You can't pay any attention to what she says."

"What was it?" Becky asked, and though I was afraid to say anything, I seconded her question by vigorously nodding my head.

"Hush up," Mother said, giving a light, warning slap to Becky's shoulder blade, "or I'll send you both outside."

Now my father spoke up. "Listen, Kathy," he said, "we ought to just call John Ray down at the bank. He'll come get her, and that'll be that."

"I've a mind to call the police," Mother said, and I looked at her curiously. She had sounded hurt.

"She hasn't done anything," Dad said gently. "And anyway, it's none of our business."

Grandma pressed her hands together, as if to stop their shaking. "Oh, if you'd heard what she told me, once I brought her inside. I gave her the iced tea, and a little saucer of butter cookies, and for a while she sat there on the sofa, with me right beside her, and she just talked in the sweetest way. Said she was just out for a walk this afternoon, but hadn't realized how hot it was. She said the tea was delicious, and asked what kind I bought. Hers always turned cloudy, she said. And I'd started thinking to myself, This woman isn't crazy at all. She dresses peculiar, yes, and she should bathe more often, but people have just been spreading ugly gossip all these years, exaggerating everything. Anyway, I gave her more tea, and tried to be nice to her. She kept looking around the room, saying how pretty it was. She noticed Jacob's pictures, and couldn't believe he'd done such beautiful work. She asked if I still missed him, like she missed Mr. Longworth, and if I ever got lonesome, or frightened…. And it was then that she changed, so suddenly that I couldn't believe my ears. She started talking about John Ray, and saying the most horrible things, but all in that same sweet voice, as if she was just talking about the weather. Oh, Kathy, she said John Ray wanted—wanted to kill her, that he was going to take her into the attic and chop her into little pieces. She said he beats her, and sometimes won't let her eat for days on end, but by then she'd started using her husband's name—you know, mixing up the names. One minute she'd be saying Carl, the next she was back to John Ray. And pretty soon she was just spouting gibberish, and she'd started that crazy singing of hers. She said did I want to hear a song, and that's when I came to phone you. I didn't know what to do—I didn't—"

Tears had filled her eyes. Mother reached out, taking both her hands. "Never mind, you were just being kind to her," she said. "Bert's right, of course—we'll just call John Ray, and that'll be that."

Grandma couldn't speak, but her blue eyes had fixed on my mother's with a frightened, guilty look. It was then that Mrs. Longworth's eerie trilling stopped, and we heard, from the sofa: "Bert's right, of course, we'll just call John Ray. And that'll be that." The voice was sly, insinuating—it had the mocking, faintly malicious tone of a mynah bird.

I looked at Dad. His face had reddened, his mouth had fallen partway open.

"Would you like some more tea?" Grandma asked, in a sweet overdone voice. She inclined her head, graciously, though it was clear that she couldn't bring herself to take another step toward Mrs. Longworth. But the crazy lady didn't seem to mind. She cocked her head, and at the very moment I feared she would resume her weird singing, she said in a casual, matter-of-fact way, "No thanks, Paulina. I like the tea, but it isn't sweet enough." And she smiled, rather balefully; her teeth looked small and greenish.

Grandma began, "I could add more sugar—"

"Do you have Kool-Aid?" Mrs. Longworth asked. "That's my favorite drink, but my son won't let me have it."

"Yes, I think so," Grandma said, uncertainly. "I'll go and look."

"Red, please," Mrs. Longworth said. "Red's the best."

Grandma hurried back to the kitchen, leaving the rest of us to stare awkwardly at the old woman, while she looked frankly back at us. She had a childlike directness, but her eyes glittered, too, with the wry omniscience of the aged. Particularly when she looked down at Becky and me, her glance seemed full of mischief, as though she were exercising her right to a second childhood. And there was something in her glance that I could only feel as love, born of some intuitive sympathy. Young as I was, I remember sharing Grandma's thought: This woman isn't crazy at all.

For the moment, her attention had fixed on Becky. She held out a dirty, clawlike hand, as though to draw my sister closer by some invisible string.

"You're a pretty girl," she said, in the tone one uses for very young children. "Such pretty hair, and those cute freckles.... I used to have freckles, when I was young. I was a pretty girl."

She shook her head, as though hard put to say how pretty. "And I had nice dresses, cotton and gingham, all trimmed in lace. I'll bet you like pretty dresses. Your little nose is turned up, just like mine was."

Becky looked spellbound; her face had paled. "Thank you—thank you very much—" she stammered.

"Would you like to have some of the dresses I wore?" the old woman asked. "They're up in the attic, in a special trunk. We'll steal the key from John Ray. The dresses are safe, no bloodstains and none of them ripped. You could wear them to church, or when the young men come calling." She raised one finger of the still-outstretched hand. "But you'd have to bring them back. You couldn't steal them. We'll sneak them back late one night, when John Ray's asleep."

Becky tried to smile. I could see how scared she was, and I stood there hoping Mrs. Longworth wouldn't turn to me. Somehow I felt safer, being a boy.

"I—I don't know—It's real nice of you—" Becky couldn't put her words together.

"And you still have pretty clothes," my mother said suddenly, stepping forward. "That's a lovely shawl, Mrs. Longworth."

The crazy lady glanced down; she pulled the shawl tighter around her shoulders, as though she'd suddenly felt a chill.

"I had a cashmere shawl, pale gray," she said, "that my husband gave me. It was before John Ray was even born. Mr. Longworth went up to Memphis, and afterward he showered me with presents. An opal ring, too. And a set of hair combs. I was a pretty woman, you know. I still wear shawls, but it's not the same. This one's green."

She spoke in a circular, monotonous rhythm, as though reminiscing to herself; as though she'd spoken these words a thousand times. It was a kind of singsong. I thought again of her birdlike trilling.

"Well, it's very pretty," Mother said.

"It's *too* green," the crazy lady said, "but I think it hurts John Ray's eyes. He has weak eyes, you know. When he goes blind, I won't have to wear it."

Grandma came in from the kitchen, carrying a tray with six glasses and a large pitcher of Kool-Aid.

"It's raspberry, Mrs. Longworth," she said as she put the tray on the coffee table. Her hands still shook, and the glasses clattered together. "I hope you like it."

She poured a glass and held it out; Mrs. Longworth grasped it quickly, then took several long gulps. She closed her eyes in bliss. "Oooh!" she cried. "Isn't that good!"

Grandma maintained her brave smile. "Kathy, would you and Bert like—"

"No, Mother. We can't stay long, and Bert has a phone call to make. Don't you, Bert?"

"Yes—right," Dad said awkwardly.

"How about you kids?" Grandma said. She was trying gamely to make all of this appear normal; then, perhaps, it would somehow *be* normal. That was always Grandma's way. But, much as I loved her, I was afraid to join in anything the crazy lady was doing. Like Becky, I stiffly shook my head.

Mrs. Longworth emptied her glass, then held it out to Grandma. "More, please," she said. While Grandma poured, she said (again in that matter-of-fact way): "You might not believe it, but I don't get good Kool-Aid like this. John Ray says it rots my teeth and my brain. I can drink water, or coffee without sugar." She made a face. "And if I don't drink it, John Ray gets mad. Now Carl, he never got mad. But my son is going to cut me with a long knife one of these days, and hide the pieces in the attic, all in separate trunks. When it starts to smell, he'll throw the trunks in the river."

She took the second glass of Kool-Aid that Grandma shakily handed her. Then she sighed, loudly, as if the details of her gruesome demise had become rather tiresome. "My son works in a bank," she said, "and his teeth are big and strong. So he can have sugar. If I try to sneak some, he pinches my arms, or hits me with a newspaper. That hurts, because he rolls it up first and makes me watch. The pinches hurt, too, but not always. He works in a bank, and so he knows all about locks and trunks and vaults. He has a map, so he can find the river when he needs it. I should be able to have red Kool-Aid, and to sing. I used to sing for Carl, and sometimes I sang to John Ray when he was a baby. Now, he's tired of taking care of me. He says, Don't I have a life to live? Don't I?" Again she spoke like a mynah bird, pitching her voice very low. "That's what he says, and that's why he wants to cut me into pieces, and why I have all these bruises on my arms. You want to see them? It's not fair, because my singing is pretty. Carl said I had a prettier voice than Jenny Lind, and he heard her in person when he was a boy. He's dead, though. You want to hear me sing?"

She stopped abruptly, her eyes widened. She waited.

"Would you like some more Kool-Aid?" Grandma asked, helplessly.

"Bert, you and Jamie go back into the kitchen. We'll wait out here with Mrs. Longworth." My mother gestured to her ear, as if holding a telephone.

Dad said, "Come on, sport," and I joined him gladly. I glimpsed Becky's look of envy and longing as we escaped into the dining room, and finally back into Grandma's tiny kitchen.

"What's wrong with her? Why does she say those things?" I asked breathlessly, while Dad fiddled with the slender phone directory. I tugged at his arm, like a much smaller child; my heart was racing. I wore only a T-shirt and short pants, and I remember shifting my weight back and forth, my bare feet unpleasantly chilled by the kitchen linoleum.

"Just simmer down, son," he said, tousling my hair in an absent-minded way. Frowning, he moved his eyes down a column of small print. "Ah, here it is. First National." He began to dial.

I didn't understand it, but I was on the verge of tears—angry
tears. When Dad finished talking with John Ray, his eyes stopped
to read the little chalkboard hanging by the phone. "I can't believe
it," he said, shaking his head. "It's still there."

Grudgingly, I followed his gaze to the chalkboard, and for the
hundredth time read its message, in that antique, elaborate hand:
*Paulie, Don't forget Gouda cheese for dinner tonight. I'll be hungry
at six o'clock sharp. (Ha ha) Jacob.* If Grandma was out when my
grandfather came home for lunch, he would leave her a note on
the chalkboard. But he hadn't lived to eat that Gouda cheese—he
was stricken at four that afternoon, and died a short while later—
and Grandma had insisted that his last message would never be
erased. Mother disapproved, saying it was morbid, and more than
once I'd seen Grandma's eyes fill with tears as they skimmed across
the words yet another time. But she could be stubborn, and the
message stayed.

"You'd know it was still there," I said, sniffling, "if you ever came
with us to visit Grandma. But you're always gone."

The resentment in my voice surprised us both. My father's
clear brown eyes flashed in an instant from anger, to guilt, to
sorrow. He shook his head; the gesture had become familiar lately,
almost a tic.

"Well, Jamie," he said slowly, licking his lips. "I guess it's time we
had a little talk."

And for five or ten minutes he did talk, not quite looking at me,
his voice filled with a melancholy dreaminess. He told me how
complicated the grown-up world was, and how men and women
sometimes hurt each other without wanting to; how they
sometimes fell "out of love," without being able to control what was
happening. He knew it must sound crazy, but he hoped that
someday I would understand. Things were always changing, he
said softly, and that was the hardest thing in the world for people
to accept. Even my mother hadn't accepted it, not yet; but he
hoped that she would, eventually. He hoped she wouldn't make it
even harder for all of us.

The speech was commonplace enough, though startling to
my young ears. As he spoke I kept thinking of Mrs. Longworth,
and how she'd talked of her husband who had died, and how

everything changed after that. I felt the cold, sickish beating of my heart inside my slender ribcage.

"But will Mother turn crazy, like Mrs. Longworth?" I asked, imagining myself, in a moment of terrified wonder, turning mean like John Ray. "Is it always the ladies who go crazy?"

Dad looked stymied; nor did I know myself what the question meant. I wouldn't even recall it until decades later, visiting my sister Becky in the hospital, where she was recuperating from a barbiturate overdose after the disappearance of her third husband. It would come back to me, in a boy's timid, faraway voice, like the echo of some terrible prophecy, a family curse. After a moment, though, my father reacted as though I'd said something amusing. Again, he tousled my hair; he smiled wearily.

"No, son," he said gently. "It's not always the ladies. You shouldn't let Mrs. Longworth get to you."

"But she said—"

"She's a crazy old lady, Jamie. She has nothing to do with us—don't pay any attention to what she says."

Hands stuffed in my pockets, one foot rubbing the toe of the other, I stood looking up at him. There were questions I wanted to ask, but I couldn't put them into words; and I somehow knew that he didn't have the answers.

"Now," Dad said, with a false heartiness, "why don't we—"

It was then that the kitchen door swung open, and there was my mother; she looked back and forth between Dad and me, as though she didn't recognize us.

"Honey? What is it?" Dad said, panicked.

"We—we couldn't stop her," Mother began, wildly. "She took off the shawl, then started unbuttoning her dress, that filthy dress—"

Dad crossed to her; he gripped her firmly by the upper arms.

"Calm down, Kathy. Now tell me what happened."

My mother was trembling. She said, haltingly, "Mrs. Longworth, she—she said she would show us, prove to us how cruel John Ray was. Before we could say anything, she started undressing. She undid the dress, then slipped it down to her waist. We—we just stared at her. We couldn't believe it. There were bruises, Bert, all over her arms and back. Big purplish bruises, and welts.... And she said, *John Ray did this*, in that little singing voice of hers—"

Dad had already released her arms. He went to the phone and dialed again. For a moment my mother's eyes locked onto mine. I'd never seen her lose her composure before, yet for some reason I was filled with a remarkable calm. From that moment forward, everything was changed between us.

"Oh God," she whispered, grief-stricken. "How I wish Becky hadn't seen."

Dad hung up the phone, then led us back into the living room; he kept one arm draped lightly around Mother's shoulder. John Ray had arrived, and sat on the sofa beside Mrs. Longworth. Her dress and shawl were in place, so it was hard for me to envision the scene my mother had described. Mrs. Longworth sat staring blankly forward, as if her mind had wandered to some distant place. John Ray held one of her hands, and sat talking amiably to Grandma. He was a big-chested man, almost entirely bald, and had teeth that were enormous, white, and perfectly straight. He smiled constantly. He was telling Grandma about all the times his mother had been "naughty," wandering into a department store, or a funeral parlor, or a private home. He hoped she hadn't been too much trouble. He hoped we understood that she meant no harm; that for years she hadn't had the slightest idea what she was doing or saying.

A small, terrible smile had frozen onto Grandma's face. She stood near the front door, her arm around Becky, who looked pale and dazed.

"She—she wasn't any trouble," my mother gasped.

"Oh no, none at all," said Grandma.

There were a few moments of silence, during which the five of us stared at the Longworths, John Ray giving back his imperturbable smile and Mrs. Longworth seeming lost in the corridors of her madness, her mouth slightly ajar, her hand resting limply inside her son's. I tried to picture John Ray beating her, or shouting his threats of a gruesome death. I decided it could not be true.

When the police arrived, neither John Ray nor his mother protested. The officer spoke to Mrs. Longworth by name, and returned a few pleasantries to the smiling John Ray. As he followed them out the door, the officer gave a knowing, barely perceptible look to my father, who nodded in acknowledgment, then turned his attention back to us.

"Well," he said, jovially, "why don't we all go out for an ice-cream sundae?"

Beyond that, I can't remember clearly. I don't believe that anyone, including myself, ever talked about the incident again; there was a tacit assumption between Becky and me that we would not resume our spying on the Longworths, but they continued to be tormented by other kids we knew. I remember feeling, for years afterward, that life had become disappointingly routine. Evidently the police hadn't charged John Ray: he was still working at First National by the time I left home for college. Nor had anything untoward happened to Mrs. Longworth: one night, about three years after wandering into our lives, she died peacefully in her sleep. It was whispered around town that John Ray was wild with grief.

By then, the tensions between my parents had all but vanished; my father's unexplained absences had stopped, my mother no longer seemed angry or depressed. Grandma stayed absorbed in her garden, her knitting, her memories. Becky had plunged headlong into her adolescent social career, and with great effort had obtained her obsessive goal: popularity. It seemed that I alone had changed. Violence had failed to erupt, and I became uneasy, tense, and vaguely suspicious. If I could have foreseen what would happen to my sister, I would not have been surprised. Like her, I left the South as soon as I was old enough, relocating to a big, overpopulated city where violence is commonplace. Although I often worry about Becky, and Mother, and even Grandma, I know there is no reason to feel guilty, just as there is no logic to the dream I've had, recurrently, for all these years: a dream in which I open a door to find the three of them perched on a sofa, cocking their heads from side to side, trilling their songs of madness and despair.

Leavings

On Claire's first morning back in Georgia, she found a feather lying in the bottom drawer of the squat, smallish chest—a "chifforobe," her aunt Lillian called it—where Mack had stored all his things, and at first she didn't react. Slowly she twirled the feather between her fingers, noting its undiminished sheen of pale silver, shading to white at the edges, and the stem shiny and hard as a thumbnail. A pigeon feather, preserved for all these years. Sleep-muddled, or perhaps a little dazed from yesterday's journey—the long flight, the jolting car trip with Lillian into this lush, dim, unforgettable countryside, the rather embarrassed reunion with Lillian herself—she merely gazed at the feather with her mint-green eyes, moved as if to replace it in the drawer, then abruptly walked to the made-up bed and dropped the feather inside her purse. She stood there, neatly dressed, a trim and competent-looking woman of thirty-six, bathed in the golden, nearly palpable sunlight pouring in at the white-curtained windows: stood waiting, as if curious about the reaction that did not come.

Though it was scarcely eight o'clock, Lillian had their breakfast already laid. "Did you sleep well?" she said airily when Claire entered the room, but of course she did not wait for a reply. She had the brisk, single-minded energy often found in elderly women of the rural South, her voice a singsong, her movements insouciant and quick. She arranged the platters of eggs, sausage, toast; she poured grapefruit juice from a pitcher. Claire, standing quietly behind her chair, wanted to begin: "I found a pigeon feather in Mack's drawer. When we were children..." But she pictured the furrowed, discouraging stare Lillian had given her last night when, waiting in baggage claim for her luggage, she'd rasped out, "Oh Lillian I'm so sorry." There had been a sickish pause, then that inscrutable wordless look. And then Lillian had asked if she'd had a pleasant journey.

Now Claire said, "Quite well, thank you. This certainly looks delicious."

Lillian sighed. "It's not up to snuff," she said, "but I've been on the phone with that man about the sale. I told him we could have it Sunday, now that you're here to help."

Claire sat, keeping her eyes lowered as she fiddled with her napkin. Lillian's matter-of-fact voice jarred her nerves, though she told herself that her aunt's pragmatism was a healthy sign in an old woman who had lost her lifelong companion and only child, and who was about to be uprooted. Even as a girl she had noted Lillian's air of invincibility, the impression she gave of relentless forward motion. To Claire herself clung a reputation for level-headedness, containment, and for long stretches of her life it seemed she had no nerves. Yet now they jangled. She sat quietly as Lillian, absorbed in buttering her toast, talked of the sale, the professional auctioneer who would drive over from Macon, the work that was in store for herself and Claire during the next few days; more than a decade had passed since their last visit, yet Lillian chatted as though they shared breakfast every morning. It had surprised Claire, at first glance, how little her aunt had changed: still the florid face, set with eyes unexpectedly hard and blue, framed by thinning whitish hair; still the mottled, quivering flesh of her upper arms, exposed by a short-sleeved housedress. She was capable, domineering, superficial, vulnerable, and doomed, Claire thought, knowing that the superficiality was deliberate, Lillian's way of deflecting any move toward intimacy or candor.

Now her aunt glanced at her, with a half-guilty look. "I do thank you, Claire," she said softly, "for taking the trouble to come down."

"I'm glad to help, of course," Claire said. "My only hesitation was—"

"It'll sure relieve my mind, putting all this behind me," Lillian cut in. She was pouring herself another cup of coffee. Claire, her senses sharpened, knew the "all this" meant more than the sale of the nursery and house where Lillian had lived for thirty years, and more than the coming days of upheaval and backbreaking work. Suddenly Claire thought of the pigeon feather—its marvelous plainness, its delicacy. Impulsively she said, "Lillian, I found a feather upstairs that Mack had saved since we were children. One summer he kept a pigeon coop, I'm sure you remember it, and we—" but she broke off, for again Lillian had given her that leveled steely gaze.

"Claire, don't even bother," she said. "I won't ever forgive that boy."

Yet he was not a boy, as Claire had understood many years ago. It was the summer her mother died: she was fourteen, Mack a couple of years older. Though Claire and her mother had always lived in town, and had not seen much of Lillian and Mack, she'd known from the day her mother entered the hospital that she'd end up "out on the farm." That was how her mother referred to Lillian's place, though it was a nursery rather than a farm. "I know your mother never liked me"—these had been Lillian's first words to Claire as they drove home from the funeral. "My own sister, yet," she'd sighed. "I guess it's because I moved out here, became a country girl," and she'd given her quick laugh. Even then Claire had known that Lillian's never having married Mack's father, whoever he was, was the real reason her mother had remained cool toward Lillian through the years. Claire's mother, though good-hearted in her way, had been above all respectable: she'd married a local attorney, had become a regular churchgoer, and after being widowed at an early age had raised her daughter quietly in her small clapboard house near the edge of town. Her sister Lillian, out there in the countryside among all that unchecked greenery, all those cultivated, sickly-bright flowers, was something of an embarrassment.

As for that peculiar son of hers, that Mack: he was not even to be acknowledged.

Yet Claire, once she had settled in and sensed Lillian's attention straying back to the nursery and her current male companion, had been pleased when Mack had taken her under his wing, as though she were the little sister he'd always wanted. From the first she'd sensed how lonely his life had been until now—the nearest farm was half an hour's walk—and she'd passively, if rather coolly, accepted his affectionate enthusiasms, listened to his eager monologues, and tried her best to overlook his rather clumsy, unprepossessing manner and appearance. In later years she'd often marveled at how unlike they'd been—Mack so garrulous, open, artless; Claire so watchful, composed, and withdrawn. Yet that summer he'd devoted himself to her, and she'd never felt the lack of other company. He took her on lengthy tours of the hothouses, naming each flower or seedling and detailing the care it required; he took her roaming through Lillian's hilly, verdant acreage ("a gift from some man," Claire's mother had snapped, when Claire had innocently inquired), with its bewildering array of kudzu, vines, and mosses, its towering elms and magnolias; and he let her join in the various "projects" that Mack always had in hand. Out behind the main hothouse, he had his own small garden, neatly tended rows of peas, squash, string beans. In an old potting shed he kept and cared for a mongrel bitch and her three puppies, having found them all abandoned one day on the oiled road leading into town. He'd made the dogs comfortable with straw and old blankets, and each evening made a game with Claire of sneaking out food from the supper table, usually adding a "dessert" of stale bread crumbled and mixed with milk. (Lillian, who was tight with her money and unsentimental about animals, grudgingly allowed him to keep the dogs when she finally discovered them: even four years later, when Claire went off to college, all the dogs were well and thriving under Mack's care.) And there had been, late that summer, the pigeon coop Mack had built, with Lillian's reluctant approval, on an edge of the property farthest away from the nursery.

"Those ugly, smelly old things!" Lillian had cried, when he brought the half-dozen birds in from town. "You keep that coop out of my sight, Mack, and out of my customers' sight, too. That's a good way to scare off business!"

Mack had looked at Claire, and they'd both giggled. They were always giggling together, like much smaller children; though in a way, as Claire sensed at about this time, neither of them had ever been a child.

One day, after the pigeon coop had been in place for several weeks, Claire came home from school to find Mack peering anxiously inside.

"What are you doing, Mack? Is something wrong…?"

The coop was an enormous, complex structure for so few birds: made of two-by-fours and chicken wire, it was seven by nine feet, six feet high, complete with four "windows"—also covered with wire—and both a front and back door. Mack, shirtless and dressed in overalls, was gazing up at one of the pigeons; it was perched quietly near the feeding trays, its eyes closed, set apart from the other five who strutted noisily about the cage.

"He's sick," Mack said, not glancing aside. His hands clasped the side of the coop, fingers curling through the wire holes.

"Are you sure?" Claire asked. She came up beside him, squinting inside. It seemed to her that the bird was simply resting.

"That bird's gonna die," Mack said hoarsely.

Claire glanced at him, alarmed by something in his voice she had detected before, but had not really thought about. It was a childlike, gurgling sound from the back of his throat, the sound of defeat or of a grief beyond tears. Mack was a tall, sturdy, dark-haired boy, and handsome in his way—muscular arms and shoulders, a long well-molded face, green eyes that were thickly lashed. Some people, even his mother, insisted that he was "slow," and it was true he'd quit school long ago, but Claire had never heard him say a foolish thing; he knew about animals and plants, and could work well with his hands. The misapprehension of others probably arose from his childlike moodiness—he was exuberant and gay one minute, and might seem to be choking back tears the next—or from his quick, eager grin, or from the general absence in Mack of cunning, malice, or any sense of the future. It did seem an assumption, somehow, that he would never leave this place, that his days would always be divided between his rambling, boyish pursuits and his being "a help to his mother." Until that day at the pigeon coop, Claire had never questioned any of this. Mack was rare, special, and he loved her; at school she was like the other kids (though perhaps somewhat shyer, more "citified" than most), but at home she was Mack's partner, his playmate, his "perfect friend." For, out of the blue, he had called her that one day, reaching out to touch a whitish-blond strand of her hair.

Now he had begun crying, as Claire watched in horror. He still had not looked at her. In the way he stood there, grasping the chicken wire as though it were a prison wall, gazing through tears at a sickened bird that now seemed—for she still possessed, back then, the ability to see with Mack's eyes—so much more than a bird, and making that pathetic, heartrending noise at the back of his throat: in his posture and grief Claire saw not the momentary fit of a child, but a man's abiding, incommunicable sorrow, sharpened by frustration or longing, wordless and even soundless but for the unashamed gurgling in his throat that was the sound of someone trying to wake from a nightmare, she would later think, grasping for a metaphor; or the sound of a drowning man.

That day she'd had no metaphors, only a sudden coldness in her heart. Stepping back from him, she'd said cautiously: "I've got some homework to do, Mack. I'm sorry about your bird...." It was that moment, the moment she'd said *your bird*, from which she dated her treachery, her becoming part of the great world Mack would never acknowledge or understand. He hadn't answered her, and she'd hurried away from him and the coop, but it turned out that Mack either hadn't grasped what she'd said or hadn't cared. For only a few days later he came into her bedroom, shyly, holding two of the dead bird's feathers in his calloused palm. "Let's always keep them, all right?" he said, holding one out to Claire. "Keep them for as long as we live...?" Claire had taken the feather, intrigued; had twirled it in her fingers. The idea charmed her, and she'd smiled back into her cousin's anxious, shining eyes.

"All right," she said.

Late on Friday afternoon the telephone rang, startling Claire. She and Lillian had been working since dawn, packing boxes, supervising the men who had come for the nursery stock, and after lunch Claire had come into the living room—she couldn't remember why—and had collapsed onto the sofa. Five minutes, she'd thought drowsily. When Lillian appeared at the door to announce that Claire's husband was on the line, she added a censorious smirk. "It's past six o'clock, you know."

Dazed, Claire hurried from the sofa to the oak telephone stand in the hall. She fought past cardboard boxes, grocery bags filled with trash.

"Hello? Jeffrey? What are you—"

"Yeah, it's only me," her husband said dryly. "I called to see how things were going."

"What? I just woke up—"

"You were sleeping? In the middle of the day?"

"Yes, I took a nap," Claire said, glancing around. She could sense Lillian's presence somewhere behind her, monitoring every word. Or had she picked up an extension?

"But you never take naps," Jeffrey said. Already his voice was peevish. She pictured him on the bar stool, in his typical after-work posture: sleeves rolled up his big arms, fleshy face shadowed by the day's growth of beard, his left hand curled around a scotch and water. An air of exasperation, defeat. When he returned home, Claire was usually fresh from her bath, scented, and had begun preparing dinner: her talk, her busy movements often revived him.

"I was tired," Claire said. "We've been working since early this morning."

"What about Lillian?" he asked.

"Oh, she's fine. She's holding up better than I am, I think." If Lillian were on the extension, Claire thought, she'd grasp Claire's meaning. Though Jeffrey, of course, did not.

"I told you, Claire. I told you the whole trip was a bad idea, that too much time had passed—"

"I wanted to come back, Jeff."

"And anyway, it's obvious she doesn't need you."

"She *does*, Jeffrey. And it's not just that. I want to be here."

"Claire, I don't—"

"I used to live here, remember? It's all being dismantled now, and I can't just ignore it."

Jeffrey paused, stymied. She heard the clink of ice cubes, a thousand miles away, as he gulped his cocktail down. She wondered how many it would take, with Jeff alone in the house. She knew she ought to be there, too; but she'd become selfish about the past, wanted to meet its demands for a brief while. If she wanted to tend to Jeffrey later, she could.

"Jason called," her husband said. "I didn't know if I could give him the number down there."

"Of course you could!" Claire cried, irritated. Most irritating was her husband's torpor, the deadly calm of his voice. Jason was their twelve-year-old, off at boarding school and very unhappy, very lonely, and it had recently occurred to Claire that Jeff had begun to use him, trying to heap guilt upon Claire to balance his own guilt. At thirty-eight he was a fairly successful insurance lawyer, but had been getting the impression that the firm no longer believed in him, would keep him on the routine cases; the result had been an increase in his drinking and an unexpected aptitude for malice. For a while Claire tried to assuage his guilt, denying his idea that he'd "failed" her and Jason, insisting that their diminished sex life was only a temporary result of stress; but like the drinking, the guilt had gotten beyond them. When he turned it outward upon her, and then upon Jason, she had lost sympathy. In recent weeks they'd begun discussing divorce, though not seriously. The divorce was as vague in Claire's mind as the European vacation they'd been promising themselves for years, or as the memories of her life before Jeffrey, memories which had turned out so manageable, so disappointingly tame.

"I was going to call him anyway, later tonight," Claire said coldly. "I'd better go now."

"But when are you coming home?" her husband asked.

"When I finish all this," Claire snapped. "I don't *know*."

"But—"

She put down the phone. Exasperated, she ran her fingers back through the short, plainly cut whitish hair that gave Claire her look of severe competence. Mostly she was annoyed with herself for having napped, when there was so much work to be done. She went back to the kitchen, where Lillian was packing dishes into an enormous wooden crate.

"Why don't you rest for a while, Lillian? Let me do that."

Grunting, the old woman lifted her arms for more dishes. She didn't look around.

"No time for restin'," she muttered.

Claire fell in beside her, and the two women worked steadily through the evening. Now that Lillian had begun this project, she had a grim determination to finish, and it displeased Claire to understand that she'd inherited the trait. Since arriving she'd been forced to visualize again the two poles represented by her mother and aunt—her mother's genuine, sanctimonious affection that even now, so many years after her death, gave Claire a thrill of loathing, and Lillian's permissive carelessness in which Claire, at fourteen, had felt acutely the lack of specific warmth—and to see, in fact, more of Lillian in herself than she'd ever imagined. The poise, the oblivious strength, the impression of coldness—Lillian presented these to the face of her upheaval, just as Claire had moved so calmly, in recent months, through the gradual dissolution of her marriage. Despite many opportunities, and a few specific hints from Claire, Lillian had been unwilling to discuss Mack's suicide except as a set of facts, and as it represented a natural turning point for her. Mack had borrowed a neighbor's shotgun, she said; he hadn't left a note, and had been considerate enough to go far back into the woods. Lillian had considered selling the place for years, so now seemed the appropriate time. It was then Claire had mentioned that she might be getting a divorce soon, might leave everything behind and move away from Philadelphia, maybe even back South, but Lillian had shrugged as if this were only the natural course of things.

When they'd finished packing in the kitchen, having sorted out the few items Lillian wanted to keep for her small apartment in town, Claire suddenly asked her aunt if she might keep the feather she'd found in Mack's drawer. Lillian, who had begun to tire in spite of herself, turned slowly from the set of wine glasses she'd been marking for the sale. Sourly, she smiled at Claire.

"What would you want that for?" she asked. "A filthy thing like that?"

Her aunt's smile, so ghastly and incongruous, paralyzed Claire.

"It's just a feather," Lillian said contemptuously. "Something he plucked off a dirty pigeon, twenty years ago. I thought you had more sense."

"I—I just wanted it," Claire stammered. "I put it in my purse, but if you want it back—"

"Hell, I don't want it. Everything that boy left is going in the sale, I told you that. Clothes, tools, that old album full of worthless stamps—everything. I ain't taking nothing of Mack's along, when I move to town."

Claire's anger came quickly, as it had when she'd spoken to Jeffrey on the phone. She despised his self-pity, and now she despised her aunt's pretended callousness. Which was, she thought, another form of self-pity.

She said, in a steely voice, "Then you don't mind if I keep the feather."

Lillian shrugged, the ugly smile playing again at her mouth, then turned with the box of wine glasses toward the dining-room door.

"I don't care what you do," she said airily.

I don't care what you do. The phrase had always been a signature of Lillian's, her way of sidestepping emotions or awkward moments she couldn't handle, and had revealed an attitude that Claire, even as a girl, had cautiously admired. She liked the bravado, the hint of dangerous freedom. During the years she spent with Lillian and Mack it often occurred to her that she knew of no one like her aunt: women she encountered from nearby farms, her girlfriends' mothers, even her own dead mother seemed to her imagination pathetic figures trapped inside narrowed, sour lives, an atmosphere of constriction and fruitless care. Yet there was something in her aunt, too, that chilled her. She felt it most during her last weeks before college, when she would overhear Lillian remarking on the phone, "Now that Claire's leaving…," or complaining that there was no one to do Claire's Saturday chores at the nursery. "I'd hoped that Mack could take over," she said to Claire one day, sighing. "But that boy gets more and more useless as time goes by…."

Much as Claire hated hearing this, she knew it was true. Mack had continued his eccentric, childish pursuits, though he was past twenty; he'd grown careless about watering the plants, or doing repairs to the sheds or fences. On Saturdays, Lillian's busiest time, when it was Claire's job to keep track of the money and Mack's to load the customers' purchases into their trunks or pickups, he would usually have wandered away before noon, and that evening they'd find him on the back porch, whittling crude little statues out of a piece of rotted fencepost, or playing stray tuneless melodies on a toy guitar he'd gotten one Christmas as a child. Lillian would breeze right by, contemptuous, as though he weren't worth scolding. Sometimes Claire would stop to talk, but Mack couldn't pretend interest in her activities at school, and Claire was bothered by the way his eyes had sunk inward, as if through exhaustion or excessive dreaming, and by his snarled hair and dirt-encrusted nails. Claire had become a blond, tanned, popular teenager, particularly since the local kids knew her mother had left behind some "money"—the word spoken in a hushed monotone— and that she was among them only for a time. Very few of her friends even knew about Mack, and anyone she brought home probably assumed he was a hired hand; Claire noticed that her friends didn't really see him, even though he might be sitting at the kitchen table as they passed through to Claire's bedroom, and Claire saw no point in introductions, explanations, complicated attempts to describe the person Mack was. She wasn't ashamed of him; she simply knew that he couldn't take part in the mainstream of her life. When they were alone she talked to him, gaily, or asked him idle questions, as though they were children enclosed forever in a paradise of flowers and sloping green hills, children whose bond no meddlesome adult or passage of time could sever. Yet even these occasions grew less frequent, since Claire was in fact a bright, self-reliant teenager and Mack a prematurely aging man, morose and whimsical and doomed. It was on a Sunday evening, about three weeks before she left for Vanderbilt, that Claire understood how relieved she was to escape this place. She and Mack were sitting on the back porch, around sunset, and he had turned to her with his dark, doleful eyes to ask quietly: "Claire, why does everything have to die?"

Her first impulse had been to laugh, as one laughs at the ingenuous query of a child. Yet the moment passed, and Mack sat waiting tensely, almost severely, staring at Claire's mouth. That was a habit of his—he stared at your mouth after asking a question. Claire bit her lip. She gave a strained smile.

"Well, Mack ..."

She'd been thinking about a boy, Jake Summers, who had taken her to the senior dance and had "liked" her all this year but who didn't seem sufficiently upset, Claire thought, about her going off to college. When she'd teased him about this he'd said, using an odd phrase, that for a long time he'd known it was an "established fact." That's what Claire's mother had saved up her money for, wasn't it? Claire had smiled at Jake, uneasily; had nodded. Out on the back porch, that mild August evening, she summoned back the same uneasy smile for her cousin with the bruised-looking eyes and the darkness in his veins. Behind them, in the kitchen, Lillian was clanking dishes together as she got their supper. How she longed to escape these people! She answered Mack by saying evenly, as though she were reading the words off a blackboard, that death was part of God's plan; and for the first time in her life despised herself.

Yet the moment passed, and Claire's mind quickly filled with other cares. In those last, hurried, dreamlike weeks, she had been almost too busy to notice Mack. There was the constant sorting of her clothes, her indecision over what to take, what to leave behind; there were shopping trips to town, for additional clothes; there was a visit to the bank accompanied by an unusually solemn Lillian, where the money Claire's mother left had been accumulating all these years. There were forms to fill out, sent by the University. There were stationery, supplies, and the occasional odd item to buy—a reading lamp, a waste basket. There were long stretches of time passed at her bedroom window, hours of excited or languid daydreaming, harmless fantasies about her roommate, her teachers, her first college boyfriend. In all this pressure and elation, this breathless forward-looking, Mack had almost no part: he was at the periphery of her life and even of her vision, a shadow appearing at the far end of the hall, startling her, or a slump-shouldered figure trudging through a distant field, darkening the corner of her eye for an instant as she bounded out the kitchen door. Yet when they did come together—at mealtimes, usually—

Mack behaved as if nothing were different, evidently feeling no sense of loss or betrayal. So Claire told herself, and smiled brightly at him over Lillian's blackberry cobbler, and listened to him talk about a lame squirrel he'd found the other morning, his dark-ringed eyes hectic in their sockets, his beautifully molded mouth with its decaying teeth and his strong, soiled fingers moving jerkily as he talked, wanting to communicate the entire experience to Claire. "And it wasn't but three days ago," he said shyly, pleased with himself, "and this morning he was hoppin' around outside that box, playin' in the hay. His coat's come around, too. All nice and shiny." Claire smiled, and asked every question she could think to ask, as if compensating for all Mack's future projects for which there would be no one to show any interest. She comforted herself, at least, by thinking that he hadn't asked again about death. The question meant nothing, she told herself; it was the idle query of a child.

And so the time came for leaving. Mack and even Lillian had gotten dressed up—this touched Claire—and they helped her load the two big suitcases into Lillian's old Plymouth, then drove her into town where she would catch the bus for Nashville. Lillian, as Claire might have predicted, was awkward at goodbyes, and had roughly brushed her niece's cheek as she muttered something about coming back to visit. Then, stepping back, she said in an overloud voice: "Why, she won't be gone for long—tell that to Mack, Claire honey, cheer him up a bit! She'll be here a month at Christmas, then all next summer, and once she's had enough of schoolin' she'll be back for good. Ain't that so, Claire?" And Lillian, betraying herself, threw back her head and laughed, something Claire had never seen her do in her life.

Claire turned slowly to Mack. Uncomfortable in his musty dark suit, and the starched cotton shirt with no tie, he stood shifting his weight from one foot to the other. In the morning sun outside the depot, his face looked more shadowed than ever, as if a little oblong cloud had perched just above him. He'd cut himself shaving, Claire saw. She reached out to touch him, and not exactly meaning to, brushed the tiny scratch at his jaw-line. Alarmed, she drew back her hand. "Goodbye, Mack," she said quickly, embarrassed, and tiptoed up to kiss his other cheek. It occurred to her that she'd never come this close to him before. He smelled of the outdoors, of the long, sweet grasses carpeting the hills, of the pleasantly rotten dampness of black soil. His eyes were clear as rainwater, but they filled. "Gonna write me every day?" he said hoarsely. By now she sensed the anxiety in him, a voltage she suddenly imagined could send his black-suited limbs flapping like a scarecrow's. She touched his shoulder. "It's all right, Mack, don't worry. I'll write all the time, and I'll be home for visits. Just like your Mama said." Lillian had stood aside during all this, pretending interest in the activity inside the depot, but Claire watched as Mack shot his mother a quick, resentful look, of the kind she'd never seen from him. Her heart gave a queer leap, then just as quickly sank. "And I'll call you, too," she added lamely. "On the telephone."

Wiping his eyes, Mack stepped back. He'd straightened his shoulders, assuming an air of dignity that tore at Claire's heart. Suddenly she felt, as she hadn't in years, that he was central to her life—her childhood playmate, her unassuming teacher, her silent, bruised-looking friend. Yet it was not true, as she supposed even then, that she would return to him, or that they would evolve into anything beyond what already seemed a twilit, vaguely haunted past. Though she did come back for several visits during her college years, and wrote bright, simply phrased letters to Mack whenever she could, it was her new interests that absorbed her: a year-long passion to become an archeologist, which evolved out of her crush on an art-history professor; in her sophomore and junior years, her apartment and roommates and exhausting summer job with a fashion merchandising firm (Claire had majored in business, finally, and never returned to Georgia for the summer because of her need, as she put it in a letter to Lillian, to get "real-life experience"); and, finally, her relationship and impulsive marriage, near the end of her senior year, to a handsome pre-law major from Philadelphia, who whisked her off so quickly to a book-filled, stylishly ratty apartment, less than a mile from Penn, that she wasn't even able to attend her own graduation. There had been cards, phone calls, small gifts exchanged between her and Mack; there had been one or two visits after her marriage, during which she talked easily with both Lillian and Mack, warning herself against even the most justifiable condescension. She had moved beyond them, of course. Happily married, pregnant, with no particular ambitions for herself beyond leading a life both intelligent and sensual, she had the emotion toward them one has toward old black-and-white photographs, suddenly encountered after many years: a sense of amazement or even dismay, but little more. By the time Jason had become an energetic toddler, Claire always had an excuse for not visiting; and gradually Lillian stopped asking her. They'd been out of contact for several years when Claire received the telegram about Mack—which had been brief and tersely worded, even for a telegram.

Though she couldn't have predicted all this when she was eighteen, and boarding that whinnying Trailways bus, it might not have surprised her. Sitting at the tinted window, she felt already detached from them as they stood out in the sunlight, both squinting as they passed their gaze along, unsure which window was hers. Several times they both waved, vaguely, and she waved in return, but she was never certain that they saw her. The bus was so high up, so impersonal. It wasn't until it had left the depot, and was already on the interstate heading north, that Claire let her gaze stray from the window and looked down to see the small but unmistakable bloodstain on her forefinger. Her first reaction had been to wipe at it, horrified, or to hurry back to the restroom and scour her hands. But she hated herself for this, and in a moment her heart quieted. She'd always been a sensible girl, and she simply waited, leaning back her head and enjoying the scenery, until the bus made its first stop and it was time for Claire to wash her hands for lunch.

"Claire, there's something that don't seem quite right," Lillian said.

They were standing in the near-empty living room: the sale was over. The auctioneer, an unsmiling potbellied man in his fifties, had set up business on Lillian's back porch, having brought a card table, an ancient filigreed cash register, and a couple of slack-mouthed assistants. These younger men, in their early twenties, had kept disappearing into the house and returning with more of Lillian's goods, and each time something was brought out the

auctioneer would turn to the gathered spectators and exclaim—
not very convincingly, Claire thought—over its beauty or value.
While Lillian and Claire waited at some distance, under the shade
of an old pecan tree, people had arrived and formed a semicircle
around the porch, a few having brought lawn chairs and jugs of
lemonade. The day was hot, cloudless. From under the tree the
two women watched in silence, dazed by the incessant work of the
past few days and feeling detached from the sale itself now that
their own work had abruptly ended. It surprised Claire that almost
everything went quickly—one by one the auctioneer cried "Sold!"
over the washing machine, Lillian's china cabinet with the beveled
glass panels, Mack's small, squarish bureau. Each item looked so
diminished, Claire thought, so pathetic as it was brought out of the
dark kitchen into the glaring noontime sun. With a folded
newspaper, Lillian stood fanning herself. She did not seem to mind
that most of the buyers were people she'd known for years, town
neighbors and longstanding customers of the nursery. She'd only
commented that the auctioneer's two assistants looked "pretty
shiftless" to her, and she remarked, sighing, that maybe she should
have kept her good china, in case she ever had company in town.
Then she'd laughed, shortly. Claire hadn't replied.

When the auction was over and the small crowd had dispersed,
the auctioneer handed Lillian her share of the cash and within ten
minutes had driven off in a late-model paneled truck, the two
assistants following in a badly rusted van with dark-tinted windows.
Absently, the two women moved inside and began wandering
through the empty rooms, noting the paltry leavings of the sale,
remarking that in Lillian's new apartment the few items marked
"Not for Sale" would not look so tiny and insubstantial as in these
overlarge rooms. In the kitchen there were still the breakfast table
and four chairs; in the dining room a small mahogany hutch; in
the living room a wine-colored loveseat, an old fringed rug, a few
chairs and lamps. It was here that Lillian stopped cold, frowning as
she passed her gaze slowly around the room.

"What do you mean?" Claire asked. "Is something still here that
you wanted sold?"

"No," Lillian said. "I don't know, but there's something not
quite right."

Claire crossed the room to stand beside her aunt. "It's just that everything's gone," she said gently. "The room looks so big, so barren...."

"No," her aunt repeated. A note of asperity had entered her voice, as if she resented having to speak to Claire at all. In these last days Claire had treated her with tact, even with deference, not presuming to ask anything further about Mack: though it was a fact—and one she resented, mildly—that she'd begun to think obsessively of him. She'd had to content herself with imagining (idly, as if she were creating a story that might never have happened) a slow transformation in her cousin through the years: a gradual dawning of his consciousness as time passed, facing a vision of himself as one of those lame animals caught somewhere in the obscurity of these hills, where no kind stranger would ever happen along; or suffering an equally slow encroachment of the darkness, a constriction and a narrowing, until the neat depthless circle of black inside a gun's barrel had concentrated all the reality Mack would ever know. These were identical answers, Claire thought. Any supposition of hers arrived at the same unknowable—and undeniable—conclusion. So there was no reason to bother Lillian, who doubtless had torments of her own, and Claire had simply helped her with the work as if she were a servant, obedient and quiet, joining in idle conversation when Lillian seemed to want it, privately counting the days until the auction. Their only argument had centered on that, in fact, because Claire had informed her aunt that she intended to leave that very night, when the cleaning and packing and the auction itself would be over. Lillian had claimed to need help with the move into town, but Claire pointed out that the movers would arrive on Monday morning, that there would be precious little to unpack, and in any case the landlord at Lillian's new apartment house could help her if any problems arose. Claire really should fly back at once: she was separating from her husband, she told Lillian frankly, and needed to find an apartment of her own.

Now she waited patiently as her aunt continued to survey the room. "I don't know," she was muttering, "I can't understand it, but there's something—" and then, abruptly, she stamped her foot. "Claire, look over in that corner—why, it's the television set."

"What? Do you mean—"

"Gone," said Lillian. "Stolen."

Alarmed, Claire stared at the empty corner where the color television set had rested on a small end table. The table, dusty and nicked, was still there.

"But there must have been a mistake," Claire said. "The auctioneer must have thought—"

Lillian clapped her hands, then walked to the front door and opened it. She peered outside, as if expecting to find the culprits waiting on the porch to be discovered. "Told you they were shiftless, didn't I?" she said, glancing back to Claire. Her eyes gleamed with satisfaction. "While we were all out back, those boys were taking things out the front door—setting them in that old van, I'll bet. Stealing me blind!"

"Oh Lillian, I don't think—"

Her aunt shook her finger, as if Claire had been complicitous in the theft. "Now listen, that TV had one of them red tags on it, big as life. *Not for sale.* You put it on yourself, didn't you? Eh?"

"Yes," Claire said quietly.

"And you didn't see them bring it out back, did you? There wasn't any television set put up at the auction, was there?"

"No," Claire said.

"That's right," said Lillian, slamming the door. "No tellin' what they got away with."

Helplessly Claire followed her aunt back through the other rooms, able only to shake her head when Lillian pointed inside the hutch where a valuable figurine had stood, a gift from some long-ago admirer; examining the shelf, Claire could see a small clean circle in the dust. In the kitchen there were service pieces missing. "Only silverplate," Lillian said, pointing to an empty cabinet beneath the sink, "but still." More than anything Claire was paralyzed by her aunt's manner—unsurprised, grimly jovial, as if the discovery of each theft helped confirm a theory she'd been trying for countless years to prove. She was a big, strong, willful woman in a brightly flowered dress, her white hair drawn back carelessly in a bun, the back of her neck damp with perspiration: following, Claire felt silent and insubstantial as a ghost. Lillian's manner reminded her of her husband's on those nights when he drank straight through dinner and into the night—the cynicism, the rancor, the wayward energy that seemed to arise out of helplessness itself but was no less prodigious for that. Claire's own energies were controlled, efficient, lacking in much emotion; she was a born manager, cool and diplomatic. She thought to herself, clearly, that she did not understand these other people. She allowed Lillian to lead her upstairs, thinking *By this time tomorrow I'll be home*, but Lillian had stopped her at the bedroom door. She said something intended, probably, as "Hah!" but that came out diminished, as if the sound had strangled in her throat.

Claire came forward, then briefly closed her eyes. The room had been torn apart—drawers flung out of the bureau, their contents strewn along the floor; the mattress had been lifted partway off the bed, then dropped; some boxes and suitcases in Lillian's closet had been ransacked. She and Claire moved slowly into the room. At last the old woman seemed chastened, but Claire could not comfort her: she could barely contain her own sense of outrage. As a child she had played with Mack in this room, getting into Lillian's makeup and jewelry, giggling; once she'd even dressed Mack in one of his mother's loudly printed dresses, had squealed with laughter as Mack stood there snickering and blushing. Suddenly it came to Claire how many lovers of her aunt must have stayed in this room, slept in that very bed. Neither Claire nor her aunt were particularly sentimental, but nonetheless they stood there a long time. Claire's heart pounded. Her fists were clenched at her sides.

Lillian said, finally, "My, my ..."

"They'll be easy to catch," Claire said, severely. "We should call the police right away. They couldn't have expected to get away with this."

Lillian was walking around the room, lifting items and then dropping them, shaking her head. "Why bother?..." she said vaguely.

"But you have the man's number," Claire said. "It must have been one of those boys he brought with him, I doubt the auctioneer himself had anything to do with it. If you'll just call him—"

"No," Lillian said sharply. "Let them have it. Let them do what they want with everything, with *me*...." To Claire's horror, her aunt had begun to whimper. She stood by the night table and abruptly held up an object—a white straw purse. "Look, they even emptied this, not even a Kleenex left...." Lillian turned the opened purse upside down; nothing came out.

With a startled cry, Claire turned and ran out of her aunt's bedroom and down the hall to her own room. Her heart beat wildly, like a maddened bird inside her chest. She thought, *This isn't me, this isn't happening*— At the doorway she saw that the small, scantily furnished room had not been ransacked; perhaps they had spared her.... But entering she saw it, fallen to the floor beside her bed, her own small navy handbag with the white trim. Before she bent over, numbly, to pick it up, she could already see that the clasp had been opened. She lifted the purse; without looking inside, she turned it upside down over the bed. Nothing happened. Then she rooted inside with her fingers, almost ripping the satin lining, but in their rush they had taken everything, her wallet and lipstick and keys, her small address book and her packet of traveling tissue, and even the small worthless feather it had taken her twenty years to lose.

Weakly she thought, *Mack...*, but it was too late for that. She dropped her purse on the bed, she left the room and tried to console her aunt. Lillian had already recovered, but Claire offered to phone the auctioneer. When she called, the man told her gruffly that those "sorry fellers" had disappeared: he'd hired them just last week, he was sorry if they took advantage but he couldn't be responsible, it was hard to get any decent help these days.... As the man spoke, Claire listened numbly. When he stopped talking she simply hung up, not knowing what else to do.

They decided not to call the police. There was no point, really; they were already exhausted, and the chances were slim that the police would recover their property. So they cleaned up the house, made themselves a light supper, and Claire had her suitcase—the thieves hadn't touched it—packed and ready by six o'clock. Claire told her aunt, in a sensible voice, that after all the purse had contained nothing that couldn't easily be replaced; there had been less than fifty dollars in her wallet and she would cancel the credit cards; the airline ticket, thank God, was tucked safely inside a compartment in her suitcase. Probably the thieves had dumped the contents of both purses into a box, hurrying, not troubling to examine what they were stealing. But there was no point in chasing after them, Claire said, let them have whatever they wanted.... Lillian hadn't replied. The matter was settled. On the way to the airport the two women talked idly, as people do when they know they will never meet again, and on the plane Claire felt a miraculous calm overtaking her, as if by returning home unburdened, empty-handed, she had become innocent once again.

Wildfires

The phone calls from Dr. Bucknell and from Gerald's brother, Stan, come during that same afternoon. It is late August, and Janet has spent much of her day staring at the ragged, sloping lawn and dispirited trees outside her office—the green landscape is baking away, she thinks, everything left an indeterminate yellow-white. A death-color. The green has been drawn upward into the superheated air, dissolved in the fierce brilliance of sunlight. She is startled by the telephone calls, and made to feel rather guilty, for both calls focus on her husband—I'm phoning you about your husband, Mrs. Stillman, hello, Janet, I'm calling from the bus station, how is Gerald? Both startled and guilty, yes, for she understands that she had successfully avoided thinking of her husband during most of that day.

Stan is a tall, strapping kid of nineteen, the kind who can drain a tumbler of iced tea in two or three swallows. Janet pours him a second glass, feeling disconcerted by his presence although she has known of his visit for five or six weeks. It will be good for Gerald, his mother half-yelled into Janet's ear, through the crackling of long distance; they don't get to visit enough, they need to get reacquainted. Stan's such a sweet boy, old Mrs. Stillman had said, but Janet had not felt stung by the implication that Gerald was not—only mildly disappointed. After all, mothers always favored the baby of the family, didn't they? Janet would never know, yet such a small residue of affection for Gerald, after all that had happened, did disappoint her. Easy to say she'd have been a more loyal mother, but wasn't it true?

It is touching, nonetheless, that Stan has talked of little besides his mother since his arrival. He tilts back in the kitchen chair, a piece of ice held in his back teeth. "I swear, she cried a bucket," he laughs, sentimentally. "'Cause I'm the youngest one, I reckon." He crunches the ice.

Janet sits down with her own tumbler of ice, and a diet soft drink. "Well, you'll have to make her proud."

"Yes'm," he says, and Janet could swear a mist covers those artless blue eyes. "I reckon I will."

Wanting to break the tension Janet says, with a little laugh: "Stan, please don't call me ma'am!"

Stan has the country boy's radiant grin; it spreads from ear to ear. He flushes crimson. "It's okay," he says, winking. "I didn't mean you were old or nothin."

Stan is moving up to Atlanta from his boyhood life, the only life he knows, in order to attend Georgia Tech. Like Gerald he's big-boned, his yellow-gold hair cut short; unlike Gerald he's trusting, open, ready for a good life. He doesn't know anything, and Janet thinks maybe his mother's ambitions are a good idea, after all; even if he flunks out of college, he'll meet a few people different from himself, understand himself as a south Georgia farm boy and decide to go back. Janet wishes this for him. Gerald, she fears, has forgotten his extreme youth. She can't remember his last reference to the farm, his childhood.

"It's real nice of ya'll to invite me up," Stan says. "But don't worry, the dorms open on Monday and I'll be out of your hair."

"Oh, you're no bother," Janet says, laughing. Why is she taking this jaunty tone with him? she wonders. She is almost flirtatious.

"But I mean it," he says. "Everybody needs their privacy, married especially. Once I get to the dorm you won't know I'm in town."

Janet puts down her glass, feeling alarmed. Old Mrs. Stillman isn't behind this, she knows; she'd wanted Stan to move in with Gerald and Janet, claiming the arrangement would be "good for everybody." Janet understands with a pang that Stan does know a few things, after all. She'd seen his gaze cut downward on the word "married," and she wonders what Gerald's mother and the rest have said about them, what whispered conferences have taken place. And now the commonplace thought arrives with a jolt: Yes, she is married to Gerald. When they eloped at eighteen, Stan was only a toddler.

"We—we hope to see a lot of you," Janet says blankly.

"I'm looking forward to visiting with Gerald," Stan says. "When will he be home?"

She wakes, startled. The telephone, the doorbell...? Today at work, Friday, she'd fallen into a daze, nearly mindless, as often happens on these summer afternoons. She is head of the drafting department for a medium-sized construction firm, and she does enjoy her work, especially since they moved to a new building adjacent to a shopping mall and only a few blocks from where Gerald and Janet live. Now that she has her own office—the cubicles of her subordinates are down the hall—she often falls into daydreams, stares blankly out the window, unaware of time and genuinely unconscious of herself; even when she is working hard, she has begun to notice, she is similarly abstracted. One day she had joked with Gerald, trying to comfort him, by saying her work was moronic: it required skill, but not really much thought. Gerald has complained for years that his own work is meaningless, but he hadn't liked the joke. "If that's the case, why don't you quit?" he said, irritated. She didn't dare respond that they needed the money—though she wanted to—since she makes twice what Gerald does, and that's another sensitive issue. "Maybe I will, one of these days," she'd said vaguely, and then she laughed. Gerald gave a little smirk and left the room.

But today she hadn't been working, just staring out at the colorless landscape. The jangling phone had startled her, and when a deep voice said, "Mrs. Stillman, this is Dr. Bucknell," for a moment her pulse raced. Then she understood. She quieted. "As usual, it's nothing," Dr. Bucknell said, rather shortly, and Janet could only say, "Yes. Thanks for your patience." The line went dead.

Now, deep into the night, she understands that the phone hadn't rung, nor the doorbell. Across from her Gerald sleeps heavily in his own twin bed, face down, one arm thrown across the top of the pillow. In the distance she hears something: a car's squealing tires, a horn honking, then a bottle shattering against pavement. Neighborhood teenagers, she thinks. Friday night. Janet's face is unlined but she is thirty-nine years old, and alarmed by such things.

She lapses back into the pillow, remembering Gerald's paranoia those first few years, his jumping like a wild man at the slightest abrupt noise. (Just part of the "shell shock," people had said—even the doctors. It would go away soon.) Then followed the years of depression, his hypersensitivity leaking into a great dark hole, into oblivion. And now the petty grievances, the fatigue, the hypochondria of an old man. Perhaps the phone rang inside a dream, Janet thinks, making her nerves sing, her heart pound. Perhaps she has caught her husband's earliest symptoms, after a lapse of years.

She remembers the uneasy, somehow knowing way Stan had pronounced the word: Married.

Sunday is never an easy day, and now there is the pressure of company in the house. Stan sleeps long and deeply, like an infant, but Janet is up by eight o'clock, making coffee and setting out the breakfast things while Gerald sits at the dining room table, rattling the big newspaper page by page.

He has been reading items aloud from the Arts & Entertainment section, trying to find something to do with Stan this afternoon. He brings up a movie, then a play, but Janet points out that Stan is new to Atlanta, shouldn't they show him something of the city? Gerald makes a grunting noise of assent. He rattles another page.

Janet makes the coffee, each movement deliberate and slow. She is stalling, she muses, but against what she isn't sure. Yesterday was somewhat awkward, made tense by the need to entertain Stan and also assure him that all was well, but she'd been surprised to see Gerald relax in his presence, even fall for a few brief moments into his old, kidding ways. She'd had, here and there, heartrending glimpses of Gerald at nineteen, and the buried memory revealed that he hadn't been so different from Stan; a little thinner, a little smarter, but really the same eager, innocent kid. Yesterday they went to a baseball game, and she'd watched as Gerald and Stan jumped up at the same moment to cheer a ball sailing out of the park; she'd seen their identical Adam's apples bobbing as they downed beer after beer. Later in the day Gerald had seemed to tire, the burden of talking with Stan gradually shifting to Janet, but naturally Stan hadn't noticed: he'd sat in the living room eagerly talking about his future, about the university and the girl back home he hoped to marry, about his excitement at finding himself in this enormous city.

"Pretty soon I'll be a real slicker," he'd said to Janet, winking and cocking his head toward Gerald. "Just like my brother here."

Gerald had been staring, dazed, at the television set: another baseball game. Though they'd turned off the sound right before dinner.

"Brother, be happy the way you are," Gerald had said flatly. He hadn't taken his eyes from the set.

Now, pouring her and Gerald's first cup, she looks at him through the kitchen doorway. "I've got an idea," she says. "How about the museum?"

Gerald pauses a long moment, as he generally does after Janet speaks. "But that's indoors," he says, turning back to his paper. "I thought you wanted him to see the city."

"But Gerry, the museum is the city," and for a moment her hand, lifting the cup to her lips, trembles in anger. She takes a deep breath, understanding that really this is an old argument. When the highly publicized new museum had opened, Gerald had refused to go because of the long lines. Later, as national articles began to appear detailing the innovative architecture of the museum building, and the dramatic additions to its permanent collection, he'd scoffed at the publicity. So Atlanta was becoming an international city, was it? We were leading the way toward the 21st century, were we? He'd made some crude references to the city's racial problems, its street people, its violence after dark. It pained her to see his anger so unfocused, so desperate, but she hadn't known what to say. They still hadn't visited the museum.

"And besides," she adds now, "it's time you and I went, too. It'll be fun for all of us."

She has approached him from behind, talking in her smooth caressing voice all the while: an old habit, taking pains not to surprise her husband. Yet he looks up with a child's pained, wondering face, as though "fun" were an obscenity shouted in viciousness or anger. Fortunately for Janet, Stan comes in from the hall at that moment, and they both look up. Wearing only his blue jeans, he rubs his puffy eyes with one hand, scratches his flat belly with the other. His arms and chest are huge, Janet sees, the skin a smooth pinkish-brown around the sculpted muscle.

Stan says, yawning, "Hi everybody, what's for breakfast?"

Once a young woman of considerable fire and passion—so she had enjoyed thinking of herself, in the days when she might toil for eight or ten hours straight over one of her canvases—Janet often consoles herself by remembering that "art" was more noticeable as a feature of her youthful persona than it was evident in her finished paintings. Having diverted that single-minded energy into a job that demanded skill but not art, a marriage that required more tact than love, she now looks indulgently upon her extreme youth—the oversized paint-spattered flannel shirts, the ostentatious disregard for makeup or her hair, the late hours of work that shocked her early-rising parents and then her young husband, from whose side she would steal away, at one or two in the morning, for a few additional, fervid hours. The resulting canvases were really quite tame (once or twice a year, Janet visits the basement and opens again the big waterproof locker, then returns upstairs half an hour later, chastened) and what gives her the sharpest throe of nostalgia is not the thought of what might have been, but rather of who she was. Perplexed or not, Gerald often woke again when she returned to him, as if roused by the fever that glowed in her veins while she worked, their mutual passion incendiary in those few months as it had never been since. She often thinks, in these late and diminished times, of her early fervor as an artist, of her passion with Gerald, and finally of the war itself as a series of quick fires, outbursts of feeling that defied containment, exploding the flimsy boundaries of flesh and time. Although Gerald had suffered no physical injuries, and though nothing prevents Janet from buying an easel and canvas tomorrow if she chooses, there are silent moments between them when she caresses his body slowly, reverently, as if the limbs had been blasted, the skin irreparably scarred; or he will hold and fondle her artist's hands as if they were a pair of dying birds.

Though Gerald loves his brother, it's clear to Janet that Stan makes him uncomfortable; the sooner this visit is over, the better. Perhaps the Sunday morning routine, in Gerald's mind, has made the unlimited expanse of Stan's future too painfully clear. Paging through the newspaper, he glances at neither Stan nor Janet; his deeply set eyes seem half-closed, wincing. The same expression, Janet thinks, as when he opens the drapes in the morning to a flood of sunlight. Not long ago he remarked that he prefers cloudy days.

Janet has been telling Stan about the museum, and he reacts with polite interest. Now he sees Gerald bending over the paper, however, making a series of dark slashes with the ballpoint gripped in his hand.

"What's that, the want ads?" Stan asks, in all innocence. "You're not job-hunting, are you?"

"So will you, soon enough," Gerald says.

Stan looks at Janet, puzzled.

"He likes to keep his eyes open," she explains, noncommittally. "You never know what will turn up."

"But what about those government benefits, bro?" Stan asks, though the joshing tone doesn't suit him. Gerald says nothing.

"I think he's bored with it," Janet says, rising. "How do you like your eggs, Stan? I'd better get started."

Stan follows her into the kitchen, and though their voices are audible from the dining room she can take a different tone in here.

"His co-workers are much younger, most of them," she tells Stan, "and I think he feels outnumbered. There's no communication, it's a big office and very hectic, and after all, the work isn't very fulfilling..." She goes on to explain, in her quick rushing voice, that although he still works in the government welfare office, he seldom gets to meet with clients. Most of his time is spent operating a word processor, and filing an endless stream of papers. Stan clucks his tongue in sympathy. "Gee, that's a shame," he says.

Janet doesn't tell him that Gerald has been on probation three times for "excessive sick leave," or that his supervisor told him bluntly that he would never be trusted with work requiring interpersonal skills. She doesn't tell him about the morning last spring when Gerald found an unsigned note in his mailbox at work: BABY KILLER it had read, in big block letters. For all this, she can't really explain why she hasn't encouraged his job-hunting, or that she knows he isn't serious, anyway. He has returned from all his interviews over the years with the same grudging attitude, assuming he hadn't done well, pointing out flaws in the interviewer or the position or the company in the same way he discovers imaginary flaws in his body, then makes new appointments with Dr. Bucknell week after week. As with his job problems, Janet is neither sympathetic nor unsympathetic about her husband's hypochondria. She makes the doctor appointments when he asks her to; she reports the test results when Dr. Bucknell finally calls back. There is nothing more she can do, Janet thinks. Before long they will need to change doctors.

Now Gerald's brother does something which, at the moment, astonishes her, though later she'll look back and wonder at her own surprise. He comes from behind her, while she is cracking eggs inside the bowl, and draws his bare arm up along her side. He says, bending to her throat, "It must be tough for you sometimes, huh?" and so weirdly mingles dastardly bravado and countrified awkwardness that she might laugh if she hadn't experienced any deeper reaction. As he presses his solid chest against her back, crushing her on both sides with his biceps, her girlishly warm, swooning response causes her to drop an egg unbroken into the bowl. It makes a small, insulting splash. Her eyes closed, she manages, "Ger back, Stan, please get back." And instantly mourns the loss of warmth, of solid male heat, as it retreats into the empty space behind her.

Janet drives them to the museum, all three of them packed into the Stillmans' Cutlass, the air conditioner blowing at high speed. It has been years since Gerald drove a car; he takes the bus to work, and Janet does all the other driving. Today Stan had offered to drive, but Janet quickly shook her head. Now he sits behind her and Gerald on the backseat, like their overgrown child.

"Guess I might as well tell you," Stan says sheepishly. "I've never even been to an art museum."

"This one is fairly new," she says, turning onto Peachtree Street. "It's quite spectacular."

"We haven't been, either," Gerald tells Stan.

"Not to this one," Janet says. "We went to the old museum, of course. Quite a few times."

"I don't remember one of those times," Gerald says.

There is an awkward silence. Janet doesn't know if he is needling her, deliberately, which isn't like him; or whether this is an obscure reference to the memory loss, both short-term and long-term, that he frequently claims as one of the results of his war experience. Janet finds both possibilities unsettling and decides to change the subject.

"Maybe you'll decide to take an Art History course, when you're a junior or senior," she says to Stan. "You know, as an elective."

"Well, maybe I could," Stan says slowly.

"He's going to study biology, remember?" Gerald says. "Why would he—"

"I meant as an elective," Janet repeats. "For his own enjoyment."

Gerald looks straight ahead, saying nothing. He is wearing sunglasses.

After a moment Stan says, "Well heck, why not? I could do that."

They park on a side street only a block from the museum. As they join the other Sunday afternoon strollers on the broad sidewalk, Gerald lagging a few steps behind Janet and Stan, Janet begins to feel a buoyant, light energy filling her, especially her legs. They feel elastic, springy, but she tries not to walk too quickly. At the museum entrance, Gerald keeps his sunglasses on while Stan gallantly pays their admission. They wander inside, a little dazed by the cool glaring whiteness of the walls, the pale flood of light from the numberless windows and skylights. The interior gives an illusion of weightlessness, a pleasant nullity, despite the hundreds of milling visitors, the spiraling walkways, the incessant vague rush of whispered voices, exclamations....They stand on the ground floor, staring upward at the walkways that lead in a slowly ascending circle around the dome, rising to three additional floors. Watching as visitors ascend the ramp, Janet feels a familiar stab in her abdomen: the half-pleasant vertigo that has plagued her since childhood. Despite herself, she is eager to begin ascending the ramp.

Then she turns, abruptly, to see Gerald and Stan waiting next to her, looking helpless and bewildered.

"Isn't there a tour or something?" Gerald asks, embarrassed. "I hate just wandering around a place like this."

Janet gathers her patience, takes one of the brochures at a desk marked "Information," and pores over it quickly.

"The next floor is furniture and decorative arts," she explains, "and the main collection is above that. Why don't we start up the ramp—"

"No, let's go this way," Gerald says. He points to a sign at one end of a long corridor: ELEVATOR. "It'll be quicker."

Janet looks longingly at the ramp, fascinated by its weightless suspension around the inner shell of the building. People on the ramp appear to spiral upward along the walls, released from gravity. "But—"

"You take the elevator, Gerald," Stan says. "We'll meet you upstairs."

And they separate before Janet can react. Gerald trudges toward the elevator.

"Janet, I wanted to talk for a minute, anyway," Stan says. "Listen, I really don't know what got into me, you know? Maybe it's because—"

He continues to apologize, awkwardly and at length. Janet scarcely listens. She is fascinated by this building, its cunning yet somehow beneficent design, seeming to cleanse one's vision of all biases of weight or color; having entered this place, she is ready to see. Though smiling at her own thought, she knows it is true. Every few steps up the ramp she gets a new perspective, enabled to see the enormous atrium on the ground floor, a grouping of porcelains on the second floor; and now she glimpses the majestic stillness of the European paintings just coming into view, lined along the pristine walls in their own weightless glory, enthroned like a row of grandly gazing monarchs. In a single glance she picks out Renoir, Van Gogh, Delacroix, Toulouse-Lautrec...."Here," she says, touching Stan's hand. "This is the floor we want."

As they leave the ramp Stan asks, whining, "But you understand, don't you? Please say—"

"Oh yes," she says carelessly. "Of course."

In 1972, shortly after finding his present job, Gerald had seemed to take hold of himself: it was time, he said, to put the past behind him. He was sensitive to his wife's condition, he told her. He understood her distress. Recently Janet had quit art school, abandoning her dream of teaching part-time to gifted children while simultaneously developing her own talent. She'd never worked with any real sense of discipline, or direction; she'd never had her own teacher except in the enormous public high school she attended in an Atlanta suburb, and that wasn't an atmosphere conducive to serious work. It was the summer after high school that she began her "bohemian" period, staying up till all hours and wearing her sloppy clothes, and that same summer she met Gerald when he was in town for a big weekend with some of his pals. They were engaged within two weeks, married within another month. It was during the two years of Gerald's tour duty, which followed almost immediately, that Janet had the time to think of her life and her commitments, and to understand that her love for her husband somehow transcended everything. She was left dissatisfied, a little bitter, but certain in her self-knowledge. When Gerald returned to her, hardly the same person as before, they struggled along for a while on his benefits and her part-time salary as a cocktail waitress—the last vestige of her bohemian indulgence—but she wasn't making progress anyway, she felt; her canvases seemed to her lifeless, arid, each new one a tedious variation of the last. When her husband, whom she loved, continued to flounder in the confusion of his memories, his dreams, his terror, she abruptly quit both art school and the cocktail lounge; within weeks she had an entry-level drafting position, and to her gratified surprise Gerald began immediately to improve.

He began to share some of his experiences with her, something he had never done those first few years. He used those over-familiar words from the evening news—napalm, Tet, Khe Sanh— but in her husband's flat, disaffected voice they had the force of some exotic and furious language, making her heart beat with morbid excitement, with its own fury. He was cool, non-judgmental, failing to use the word "atrocity" though she listened and hoped for it, but he told her of the bombing of a small village, deep in the Hue province; of thatched-roof huts bursting into flame as their occupants scurried out into the surrounding brush; of the way the fires spread, so easily, to the brush itself, so that Gerald could pause and hear the screams, hear the desperate trampling rush, then look upward to see the dull, hanging smoke like a soiled thumb-print on the sky. On any day, walking through the jungle, they found charred patches of ground, as though a cancer had erupted out of nowhere, eating everything in its path, then dying mysteriously as it began. They found bodies, of course; all ages, sizes; some blackened to cinders, scarcely identifiable at all, others clean and whole, unmarked, the cause of death another mystery, not that anyone was curious. We never buried anyone, usually we didn't even stop, Gerald had said, in a dry rasping voice. I don't know, somehow it didn't seem so bad—not at the moment. They were just part of the landscape.

Janet listened patiently. Out of long habit, she stored the imagery away, although knowing she would never use it; she felt herself and Gerald involved in a process, perhaps, by which she could share his pain, story by story, image by image. But as months passed he became worse instead of better. If she spoke unexpectedly, he jumped half out of his chair; if she suggested their going to a party, he looked at her with half-incredulous horror, or he laughed bitterly. He began visiting a psychiatrist, who prescribed antidepressants. He meditated alone in his room, playing a cassette tape with his doctor's murmur guiding him along, step by step. Late at night he wandered the house, his bare feet thudding heavily, while Janet lay staring at the ceiling, helplessly monitoring his progress through the rooms. Now the kitchen, now the living room. The small half-bathroom off the hall. Again the living room. Janet's eyes were opened wide, unblinking. She would lay thinking about those wildfires, sprouting randomly through the tree-covered hills. Imagery rose in waves like the undulating hills themselves inside her brain, riddled with smoke and flame, some primordial landscape stubbornly refusing to metamorphose into anything shapely or coherent. At her sides lay her white hands, unclenched and still. They drifted gradually, Janet and her husband, from a perspective to which the future seemed a barely possible deliverance toward a place whose past, present, and future did not seem distinct; one could use, really, a single word to designate them all. Only the week before Stan's arrival to begin his college studies, Gerald had woken her from a sound sleep, his face a half-moon floating above her bed, and that night it had been her turn to jump. "My God, you scared me half to—" "Janet, shh," he said, and she had the strange thought that he'd been drinking, or was simply talking in his sleep. Yet she saw the opened slits of his eyes, a concentration of the surrounding dark; she saw the tension in his posture, in his white shoulders and downturned head as they hovered in her terrified vision. "There's still time, isn't there?" he said. "You remember, we talked about the baby, we said maybe in a year or two.... Janet? Are you listening?" Then he'd made a choking sound, and had turned his head to cough; she had risen gently from the bed and taken hold of him. He said nothing more, allowing her to lead him back across the room, toward his own rumpled bed. She got him settled in, aware that he was already sleeping, certain that he had not really woken; but sleep did not return so easily to her. She lay for a long time, her eyes open. She had performed that ritual countless times—returning him like a frightened child to his bed, soothing him however she could—but it had been years since either of them had mentioned any baby.

For a while Stan follows her, like a docile child. He shifts his weight from side to side; he makes vague, appreciative comments. "Now *this* is nice," he says. In the packed, complicated silence of this room, his enthusiasm is jarring. "I like this a lot."

"Yes, it's beautiful..." Janet says. They are standing before a large statue—Randolph Rogers, "Nydia, the Blind Flower Girl of Pompeii." Slowly Janet circles the sculpture, amazed by the compressed urgency of the girl's posture. She is hunched forward, eternally poised in flight, her limbs and drapery conveying an elegant containment in her fear, a tragic integrity. Janet stops before the girl's face, the smoothed-over sightless eyes. She imagines such a girl, a blind girl hearing cries all about her, sensing the supernatural onslaught of heat, destruction, death; the girl's emotion is somehow preserved here, in the white glittering stone.

Her fingers itching, Janet reaches to touch the girl's eyes, but Stan grabs hold of her wrist. "See the sign?" he whispers. "You're not supposed to touch anything."

She drifts away from the statue, toward a long row of Impressionist paintings. Monet, Renoir, Degas.... "Look, oh look at this," she breathes. It's a painting by Renoir, "Mademoiselle Legrand." A shy, hauntingly beautiful young girl of about twelve, her hair a glorious light-filled auburn, a tiny jewel glittering at her finger. The face conveys timidity, innocence, an eerie poise. The child will become a child-woman, Janet thinks, fascinated by the balancing of elements— the child's elegance and beauty, the artist's sense of doom.

At her side, Stan is growing restless. "Shouldn't we find Gerald?" he says. "Is he—"

She refuses to hear him; her awareness is filled by these glorious paintings. She moves from one to the next, feeling herself alone at last, cut loose, floating—how was it possible that she'd stayed away so long? That the pictures hung here, day in and day out, without her coming to pay homage, to match their exhilaration with her own? Now she stands before a small, unfamiliar painting by Van Gogh—"Woman in a Wood." At first glance an unappealing work, heavy with dark greens and browns, muddy-looking. Like the numberless trees, the woman is little more than a stilled column, a slab of paint applied rapidly, angrily. But entering the picture, Janet feels its power. The woman is trapped, of course; even the sky offers no hope in this landscape so rampant with life, claustral, entangling its human victim. Janet can readily imagine a pinprick of flame arising somewhere in those woods, spreading rapidly, cleansing the landscape of all good, all evil. She takes a deep breath, then another. Trembling, her hand floats toward the painting, one finger outstretched as if touching the woman, or the slab of paint that represents the woman, might somehow comfort her—the way her mother had comforted her when she was a child, waking in tears. It's only a dream, Janet—only a dream. But as her finger nears the canvas, she feels a man's hands enclosing her waist; his breath is warm against her throat. She turns around, startled and angry.

"What are you—"

"What's wrong?" Gerald says, confused. Clearly, he is more startled than she.

"Oh, it's you—but you shouldn't—"

She breaks off. Can she blame her husband, really? But neither can she make him understand, of course, or even communicate her exhilaration, her sense of power. She gives him her old smile—conciliating, mildly hopeful.

"Where's Stan?" she asks, but she is watching Gerald. There is something strange about him; he seems shy, boyish. He has removed the sunglasses, revealing eyes of a pale, aching blue. Have they always been that color? she wonders. He takes one of her hands and kisses it.

"Could we leave?" he asks, gently. "I can't look at this stuff...." His voice is flat, apologetic.

"You mean—the Impressionists?" she says. "Or—"

"All of it," Gerald says.

They find Stan and walk soberly back to the car. For several minutes they sit awkwardly silent, but then Janet says: "I'm coming back, you know. I'm coming back next Sunday."

They are stopped at a red light. Her hands rise to her face, fluttering—but why should she be nervous? She has not spoken in anger, but as if she were alone in the car.

Following a stray impulse, she puts down the visor and stares for a moment into the small mirror. She sees a blond-haired, reasonably pretty woman, wearing an unreadable expression. Tense, expectant, insolent? She is pale, perhaps too pale, excepting the small, feverish blossoms at the tops of her cheeks.

How long since she has stared into a mirror? she wonders. But yes, there she is. She remembers.

Gerald had turned toward the rear of the car. "So, how do you feel about tomorrow, eh?" he says to Stan, who leans forward, his big arms along the top of the front seat. "It's a big day, isn't it?"

Janet hears the falsity, the desperation in Gerald's words to his brother; they spark a flame in her heart so sudden, so merciless, that she literally clutches the wheel.

"Yeah, I'm looking forward to it," Stan says, grinning. "I'm looking forward to everything."

The Metamorphosis

Tiny distant lights, prickling this soft, uncertain, rumbling darkness—star lights, spot lights! She thinks: here it all begins. He thinks: *here I am, again.* That portentous hush, little flickers of light near the ceiling—wavering, dancing, mocking a night sky to still the waiting hundreds in suspense, to quiet their voices and widen their eyes for *her.* For Lacey. Who also waits, not knowing herself when the tiny ceiling stars will vanish and give way to the light-flood and her own radiant smile and thunderous welcome.

She waits, her heart pounding. The normal lighting disappeared to prepare for her, voices fell into expectant silence—broken only by scattered whispers, exclamations, giggles—and now she stands onstage, alone. Invisible except for the weak unpredictable lights hovering far above her and reflected by her sequins if she breathes; or the sudden flare of a match being struck, out there; or the faint glimmering of cigarettes in the distance, moving in slight dizzying patterns. When the lights go up she must smile, she must not scan the audience except in her vast, sweet, impersonal gaze that takes in all of them, loves them all. How she loves them! She thinks: look at them but don't see them, their faces. Don't really see. He thinks: *I am afraid.*

But darkness persists and she sees nothing, no one. How she once reveled in these brief breathless moments just before the lights, the cheers…her heart had pounded in excitement, not in

fear. Her heart pounds, hammers. What had Teddy said?—
"Sweetheart, don't be afraid—it's not the same place anymore, not
to worry! This is your homecoming, they all love you, everyone
loves you!" "But what if I look out there and see—and see—"
"Lacey, don't worry! I'm taking care of you now, nothing should
make you afraid anymore—you're well again and gorgeous as ever
and you're coming home a star—they'll love you, they'll worship
you! You're a goddess, Lacey—nothing less." "But—" "No buts:
a goddess."

Teddy's words are like bits of ice shooting through her veins.
The air reeks with Fear and she can smell it. He gave her something:
small orange capsules. She took them greedily—two, three, five,
she can't remember—so that now she feels the Fear but can't
remember why. Something out there, something dangerous, but
there is a constant faint buzzing in her head and a slight film over
her eyes and she will be all right. When the lights go up she does
not want her eyes to flick outward to the crowd as if searching
for someone, for one particular face. Nothing is there, nothing
her eyes could catch onto. Past is past. Four years since she stood
here last, since then she has played clubs in countless major cities
in the States and in Europe, she is Lacey Clarke, Lacey, a star,
the queen of all queens and adored by everyone. They worship me,
she thinks.

He thinks: *she is a star and no one can hurt her, not anymore...*

A tradition: walking onstage in silence, in darkness; but they
know. It excites them, her presence they cannot quite see. Only a
teasing flash of sequins, so many minutes of suspense! Most of
them, tonight, have probably never seen her. But they love, adore,
worship her. A goddess! They know she began here long ago—in
this dingy, smallish club in the seedy section of a mid-sized,
unglamorous city—and went on to New Orleans, Atlanta, New
York, London Amsterdam Paris and wowed them all. She didn't
have to come back here and so they love her all the more. They
remember the story in *Newsweek*, what an honor! *Lacey Clarke:
Dragging Her Way to Stardom.* Her picture—those wide-set violet
eyes, the blond flawless waves of hair, that angel mouth!—was
placed alongside that of John Wesley Herrington, a nondescript
young man in glasses who stared dully out of a black-and-white

photo, probably from a high school yearbook. The caption read: "John Wesley Herrington/Lacey Clarke: The Metamorphosis." She remembers how popular it became, putting the pictures side by side. She remembers feature stories in the New York *Times*, the Washington *Post*, the Cleveland *Plain-Dealer*, the Atlanta *Journal-Constitution*, the Dallas *Times-Herald*, even three staidly written columns in *The New Republic* with the two pictures placed neatly above them, side by side. She read all these stories cynically, her eyes narrowed; or Teddy would read them to her, while someone did her makeup. Together they laughed over all this publicity, since it helped make them rich and was so absurd...and she laughed to herself, privately, because the newspapers and therefore the world would never understand who she was or why she created such love, they could never understand these sweet moments of fear just before the music, lights and cheers, their crude perceptions could never sharpen down to moments such as this!

Yes, she thinks, the darkness is pulsing with love—and at once the Fear subsides. Whispered conversations continue, out there; she senses the excitement in their voices. She can be anyone, her act is carefully planned of course but she can be anyone at all: she can be a goddess of her own making, she can be Diana Barbra Liza, or she can simply be *Lacey* for they will accept even that, she is that big a star. She feels the tension rise, here in this large room and its enveloping darkness pierced by the tiny star-lights and her sequins and the match-flares, everything hinted at and nothing disclosed, she feels a tingling in the muscles of her thighs, her calves, something burns half-pleasurably in her throat and she feels a bright ecstatic stinging in her eyes. Tears. Such love and excitement and tension can hardly be withstood, the moment is too rare, too brief, too fleeting—and the past is past, forgotten, she is home again and she is loved and everything is reborn, she feels something like a small exquisite flood deep inside her—only a flood of love!

In an instant music blares and the crowd cheers and her body sparkles in light.

She thinks: I am loved.

He thinks: *I do not exist.*

* * *

"God, you were so fine. So beautiful..." For once he isn't screaming: his voice is a reverent whisper.

"Don't call me God," she jokes. "I'm a girl."

Teddy lowers his eyes. "A goddess. A goddess."

"I'm tired, Ted."

"But of course, you worked hard—a solid hour. Can't you hear them?—they're still cheering, Lace. They love you. They want you."

She sits in a rickety chair before the oversized mirror that accompanies all her travels; the mirror is surrounded by light bulbs that make her face eerily bright. The dressing room itself is decrepit, ugly, dirt in all the corners, paint needed everywhere, but she pays no attention to that. She remembers the first night she'd used this room, four years ago—she'd thought it grand enough. Now she sees only herself and the mirror, they are in love, she has forgotten why she is here. She has forgotten everything.

Teddy hands her something: two orange capsules.

"No more, Ted."

"But the second show isn't for two hours, Lace. You don't want to lose it. Don't forget Amsterdam."

"But I *want* to forget Amsterdam—"

"God, how they loved you. They were so hyped for the second show, I thought they'd tear the place apart when you canceled. I hung around, listening to them, while we were waiting for the ambulance—I thought they'd burn the place down!"

She stares at Teddy: a big man, wearing glasses with heavy black frames that are always sliding down his moist nose. She watches Teddy sweat. He is very excitable and he sweats uncontrollably, he never stops sweating. He manages her tours and promotes her career and soothes her fears and stands just backstage at each of her shows and shouts praise at her constantly and always sweats. He *loves* her. She'd found him in New York, when it looked as if her career might be flagging, he'd fallen in love with her at once and since then they'd spent every moment together. He must be forty-five at least, though she isn't certain. Neither of them asks questions. He's never met John Wesley and he doesn't want to.

"Relax, Ted."

But when she says these words her voice wavers and she wonders if he can tell. She does need the capsules. But no. No. She remembers Amsterdam. Toward the end of the first show, that night, her eyes had stuck without warning on one of the faces out there, they stuck and could not move: she stared. Stricken, paralyzed. Who was he? He wasn't smiling like everyone else. He wasn't swaying with the music or leaning forward eagerly into her magnetic presence onstage or shouting cheers and encouragement like everyone else. He sat back, scowling. He watched her. She froze. She finished the number in her chilled flesh, her eyes widened with terror, her legs stiff as a doll's.

Backstage Teddy said, "Honey, what happened?"

"He's there. He's—out there."

"Baby, *who* is out there? Who is this guy—?"

"I—I—Ted, cancel the second show. I can't—I—"

"Is it somebody you know? Lacey?"

She pushed past him. She locked the door to her dressing room and stood there, panting. Already Teddy was pounding at the door. *Lacey, sweetheart, open up—Lacey, I love you, I—* She tore off her wig and threw it in the corner. That face: sometimes she becomes careless and her eyes flick out toward the crowd and one of them catches at her, one particular face. She remembered how he scowled. His mouth a thin dark supple line. That mouth was like a small crack, her eyes had frozen onto it, on that little dark squiggling line like a dangerous crack of unreason, a dark delicate river that might lead her riveted eyes away from here, out of herself entirely... she could not look away. Mechanically, her own mouth had continued moving to the recorded voice blaring out from somewhere but the movements of her body had slowed, weakened, she stared at his dark unsmiling line of a mouth and then, with a quick jerk, glanced back up into his eyes, terrified. They stared. A recognition.

She remembers Teddy's hysterical voice, outside. With a cloth she had wiped off her makeup, pawed at it viciously like a child trying to wipe away dirt; she was careful not to glance into the mirror. Her skin hurt. She ripped off her earrings. *Lacey, Lacey, please unlock the door—please answer me. The crowd loved you, sweetheart—there's no one out there, no one bad—don't be afraid—* She had heard the muffled hammering of her heart.

She hears it now: it is telling her something.

She says to Ted, "I feel like hell. Did you have to bring up Amsterdam?"

"I'm sorry, sweetheart."

She tries to be ironic. "They want to eat me alive, don't they? Don't they want that, Teddy—to eat me up until there's nothing left?"

Teddy snickers.

She thinks about the crowd—usually she doesn't mind them. Most of them are lonely, unbeautiful pricks, she thinks sadly. Most of them would slit their throats if she asked them to. She makes a mental note for her next act: ask one of them to slit his throat, get him onstage, smile, raise a flirtatious eyebrow, hand him a razor blade and say in that sweet simpering voice: *Slit it, honey. Slit it for Lacey.* It would be justice after all, for hasn't she wasted too many nights of her adult life in crowds like these, waiting for something, always waiting?—even before she became a star. Especially then. She remembers John Wesley at eighteen, searching among those faces every night for the perfect man, the ideal—he was there, of course! Somewhere! It was only a matter of time. Poor John Wesley, just out of high school, sneaking away from the house after his parents had gone to sleep, still wearing a crew-cut—hopeless, living on hope. He had wised up, eventually. The faces had turned into fearsome masks, eventually, and he began wearing one himself. John Wesley found four lovers in the crowd and died four separate times and was reborn.

He became acquainted with the Fear.

As a child, he had not known fear—though he'd been a disappointment, certainly, that was always made clear. What was it his father called him? "The runt"—of course, he was *the runt of the litter.* Frail, sickly, with that unaccountably girlish face. His older sister, Marcia, had dressed him in her own clothes one rainy summer afternoon and he'd never forgotten it: only ten years old, yet he'd stared into the mirror in fascination at the long pale-yellow dress, the pinkened lips, the powdered flawless skin. His eyes had gone wide in disbelief. A transformation. "Johnny, you look just like Marilyn Monroe!" his sister screamed, delighted. He himself had not screamed—he only stared and stared. Years later, when the idea of performing first entered John Wesley's head, his mind had reeled back to that afternoon in his childhood and to Marcia's delighted, half-envious stare....

Onstage at twenty-one, in that seedy ordinary club, her first appearance, she had seen him at last: her eyes had caught on him.... But he had changed: there was no love in those eyes. It happened again in New Orleans. And in San Francisco. In Amsterdam, finally, Teddy had pounded on her door: *Sweetheart, why don't you answer, please say you're all right. Who's out there, Lace?—I won't let them hurt you, don't worry—Lacey? Lacey? — Hey! You guys! Somebody do something, help me break down this door—go get somebody, a locksmith—oh my poor Lacey, oh God— please, sweetheart, talk to me—just one word—one syllable—*

She was dazed with fear and she'd made a mistake. Slouched at her dressing table, trying to ignore Teddy, she had glanced for an instant into the mirror. She saw: something horrible, grotesque, freakish, only a mass of smeared blues, pinks, reds like blood dried but still bright, tiny lurid black rivers streaking down her cheeks. She stayed silent, staring. They looked like tiny cracks in a doll's face, but they moved. She bared her teeth. Her hand reached for something—a bottle of sleeping pills, bought in London at the "chemist's" but still half-full—but she did not move her eyes. She stared. The rivers widened into little faint ribbons as her face got wetter, she heard her own whimpering, a sound that did not seem to be hers at all—a man's unaccustomed, belabored whimpering— and she ignored Teddy's hysterical banging on her door. She swallowed pills without water. Four pills, then four more. Then six. Eight. They were small pills with a slick coating and went down easily, the bottle was soon empty, she let herself slide down into her chair until she could no longer see that face in the mirror and then, somehow, she was on the floor, holding onto the curving legs of her little vanity table, sobbing....

Now she thinks: there is something out there, it wants me, it doesn't love me at all but it wants me—

"Relax, Lace, do you hear? Shouldn't you take something? Lace?"

She stares at Teddy. "No second show," she says coldly.

"But Lacey!"

"No—I can't do it."

"Baby no, you're just upset—I shouldn't have brought up Amsterdam, I'm sorry. Listen Lace, they love you. I love you. Not to worry, Lacey, not to—"

"Call me John," she says.

He stiffens. "Don't lower your voice like that, honey, it's not like you, you're too beautiful for that kind of voice, I can't stand—"

"I'm through with this, Ted," she says. "It scares me. The crowd scares me. There's something they want—I don't know, but sometimes I see one of their faces, accidentally, and I realize what could be out there, that anything at all could be out there, waiting...."

"Honey, I don't understand you."

"Once I thought it was a man out there, a certain man. And I'd find him. I'd be beautiful and he'd see me and we'd find each other."

"But what about me?"

"Then I began to see other things, something in a pair of eyes, or the gesture of a hand, or someone's mouth—sometimes I get so afraid—"

"Lacey, this is nonsense!" Teddy is angry. He stands up and moves around the room, irritated, pacing. He says, "You remember what Dr. Adcock said, that time—a neurosis, Lace. It's only a neurosis. You've got to fight it. Now look." He pauses rhetorically, standing over her until she raises her meek eyes. Her brain is blank, she is listening. His long white finger points and nags. "You just look: you don't need this. You don't need to be told anymore—you've beat this once and you'll beat it again. You *know*, intellectually, that no one is out there, that there's nothing to be afraid of, that no one wants to hurt you. So you don't have to let this happen. This is life, Lace: overcoming fear, struggling through this shit. You've got to live your life!"

"But this isn't my life, it isn't real—"

"Of course it's real—you're a star!"

"But I wish—I wish I could give them something—something real. Not Lacey. Not going through someone else's movements and mouthing someone else's words. But I know they wouldn't love me then—they only love Lacey."

"But Lacey, Lacey—that's who you are."

She thinks: No.

He thinks: *You've got to live your life!*

She shakes her head, staring at the floor. There is a silence.

Teddy bends down. "Sweetheart, just take these. They'll help you through. You know the doctor said it's all right—they're just to help you through. Lace—?"

She lets him lay the capsules in her palm.

He smiles. "On with the show?" And when she nods he smiles again, he backs away in deference: "I'll go away for a while, honey, let you get freshened up—take your time, Lace, you've got an hour—call me if you need me...." He backs out the door.

She thinks: Bastard. She gets up and goes into the toilet, watches the pills swirl down. Bastard!

He thinks: *I need you....*

Nothing to fear, she thinks. The show is almost over and she writhes in light—the final number! She floats around the stage in white chiffon, yards and yards of it, trailing a white feather boa she uses on the crowd to make them laugh. One moment she is simpering, coy, a tease, the next she opens up and has them on their feet, cheering. Lacey! *Lacey!* They cry out her name, they are frenzied and ecstatic and in love with Lacey. She smiles, feeling her lashes touch the tops of her cheeks, swaying with the music, knowing they are in love with her every movement. When she looks out she can glimpse, far in the distance, posters covering the walls of the club—announcing the homecoming appearance of Lacey Clarke, her name in high, pink, swirling letters! As she passes her sweet vapid stare among the crowd she notices some of them wearing large round buttons, pink letters on a white background: I LOVE LACEY. There is nothing to fear out there, she did not take the pills and is perfectly clear-headed and she even lets her eyes rest upon their faces, their eyes, their smiling mouths, but there is nothing to fear. The number is coming to an end and the lights are hot, bright, glaring, she can scarcely see but knows they have risen to their feet, cheering, stamping, calling her name—

Shouting, *Encore! Encore!*

Of course the show must not end, they want more, more. Always more. She bows and grins, she keeps them in suspense, and finally signals to the rafters: of course she will oblige. It is planned. She senses Teddy in the wings, smiling. The lights grow softer now and the music starts up again and she begins to "sing" in a strident, strong, sarcastic voice—"Free Again." Her favorite song because she never knows if they believe the words.

They are listening but still they seem tense, expectant, barely restrained. She moves, gestures. Grimaces. She is giving them everything but still it is not enough. Her heart hammers in glee. They love only the mask of her but that is all right—she is a symbol, an ideal, a star. She knows they too are wearing masks and she has often thought, up here, working her heart out, how necessary are these brash outlandish masks, how indispensable to protect the secret, feeling self. Smiling onstage. Backstage her makeup streaming away in tears, sweat, grimaces of fear.... She understands it now. She is all right. She sings:

> *Free again...*
> *Lucky lucky me, I'm free again...*

But something is happening—the song is winding down, ending, the last song, but they will not let her go. They are chanting something: *We want Lacey! We want Lacey!* Where is the music?—somehow the record is over. It is over too quickly. The crowd cheers, stamps, screams. *We want Lacey!* Yet here she is, in full view. What do they want? She stands there, trying to smile, to make a joke of it—she does a little dance. She rolls her eyes. But this does not appease them. *We want*— Finally her smile dissolves. She stands there awkwardly in the hot lights; she feels a dribbling of sweat down her back. Cold insidious moisture breaks out on her temples. What is happening? Her body seems awkward suddenly, exposed, swaying slightly...the violent heat of lights bears down, she breaks into sweat. The crowd is screaming, calling—she can't make out the words. She turns to them, her arms spread wide in a helpless gesture, an appeal. She begins to speak: "Please—I want to say that I love—no, please—please listen—I want—" But from a distance, of course, she appears to be moving her mouth silently, they cannot hear her words; she knows this but keeps on. "Please wait—no, please wait—" They yell, applaud, jeer. She squints out, trying to see past the lights, trying to make contact with something out in that total, restless, wavering darkness.... Then there is a throbbing in her temples, making her throat ache with fear and her eyes widen in fear and her bones chill with fear: her eyes stick on something. A smile. His smile.

Behind her she hears a familiar voice, probably Teddy's, stage-whispering her name—somehow she hears it through the crowd. Their cries. Hissing, chanting. *We want—!* She thinks: Is this love? He thinks: *Is this love?* The music has vanished, drained away into that little crack between his lips, that blackness, that tiny river…she stares, fascinated. The crowd has gotten to its feet but she has no eyes for them. She stares. Somehow they are closer: the darkness, the vast sea of faces, like living pale flares in the darkness, bobbing. The bright lights vanish. She discovers she is no longer onstage but is being sucked down gradually into them, she feels hands upon her, she knows that the minute crack of unreason has ballooned around her—how has this happened? Her eyes are suddenly freed and they dart all around, like a frightened bird's.

She imagines herself in the eye of a hurricane, feeling nothing. Harsh, high voices all about her, raucous, greedy, a cacophony strangely distant, unreal. She ignores it. She is pushed and turned and mauled. Her eyes rest on nothing, she sets them free. She hears her name in the screaming calls of voices, a frenzy of callings, she feels deft hands paw at her from all sides, pummeling, she sees the white chiffon go drifting across the darkness in shreds, like delicate white birds fleeing a tempest. Hands tear at fragments of the dress that still cling to her body until there is nothing—she feels her wig sucked away, her earrings yanked off, her shoes wrenched from her feet, something twists and tears at her stockings, something yanks at her underwear, something dangles out. She drifts in this dark turbulent sea of noise. Fists appear, pummeling, angry, then retreat dripping red. She glimpses a face: its bloodied nose, glasses aslant (broken?) across it, eyes white with terror. "Lace, grab my—" The face dissolves back, disappears. She is pounded, clawed, mauled, hands on all parts of her body, poking, prodding, getting in…. Someone's teeth raze her cheek: a bright spurt of blood. She wants to say, to scream: "But I love…" but she cannot say these words, they are a lie, all the love is being sucked out of her, drained out, like energy sucked out of stars until they become great black holes, ugly pockets in the universe. Now something flashes before her eyes: a blade, a knife blade rising out of the dark like a silver fin approaching on a black sea.

Teddy's face appears again—strained, contorted. Struggling. He takes her arm. "Lace, hold on to me—" He won't let go, she thinks, won't let me be free.... And then she feels it, the harsh bright stab of pain. It spreads downward through her legs and up through her chest, her arms, up her aching throat to her wide, blank, staring eyes. The pain cleanses her—it is pure, absolute, a miracle.

Her eyes roll back inside her head.

The crowd sends up a cheer. Something bloody is passed from hand to hand, in triumph.

Teddy holds on, pulls her slowly away. Naked, battered, inhuman, like some hideous plucked chicken, some great bleeding insect—he pulls it away slowly, back toward the stage. And it seems he will pull it free, drag it away and backstage and into hiding, for the crowd does not notice and continues with its festival.

II

from *A Friendly Deceit*

The Boarder

People enter your life in the oddest ways!—something I've often observed to Ralston, without his exactly agreeing. Ralston is my husband: fifty-five, soft-spoken, and solid as a brick building, but he isn't much for philosophical remarks or stepping back to consider the long view. He just plows right along, one day after another, and you've got to admire that. He likes most people, but doesn't have the easily piqued *curiosity* about them like I do, and so it's doubtful that he'd ever have met Professor Coates—in the odd way I met him, or any way at all—if I hadn't had what Ralston calls, dry-mouthed, one of my "bright ideas." In my opinion he'd also have missed a most profound and illuminating experience, though there's little chance of Ralston admitting to that.

My idea, to be plain, was that we take in Professor Coates as a boarder. He and I had met in the cleaners one day, the one I've patronized for twenty years or so, where I'd just gotten in line behind a small-framed youngish man in a tweed jacket. He stood quietly holding up a dress shirt on a hanger, the sleeves lifted up to show underarms that had been…well, pulverized, it looked like. In a snap I saw that they'd used much too strong a chemical for the underarm stains and that the young man should get a new shirt, but the clerk—a tiny, red-haired girl I'd never cared for—stood there shaking her head. And then, out of the young man's mouth, came the most amazing words: "Oh, very well. I hope you don't mind my having asked." The girl blinked, half-smiled in a smug way, and it was then I had one of my "impulses," as Ralston calls them. I just had to see that young man's face, so I stepped around and got on tiptoes (I'm a rather petite woman) to peer over the shoulder of the ruined shirt.

"I couldn't help overhearing," I began—and not to brag or go on about it, I had the manager out front within five minutes and a new twenty-dollar bill in Professor Coates's hand. The red-haired girl had left for her lunch break, in something of a huff.

Anyhow, that's how we met, and out on the sidewalk we got to talking. He interested me right away because he seemed so helpless and had such excellent manners. He spoke in this odd, kind of formal way, not off-putting or affected but like he hadn't yet got the knack of talking like ordinary people. For instance: "You were extremely kind to intercede for me like that." And a minute later: "Why, a cup of coffee at your house would be delightful. How hospitable of you." Now I found this way of talk most intriguing, especially since the man looked normal in every other respect. Professor Coates was about thirty-five, with dark hair neatly cut, and eyeglasses with thick rims tinted the same deep brown as his eyes, and slender clean hands—the nails *exquisitely* clean and well tended—and a generally shy and kind-hearted aura to him, the sort that's very appealing to a woman. And he looked at you so directly, with such friendliness and gratitude, that you couldn't help but love him right away ("love" is exactly the right word, but don't jump to conclusions: I'm old enough to be the professor's mom and besides, despite all the little digs I'm nuts about Ralston). It's just that I found Professor Coates...well, so interesting, and also vulnerable somehow, undefended. An attractive trait in that rough-and-tumble world out there, so I was tickled pink when he accepted my invitation for coffee—after all, I told him, I lived just around the corner, and no, it wasn't any trouble at all.

So we went. And sat there talking. And having coffee, and later some lemonade, followed by a plateful of macaroons. And we talked some more. The experience, I tell you, was beyond anything I could have expected. Granted, I did most of the talking at first. I told him about Ralston and his work down at the tire store, and about our daughter Sarah who had just flown off to college the month before, and about our sixteen-year-old spaniel, Lucky, who'd died in her sleep just a week before that. I said how upset Sarah had gotten, insisting that Lucky had somehow sensed that she was going to abandon her, how it was all her fault and now she wasn't going, after all!—those few days had been terrible, probably the worst we'd ever lived through as a family. Ralston had spent a couple of hours up in Sarah's bedroom, talking in a gentle, persuasive voice, and when he came out he looked gray as ashes and said that Sarah had decided to leave a week *early* for college, she'd get there the day the dorms opened and try to busy herself with— But then I stopped myself; I'd felt a little catch in my throat. "Enough of that!" I said to Professor Coates, laughing it off. "I guess you're not interested in an old lady's troubles."

This wasn't completely honest, I suppose, since all the time I talked Professor Coates hadn't moved his damp brown eyes from mine. He sat very erect, every now and then taking a small sip of the coffee, looking concerned and thoughtful; his listening so closely made me a bit self-conscious.

"On the contrary," Professor Coates said, in his polite way. "Your story is very affecting. You must have a great deal of strength."

"Strength?" I said. I didn't understand.

"Inner strength," Professor Coates said.

No one had ever told me such a thing, and I felt that I'd earned the professor's respect without even trying. Certainly I'd earned his trust, since right away—and this is what I'd never have expected—he began talking about his own past life. Somehow I'd pegged him as a timid, withdrawn type, but actually he spoke in a frank unhurried voice, the rhythms pleasant and convincing. As he talked, I imagined this as the same voice he used to teach his classes at the university. For that's what he talked about first—his one-year appointment in the History department, his heavy work load of preparing lectures and corresponding with other professors and writing a book (a long, complicated book, he said with a sigh) about Napoleon's last days. He'd moved to Atlanta in August, he said, but after two months he still didn't know much of anyone here, and he often thought that there wasn't much point— he had so much work to do, and he'd be moving somewhere else when the school year ended. The more Professor Coates talked, the more wistful he sounded. When I got up for the lemonade and cookies I said, "Go on, go on," and by the time I sat down again he'd already started talking about his parents.

Something awful had happened, he said. He broke one of the macaroons neatly in half, but then put both halves back down on the plate. The previous year, he said, he hadn't done any teaching. His mother had become very ill and he'd returned to Boston last September, to help take care of her. His father was retired but depressed—"severely depressed," Professor Coates said—and couldn't do much. Cancer, it was; a hopeless case. As the doctors had warned him, things went from bad to worse, and before Christmas she was gone. But that was only the beginning, in a way, because then he had to tend to his father, which was really much more taxing than his mother's care had been. In a slow, mournful voice Professor Coates told me that his father had died suddenly— that is, by his own hand. He didn't specify how, and of course I didn't ask. Big tears stood in my eyes; I took a swallow of lemonade to wash down the lump in my throat.

"That's—that's awful," I finally managed.

Professor Coates opened his long immaculate hands, palms up. "Thank you for listening," he said, his voice remarkably calm. "Over where I'm staying, it's pretty isolated. I really haven't made very many friends."

"Where are you staying?" I asked.

"Oh, just in the faculty quarters," Professor Coates said, shrugging. "Actually it's quite a nice—"

"Why don't you move in here?"—the question and the idea came at the same moment, but I didn't regret my words. Ralston often says that I speak before I think, but what was there to think about, really? It was the perfect solution.

"You could stay in Sarah's bedroom," I said, talking faster now that Professor Coates was shaking his head. "I've often thought to myself, we should take in a boarder, we really should"—this was a white lie, I guess, but maybe I'd *felt* it, without really *thinking* it— "and since Mr. Parks and I sleep downstairs you'd have plenty of privacy, and your own bath. You could have dinner with us, too. I'm not a bad cook, and I—"

"Mrs. Parks, you're far too kind," and I could tell by his face that he was both alarmed and pleased by the invitation. The alarm I understood—it seemed too sudden, it was ridiculous when you thought that we'd met only a couple of hours ago. I've always had faith, however, in my woman's intuition—I have this knack for seeing to the heart of a situation, even Ralston will grant me that. Sometimes you have to proceed slowly, though; you have to bring people around.

"Well, at least come for dinner tonight," I said. "You can meet my husband, and we'll talk about it."

He paused, looking pleased despite himself. "I'd be delighted to come for dinner," he said, "but as for the other—" He stopped, then reached down for one of the macaroon halves.

We would discuss the matter, of course, but I knew that the thing was as good as done. I felt happy—completely, absurdly happy. So there was nothing left to do but reach across and take the other half of Professor Coates's macaroon. We sat there for a while, smiling, chewing happily. There was nothing more to say.

Granted, the idea of a border caused a tiff between Ralston and me. I'd told Professor Coates to come for dinner around seven, thinking I'd have a couple of hours to break the news to Ralston, calm him down, win him over; but naturally he picked that very evening to stop by his brother Ferris's house for a beer, so that when he got home at six-thirty I had to explain everything in a rush. We were in the dining room, where I kept straightening and re-straightening the three plates, the silverware. I didn't much want to look at Ralston.

"Honey?" I said at last, adjusting a candle in the silver-plate candelabrum we'd gotten for our twenty-fifth anniversary, from Ferris and his wife Julie. "Shouldn't you get cleaned up? I told Professor Coates seven o'clock, and it's already—"

"No," Ralston said, from behind me.

I turned around. He looked clean enough in his work khakis, his silver-white hair combed back neatly from his crown. Yet his eyes had darkened; he looked tired and angry at once.

"Then at least change your clothes, OK?" I said, keeping my voice light. "See what I'm wearing?" And I lifted my arms, turning smartly like one of those models on TV, showing off my sky-blue linen with the gathered sleeves and hoping to get a smile out of Ralston.

"I don't mean that," he said, the twin creases between his eyes deepening. "I mean *no* to the whole idea. No, no, no."

He pulled out his chair at the head of the table, snapping the cloth napkin onto his lap. "Let's eat."

"Ralston, I've invited the man for dinner. He's a very nice man, and I want *you* to be nice, too."

Ralston put down the fork he'd been holding above his empty plate, mockingly. The corners of his mouth drooped. "For heaven's sake, Lily. Did you really ask the man to *live* with us? Without discussing it with me?"

He was weakening. I hurried over and sat in my usual chair, leaning close to Ralston and speaking in a near-whisper. "It's only for a few months, sweetie, only till the end of the school year. Then Sarah will be coming home, but in the meantime won't it be nice to have someone in the house? It's been so quiet around here."

"*You* live here," Ralston said, but I saw the little glint in his eye that meant I'd won. "So it's never quiet."

I reached out and pinched his forearm. "Scalawag," I said.

"But a perfect stranger, Lily," Ralston said. By now, even his shoulders had drooped. "A man we don't even know—"

"He's a lonesome fellow, I think," I said quickly, bringing out the ammunition I'd stored in my head all during the afternoon, "and it's the Christian thing to do, isn't it? I'm sure that Father Dalton would approve. And it'll bring a little money in, of course, and maybe he can even help around the house—you know, small repairs and such, and on top of that—"

Ralston had lifted his palm, so I stopped.

"It'll depend," he said.

"Depend? Depend on what?"

He threw me a look that said, *Dumb question, Lily!* Experience had taught me not to react to this look, so then Ralston said: "On him."

The doorbell rang.

"Fine," I said, getting up, smoothing my dress. "You'll see that I'm right, then. You'll be forced to *admit* that I'm right."

And, of course, he did exactly that, for Professor Coates was a completely charming dinner guest. He brought flowers for me, a bottle of Chardonnay for Ralston; he remarked on my dress several times and didn't seem to notice Ralston's wrinkled khakis. And if I say so myself, the meal was delicious. Swiss steak, new potatoes, Caesar salad; and my famous raspberry cheesecake for dessert. During the meal Professor Coates asked us a good many questions, but nothing personal or inappropriate; he asked about Ralston's work down at the store, he asked about our church after I'd mentioned something about Sunday mass, saying that he'd been raised as a Catholic, too, though unfortunately he had "lapsed" in recent years, and most of all he asked about Sarah, assuming that she was the favorite topic of conversation for both Ralston and me, which of course she was. This was the point, in fact, when the professor finally won my husband over. Ralston had been a bit reserved and stiffish up to now, but he leaned forward and asked Professor Coates eagerly about the college Sarah had chosen—was it really as well regarded as Sarah thought, would it give her the best possible chance for getting into law school, presuming she did well? Did most of Professor Coates's students, especially his freshman students, seem *happy* in their new lives, did they get over their homesickness quickly, did they make new friends?—and for that matter, what was college like, exactly? Professor Coates reassured him on all points, telling him about the social activities, the counselors, the sheer excitement of college life for most students. We shouldn't be alarmed at not hearing from Sarah very often—that was a good sign, in fact; it meant that she was just too busy to be homesick.

Ralston sat back from the table, satisfied. "How about some brandy for Professor Coates, Lily?" he asked, to my great surprise. "We still have that bottle, don't we?"

He meant the bottle from our little anniversary party, eight months before.

"Yes, of course," and as I poured brandy in the kitchen I heard Ralston saying to Professor Coates that if he'd like to board with us for the rest of the school year, that would be fine with him. For reply, I could hear only the professor's polite murmuring, but I felt sure that he would accept. During the dinner, it occurred to me that we had found out very little about him, and of course I didn't allude to the sad story about his parents. Having unburdened himself, perhaps he now felt embarrassed; and I wondered if his barrage of politely worded questions were a way, partly, to avoid revealing more about himself. A very shy man, this Professor Coates! And how pleasant it was, to be able to help him! Feeling a bit sly, I lifted one of the brandy glasses and made a toast to myself, for having accomplished so much in one day. The liquor burned in my throat and stomach, like the sweet glow of charity itself. Then I refilled the glass, and went back to join my husband and our new boarder.

For a long while, the arrangement worked perfectly. Professor Coates kept to himself most of the time, but he took his meals with us, and occasionally joined us for an evening of TV in the den. What a polite, well-groomed man he always was!—never a hair out of place, always wearing one of his tweed jackets and his carefully polished shoes. (Ralston and Professor Coates had made a Sunday morning ritual of polishing their shoes together, the professor his Bass Weejuns and Ralston the chunky black wing-tips he wears to church, the two looking for all the world like father and son as they worked and chatted.) Nor did he seem to mind our simple ways, commenting on how "cozy" our house was, repeating every week or so how "eternally grateful" he felt to have lived here for a brief while, just like a member of the family. I noticed how often he mentioned his departure the following May, as though reminding himself that his "family member" status was temporary, or reminding us that he didn't intend to overstay his welcome. I'd feel a bit melancholy then, but with Sarah coming home for the summer I couldn't suggest that he stay any longer and decided to just enjoy him while I could.

So, everything chugged along perfectly during the fall. Only one thing bothered me, and that was how I kept feeling I didn't really *know* the professor very well, despite all the time we spent together. When I brought this up to Ralston, he said I was being silly: Professor Coates was a grown man, he needed his privacy; and there was an age difference, too. For that matter, Ralston said, in an irksome, commonsensical voice, what does he know about *us*, exactly? We're just an aging couple who watches TV on Saturday night and goes to mass on Sunday morning. How many of *your* deep, dark secrets have you confided to the professor, Lily? I told Ralston that I wasn't talking about "deep, dark secrets," only about getting to know the man. What had his childhood been like, what made him happy or angry, what did he think about right before he went to sleep, what were his dreams about the future?—that kind of thing. You expect too much, Ralston said flatly, and then he added: Also, remember that he's not a Southerner. He's from New England, right? From Boston or somewhere? That's a different kettle of fish, you know.

There was no point in arguing with Ralston, but the truth was that the longer Professor Coates lived with us, the more curious I got. I guess I should blush to admit this, but a few times, while doing the cleaning, I lingered in his room a bit longer than necessary, knowing that the professor wouldn't return until late afternoon. (Not that much cleaning was needed: he kept his closets neat as a pin, jackets and slacks organized by color, dark things on the left, shading to tans and beiges on the right. That tickled me, somehow. His drawers were orderly, too, the socks arranged in matching pairs, the under-shorts folded and neatly stacked.) Externally the room was pretty barren: while Sarah had covered the walls with posters, lined her dresser with keepsakes and framed pictures, and kept a menagerie of stuffed animals on her bed, the professor hadn't added any personal touches. He'd bought an ordinary bedspread of white chenille, and though I offered to do it, he made the bed himself every morning. He left the walls bare, and on the dresser there were only a few magazines, a small sheaf of stationery, and a brass tray holding spare change and some matchbooks. I knew that the professor didn't smoke, so I did examine the matchbooks. They were all from a place called "The Den," with a midtown address, and none of the matches had been torn. One had something written inside: the initials "D.J." with a phone number. Probably a colleague of his from the university, I thought; maybe "The Den" was a lunch place. Among the matchbooks I also found a small strip of paper with a neatly printed sentence: "History is no more than a lie agreed upon," followed by the initials "N.B." Another colleague, I guessed, though the message didn't make much sense to me. Anyhow, I didn't go further than that. In the back of his bottom drawer, under some knit shirts, there *was* a small packet of letters, but I wasn't that much of a snoop. I closed the drawer with a sigh, and vowed not to open it again.

When Sarah came home at Thanksgiving and Christmas, the professor took off for Boston, so it happened that our daughter never met the man who'd begun inhabiting her room. The arrangement was "okay by me," she said, but she refused to stay in the room, sleeping instead on the lumpy sofa in the den. That hurt my feelings a bit, but Ralston said that Sarah was going through "a phase" and it was probably best to let her alone. Otherwise she seemed happy, though. She made all A's and B's her first semester, she had a boyfriend ("sort of," she qualified), her clothes had gotten deliberately sloppy and more colorful; and she'd started frizzing her hair, tying it together in a kind of ponytail perched on the very top of her head. For once, though, I did agree with Ralston: I wasn't worried about Sarah any longer, and when she left the day after New Year's the melancholy lasted only an hour or two. And besides, I was looking forward to the professor's return, later that week.

He came back on a Saturday evening, but almost immediately went out again. I must admit, this bothered me. I'd fixed him a nice dinner and put it in the refrigerator, wrapped in foil, but Professor Coates just said, "I ate on the plane, thank you. Quite a delicious meal." It was almost ten o'clock, but he rushed upstairs and took a quick shower, then changed into jeans and a sports shirt. During the fall he'd often gone out on weekend nights, by himself—for a movie, he said, or just for a walk around the neighborhood. Though I'd tried once or twice, I'd never managed to keep myself awake until he got home, so I knew he stayed out late. Now we were having a cold snap, though, and when I heard him move lightly down the stairs I came out from the den. "My, it's such a cold night!" I said, laughing. "Why don't you come on back, have some hot chocolate with Ralston and me? You can tell us about your trip." Professor Coates smiled politely, opening the hall closet and taking out a black leather jacket I hadn't seen before. A Christmas present, maybe, though I hesitated to ask. He looked tired; even the smile seemed a bit forced. (Now Lily, Ralston had said over the holidays, when I'd expressed curiosity about what the professor was doing that very moment, you've really got to let the man alone. He's an ideal boarder, but he isn't a—a personal *friend.* Now, I didn't agree with this at all, but I said nothing. Didn't Ralston understand that the professor was lonely? That he needed someone to bring him out, get him to talk a little about himself?) He zipped up the jacket and said, "Thanks, but I'm meeting a friend of mine. I called—um, I called her from the airport, and—" He broke off, looking embarrassed. "Oh, well," I said, flustered myself, "then don't mind me! We'll talk tomorrow—have a good time!" And he was gone.

Now I'd better confess something: I felt jealous. But, to my credit, almost immediately after that I felt happy for Professor Coates. I remembered the matchbook and amused myself with a guessing game for the rest of that evening—that is, guessing what the "D" stood for. Diane? Darlene? Dorothy? It was a pointless game, of course—there were dozens of possibilities—and I didn't even mention to Ralston what the professor had said. I knew he would be irritated if I were even thinking about the professor's private life.

So, I had to keep my own counsel where the professor was concerned. There was a lot to think about, I must say, for if anything the professor became more secretive that winter. He started missing dinner and arriving home later and later from the university, his briefcase bulging. He'd mentioned that he had a heavy teaching load this semester, and he was trying to finish his book by May, and there was so much new material on Napoleon, it seemed a new book was published every other day…. We'd stand talking at the foot of the stairs, the professor in his beige overcoat, his hands and nose reddened from the cold (though he owned a car, he walked the half-mile to campus no matter how cold the weather, no matter how I chided him), his body dragged down on one side by the weight of the briefcase. But he wouldn't put down the briefcase; wouldn't let me take his coat and damp shoes and lead him into the kitchen for a nourishing dinner, or some hot chocolate, or hot tea and lemon to keep him from catching a cold. It was seven-thirty, it was eight o'clock, I *knew* he hadn't eaten a thing but still he'd back up the stairs, thanking me anyway, apologizing, touching his glasses between the eyes in an odd gesture he had (for the glasses hadn't slipped out of place) and saying sorry, he had so much work to do, papers to grade, and some reading, he was really very sorry.... And then I'd be left standing there, my neck aching as I peered upward into the dark.

Lost something, Lily? Ralston said smartly one night, passing by.

As the winter dragged on, the professor's company got scarcer, and when he did show up for a meal—breakfast, usually—he looked awful. Except for his red-rimmed nostrils he'd gotten white as the tablecloth, that kind of dead-white people get when they don't sleep right or exercise or take any vitamins. His eyes were dull and glazed, and he'd murmur that he hadn't slept well, he knew he'd be fine if he could manage to get some rest. By now, even Ralston was getting a bit concerned, and he jotted down Dr. Hutter's name and phone number—that's our internist—in case Professor Coates wanted a checkup, or maybe something to help him sleep. The professor mumbled his thanks, folding the slip of paper inside his wallet. "I really *do* regret," he said carefully, his eyes not meeting Ralston's, "having been such poor company of late."

"My goodness, don't apologize!" I broke out, before Ralston could answer.

"You see," he began, "I've been troubled by—well, something of a personal matter that I—"

"Professor Coates," I said, reaching out my hand and patting his, "don't feel like you owe us any explanations—none whatever. Your private life is your private life, and we understand that."

I glanced at Ralston, thinking he'd be pleased, but instead he shot me a threatening look—a *scowl*, it was—that made my heart jump. Ralston isn't a big man, but he has a fleshy face, thick neck, dark quick-moving eyes, and when he gets mad that combination can be fearsome. The skin hardens, the neck thickens, and the eyes have the effect of freezing you in place. You can't move, and you can hardly speak.

"What—what I meant—" I stammered.

"Why don't you let Professor Coates finish?" Ralston said, in a polite voice that was curiously like the professor's but that Ralston used only when he was furious.

"I—I'm sorry, I—"

"Please, don't trouble yourself," the professor said, and I'd no idea what he meant. I looked back and forth between him and Ralston, but they were both looking down at their plates, embarrassed. Then the professor rose quickly, saying he'd better be off. I didn't say anything, even though I noticed that he'd forgotten to take the multiple vitamin I'd put beside his plate; he hadn't eaten his scrambled eggs, either. No sooner was the professor out the door than Ralston left, too, so I got up and started cleaning the breakfast dishes, feeling sadder and more bewildered than I'd ever felt in my life.

I stayed melancholy for a long while, feeling that I was in a kind of fog and that I didn't know what I was doing. I noticed the professor's exits and entrances—he left earlier and earlier in the morning, sometimes stayed gone until nine P.M. or later, and on weekends stayed out late at night and then slept until long after Ralston and I got back from ten o'clock mass—but I no longer went out to greet him in the hallway, or tried to coax him back into the kitchen for food or conversation. February passed, and March; we began making plans for Sarah's visit during Easter vacation, though we hadn't asked the professor about his own plans. I started worrying about what would happen if they both planned to be here—who would sleep where, would the situation be strained, and so forth. And something else troubled me: all during the fall, Professor Coates had called home frequently—at least, I assumed he was calling home, I knew he had a couple of brothers still in Boston—and I remember feeling gratified that he kept in such close touch with his family. At the end of each month, the professor would ask about the long distance charges—sometimes they were more than a hundred dollars—and would promptly write me a check. After the Christmas holidays, though, the calls abruptly stopped, and I wondered if his overwork or stress or whatever was bothering him had made him decide not to call home for a while, so that his family wouldn't worry. That would be just like him, I thought. So considerate of others, he always was. That's one thing about Professor Coates that never changed. No matter how much he kept to himself or how badly he seemed to be feeling, he always took the time to compliment a new hairdo of mine, or a dress he thought was becoming; and every once in a while, he'd repeat his thanks for having him as a boarder. These days, I didn't know how to respond, since his boarding with us had seemed to coincide with such a difficult period in his life, but nonetheless I appreciated his comments and wanted to say to Ralston—though I didn't dare—that I wouldn't have missed knowing Professor Coates for the world.

Despite what happened, I still feel that way. Now that the shock has worn off; now that enough time has passed that Ralston and I have talked the matter over, not only between ourselves but with Father Dalton down at church. It was Father Dalton, after all, who pointed out that we'd given Professor Coates a "room in the inn," so to speak, and tried to ease his way during a time of great suffering. Nonetheless it wasn't ours to judge, Father said, in response to some complaint Ralston had made (in a low, surprisingly meek voice) about Professor Coates's having been dishonest, in a way; having lied "by omission," as Ralston put it. But no, it wasn't ours to judge. I couldn't have agreed more, and was happy that Father Dalton was so understanding and open-minded. Maybe it rubbed off on Ralston, for this time I didn't get the usual smart remarks—the "I told you so," the "See what you get" kind of talk. No snide references to my "impulsiveness," my "harebrained schemes." We've reached a kind of truce, it would seem, where our different views of the world and other people are concerned. Finally, after all this time, we're even.

The shock was the main thing, I think, for in the past it was always yours truly who ended up surprised, or disappointed, or hurt by people I tried to befriend. Ralston, on the other hand, tended to be smug, as though taking in stride the quirks of other people and the world at large; nothing surprised *him*, he'd have you believe. The incident with Professor Coates did surprise him, though—surprised the hell out of him, if you'll excuse my language. It goes to show, I guess, that something good can come out of even the most tragic circumstances, and to this day I believe that the whole experience *was* illuminating, *was* profound— though Ralston certainly would not agree.

* * *

It was just another Sunday morning, in early April. I'd had
breakfast ready at eight-thirty, like always, and of course Professor
Coates hadn't come downstairs; it had been weeks since he'd risen
before noon on a weekend day. Last night, though, I'd stayed up
extra late—I was watching one of those old forties melodramas on
TV that I love so much, this one with Loretta Young—and it had
crossed my mind that maybe Professor Coates *would* come home
before the movie ended at one A.M., and maybe we would have a
little chat. But no. I turned off the set, and even dawdled in the
kitchen over some hot milk and graham crackers, but still no
professor. I went on back to the bedroom, and by the time my head
hit the pillow I was asleep.

At breakfast, Ralston and I were chatting about this and that,
nothing special, and I was just about to go and change my dress
for church, when we heard a sudden noise from upstairs. A
crash, it sounded like, followed quickly by two or three more.
Ralston had pricked his ears, his coffee cup suspended in midair.
"What on earth—" he began, but then we heard other sounds—
a series of muffled, heavy grunts, like you hear from boxers
when they're fighting. Professor Coates's room was catty-corner
on the other end of the house from where we sat, so the sounds
were blurry, but nonetheless that was my first thought: fighting.
Two men, fighting. But then I thought of soft-spoken Professor
Coates and knew I must be imagining this. Though Ralston
would often say, later, "Why did I just *sit* there," I knew he had
the same reaction. It sounded like one thing, but had to be
something else.

At such times, of course, thoughts race through your mind:
maybe he's moving the furniture around? maybe he's exercising?
maybe he bought himself a TV and is watching something
noisy and violent? But then came a loud thud that made the
walls tremble even downstairs, and Ralston and I exchanged a
wide-eyed glance. A door slammed, and we heard the loud,
thumping footsteps coming down—making a racket, I knew,
that Professor Coates had never made in his life. Then, at the
doorway of the breakfast room, he appeared: a tall, mustached
man wearing boots and blue jeans, and a very soiled light-
blue sweatshirt. He had dark bushy eyebrows, big red-knuckled

hands. I noticed the hands because he thrust one arm forward, as if pointing or accusing, his finger shaking in our direction.

"Look, I need some money," he said. "Do you people have any money?"

Ralston said at once, "Just what's in my wallet."

The young man wriggled his fingers. "C'mon, hurry up." I saw how nervous he was, his eyes reddened, his body moving constantly in little jumps and spasms. His longish dark hair looked electrified, standing out in all directions. When Ralston held out the wad of bills, the young man snatched them the way Lucky used to snap her dog treats out of our fingers. He turned and ran out of the house.

Feeling limp, scarcely breathing, I followed Ralston to the front door, which the young man had left standing open, and we stood watching as he raced Professor Coates's little car—some kind of hatchback, I think—backward out of the driveway, then down the street with a loud squeal of the tires.

"My Lord...," Ralston whispered.

At the same moment we turned, gazing up to the top of the stairs.

"Professor Coates...?" I said, but it came out as a croak and I knew he couldn't have heard.

Then Ralston squeezed my wrist, trying to pull himself together. "Wait here," he said.

He climbed the stairs three at a time, and of course I wasn't far behind. At the bedroom doorway he said again, "My Lord...," and gestured me back with his hand. For a moment, I obeyed. I heard my husband's low murmuring inside the room, as though he were comforting Professor Coates, or gently questioning him. Then I heard him talking in a louder, more businesslike voice: the one he uses on the phone.

I crept forward, just barely peeking my nose and eyes inside the doorway. This sounds cowardly, I know, but I was truly frightened; I believe that my teeth were actually chattering. And then I saw him. Lying on the bed, one arm splayed outward. His glasses had been knocked off: later they'd be found on the floor, underneath his desk. His face was pale, and there was a long streak of blood along one side of his mouth, like saliva. His eyes were open but dead-looking: glazed over. No, I thought, please God, please Mother Mary, no no *no*.... When Ralston finished ordering the ambulance, he dialed again and asked for the police. All the time I stared at Professor Coates's face: so pale, so dead-white, except for the thread of blood out the side of his mouth. His T-shirt and the mussed white chenille bedspread were also streaked with blood, stray blots and wriggles of blood, random designs. I felt myself becoming sick.

I turned and hobbled down the hall, into the upstairs bathroom.

When the ambulance arrived, they loaded him quickly. The driver told Ralston not to worry, that he was in shock but would be fine; there seemed to be no serious internal injuries. A broken wrist, maybe a couple of broken ribs, but nothing to cause undue concern....When the police arrived, they were amazingly callous; or so I thought. Later Ralston remarked, philosophically, that we led a sheltered life, that maybe we were to blame for being so shocked, so defenseless.... I didn't understand what my husband meant. The policeman who did the talking—a short, jowly man in his forties—said this wasn't unusual, not in Atlanta; this happened all the time. He seemed rather pleased, somehow. I didn't know what he meant by "this," exactly, but a part of me was too angry to speak, part of me still too frightened. I kept glancing around the room at the bloodstained bed, the broken desk leg, the papers scattered everywhere; I was already picturing myself cleaning up the room, slowly and methodically. I clung to that.

For the next day or two, Ralston and I talked very little about what had happened. Occasionally we'd give each other the same wide-eyed look we'd exchanged at the breakfast table that morning, as though we were reliving the incident together; and yet we were apart, too, because we couldn't talk about it. We didn't have the words, it seemed to me. On Monday morning Ralston did go down to the hospital, but was told that Professor Coates couldn't have visitors except immediate family members; later that day, one of his brothers would be flying down from Boston. That night, I happened to answer the phone when it rang, and it was the brother, Jason; he said he would like to come over at once, if convenient, and clean out the professor's things. He called the professor "Jim," which sounded funny to my ears. After we hung up, I stood by the telephone table a long while, understanding that we would never see Professor Coates again. After a few minutes Ralston came up behind me. "Don't worry, Lily," was all he said.

Jason Coates turned out to be a slightly older, darker-complected version of the professor; and he looked fleshier, stronger. It took him and Ralston less than half an hour to load the professor's things into the man's rented car, and then we were all standing at the front door together, awkwardly saying goodbye. Mournful and slump-shouldered, Jason stood there a long while, as though there were something more he wanted to say. And then, looking chagrined, he brought out that the professor *had* been well enough to see visitors, but he felt too embarrassed, too ashamed. He never dreamed of our having to encounter that—that acquaintance of his, Jason said, dropping his voice even more. As for the money and the damage, he would send a check from Boston as soon as he was able; and above all, Jason said, the professor wanted us to know how grateful he was for our being so kind to him, during these past eight months.

"He says he's never known such fine people," Jason said, with a quick smile. "And as for myself, I'd like to thank you, too. For being so good to my brother."

"But," I began, "I still don't understand—"

"Hush, Lily," Ralston said. "We were glad to have him," he told Jason Coates. "And you tell him not to worry. We know it wasn't his fault."

Suddenly Jason looked anxious. "You know," he said, "he has had some personal problems. There was a—a person, someone he was involved with up in Boston, and it ended very abruptly last year. Jim has a knack, it would seem, for choosing people who aren't good for him, who don't have his best interests at heart. It amazes me, really, that he found you people." Jason smiled, ruefully.

"I found *him*," I said. "But I still don't—"

"Tell him we wish him well," Ralston said. "And God bless." I could hear in his voice—though Jason probably couldn't—that he wanted to end this conversation. As he held my wrist I could feel the tension in his fingers.

"I'll tell him, and don't worry about him, *please*," Jason said, and he was gone before I could even get his address or phone number. So I never found out how long it took Professor Coates to recover, or whether he went on to another teaching post the next fall, or whether he finished his book on Napoleon. Whenever I brought any of this up, Ralston would say shortly that it didn't matter if we knew these things or not.

Anyhow, despite Ralston the incident never quite went away. For several weeks there was a change in the atmosphere, somehow; when Ralston and I talked over dinner, or during the TV commercials in the den, we sounded awkward and a bit false, like people rehearsing their lines in a play. I suspect he was thinking, as I was, that everything would change when Sarah got home in mid-May, but actually the opposite happened: for Sarah, once as talkative and carefree as her mother, had become a different person in the last nine months. She moved all her things back into the professor's room—that is, *her* room—but not only had she gotten sloppy and a bit "wild" in her dress, as we knew from her visits home, but was quieter, moodier, spending long hours alone in her room, reading and listening to music, and writing letters that she rushed out of the house every morning to mail. (During her first week home, practically her only words were the daily request for stamps, her eyes not quite meeting mine. I'd stall for a moment, staring at this girl who had once been, people said, the spitting image of me, petite and auburn-haired and, if I may say so, very pretty. Delicate, pointed features; very fair skin. But she'd ruined all this with heavy eye makeup and the frizzed hair and the bright loose-fitting clothes, and I hardly knew her. Soon enough, I began to think that Sarah—our new boarder—was as much of a stranger as Professor Coates had been.)

Finally, one Saturday morning after Sarah had taken off for the post office, I began crying over my scrambled eggs. I don't cry often, as you might guess, but when I do it's quite a sight. I can't hold back, you see. Great racking sobs, like hiccoughs. Tears running like a faucet. When Ralston said, "All right then, let's go see Father Dalton," I could only nod and let him lead me out to the car.

Mostly I've reported what Father Dalton said, but I did leave one part out, and that was about the letters. This part surprised even Ralston, I believe. You see, the day after Jason Coates's visit I was cleaning the professor's room yet another time when I saw that someone had thrown some papers into the wastebasket, and of course I recognized the letters I'd glimpsed in the back of the professor's drawer. Evidently Jason had thrown them away, and naturally I wondered about this. It seemed a callous thing to do, but maybe he knew more than I did? Were the letters somehow linked to whatever was troubling Professor Coates? Sitting in the little reception room at the rectory, I remembered that I'd recently glimpsed some letters of Sarah, too, in the very same drawer; and of course I hadn't touched them, either, much as my fingers itched. Anyhow, I told Father Dalton about retrieving the letters from the wastebasket, and noticing they had a Boston return address, but no name above the address. The handwriting was small, neat, precise; "Dr. Jim Coates" was how they were addressed. After telling him about the letters—there were five of them, all folded inside identical pale-blue envelopes—I asked Father Dalton if it would be all right (if it wouldn't be "sinful," I suppose I meant) if I opened them.

Ralston jumped in his chair. "Lily, what on earth—"

But Father Dalton had raised his hand, shushing Ralston; *he* didn't seem surprised.

"Why would you want to do that, Mrs. Parks?"

"Because—because then it might make sense," I told him. "It's not idle curiosity, I'm not a snoop," I said quickly, "it's just that it's so hard, not being able to know people. Not feeling that you really *know* another person, even when he lives right under your own roof."

"Father, she's been very upset—" Ralston began.

"Even my own daughter, now that she's home. And even—"

"Lily!" Ralston said, his neck thickening. "You're not making sense."

Ah, my stern husband, my protector!—actually, I knew him very well.

Then, for a long while, Father Dalton spoke. Again he mentioned Christ, and how he taught forgiveness without explanations, without conditions. He suggested that just as Christ's life was a mystery, so was each of ours, and no matter how we might try, there's no getting to the genuine heart of another person. Not even when they live in our own house, he added gently. But knowing one another wasn't finally important, he insisted, it might even be considered a wasted effort. All of life, finally, was a mystery, Father Dalton said, but a mystery made bearable by Christ's unstinting love.

It was a very nice speech, I guess, but Father Dalton never did get around to answering my question. Months have passed, and I still have the letters, tucked into the back of my own dresser drawer. I haven't opened them, I think, because I'm afraid they *won't* tell me much, or at least not enough, and that certainly they won't ease the hollow feeling that has gradually settled in my heart, and that stays whether Ralston is nearby or not, whether I'm having a good day or a bad one. Though I try to stay cheerful, I'm no longer the person who'll just start talking to someone on the street, as I did to Professor Coates; and even with friends of ours, even at church, I'm aware that I'm not quite as friendly, don't laugh as much. She's getting older, people must say, if they notice at all. I'm fairly sure that Ralston hasn't noticed.

So, we go about our lives. Ralston is next in line for manager down at the tire store, then retirement and a good pension in six more years. Sarah's back at college, and I guess I understood too late that she was a separate person from myself, and that we've never really known each other. Maybe we'll become friends one day, close and confiding friends...? As for Professor Coates's letters, I'm sure that I'll never read them and also sure that I'll never throw them away. When I remember them, though, I become thoughtful for a moment—it's like praying, almost—and my heart lies hollow and still as that empty room upstairs.

Fever

During the year I was ill with rheumatic fever and was kept home from school, my mother and I would spend our afternoons watching forties melodramas on TV. This was the early sixties, the pre-assassination sixties, and at that time the overheated passions of those movies didn't yet seem impossibly distant; far from inspiring cynical laughter, the aching eyes and hearts of Loretta Young, Susan Hayward, and Jennifer Jones brought to any observer, male or female, adult or child, a quietly personal thrill of recognition and longing.

That year, my mother had all but relinquished housework; she spent mornings toying with new hairstyles or phoning the dress shops downtown, hoping something new had come in; whenever someone called her, she spoke in a fey, girlish voice, as though I were not in the next room. Her manner held a new urgency, I thought, a sense of plunging, original effort, as in some desperate audition for the role she'd been born to play.

I believed she had fallen in love.

She had not fallen in love. Her afternoons weren't spent with a lover but on our living room sofa, holding my feet as we watched our movies, though often I gazed at her instead of the TV, awed by a pink silk scarf at her neck that I'd never seen, or some bewildering new arrangement of her hair. I believed she had fallen in love and at night I stared at my bedroom ceiling, another screen, watching as she drove off with the stammering mailman, or the pseudo-cheerful manager down at the Piggly-Wiggly, or the flat-topped football coach at school. These were the only men in town, that I knew of, who were young enough, and reasonably handsome, and unmarried. They weren't John Gavin or Tyrone Power, but I supposed that they would do.

I did not suppose, on the other hand, that anything had come between my mother and father. Though nearly twenty years older than his wife (a situation much more usual then), my father clearly loved her, though it seemed a fond, remote love, lacking much evidence of passion. My parents exchanged cheery-voiced hello's in the mornings and dutiful pecks when they said good night. My father was past fifty by then, his arthritis already begun, and his bedtime was usually much earlier than my mother's. By the time I was ten, he would sometimes retire before I did, leaving her and me—especially on weekends—to watch old movies late at night. That's when our addiction started, I believe. It had some vague connection to forbidden things, to emotions indulged but not acknowledged, to the release we felt—though we did not acknowledge this, either—at the sight of my father's salt-and-pepper head retreating down the hall. Half an hour later my mother and I would be making popcorn, or pouring hot cocoa, or heaping squares of fudge onto the single plate to be wedged between us on the sofa, our eyes bright as we exchanged happy but forgettable kitchen conversation, a prelude to the much deeper and abiding pleasure of the movie that lay ahead.

During the year I stayed home from school, we watched movies nearly every afternoon on the Million-Dollar Movie Showcase. Since I would have preferred to be at school, I felt something of the invalid's self-righteous indulgence, and although my mother occasionally sighed that this was a "work day," and she really ought to be doing other things, I knew that her guilt attending these lazy afternoons was itself a source of pleasure. So we were long accustomed to our routine when, late in the spring, the Showcase featured a melodrama called *Leave Her to Heaven*, with Gene Tierney and Cornel Wilde, which had a puzzling but profound effect upon my mother.

In the movie, Gene Tierney the beautiful woman marries Cornel Wilde the handsome novelist, and it seems all will be well, except that Gene Tierney is sick with jealousy at the thought of Cornel Wilde giving love of any kind to someone else. She is even jealous of her own younger sister, Jeanne Crain, a sweet girl who would never consider committing adultery with Cornel Wilde, but to whom Cornel Wilde, rather unwisely, dedicates one of his novels. Gene Tierney is not the type who needs much in the way of evidence, and the book dedication sets her dark pained eyes aglow.

Meanwhile, Gene Tierney has also become jealous of Cornel Wilde's crippled kid brother, because Cornel Wilde loves him, too, and she feels that even such exemplary fraternal love somehow cuts into the love Cornel Wilde should feel for *her*.

Finally they go to a lakeside resort, so that Cornel Wilde can write, but he insists on bringing his crippled brother along. In the movie's climactic scene, Gene Tierney takes the boy (who is about eleven, my own age as I watched this movie with my mother) out onto the lake while her husband is busy writing. As part of his physical therapy, the boy has been learning to swim, so now Gene Tierney suggests that he see how far he can swim out from the boat. When he gets into trouble and starts yelling for help, Gene Tierney just sits there, behind her dark glasses. Gene Tierney just lets the boy drown, because then there will be one less person with whom to share the love of Cornel Wilde. The camera closes in, of course, on Gene Tierney's stony expression as she watches the boy drown, and the dark glasses make the scene especially effective. On the day my mother and I watched *Leave Her to Heaven* on the Million-Dollar Movie Showcase, the host said that the movie's director had claimed that Gene Tierney should get an Academy Award for that scene alone; but, as it turned out, she lost to Joan Crawford. She was "completely overlooked," according to the host, who seemed extremely unhappy about it.

"Imagine that," my mother said, rubbing the soles of my feet in her absent-minded way. "She didn't win the award...."

I tried to make a joke. "I guess they left her to heaven," I said, but my mother didn't seem to hear.

It was May and already hot outside and my mother wore a white sundress with spaghetti stripes and lime-green piping. Her honey-blond hair was swept back on both sides, fastened with stylish gold-toned barrettes. I tried to imagine her sailing off into the sunset with Cornel Wilde, even though I knew she would prefer John Gavin. Until we saw *Leave Her to Heaven,* the movie that had impressed her most was *Back Street,* starring John Gavin and Susan Hayward. In that one, John Gavin is married to a rich but mean-spirited woman, and Susan Hayward is a fashion designer who has everything in life but John Gavin, the man she loves. At the end, he lies in a hospital, dying from wounds suffered in a car accident that was caused by his wife who was not only rich and mean-spirited, but also suicidally unhappy. By then, it's a relief to everyone that she's dead. Her being dead allows for a final scene in which Susan Hayward comes to John Gavin's hospital room and reaffirms her undying love through a blur of tears, just before he breathes a final time.

We watched that movie twice during the year I was home with rheumatic fever, and I remember that once my mother wept softly to herself over the ending, but then rubbed at the tears quickly with her fists, not wanting me to see.

That was the first time I wondered if she were in love.

By mid-May, when we watched *Leave Her to Heaven,* we had dozens of those movies under our belt, so I was surprised when she snapped off the TV and said that she shouldn't have allowed me to watch that particular one. What Gene Tierney did was simply too awful, too unspeakable, and scenes like that generated the wrong kind of excitement in your heart. (For Gene Tierney had become even more desperate; when killing off her crippled brother-in-law failed to earn her the undivided attention of Cornel Wilde, she finally proceeded to kill herself, but made the suicide look like a murder. She planted some "evidence" that suggested the sweet-natured Jeanne Crain had been her sister's killer.) My mother glanced at me, worried. Because of my rheumatic fever, my young heart was supposedly in danger, so that sports were forbidden, as were running, or riding a bicycle, or energetic play of any kind. The previous summer, while I sat in my Jockey shorts on an examining table, our family doctor had shown me a heavy medical reference book that had pictures of diseased hearts in it. This was what could happen, he said, to people who had rheumatic fever and failed to take care of themselves. Entranced, I stared at photographs of deformed hearts, so swollen and scarred, so burdened by calcified dead-white tissue that they scarcely resembled hearts at all. Coiled in upon themselves, seeming to writhe upon the page, they suggested great tormented seashells, I thought, that might have been salvaged from some other planet. There was nothing human to them.

The photographs had their effect, and from that moment on my complaints about staying home from school, about staying indoors, took on a rhetorical blandness. After watching *Leave Her to Heaven*, and hearing my mother say that exciting movies also should be forbidden, I didn't even flinch. I had grown resigned to my enforced boredom. I had no particular reason to protest, so I merely waited for my mother to explain. She had kept watching me, standing near the silent TV with her arms folded.

Instead of meeting her look, I stared at the lingering silver dot in the center of the TV screen: stared until it shrank down to nothing.

Did I know, she asked finally, that Gene Tierney had been a truly evil woman? My mother wasn't sure if the movie had made this point as clearly as it should have. She wasn't sure that she hadn't detected a bit of sympathy for Gene Tierney somewhere in the movie, though she couldn't put her finger on it.

I said that I didn't know.

Didn't know what? she asked. If Gene Tierney was evil or if the movie failed to make clear that she was evil?

I said I didn't know that, either.

I got my fun where I could, that year. I had begun developing the kind of wit, and a viewpoint on the world, that would later be termed "caustic," and my mother already had had reason to claim, wrinkling her nose, that I had better watch my mouth.

Sometimes my mother unconsciously preened before me. Now, still standing beside the TV, she made a single turn in her white sundress, letting the skirt flare a bit; I noticed then that she was wearing a new kind of lipstick that resembled pink frosting. Eleven years old, wearing my summer uniform of T-shirt and cut-offs, and possessed of a fragile heart, I half sat and half lay on the sofa, the only male audience she would ever have. (Her behavior around my father, of course, was far more conventional; by 5:30 that afternoon, the sundress and lipstick would be gone, and she would resemble a youthful version of Donna Reed.) As she finished her twirl, which was her way of expressing the drama and emotion left over from the movie, she said: "Well, you'd better *know.*" But then she came forward and tweaked my nose, in a gesture dating back to my earliest boyhood ("Look, I've got your nose!" she would cry, poking her thumb out from between two fingers. "What shall I do with Lennie's nose, I wonder?"), and then she sat in a chair, across the room. She merely sat, watching me, and I sat watching back.

This wasn't so unusual. Often we didn't know what to do with the stilled amber time between the end of the Million-Dollar Movie Showcase at 4:00 and my father's arrival home. We'd sit there in the living room, the blinds still half-drawn (to prevent glare on the TV screen), a few stray dust motes visible in the air, and we would look or not look at each other, feeling neither happy nor unhappy, knowing that unlike good Loretta Young or evil Gene Tierney or misty-eyed Susan Hayward we could do nothing with the terrible fever of the roused love inside us, which was objectless, ravenous, and self-consuming, and which left only an astonished silence in its wake, like that following the noise of a television set that has been switched off abruptly.

Finally I said, "Did she"—and I meant Gene Tierney—"think that her husband's love was like a pie, and that if his little brother died then that was one more piece for herself?"

I was thinking of a few years ago, at school, when they had used drawings of pies to teach about fractions.

"Yes, something like that," my mother murmured, lifting her arms in a sudden but languorous stretch. Her arms were no less white, I was thinking, than those of Jennifer Jones in *Madame Bovary.*

I wasn't thinking, not then: She's only thirty-two years old.

"If she was wrong," I said, "then how *does* it work?"

I spoke in the childish sing-song I often used with my mother that year, a voice implying that I didn't care what the answer was; or that somehow it was the rhythmic give-and-take of our dialogue, not the words or their meaning, that mattered. Though my mother often looked as dreamy and abstracted as if she were, in fact, in love, her voice implied that she understood this, too; she knew that we were merely pleasuring ourselves, for a brief time; that next September I'd return to school, of course, and her current phase ("just a phase I'm going through!" she had sighed once, when I'd asked about the new clothes and hairstyles) was only that, a phase, and meant nothing, just as our idle late afternoons meant nothing, and even as those forties melodramas meant nothing, really, in the context of actual people and the world.

I wonder (though I didn't then) if she was thinking of me, back in school next year, rambunctious, unself-conscious, involved in my classes and sports, perhaps finding my first girlfriend?—while she waited here.

She came back to herself, frowning; but it was a joke-frown like Carole Lombard's or Greer Garson's, implying that here was a crazy question from a crazy kid.

"How does *what* work?" she asked.

Unexpectedly, I blushed, too embarrassed to say the word *love*.

But the room was dimly lit, and I didn't think she saw the blush.

I was trying to ask did she love my father, that kindly but distracted silver-haired man who looked old enough to be *her* father.

I was trying to ask did she love him more, or me more.

I was trying to ask whether, if I were strong and robust and, at this very moment, playing football after school, instead of lying in a forced months-long immobility to benefit my useless heart, she would then love me more, or less, or the same?

I wanted to ask, Will it ever stop rocking through our veins, will anything stop it, will it ever cool down, fade away, leave us in peace, ever?

But I didn't have the words, of course.

My mother said, "No, I shouldn't have let you watch that one," but I could tell she no longer meant it. She was thinking of something else. She stared dreamily past my shoulder, as if through the wall, or into the future.

Then she said, "Gene Tierney didn't know about love, that's for sure." Her voice had strengthened, and even in the faint light I saw the flush in her cheeks and the sudden sheen in her eyes, making me wonder if she didn't feel a little pity for Gene Tierney, too, in spite of everything.

She repeated, still gazing past my shoulder, "She never even *knew* what it was."

A Dry Season

"No, you're not a failure," Eleanor says. "That's nonsense."

She sounds exasperated, downright angry, but then she laughs. A loud, ribald laugh that Nora, after fifteen years, knows not to take personally. The laugh is Eleanor's typical response to human problems: it clears the air, puts the situation in perspective.

For that, Eleanor says, is what Nora has gotten herself trapped inside. A "situation."

Nora says, caustically, "You mean I've failed even at that? Being a failure?"

Eleanor makes a gesture with her hands—fingers outspread, held clutched above her ears. Pulling out her hair.

Go ahead, Nora thinks.

"It's just that you're so intense, so damned *serious*," Eleanor says. She laughs again, though less convincingly. "You've always been that way, you know. Ever since college."

"Have I," Nora says.

Eleanor smokes thoughtfully, staring past Nora's shoulder to the parched, bumpy lawn. The lawn leads down to the lake, not quite visible through the massive ridge of trees, and throughout this stale, restless conversation with her oldest friend, her college roommate Eleanor Jenks, Nora has let her thoughts wander down to the lake, the rippling cool water. Only eleven A.M., it's already ninety in the shade. It's August, the dog days. A thick, settled heat—a murderous heat, really—has hugged the lake and its environs ever since Nora's arrival the previous week. The heat, the three of them have decided, is beyond remedy. Neil takes a cold shower after work, but ten minutes later, he says, he's covered in sweat. While he's at work, Eleanor and Nora sit out on the redwood deck, as they're doing now, sipping iced tea or margaritas in the morning shade of an enormous elm, wearing practically nothing. Short shorts, halter tops. Their hair pulled back, tied carelessly with rubber bands. But still the heat is stifling, and occasionally Nora has trouble getting her breath: last night she'd sat up suddenly in bed, gasping for air, her throat and tongue feeling unnaturally dry, parched. For Nora, only a swim in the lake brings relief, a luxurious total immersion with her limbs outspread, her head leaned back until the water laps over her calm face, her closed mouth and eyes.

"I think it's the weather," Eleanor says at last. "It's affected Neil, too, have you noticed how anxious he seems about work? He's not that way, normally. Does Mr. so-and-so really appreciate him, will the dastardly so-and-so get promoted instead, that kind of thing. He's usually good about leaving his work at the office, but lately he's been coming home with that grim look around his mouth, full of doom and gloom. And now you—"

As she talks, the ash on Eleanor's cigarette grows impossibly long—nearly an inch, Nora guesses. She has watched it obsessively, scarcely listening, yet knowing that Eleanor is the type who'll notice the ash at the last possible moment—just in time—and then flick it into the ashtray as if nothing had happened. As if there'd been no suspense, no danger. And then she'll keep talking.

"Nora, are you all right?" Eleanor says, interrupting herself. "Listen, kid," she begins, in a gentler tone, "you really shouldn't worry—" But then she follows Nora's wide-eyed gaze down to the cigarette and quickly moves her hand toward the large Mexican ashtray, already heaped with Eleanor's butts. As they sit watching in silence, the ash falls.

There's nothing worse, Nora resolves, than a boring houseguest. That evening, before Neil gets home, she changes into a white sundress she hasn't yet worn during this trip. It's the only good dress she has brought, and half-consciously she's been saving it for some special occasion; but they seldom go out, and in any case the lake people never dress for anything. Twice they have gone to a nearby tavern for ribs and draft beer; occasionally Nora and Eleanor go shopping in town, but like everyone else they wear as little as possible. Appraising herself in the mirror, she wonders if the dress looks inappropriate. Neil plans to make tacos, Eleanor will mix the margaritas, and the three of them will sit on the deck, as usual. It's true, Nora thinks, that lately the conversation has centered on Neil and Nora—their problems, their confusions. She understands why Eleanor has gotten restive. Hearing Neil's car crunching the gravel out front, Nora decides that the dress looks all right. Impulsively she removes the rubber band, then brushes out her tawny-blond hair in a few quick strokes. She hurries out to greet Neil.

In the kitchen, Neil has already removed his tie, draped his jacket over a chair. The grocery sack contains ground beef, peppers, taco shells; peering inside, Nora feels childish in her bare feet and white dress.

"Hungry?" Neil asks. He stands with the refrigerator door open. It's a tic of his, she has noticed, that he opens the refrigerator door when he gets home, whether he wants anything or not. He looks inside for a minute or two, sometimes takes out a beer or the iced tea pitcher, sometimes nothing. He greets the food, Eleanor says cheerfully, before he greets his wife. Now he takes out a diet soft drink and slowly lifts the metal ring.

"Starved," Nora says, watching him. She wants something to drink, too, but suddenly she's shy before Neil. Vaguely she's aware of Eleanor out beside the deck table, clinking knives and forks together. "How was the office?" she asks. "Any better?"

He turns around with a swift, sudden grin. Neil is tall and well-built, with only a small ridge of flesh around his middle; Eleanor claims that he's lazy, that he dislikes sports and yard work, but Nora can tell he's the type who knocks himself out at the office. He underwrites marine insurance, and frequently travels the coasts of Georgia, the Carolinas, Florida. He's tanned and light-haired, with a full, open face capable of subtleties Nora finds startling. He's six years younger than Eleanor and Nora, and ever since receiving their wedding picture a decade ago (Neil had been nineteen at the time, his hair reaching nearly to the shoulders of his tuxedo jacket) Nora hasn't stopped thinking of Neil as a boy.

"I'm not good," Neil says slowly, "at office politics. I'm only good at my job."

"That should be enough," Nora says.

"Hardly," and the grin disappears. He looks tired.

"I'm sorry," Nora says, feeling inane.

"How about you? Any progress?"

"I'm fine," she says quickly. "I've burdened you enough with my problems—both of you," she adds, hearing the glass door sliding open behind her.

Holding a half-finished margarita in one hand and a cigarette in the other, Eleanor looks startled for a moment, slightly off-balance. She's still wearing her shorts and halter from this morning, and her eyes pause briefly on Nora's dress. Then she looks at Neil, who lifts his eyebrows at her.

"Come on, you two," she says, going past Nora toward the kitchen and giving Neil a friendly poke in the stomach. "Let's cheer up, let's get this show on the road," she says, and she begins taking cooking utensils out of the cabinet. At the same moment, Nora and Neil hurry forward to help.

Again that night, Nora wakes suddenly. At the very moment of waking, she'd glimpsed a dark figure—mere shadows, resolved vaguely into the shape of a man—towering over the bed, as though bending down to embrace her. She connects this figure with her breathlessness, her sudden, raging thirst. Now fully awake, she rises quickly. Putting on her light robe, she crosses to the glass-paned door that leads from her room onto the redwood deck. One hand on the door knob, she pauses. Out on the deck, sitting on the round table with both feet resting inside one of the chairs, there's a dark figure, barely discernible in the scant moonlight. He wears a pair of short pajama bottoms, and sits gazing down toward the lake. Every few seconds he lifts a cigarette to his mouth; Nora watches the tiny reddish glow, magnified several times in the circle of glass doors giving onto the deck. Nora turns the knob of her own door, slowly.

Startled, Neil glances around. "Nora? I hope I didn't wake you."

"No," she says in a low whisper. "I just woke up, I—I was thirsty, that's all."

He nods, taking a loud, hissing draw on the cigarette, which he holds tightly between his forefinger and thumb.

"There's no relief, is there?" he says. "Even now, it must be close to ninety."

"What time is it?" Nora says, faintly.

"Around three," he says.

Nora feels like a wraith, as though her dream-self hasn't yet taken bodily form. She places a chair beside Neil; he looks impossibly large, sitting on the table above her. She's forced to crane her neck, which instantly begins to ache.

"I haven't been sleeping well," she says. "Not for days."

Silently he brings the glowing cigarette down to her, and she sees that it's marijuana. The sweetish, ashen smell threatens to choke her. She shakes her head.

"We should ask Eleanor how she does it," he says, laughing gently. He draws on the cigarette again. Nora feels her eyes drawn helplessly toward its glowing tip, red-hot and dazzling in the viscous dark. "She sleeps like a load of bricks, from the moment her head hits the pillow."

"She's lucky," Nora says.

For a moment they sit together, silent. After Neil flicks the glowing butt out into the lawn, they sit watching as a few strands of parched grass flame up, then quickly die. Neil reaches down, idly, and begins kneading the back of Nora's neck with his right hand.

"It might have been a mistake," he says at last, "moving down here. We thought of it as a great escape, you know, a kind of permanent vacation. It's only a half-hour's drive into the city, but they're such different worlds. Somehow the contrast is too great, at least for me. When I'm at work, none of this seems real. Once or twice lately I've stopped at a bar before leaving downtown, as though I dreaded coming home. But then when I'm here, the office seems unreal. And unbelievably depressing."

Startled more by Neil's frankness than by his hand on her neck and shoulders, massaging her gently, Nora says nothing for a long moment. Then: "What about Eleanor? She seems to like it." To Nora's ears her voice sounds hoarse, not quite her own.

"I think she feels isolated," Neil says. "She doesn't like the weekend people, by and large. And she seldom goes near the lake."

"Then, why...?" Nora sits remembering the large, sunny condominium Neal and Eleanor had bought in Atlanta, shortly after their marriage, and how happy Eleanor had seemed.

"I think," Neil says softly, "that Eleanor believed it would help. That it might save our marriage."

Now and then Nora glimpses the barest suggestion of water, glimmering through the distant trees. Suddenly she yearns to bound toward the lake, running like any natural creature, and immerse herself in a single abandoned gesture, unthinking. The imagined coolness of the water sends a shiver along her back and arms. In a single movement she gently removes Neil's hand, rises until she stands with her face only inches from his, and gives him a dry, cool kiss on the cheek.

"I'm sorry you're unhappy," she says. "It seems to be a bad time for all of us."

She sees the astonished whites of his eyes.

"Nora?" he says.

"I'm going into the kitchen, get some ice water," she says. "Then maybe I can sleep."

When she gets back to her bedroom, she flicks on the lights for an instant, as though to dispel any lingering shadows. In her stomach she feels the nearly painful cold of two tumblers of ice water, drunk down in a matter of seconds. A minute or two later, getting drowsy, she spreads her limbs and feels herself adrift upon a fathomless dark, floating.

A week later, Eleanor and Nora go shopping in town. It's the last Monday in August and still very hot, though less humid. Several times recently Nora's face has felt mask-like, tightened by the dry heat; she feels that it could break easily into fragments, like pieces of crockery. Eleanor, on the other hand, looks plump and rosy. On their way down a steep hill near the center of town, they have stopped to peer inside a gallery window, their two reflections in the glass—Nora's willowy and ghost-like, Eleanor's more solid, firmly planted in her open-toed shoes—forming a contrast that Nora finds mildly comical.

"They're not bad, I suppose," Eleanor is saying, looking at the artwork inside, not herself in the glass. "But they have an air of sameness, don't you think?"

"Yes, but that's rather sweet," Nora says. "And comforting, somehow."

"It's disturbing," Eleanor says with finality, and gives a little shiver. From behind them, the noon sun beats on their exposed shoulders, browned and freckled from long afternoons out on the deck.

"Why disturbing?" Nora says, lightly, but they aren't really arguing. Often they disagree with each other, rhetorically. Lately they've been putting more effort into their conversation, Nora has noticed, as though each woman fears becoming tiresome to the other. The half-dozen landscapes in the window, each studiously executed and neatly framed, are by a group of local artists, all of them retired and over seventy. The paintings depict various small corners of this lakeside town, a resort area nestled into the wooded hills north of Atlanta, and it's true they might have been painted by the same artist. All show a fastidious eye for detail, a disarming earnestness; and they convey a great placid certainty—perhaps, Nora thinks, complacency. She finds the pictures quite appealing.

"I don't know," Eleanor says, stepping back. "They're not very original, are they?"

Now she does see their reflections in the glass, Nora hovering several inches taller, each woman staring briefly at the other. Then they continue down the sidewalk.

"What about you? Have you given up painting?" Eleanor asks, once they're seated for lunch and Eleanor has gotten her first margarita. "I remember the portraits you used to do, back in college. They were so lovely, so haunting...."

"Self-portraits," Nora says. "Yes, I've stopped." She laughs, briefly. "I've turned into a hack."

"Oh, come on," Eleanor says. She's lighting a cigarette, glancing around.

Nora often adopts a pretended cynicism when referring to herself, but perhaps it's a technique, she thinks, of holding to the truth. It's true that both her illustrating jobs in New York—one for six years, the next for three—had dulled her interest in her own work. There had been a crucial point, soon after she began the second job, when she felt the fatal dullness settling over her like a mantle, slowing her mind and imagination and even, it seemed, her physical being: she seemed to move through a thickening element, like water. She no longer saw very sharply; she no longer thought very deeply about what she saw. At this time she'd also begun to consider marriage. At thirty-two, she'd had a history of broken-off engagements, relationships that her lovers initiated and pursued with Nora following along, grateful but rather listless, until she reached the inevitable moment of severance. Always she'd felt apologetic and chagrined, and she had, she knew, hurt two or three people quite badly. Everyone had a personal crime, usually repeated throughout life, and this was hers. But after beginning a new job Nora had met another artist, Martin, and for the first time felt her allegiance subtly shifting from herself—her own perceptions, her own art—to this other, rather mysterious and powerful person, who seemed a force field gradually pulling her out of an outworn life into something startling and new. In short, she fell in love, and really for the first time. Martin was an abrupt, dark-haired man in his late thirties, an Irish Catholic with an explosive temper and an inexhaustible passion for Nora. After their lovemaking, he would often say that she was a passionate woman, the first he'd ever known who could equal him, who had the same hunger for life. Lying there, listening, she did feel her heart still pounding in her chest, dully, hungrily. She'd recognized the truth of Martin's words, but each time, nonetheless, the idea startled Nora. The word itself, "passion," had sounded foreign to her.

Unlike Nora, Martin had not lost interest in his work. After spending all day at the office, working impatiently alongside Nora on illustrations of living room furniture or women's undergarments, he would paint for six or eight hours after dinner, standing before his huge abstract oils like a god before his universe, looking utterly serious and sometimes—to Nora's eyes—slightly bombastic. She would come into the room late at night, slipping her arms around his waist, and urge him to bed. Usually she did not look at the painting. She found his work enormous, intimate, and violent, and the contrast with her own tame, smallish pictures—still-lifes, ghostly and rather attenuated portraits of herself—was too painful. But Martin never resented her interruptions. He would turn to her and give a quick smile, his eyes softening, his presence returning quickly to human scale. How grateful she had felt, witnessing this. What had she done to deserve him, after all? Hadn't she lived as a selfish, rather cold woman, absorbed in her own thoughts and aspirations? Hadn't she done harm to other people and then simply walked away, unscathed? Martin said that she was too hard on herself, that she was no more selfish than anyone else. Whether she agreed or not, what mattered to Nora was Martin's believing this, his curious faith in her, his acceptance. His love was both casual and profound— exactly what Nora needed. During their two years together, Nora gradually learned to use Martin's vocabulary of love—words like *completion, passion, fate*—without self-consciousness.

When Martin died by his own hand, four months ago, and only a few weeks before they planned to marry, Nora's response had not been, technically speaking, grief: rather she had been thrown back inside herself as into a foreign element that had only a dreamlike familiarity. From Martin there had been no note, no personal hint of any kind, only the tiny spare bedroom he used as his studio that had been stripped of everything, his dozens of stacked canvases, his sketches, even his books and supplies. Thrown out, evidently. Everything. Having no formal connection to him, Nora had backed off when the family arrived. She had not attended the funeral. Dull-brained again, she had left New York, had spent a month or two simply traveling around, visiting old friends without telling them what had happened, finally reaching her parents' home in Atlanta, where she had grown up. An only child, she had always felt a sense of panic and claustrophobia when visiting her parents, even during those first college vacations. She'd felt stifled by her father's determined drinking, her mother's determined sorrow; and little had changed over the years. She did not, of course, tell her parents about Martin, either. Then she remembered the letter she'd received early in the summer from Eleanor, her college roommate and still, she supposed, her best friend, who had moved out of the city, she wrote, to a place that's "lovely, peaceful, but hot as hell in the summertime. Come visit," she had added, "it's about time you met Neil!"

By now, after two weeks, she has stopped worrying about overstaying her welcome; she has become a familiar part of her friends' routine, especially Eleanor's, and more than once she has wondered how Eleanor coped before her arrival. The loneliness must have been stifling.

"But *those* things," Eleanor is saying, wrinkling her nose as she sips the margarita. "I'm really surprised, Nora."

"Surprised?" Nora says, embarrassed. She hasn't been listening. "Sorry, what did you…"

"Those pictures," Eleanor says, giggling, "by the local geriatrics. I might be expected to like them, Nora. But not you."

"Stop putting yourself down," Nora says, sharply. This habit, she has noticed, has become frequent with Eleanor, who had been all bubbling self-confidence in college.

Eleanor looks wistful. "You're right, I think I'm catching it from Neil. Or vice versa."

When the meal arrives, Nora eats very slowly, taking small bites. She doesn't really like Mexican food, which is Eleanor's favorite. After each bite she takes a long swallow of water.

She says, "You're lucky, you know, to have Neil—" But then she stops. Eleanor hasn't glanced up. "I mean, you're lucky to have each other. Especially during the difficult times."

"Yeah, but we have our problems," Eleanor says, talking between bites.

"For instance?" Nora says casually, knowing that Eleanor wants to talk.

"For instance, although Neil has conflicts at the office, I'm stuck out by the lake, where everything is so peaceful and there are no conflicts. Which becomes a conflict in itself."

"But you chose that, didn't you? Moving out here?"

"Yeah, we chose it," Eleanor says, pushing her plate aside and reaching for her cigarettes. "But the freedom we were choosing, or the fresh start, or whatever—it was just an illusion. I see that now." She lights the cigarette, nods vaguely as the waiter brings a fresh drink. "You know," she adds, giving Nora an abrupt, penetrating look, "it's really been sad and moving, hearing what's happened lately in your life, but in a way I've envied you, I really have. I've envied the way your life moves along so dramatically, from one crisis to the next, while mine just stays the same. Right now, for instance, you have a whole new set of possibilities. A new life, really. At the moment you're looking back, of course, you're still grieving over Martin, but you do have a future, and that's enviable. I hope that doesn't offend you."

"It doesn't offend me," Nora says quickly.

"As for Neil, he's a wonderful guy, but—" Eleanor pauses, her cigarette poised inches from her mouth. Nora sees that her lips have begun to tremble.

"It's all right, Eleanor."

Eleanor's eyes have filled. "Everything went stale, somehow, it just happened. I know it wasn't my fault, but still I *feel* that it was, you know? Like I failed to hold him, keep his interest. That I failed as a woman, some sick cliché like that." She shakes her head, pawing away the two or three tears. "I know better, though."

"I hope so," Nora says. And then, smiling: "Besides, I'm the one who's a failure, remember? You're stealing my thunder."

Eleanor laughs her abrupt, careless laugh, then lifts the margarita in a little salute and drinks greedily. This gives Nora the excuse to push her uneaten food away, casually laying her napkin over it, and to take another long swallow from her water glass. When Eleanor puts down her drink, there's a dab of salt perched on the tip of her nose.

"Sure you don't want one of these?" Eleanor says, her gaze a bit fuzzy as she searches out the waiter. "This place makes the *best* margaritas."

"No, thanks," says Nora, disappointed that their conversation, their genuine talk, has ended so quickly. "I think I'll just have some more water."

When Nora announces her plans, she notices an abrupt change in both Eleanor and Neil. Eleanor becomes bouncy, enthusiastic—her old self. What a wonderful idea!—she hadn't known Nora was considering settling back in Atlanta; she had assumed, frankly, that Nora wanted to live at some distance from her parents.... But now she and Neil will see a lot of Nora, Eleanor says; there are several attractive men they know in Atlanta, they'll be glad to arrange the introductions when Nora feels ready; and she'll have no trouble, of course, in finding a job, no trouble at all…. But Neil turns shy, boyish. Does she know where she wants to live? Does she have any real prospects, job-wise? He'll be glad to help her, in any way he can. He'll be glad to make use of his connections, such as they are.

It's Sunday afternoon, and as usual the three of them have gathered out on the deck, where Neil plans to grill hamburgers for dinner. For the second time Nora has put on her white sundress, sensing that today marks a special occasion, a turn in her fortunes. She feels suddenly grateful for her friends.

"Thanks," Nora says, smiling. "I went through today's paper, the want ads. If you don't mind, Neil, I need a ride into the city tomorrow morning. I might as well start pounding the pavements."

"That's terrific!" Eleanor says, lifting her glass of iced tea. The other evening, she'd made an announcement of her own: she planned to cut down on her drinking. At first, she would drink only every other day, and after a month she would stop altogether. Today is one of her "off" days, and thus far she seems to have no trouble abstaining—though she smokes even more, Nora has noticed, and her behavior seems more hectic, as though she's trying to distract herself. Both Nora and Neil have said, repeatedly, that they're very proud of her.

"Of course," Neil says. "And you may as well keep the car during the day. Just pick me up at five, and we'll drive back together."

Nora waits for a moment, feeling her way. She says, "No, I think I'll stay in town for a while. It'll be easier, really, to use Mom and Dad's spare room, and I'm sure it won't take me long to find a place."

Both Eleanor and Neil look at her, startled.

"My goodness!" Eleanor says, slapping her forehead. "Then this is your last night. Come on, Neil, we'll have a farewell party, we've got to celebrate Nora's decision, her new life…. Break out the champagne, honey. Then I'll have two off days in a row. It won't matter."

"That's not necessary," Nora says, alarmed. "Really."

Neil sits quietly, his blond head perfectly still. He gives her a sad, admiring look. "No, Eleanor's right," he says. "If you're leaving us, we've got to send you off in style."

For the next few hours, Nora feels herself inside a kind of haven, not needing to think, pampered by these two people who have both, in quite separate ways, come to love her. The champagne combines wonderfully with Neil's excellent burgers, and halfway through the meal Eleanor sneaks off to the kitchen, wearing a mischievous expression, to put a second bottle in the freezer. Neil and Nora laugh, shaking their heads. Despite themselves, they have taken on Eleanor's jaunty, devil-may-care mood, and Nora realizes how seldom in the past few weeks Neil has actually laughed. Tonight he's wearing a white knit shirt and khaki shorts; beneath these clothes his body is tanned and strong, the kind of manly physique on which clothes look a bit awkward and out of place, but at the same time he's a blond, grinning, overgrown boy, indulging in forbidden pleasures. Though both Nora and Neil are sparing drinkers, tonight they keep pace easily with Eleanor.

They open the second bottle immediately after dinner.

"But it hasn't chilled yet," Nora protests, laughing.

"Come on, don't be a party pooper," Neil says, sampling the first glass. "Umm," he says. "Delicious."

"Yep, it's cool enough," Eleanor says, tasting. She laughs brightly.

They begin proposing toasts.

"To Nora's new job," Neil says, his pale-blond eyelashes quivering for a moment. Nora doesn't know if he's still shy with her, or if he's simply getting drunk. "Long may Nora prevail!" he adds with a grin.

Nora lifts her own glass, which feels weightless in her hand. Her entire body feels light, buoyant. "To Neil, future company president," she says. Sipping, she peers at him over her glass.

"President?" Eleanor says, facetiously. "Hell, why not chairman of the board?" She gestures toward the center of the table, drains her glass and immediately pours another.

"Well? What else?" Eleanor asks.

Neil and Nora share a long, embarrassed moment: they don't know how to toast Eleanor. Stealing a quick glance at him, Nora sees the faint blush climbing into Neil's cheeks. And she looks away, keeping her eyes downcast.

"Wait, I know," Eleanor cries. "To friendship!"

When she wakes, much later that night, there are no shadows above her bed, no uneasy dreams trailing off behind her. Her heart beats steadily. Calmly. As a small girl, hearing her father mount the stairs late at night, muttering to himself and stumbling into the banister, into the walls, Nora's mother trying to shush him until she'd gotten him inside the bedroom and discreetly closed the door, Nora would lie still for a long time, hearing nothing but her frail, stubborn heartbeat. What kept it beating, exactly?—what gave it such a brave, relentless life of its own, so that Nora lay cringing in terror, only nine or ten years old, dreading the unholy persistence of her own heart? How long, she thinks now, that memory had stayed buried, how many times she had lain beside Martin, feeling both terrified and exultant, without recalling herself as a child, lying in bed alone, in utter incomprehension…. After lovemaking Martin would fall asleep, almost immediately, leaving Nora alone, her heart still pounding madly, convulsed and sore after the violence of their passion. She remembers the acute loneliness of those moments, and how she longed to wake him, and how her lust seemed to arise again, so quickly, her mouth and throat turning dry, patchy, her thirst becoming so urgent, so relentless…. Now, shaking her head as though to dispel this memory, she finds her sundress (looking ghostly but familiar, draped over a chair drenched in moonlight) and lets it glide down along her body, then rakes her hair backward with the splayed fingers of both hands. She hurries to the glass door and steps out onto the deck, and of course there is Neil, sitting there quietly, smoking.

This time, he doesn't turn around.

"Neil?" she says, and then, thinking she spoke too softly, "Hello, Neil? Couldn't you sleep?"

When he rises, she sees that he's wearing a bathing suit: white, with a small insignia on one side. The trunks, like his hair and bare chest and shoulders, glimmer faintly in the moonlight.

"Come on," he says, holding out one hand. He doesn't look at her.

Gingerly, they move down the grassy slope toward the trees, the water. Their feet bare, they pick their way among rocks, small bumps and ridges in the earth, sudden hollows. Nora thinks they must look like children, a pair of blond children holding hands, dressed in white, moving down toward the lake…. Now Neil makes a casual, quick gesture: throwing down the cigarette. Isn't that dangerous? she wants to ask. Out here where the grass seems so parched, the trees so desiccated and forlorn? It's so hot and dry, such a dry season…. But she says nothing. Now they are emerging from the trees and there is the water, seeming limitless as it stretches before them, winking in the moonlight. From somewhere out in the water—perhaps it's the water itself, Nora thinks—comes a dull but persistent roaring, like the crashing of waves but much subtler, more sinister. Like something strong but muffled, Nora thinks; like the crashing of a distant wave, a distant heartbeat.

They stand at the edge of the water, their hands linked.

"Neil?" she says, looking up at him. She should feel alarmed, she reasons, and yet she doesn't. She senses a dangerous peace, flooding her. "Neil, are you all right…?"

Now he does something surprising: he laughs. He drops her hand and rubs at his eyes, laughing. A child's gesture, Nora thinks; a gesture of dismay.

"Oh yes," he says. "I'm wonderful."

She doesn't understand his mood: only a few hours ago he'd been so jaunty, so cheerful. The three of them had sat toasting one another until the second bottle of champagne was gone, and then Eleanor had made up a batch of margaritas. Though the liquor and salt made her tongue contract, made her thirstier the more she drank, Nora had kept drinking right along with her friends. She was glad to see them so happy, so carefree…. Perhaps her visit had been good for them, Nora thought. For once, perhaps she'd been at the right place at the right time. Then, around ten o'clock, something happened that disconcerted Nora: Eleanor began to complain of being tired, and she asked Neil to massage her shoulders. Neil rose instantly, and stood for five or ten minutes behind his wife's chair, massaging her gently. What disconcerted Nora was the quick, undeniable pang of jealousy that rose in her.

She felt relieved when Eleanor reached back and stilled her husband's hands. "Shall we continue this indoors?" she'd said, slyly. "I don't think I can sit upright another minute." And Nora had risen quickly, saying she had to get to bed, herself; tomorrow would be a tiring day, after all. So it had ended. The farewell party. The celebration. Somehow Nora had known, as she prepared for bed, that her sleep would not last through the night.

"You're being sarcastic," Nora says, lightly, "but you *are* rather wonderful, you know. Eleanor thinks so," she adds, hating herself.

"Eleanor would think so," Neil says, "no matter what I did."

"Don't underestimate her," Nora says quickly. She's said the same thing, she remembers, to Eleanor herself.

"I won't," Neil says, in the hoarse, half-desperate tone Nora recognizes very well. When he turns to her, reaching out his arms, she steps back neatly. The moment is more than difficult, somehow; it's impossible. She turns and walks to the edge of the lake. Then, not knowing what else to do, she wades out a few yards, feeling the water begin to drag at the hem of the sundress.

"Nora?" he calls after her, bewildered.

She keeps wading, quickly, till she reaches a depth of three feet or more, and then she turns back toward shore and lets her legs collapse beneath her. The skirt balloons around her shoulders and she thinks, giddily, *Ophelia.* But she isn't drowning. The water feels wonderfully cool at her throat, her shoulders and breasts, and is actually quite cold around her legs. She has parted her knees and feels the cold water moving deliciously between her thighs, a quick, cold, friendly current; she moves her legs and arms slowly, dog-paddling, enjoying this sensation in its fullness, its purity. Then she hears a loud splashing, which stops as abruptly as it began. "Nora? What are you—?" But she can't see: her eyelids have fallen shut, and in a graceful, arcing motion she leans backward and lets her head sink beneath the surface of the water. When she lifts up again, she pushes her hair back with both hands, smiling. She spurts out a mouthful of water and lets her eyes blink open.

For a moment she sees the woods beyond Neil, beyond the shore, suffused in terrible flames. She remembers the cigarette Neil had thrown down, and sees Eleanor come running down toward the water, waving her arms. Eleanor screams "Fire!" and then comes to a stop near Neil, who ignores her, and begins jumping up and down comically, stamping her feet. "Look what you've done, you two! You've destroyed everything! That's just what you wanted, isn't it?" Nora smiles at this vision, which quickly vanishes. Now she sees the shoreline during the day, in springtime: the massed gatherings of elm, oak, and white pine, the swaying grasses, the darkish-red glintings of the earth beneath. A landscape that Nora herself might paint, perhaps, trying to accentuate its packed, overabundant life, its look of quiet foreboding. She hasn't painted, hasn't *really* painted, in years, how odd she should think of that now…. She cups a handful of water and splashes her face, smiling, blinking her eyes as the water rushes along her cheekbones, the sides of her parted mouth, her aching tongue, and she thinks: Yes, how clearly she sees. She sees everything.

Neil has waded only a few feet into the water and stands bewildered, dull-looking. Moonlight gleams along his hair, his shoulders. He's quiet, muscular, and beautiful, but what's wrong with him? Why doesn't he come running wildly into the water, why doesn't he save himself?

"Neil, I love you!" she cries. She splashes at the water with both hands, like a child.

Neil stands with his feet in the lake, staring.

Escalators

I

My Aunt Dinah has a crippling fear of escalators. She has many fears, both rational and irrational, and at fifty-two has decided to begin conquering them, one by one. She is afraid of crowds, she is afraid of people dressed in costumes (even Santa Claus, even small children on Halloween), she is afraid of loud and startling noises—firecrackers, especially. On the Fourth of July she stays indoors and plays Handel's *Water Music* while running the dishwasher and vacuuming the rugs. We laugh about these things, which doesn't mean that her fears aren't genuine or that her suffering isn't acute. For some years she has been seeing a therapist, who prescribes nerve and sleep medications (which she once said, with her low trilling laugh, were her "dearest friends—except for you, Gary"), but I was the one who suggested she begin working on her phobias. Despite everything Dinah is a strong woman and I wasn't surprised when she agreed at once.

But we should be realistic, she said. We should begin with the small ones first.

So we go to the mall one weekday morning, arriving early enough so that the mall corridors are open but the stores are not. We are not so much avoiding crowds—our city's single mall is seldom crowded on weekdays, even now in midsummer when the

teenagers are roaming free—as we are hoping there will be no one
to witness our attempts to ride the escalators. Whether our efforts
would appear comical or pathetic to a stranger I don't know, but
wanting an objective opinion about Dinah's phobias, I phoned an
old college friend over in Atlanta who has a thriving hypnotherapy
practice. After I explained the situation, he said he thought Dinah
would probably resist hypnotic suggestion, but he did think an
outing to the mall was a good idea, and he offered some pointers.
Try to appear relaxed and comfortable, he said, and indulge her
whims in every way not directly related to the object of phobia. Be
supportive and patient. Don't rush. Take breaks. Above all, don't
indulge in censorious or punishing behavior if she fails. And he
said a good deal more. There are so many instructions to
remember that by the time we reach the mall I'm at least as
nervous as Dinah.

"Dinah, are you OK?" I ask while we're still in the car. "Do you
still feel good about this?"

Close-mouthed, she nods. She has dressed up for the occasion,
which I find touching: a sleek luncheon dress of navy silk, a
crocodile handbag with long straps, girlish white cotton gloves with
pearlized fasteners. Her erect posture and careful makeup and
chic new hairstyle—short in the back, elaborately fluffed about her
forehead and ears—add to the impression of formality blended
with terror.

"Because you don't have to," I say, by now hoping she'll change
her mind. (What am I trying to accomplish today? I'm wondering.
Have I really been thinking of Dinah?)

"No, I'm fine," she says, expelling the words like a gasp. "Let's
go, honey."

Already the heat is stifling. As we escape sunlight into the
dimmed lower-floor entrance to the mall, I have a brief impression
of cave-like unreality that makes this outing seem both less perilous
and less significant. Evidently Dinah shares this perception, for she
touches my elbow and chats amiably while we drift toward the
escalators, as if we were an ordinary pair of shoppers. Usually
people assume that we're mother and son, and today I must seem
her inevitable offspring in my beige linen jacket and Bass Weejuns,
my stalwart but still vaguely boyish appearance. I even have my

aunt's rosy coloring, her light-blue eyes, her willingness to raise her top lip at an instant's notice in an affable smile. Dinah's the envy of all the other little old ladies, she jokes, whenever we go out for dinner or a concert. Though she plays bridge on alternate Saturdays and belongs to a Great Books club, she goes out of her way to avoid introducing me to her friends. "I'm not *that* addlepated," she laughed once, with a little twitch of her mouth. "There's not one of those girls who wouldn't love to whisk you away," she said, "even the ones who have sons. Especially the ones who have sons."

She laughed again and I laughed with her, not quite sure what she meant. Dinah's son, Avery, had died when he was ten, killed when he tried to cross an old two-lane highway on his bike. I'd been waiting on the other side of the highway, safely across, and in his hurry to catch up Avery hadn't seen the farm-livestock truck barreling toward him; he'd been killed instantly. I didn't think Dinah was really referring to Avery, whom she hadn't mentioned in so long people might have assumed she'd forgotten him. But I knew that Dinah dreaded her past, her memories, far more than she feared loud noises or moving stairs.

Soon enough, we're standing at the base of the escalators, Dinah gazing up toward the second floor while I stare at Dinah.

"It's so early," she says, "I thought maybe they wouldn't have turned them on yet. I thought maybe I could practice—you know, when they're not moving." She speaks slowly as if trying to stall.

"That'd be fine," I tell her. I point behind us. "You could practice on the regular stairs."

Already she's shaking her head. "Nope," she says. "I came here to ride these stupid things, and I'm going to ride them."

I'm startled by this sudden resolve. Driving over, I'd deliberately talked about other things but had tried to remember when her specific fear of escalators really began. It had always been one of the phobias she joked about most freely, describing her futile attempts as a young woman to ride the escalators in the old Rich's department store in downtown Atlanta. "I'd stand off to the side for a while," she'd say, "and watch how other people did it. I knew the trick was that you paused, chose your step, and hopped on. But with me, I'd always lose my footing, and by the time I settled on one step, my back foot was lost out behind me somewhere, and then my knees would buckle, and I'd try to get back off. If I couldn't do that, I'd just freeze with one foot in the air, hanging on for dear life." She'd laugh brightly, even standing to act out the fiasco, crooking her dainty elbows and knees. "And *then* there was the matter of getting off. I'd try to hop off like everybody else, but I was either a beat too slow or too fast, and I'd think I was off but still be on, still moving, or else I *was* off but would hit the floor at a strange angle and twist my foot or lose my balance or think I was falling when I wasn't. I'd get that strange feeling you have when you're half asleep, that the floor is about to slam you in the face."

And besides getting on and off, she said, there was the possibility of getting your shoe stuck in the gears, wasn't there? Or what if that darned moving banister caught onto your sleeve? Or your bracelet? You could lose an arm or leg quick as that, she was sure—you could lose your life! She told this story often and everyone would laugh, including Dinah, though a hollowness settled in her eyes that only I could see.

So I flattered myself, anyway. Since Dinah and I are each other's sole surviving relative, we've become accustomed to the idea that we have some exclusive, blood-deep understanding of one another. Dinah's infrequent beaux—those hardy enough to pierce her cheerful but outright indifference to romantic attachments— have never lasted more than a month or two, quickly becoming the objects, poor men, of our after-dinner hilarity, as Dinah describes some instance of coarseness or self-importance or otiose presumption that destroyed any chance of intimacy or, for that matter, friendship. For my part, my longstanding relationship with a woman named Karen Reynolds, a colleague at the investment firm where I've worked for the past eight years, depends on her understanding that some slight need of Dinah's might call me out of town at any moment, possibly for a protracted length of time. I've clung to the idea that I'm indispensable to Dinah, though probably it's the other way around. Often I make the hundred-mile drive to Dinah's for no reason, exchanging my striving, sharp-angled city life for Dinah's unchanging quirks and obsessions—her definite fears, her inchoate longings. Is she more than a fixed point, a reference point? After some time in Dinah's company the mental image of my cluttered office or Karen's attractive, impatient face brings a sudden *frisson* of denial, an amnesiac's puzzlement at the thought of some other, established life.

So I'm thinking, guiltily, that I have encouraged this adventure of Dinah's out of some base need to justify myself, to provide the fiction of some forward—or upward—motion in her life. I clasp her elbow gently, whisper temptation in her ear.

"You don't have to, Dinah. You really don't."

Despite her last words, Dinah looks far from resolute. We've stood here for five or six minutes and twice have stepped aside to let someone pass. Dinah watches the gently rising backs of these other people—these normal people, she must be thinking—with a child's dark wistfulness. She takes an audible breath, then sinks back into the arm I've drawn firmly around her shoulder.

"Maybe in a minute, Gary," she says. "Let me rest a minute."

"That's fine," I say. "We've got plenty of time."

I follow Dinah's mesmerized gaze back to the escalators, to those bottom few steps rising implacably out of the floor as if bearing an opposing, fateful message: there isn't much time, it's now or never. Dinah seems to ignore this message, her shoulders limp beneath my arm. She removes a scented handkerchief from her purse and pats her cheek, then replaces the handkerchief, sighing.

"You know, Gary," she says, in a tired voice I don't recall hearing before. "These outings probably aren't a good idea. I hate to say this, but—"

She hesitates, and I offer no encouragement; surely she feels the stiffening of my arm. I'm pondering her phrase, *These outings*, fearing that she means more than our plans to work on her phobias.

"I remember how Lucy used to go on and on," she says, "about your future. Gary would do this, Gary would do that—he'd be a baseball star, he'd be President of the United States!" She laughs, vaguely. I keep my arm around her shoulder although I want nothing more than to withdraw it. Dinah's younger sister Lucy, my mother, died the year before Avery's accident out on the highway. She died by her own hand, taking an overdose of pills one Sunday morning after Dinah had taken us boys to church and Sunday school. My father had abandoned us long before, in much the same way Dinah's husband, Uncle Winston, had left town (as I'd gathered from stray, overheard conversations between my parents) before Avery was even born. No farewells, no warning of any kind. Not even a note. So, in what seemed a natural arrangement at the time, my mother and I had moved in with Dinah and Avery. All around us, people clucked about the shame of those darling Barrett girls, the prettiest girls in town when they were young, having suffered such a fate. The idea developed that their beauty—a vulnerable, almost sickly beauty, people said—was the kind that seemed destined to be disappointed, blighted after a short time of splendor. But they had their daddy's money, at least. They had those darling little boys, at least, who would eventually grow up to take care of their mothers.... Until this moment, watching the escalators rise into some darksome rarefied sphere, some higher stage of being it almost seemed, I hadn't considered that over the years Dinah and I had formed a pact, unspoken but virtually sacred: that neither of us would recall, either by direct or oblique reference, the ghosts of the dead. I couldn't remember the last time Dinah had spoken my mother's name, and only now did I understand how foolhardy was this morning's venture, what a wayward and unreasonable longing had brought us to this juncture in our lives.

"Dinah, let's go home," I tell her.

She hasn't lost her thought, however; she has only been gathering strength.

"It's not fair to you, Gary," she says, her voice steady, lacking its customary lilt. "I've held you back, I know that—but you're still a young man, after all. You and Sharon should get married, you should have children—"

I give a quick, barking laugh that resonates strangely in the mall's open dark spaces. "It's Karen," I say. "Her name is Karen."

Though they've met several times, it isn't so odd that Dinah should mistake my friend's name; whenever my aunt and I are together, it could be said that Karen joins, temporarily, the company of Avery and Lucy and the others. We seldom refer to her.

Dinah takes out the handkerchief again and this time wipes her brow.

"I'm sorry, honey. I guess that proves my point."

"And we don't want children," I say, almost curtly. "Neither of us wants that."

Dinah squeezes my arm. "Don't be mad, honey," she says. "We've needed to have this talk, you know. For a long time."

We still haven't looked at each other. My vision has blotched, watching the endless rise of the escalator steps—each made to hold a human form, each empty this morning. I suppose Dinah is watching the escalators, too, her blue eyes gone watery with bewilderment, or some dismal recognition.

"I started thinking about this—about all of this—on the day we first began talking about my phobias. You know, about getting rid of them. Then I talked to Dr. Shields about it. I hadn't mentioned you very often before, and he asked a lot of questions. Anyhow, it all came tumbling out, and that's when I knew— I knew—"

"Aunt Dinah," I say calmly, "you shouldn't get upset."

She pauses, taking deep breaths. Again that impression of recouping, gathering strength. Has the doctor taught her that? Will she report back to him, during their next session? *Dr. Shields, I did try to talk with Gary. He wasn't too receptive, but I think we've made a start....*

"I'm not upset, Gary," she says, with a hint of condescension. "Not at all."

My heart tenses. "All right, then, why don't we get this over with? Why don't you hop on?"

I gesture with cruel nonchalance toward the escalators.

Aunt Dinah seems to know that the moment has come. She steps out of the restraining circle of my arm and approaches the base of the escalators. She removes one of the white gloves and reaches her brown-spotted hand toward the ascending banister, touching it once or twice, lightly. She starts to turn around, to glance at me, but she doesn't. Watching her fluffy dark head, the curve of her pale neck that still looks fragile and lovely, I feel my heart begin tightening, contracting. I'm aware that my fists are clenched and that I'm holding my breath.

One hand touching the banister, Dinah watches her feet and after a beat, or two beats, steps onto the escalators.

Almost at the same moment, there is a whooping noise from somewhere above. Near the top of the escalators, descending out of the shadowy second floor, I see a boy in glasses carrying a waxed cup filled with Karmel Korn. He's about ten, wearing blue jeans and a horizontally striped red-and-white T-shirt, and at first I'm sure that I'm hallucinating. The boy is smiling, munching the candy, as he sidesteps quickly down the same set of escalators that Aunt Dinah, clutching the banister, is bravely ascending. He seems to be playing a game, seeing how fast he can descend against the implacable upward current of the stairs. Moving nimbly, monkey-like, he is chuckling to himself and does not seem to notice Dinah, though they are on a direct collision course and though Dinah has summoned the temerity to release one of her pale quivering arms and begin gesturing wildly, trying to get the boy's attention. I'm still convinced that I'm seeing things until I hear, from the second floor, a woman's voice: "Do you hear me, Jeffrey? I said no, you'll get yourself killed, you'll—" But her voice breaks off, hopeless; her son is already halfway down the "up" escalators, moving rapidly. When it seems certain that he will crash into Dinah and send her sprawling, the boy hops agilely to the other side and goes past her, still chuckling, still sidestepping with uncanny skill. He has almost reached the bottom when I think to glance upward again, where I just have time to see Dinah's diminished form—head slightly bowed, shoulders slumped—move safely off the top of the escalators, onto the second floor and out of sight.

"Hey Mister," the boy says, tugging at my sleeve. "I came down the wrong way, did you see that? Pretty good, huh?"

I am thinking, bitterly, that she didn't once look back.

II

When I leave home for the first time, a few weeks shy of my twentieth birthday, I am not afraid, exactly. But I am concerned. Apprehensive. Though I "took a year off," as the jaunty phrase goes, after high school, and helped Aunt Dinah sort out her tangled financial and personal affairs, I did not feel good about leaving her.

Deciding against a prestigious northeastern school, I enrolled in the state university in Atlanta, only a two-hour drive away.

During those first weeks of school I am not homesick, exactly, but I feel oppressed with a vague sense of guilt. All during the summer my Aunt Dinah's nervous problems—insomnia, night fears, fainting spells, abrupt mood swings—had worsened, but when I suggested postponing college another year, Dinah quickly brushed her own worries aside. She invoked my excellent test scores, my sparkling future. She became cheerful and forward-looking, exactly the opposite of the way I feel during September and most of October.

When I call home each night, using the battered pay phone down the hall from my dorm room, I have trouble believing her brave assurances that she's fine, perfectly fine. The medication is helping, she says. Dr. Shields is a wonderful man, and Father Hopkins calls or visits several times each week. Listening, I shift my weight uneasily. Her voice sounds timid and far away. As the weeks pass, I find it more and more difficult to concentrate on my freshman courses.

When Father Hopkins telephones, one Thursday afternoon in late October, I'm almost relieved. I pack an overnight bag, but during the drive home I decide against continuing with college, at least for this year. Since my mother's suicide, eleven years ago, and the death of my cousin Avery so cruelly soon after that, Dinah and I have developed a close and mutually supportive bond. My only reason for attending college (though I haven't said this to Dinah, not in so many words) is to study business, so I can do a better job of handling Dinah's investments. When I reach twenty-one, there will also be the stock and bank accounts my mother left in trust. These are responsibilities I take very seriously, as I suppose I take most things seriously. (During my six weeks on campus, I've gathered that I'm not your typical college student. I've grown accustomed to the kidding of my dorm-mates, who insist that I think and brood too much. They've coaxed me out a few times— to get some pizza, to drink a few beers—and though they're pleasant company, I have trouble paying attention to their friendly banter, their endless jokes. As I drive home their laughter rings in my ears, brittle and unreal.)

I'm startled by the number of cars parked outside Aunt Dinah's house. Helplessly I recall the days after Avery's funeral, when the cars of family friends and hangers-on clogged the circular driveway. Bearing flowers or covered dishes into the high-ceilinged parlor, the ladies hugged and wept over Dinah, while their embarrassed husbands chucked me under the chin and mumbled that I was "the man of the house" now, that they hoped I'd be good and strong and brave. (This was, of course, our family's second funeral in less than a year, but when my mother died there had been no such outpouring. Father Hopkins had officiated at her service, too, but it had been extremely brief and attended by only five or six people. In the ensuing weeks he had leaked out the news gradually, discreetly, prompting Aunt Dinah to remark how much tact Father Hopkins possessed, how much foresight and wisdom. At school, eventually, I endured a few cruel jokes and blunt queries, but in general my mother's suicide was a non-event.)

When I come inside, everyone rises except Dinah herself. My eyes dart immediately to her overstuffed easy chair, where she sits looking blurry and distraught. I say "blurry" because her hair is mussed, her makeup uneven, her eyelids and lips trembling—the opposite of her usual well-groomed, focused demeanor. Father Hopkins comes forward and pumps my hand, expressing hearty thanks. "We've had quite a time of it," he says, in the jovial manner he uses for crisis situations. He's a burly, big-chested man, with a head of silver-gray curls; his skin is coarse and flushed. Although Aunt Dinah secretly dislikes the Episcopalian service and seldom goes any more, Father Hopkins visits often, as though she were his most faithful parishioner; suddenly I wonder if he's in love with her, either knowingly or not. It's not a bizarre thought, really. Also seated in the room are Dr. Shields, who has twice proposed to Dinah, and a "beau," as she always calls them, whose name is Martin, or perhaps Morton—I can't remember. It probably doesn't matter. He's thin, dapper, and sad-eyed, perched in a straight-backed chair nearest Dinah. Dr. Shields is about Dinah's age, blond, handsome, but weak-looking. He sits on the antique brocaded love seat, cracking his knuckles. These two men stare at me, with a kind of dull envy, as Father Hopkins leads me over to Dinah's chair.

"What happened?" I say, pleased by the sound of my cool, clipped voice, which cuts through the muggy emotional atmosphere in the room.

"Oh, honey," Aunt Dinah says ruefully, reaching out a white fluttering hand. For a moment we simply clasp hands, while the others look on, slack-mouthed.

Even in a somewhat disheveled state, Dinah's beauty is nothing short of spectacular. Her glamour has always been a matter of small but heartrending details—the fragile jaw bone, the just-exposed tips of her ear lobes, the deliberately arched and penciled brows above her dark, quick-moving eyes. Speaking softly, she lifts the brows into tiny, V-shaped peaks.

"Oh, honey, your auntie did a stupid thing."

Her eyes fill, and at the same moment she gives an inconsequent laugh.

"Dinah?" I say, worried.

"I've given her a sedative," Dr. Shields says, from the love seat. "She's much calmer than she was."

"I'm not sure about sedatives," Father Hopkins says, frowning. "I'm not sure they're good for her."

"Poor Dinah," says Martin, or Morton, clucking his tongue and shifting his body sympathetically in the chair. "She went upstairs this morning—up into the attic I mean—and she—"

Dinah flutters her hand once more.

"Let *me* tell Gary," she says, her eyes roving about my face quickly, hungrily. I know what she is feeling, for I feel the same: we have missed each other tremendously. Despite her edict against weekend visits until Thanksgiving—she didn't want to "depend" on me, she wanted me to plunge fully into my exciting college life—there hasn't been a Friday when I haven't wanted to come home, for my sake as much as hers.

"Go ahead," I say gently. "Tell me."

She laughs briefly, trying to settle herself, and takes a deep breath. Behind me, I can sense the sharpened attention of the other three men. There's a tension, a general anguish in the room.

Dinah says, haltingly, that she'd gone up into the attic that morning. Wanting for something to do, she had boxed up some things of mine—old sweaters and scarves, a pile of high school memorabilia gathering dust in the back of my closet—and had taken the boxes, one at a time, up the rickety wooden stairs from the second-floor landing. In the attic, she says, the air was incredibly musty and overheated. Somehow, up there, it was like another world. Once she had gotten the last box upstairs, she felt how drastically her mood had changed. Whereas she'd felt "at loose ends" earlier that morning, and a bit melancholy, now she felt energetic and spry, as though her physical labor had helped her break through the lassitude of recent weeks. Having stowed the boxes away, she obeyed a sudden impulse and went over by the attic's tiny window, whose thick piece of glass—octagon-shaped, tinted a pale amber—allowed only a dimmed, hazy vision of the yard and street below. Dinah says, hesitating, that she felt a chill enwrapping her shoulders at that moment, despite the intense heat and her own sense of energy and power. She'd been thinking how her view out the attic window resembled one of those old, sepia-toned photographs from her grandparents' days, and at that moment she noticed, beneath the window ledge, an old beechwood crate whose contents—the lid was open—snagged her attention at once. Before she quite knew what was happening, she had reached into the crate and removed several bulky envelopes filled with photographs—some of my mother and myself, but mostly pictures of Avery. She says anxiously that she shouldn't have looked at them, she *should* have dropped them as though they were burning coals, but soon enough she was going through the pictures one by one, greedily, the yellowish glare from the window tinting the photographs so that *they* appeared sepia-toned, much older than they were and somehow absolved of harm. There was Avery at his fifth birthday party, wearing his first pair of glasses and smiling from behind a lighted birthday cake. There was Avery standing next to me, a year or two later, after a neighborhood baseball game. Avery looked slight and exhausted, she says, his glasses askew, a smear of dirt along his cheek, while I looked tall and athletic and smug—Dinah uses that odd word, "smug," without glancing at me—as I stood with my chest pushed out, my arm around Avery. She found a picture of my mother—"Lucy was so lovely, so young-looking!" Dinah cries—with Avery and me perched side by side on her knees. And there was a shot of Avery out in the back yard; he was holding a butterfly net, she whispers, so it must have been taken after his tenth birthday, not long before he died.

Dinah says that she put the pictures away, after that one. She knew that in another box to her left, marked "Toys," was the butterfly net itself, and his coin collection, and his coloring books. One of the coloring books, I suddenly recall, had Bozo the Clown on the cover, and I remember how Dinah would shudder whenever she saw it, and how Avery would laugh. I can imagine Dinah opening the box and seeing that coloring book and literally dying of fright, but fortunately this did not happen. By this time, Dinah explains, the chill she'd felt had intensified and she'd begun trembling. At some point she had also started weeping. She backed away from the window and went awkwardly down the stairs, stumbling once or twice, getting to the bottom in a state that she ought to call, she supposes, "outright hysteria." On the second-floor landing, the door to the attic stairs closed, it was her ordinary surroundings that seemed unreal. She was shivering uncontrollably, she was sobbing, she knew that she'd made a terrible mistake and that she needed help at once. So she called Martin— she says the word distinctly, "Martin"—and Martin called Dr. Shields and Father Hopkins. Though she begged Father Hopkins not to bother me, the priest had insisted. All three men told her that she didn't look well, she'd suffered a tremendous shock and needed all the support she could get.

"Anyhow," Dinah says, her eyes watery again, apologetic, "that's what happened. Your auntie made a stupid mistake, and it's everyone else who pays."

"Don't be ridiculous," Martin says at once, from behind me. "Don't say such things."

He sounds angry, but no one pays much attention.

"We're glad you're here, Gary," Father Hopkins says.

"Your being here, plus the sedative," Dr. Shields says, "ought to make her good as new."

Aunt Dinah is looking at me, as though alarmed that I haven't said anything.

I lean across and kiss her cheek, whispering in the same breath, "I'm home. Please don't worry." Then, feeling self-conscious, I excuse myself by saying that I want to shower and change my clothes. There's a murmur of agreement—of course, of course. Dinah says to take my time—she's fine now, she really is. As I move slowly up the stairs, feeling deathly tired, Father Hopkins calls out something cheerful and encouraging, but I can't make out the words and I don't bother to turn around.

Upstairs I take a long, hot shower; then I change into slacks and a soft cotton shirt. Still feeling tired, I decide to lie down for a while, but for some reason I leave my room and go across the hall, to the seldom-used bedroom next to Dinah's. When we were boys, Avery and I had shared this room, which is still furnished with twin "youth" beds and identical pinewood chests of drawers. I drift toward my old bed and lie down, raising dust and an odor of disuse from the tan chenille spread. Lying on my side, I gaze across at Avery's empty bed. When we were very young, our mothers would often send us upstairs for afternoon naps, and we would lie here fully clothed, not even removing our shoes. We talked idly but doggedly, refusing to fall asleep. An hour or two later we would reappear downstairs, ostentatiously yawning and stretching our arms. At that age, the temperamental differences between us were not so pronounced, and there must have been a particular fondness between myself and Avery. Our mothers, at that time, looked so much alike that they were often mistaken for twins. Gazing across at the empty bed, idly remembering, I become drowsy despite myself, and feel gently suffused in a gauze of memory, desire, and longing; then, opening my eyes, I have that abrupt, plunging sensation, as of a helpless fall through space. My limbs jerk, my heart races, but when I land I'm still on the bed, still lying on my side.

Then, for a brief moment, I do glimpse Avery in the other bed. He's lying on his side, too, and staring across at me. He's nineteen now, neatly dressed, still wearing thick glasses, and he stares expressionlessly with his slightly magnified eyes. I think how peaceful he looks, how white and untouched and whole.

I rise from the bed and drift out to the top of the stairs. From the parlor below, I hear conversation, laughter; Dinah's high trilling laugh cuts through the muddled deeper voices. Looking down at my bare feet, feeling detached and emotionless, I begin descending the stairs. As I move downward, the heads and chair backs of Dinah's guests are visible beyond the curve of the banister. Straining, I can now make out what Dinah is saying. With clever, charming self-mockery, she is talking about her lifelong fear of escalators. By now the story must be familiar to all three men, but nonetheless their laughter sounds genuine, filled with masculine delight. I can't quite see Dinah, but I can picture her antics as she stands with her arms flailing, one leg bent in mid-air, her eyes widened in exaggerated fright.

Imagining this, I now have the thought that it's not myself descending the stairs; rather it's my cousin, Avery. That's why he's moving with such quietness and stealth, awaiting the moment when he reaches the parlor door and catches Dinah in this mood of hilarity, her limbs distorted, her male audience held in thrall. Then Dinah's eyes will bulge, her cheeks sag unbecomingly, as her make-believe fear turns to stunned disbelief and then to outright horror.

As I come off the stairway, this unbidden fantasy vanishes as quickly as it came. I'm shaken by the experience, of course, especially by its suggestion of hostility toward Dinah, but I don't feel particularly surprised or even displeased. When I come into the parlor, Dinah continues her antic monologue and none of the others glance around. Taking my seat I feel weightless and happy, insubstantial as any ghost.

III

One Saturday morning when I am twelve years old and my cousin Avery is ten, we decide to take our bikes and go out riding. Though Aunt Dinah has forbidden us to go past the circular driveway, it's fairly early and Dinah is still sleeping—"getting her beauty rest," as she likes to say, with a wink at us boys. I use this same wink on Avery when he pauses at the edge of the driveway, one foot on the ground, and says he doesn't like disobeying his mother. Aah, I tell him, what she doesn't know won't hurt her, we'll be back before she's even awake—and with a whoop I start pedaling down the street, yelling for Avery to hurry up, come on! After a moment's hesitation, he does.

We pedal slowly through the residential streets, where most of the houses, like Dinah's, are set far back from the road, with curving snakelike driveways and huge porches. One day last summer Avery had tumbled off our own porch and gashed his forehead on the bottom step; the cut took eleven stitches, one for each of the brick steps leading down from the porch. The day after Avery's accident, wanting for something to do, I had counted the steps and had examined the bottom step for traces of Avery's blood—but there was nothing. Aunt Dinah or our part-time maid, Flora, must have already washed the blood away.

At school the kids taunt Avery for being so clumsy, and I always take up for him. Several times I've gotten in fights with bullies from Avery's class, and I've won every fight. As we're riding along through the neighborhood, though, I can't help teasing Avery and showing off—lifting my hands from the handlebars and folding them nonchalantly across my chest, zigzagging the bike at dangerous angles along the pavement. "Hey, try this!" I call out to Avery, riding circles around him, laughing. "See if you can do *this*," I cry, not quite understanding the savage joy that's coursing through my chest and limbs.

"Cut it out," Avery says. He rides with his thin shoulders slumped above the handlebars, steering cautiously, frowning. He wears thick black-framed glasses, and at school some of the kids call him "four eyes." I wish I could keep Avery from acting like a sissy, becoming an object of ridicule, but if anything he gets paler and skinnier, and becomes more of a Mama's boy, with each passing year. The kids tease him about our family situation, too, and even about what happened to *my* mother—though they wouldn't dare say a thing when I'm around. I inherited the strong build and bony, sharp-looking features of my father, Jimmy, who left town several years ago, on one of his "sales" trips, but never came back. Avery's father had left Aunt Dinah before Avery was born, so neither of us kids remembers him, but in pictures Dinah keeps in her lingerie drawer he looks like a grown-up version of Avery, his face smooth and girlish-looking, his hair and even his eyelashes a delicate pale blond. So I've always felt a bit superior to Avery because of our different fathers, and it's clear that others sense the difference, too. Even Aunt Dinah has remarked that

Avery and I don't look like blood relatives, that we don't favor each other or share any traits or behavior whatsoever.

Now that I've turned twelve and will be transferring out to the junior high school next year, leaving Avery to fend for himself in the fifth grade, I know I shouldn't egg him on—but this particular morning I can't help it, somehow; I'm too cheerful and full of energy. When we cross Main Street and start riding along the little-used oiled road that runs parallel to the highway, I call out again, "Come on, Avery, pedal faster, try riding with no hands—look here at me, look how easy!"

Avery glances over, mistrustfully. "Cut it out, Gary," he says. And then, after we've crossed the railroad tracks—Avery getting off his bike and walking it across, while I jolt over the tracks at high speed, bouncing and laughing—he comes to a stop and just stands there, with his usual woebegone expression. He waits for me to ride back and then says, "Come on, Gary, we'd better go home."

"What for?" I ask, riding around him in small neat circles, so that he never knows quite which way to turn. I'm wiping my forehead with the back of my hand (even this early in the morning, it's fiercely hot in mid-August), feeling irritated that Avery hasn't even broken a sweat. He stands there with his white knuckles gripping the handlebars, looking pale and sullen.

"What's the matter?" I ask him. "You afraid of something— afraid to go riding, get too far away from Mommy?"

"Cut it out," he says again, but he looks away and I can tell he's really bugged. Another nickname they have for him at school: bug-eyes. Avery's glasses make his eyes look bigger than they are.

"Come on," I say, in a friendlier tone, clapping him on the shoulder, "let's cross over the highway and go out the farm road a bit. There's some great hills out there, you can get going really fast."

"We're not supposed to be *this* far," he says, his lip curling downward a little, which means he's about to cry.

"OK, how about this," I tell him. "There's a big pecan tree up on that hill," and I point across the highway. "You can sit under the tree, in the shade, and I'll go zooming up and down the hills. I'll do every trick in the book, all for you—you can just watch. I'll even show you how to do a couple of things—you know, the easier ones. Come on, Avery, it's too soon to go home."

There's a sudden urgency in my voice, combined with the persuasive salesmanship I've inherited from my charming but long-gone father. Despite everything, I know that Avery looks up to me; even "worships" me, as Aunt Dinah claims. So I know already—as I keep circling Avery, and cajoling him, and making promises in a buoyant, cheerful voice—that I'm going to get my way.

IV

In her rare moments of pique, that's what my mother would say about her sister—that Dinah "always got her way." Though the Barrett girls had been equally pretty, and were sometimes mistaken for twins, their temperaments were dramatically opposite: Lucy had been a quiet, withdrawn girl who never made a fuss and disliked attention of any kind, while Dinah had been the perverse but lively "belle," flirting at some point with every available man in a fifty-mile radius of town, and with some who weren't so available. Despite their beauty and the fortune each inherited at the death of their father, no one was surprised that both girls had married unwisely. Lucy accepted that grinning charmer, Jimmy Wheeler, after only two dates, falling in love precipitously and madly in the usual way of melancholy girls, but within months had resigned herself not only to his endless "sales" trips but to a considerable amount of philandering right in her own hometown. It was to Lucy's scandalous victimization, in fact, that Dinah would later ascribe her own ostracism from the polite Southern social circles into which the girls had been born. From what I've been able to gather (Dinah being much less forthcoming about her own emotional history than about my mother's), it appears that Avery's father, far from having abandoned his wife and son, might actually have been banished from their presence; certainly his photographs suggest a dependent, besotted admirer of the kind Dinah still keeps about her—albeit at a safe distance—to this day. I've often distrusted, in short, her melancholy references to the time when Uncle Winston "took off," or her patient explanations to Avery that his father was a romantic wanderer, the type who couldn't be held down. This description, of course, fit my own father rather than Avery's.

By the time I learned with some degree of certainty what had really happened, our lives were already set: my mother and I had moved in with Dinah and Avery, where the four of us lived in relative isolation, getting few visitors except for unshakable admirers of Dinah like Father Hopkins and Dr. Shields. Once her divorce came through Dinah did occasionally have a "beau," as she'd already begun calling them, but when these men began phoning too persistently Dinah would no longer encourage them, and if we boys were present in the room would even make faces into the phone, keeping the receiver covered with one palm to cover the sound of our laughter. (Even Avery would laugh, looking from his mother to me as if trying to discover what was so funny.) As for Lucy, she disliked her sister's coquetry but seldom objected, and she actually seemed to approve my growing closeness to my aunt, gladly retreating to her room and allowing Dinah to run the house and the daily lives of us boys. By the time we were both in school, my mother spent almost all her time sequestered, showing up only for mealtimes and an occasional visit to church. It did not strike me, at the time, that my mother was desperately unhappy. Dinah had explained to both Avery and me that some people were merely "reserved," liking to keep to themselves and read a great deal and think their private thoughts. I had noticed how Avery's pale, big-eyed face had seemed to brighten in my mother's presence, and how he would sometimes accompany her back up the stairs, the two of them talking in quick, confiding voices. So I had assumed that, by some quirk of nature, Avery took after my mother, while I took after his. It didn't seem to matter, somehow. Our daily routine was stable, predictable; we had all settled comfortably into our separate lives.

At about this same time—a year or two, I suppose, before my mother's death—Dinah began developing, or at least began talking about, her various phobias. One Halloween when Avery and I presented ourselves for her inspection (one of us dressed as Bozo the Clown, the other wearing a crimson devil's suit, complete with pitchfork and horned mask) she had taken two or three steps backward, truly alarmed. "Gary? Avery? Who are—Which one is—?" Her skin had gone white, and even her pupils had shrunk to tiny points inside the whites of her eyes. Since I was already a couple of inches taller than Avery, I had trouble believing she couldn't tell us apart. Nonetheless I'd grabbed Avery's arm and dragged him out the back door, and I made sure we removed our masks before returning that evening from trick or treat. Only a couple of months before that, Dinah had displayed in spectacular fashion her fear of escalators. She had driven us boys into Atlanta to buy school clothes at Rich's, and while the three of us were ascending the escalators toward the boys' department, Dinah had suddenly lost her nerve: her knees had buckled, her purse dangled off her wrist at an awkward angle, she somehow had her feet on two different steps and her face, wide-eyed, wore a look of abject terror. When we reached the top Dinah stumbled off, and stood panting for a few moments, her shoulders bent, while Avery and I watched helplessly. This turned out to be Dinah's last attempt to ride the escalators. That evening, in our bedroom, I remember how angry and bothered Avery seemed. "Why is Mama so afraid of things, what's *wrong* with her?" he asked, his eyes bulging behind his glasses. I remember feeling queasy and empty, and to cover this I threw a pillow at my cousin, trying to distract his attention. I knew I couldn't explain.

It often seemed, in fact, that Avery could perceive things the rest of us couldn't. In the ten-month interval between my mother's death and Avery's own, Dinah had often remarked on this, bewailing the fact that we hadn't listened to Avery, had discounted his anxiety as the whining of a sickly nine-year-old. For that morning, as the three of us were getting ready for church, Avery had kept saying that someone should check on Aunt Lucy. Although she hadn't shown up for breakfast, this wasn't really unusual: my mother had begun using sleeping pills, which sometimes kept her unconscious throughout the morning. Avery insisted that Aunt Lucy had wanted to go to church this morning, she'd attended the previous few Sundays and wanted to become a regular churchgoer again, but both Dinah and I had brushed him off. "Honey, let your Aunt Lucy sleep," Dinah had said, adjusting her hat and gloves in the hall mirror. That morning, I believe, she had never been more beautiful: her dark hair dramatically upswept, her skin taut and glowing, her figure trim, compact, but sensual in her close-fitting spring dress of yellow linen. Behind her, dressed in my navy blue suit from last Easter, I said quickly, "She had trouble sleeping all last week, so she's probably just catching up. It would be stupid to wake her, Avery, just when she's getting some rest." "That's right, Gary," Dinah said, but I noticed how Avery kept glancing toward the stairway, as if he would suddenly break away and go flying up the steps. So I went over to him, clamping a hand on each shoulder. "Race you to the car," I said. "Last one there's a little turd!" I added, laughing. Avery had no choice but to run off behind me, as Dinah called after us, "Gary, what awful language!—and on a Sunday!"

It's possible that, almost a year later, when I taunt and tease my cousin about riding our bikes out past the highway, I am recalling that Sunday morning. For who understands, finally, the sudden warps and sinister promptings of memory? Certainly I am visited, at the oddest times, with a procession of images rising into my awareness slowly, implacably, with the mechanical certainty of fate itself: once we'd returned from church, Avery rushing downstairs with a white, wrenched expression, saying wildly that Aunt Lucy would not wake up, would *not* wake up; the arrival of Dr. Shields, then the ambulance; the covered stretcher borne carefully down the stairs by a pair of black paramedics, who looked rueful and embarrassed; the visit of Father Hopkins to discuss the funeral services; and then the funeral itself, so meager and quickly accomplished that afterward it seemed, eerily, that Lucy Barrett Wheeler might never have existed. Yes, when Avery and I do pause beside the highway, each resting on one leg as we await a break in the traffic, I am remembering clearly Avery's pinched, woebegone look during the funeral service and in the days that followed, a look of diminished hope that suggested the extremes of both innocence and fear.

"Now we can go," I tell him, raising my foot to the pedal. "Right after this station wagon passes."

"Wait, Gary," Avery calls after me, in his thin whining voice. "There's too much traffic, it's too dangerous—"

But I don't listen; I push hard on the pedal, and the moment the wood-paneled station wagon is past I shoot across the highway, letting out a wild whoop, crossing easily before the next car, its horn honking and brakes squealing, rushes by.

Across all this noise, Avery is mouthing words from his side of the highway, clearly angry and offended, but rather comical at this distance. I fold my hands together and lift them above my head, in the sign of victory. Then I yell: "Come on, Avery, you can make it! Let's *go!*"

Now Avery looks doubtful, fearful; cars and trucks are whizzing past, and it seems there's never enough of a clear opening for him to cross the highway safely. Nonetheless I stand waiting, resting my weight on one leg, feeling strong and confident and even, somehow, exultant. I can feel the blood coursing swiftly through my legs, my heart, I can feel the pulsebeat at my throat keeping time to my words: "Come on, Avery, don't be a little chicken-shit! Look, there's plenty of time between cars if you hurry, so come on, will you? Come *on!*"

His expression changes again; he looks across at me, gloomily, his eyes the fixed dark points I remember still from last October, the night before my mother's death. It was past midnight, I suppose, when the telephone rang, and we were all upstairs except Dinah, who had just gotten home from a date. By the time she answered, in the downstairs hall, I had risen from bed and drifted to the top of the stairway, where I could see only the hem of her red silk dress, her shapely ankle, her black patent-leather stiletto heels. But her voice wafted clearly up the stairs, and within seconds I knew that the caller was my father. "But why now, why *now?*" Dinah said, in a kind of soft wail. I remember only snatches of the conversation. At one point Dinah said, sarcastically, "Aren't you calling for Lucy, really, but you're afraid to admit it?" And a bit later, low and wounded: "It's not in my nature, you know that, I've always *told* you that. You want too much, Jimmy, you always wanted too damn much...." It was then I felt, beside me, the ghostly apparition of my cousin Avery, wearing his thin cotton night shirt, giving me his dark fixed immutable gaze that achieved a spectral power in the scant light cast up along the stairs. Even as I heard, from behind me, my mother's door softly closing—I hadn't known, until that moment, that it had stood ajar the whole time—I felt a paralysis in my limbs that prevented my calling down to Aunt Dinah, pleading for her to rush up the stairs in all her dazzling light and beauty, and that likewise kept me from fleeing downstairs to her. I felt immobile, frozen in place. Between us there was not a mere flight of stairs but an irreparable distance, a gulf between two worlds, and my cousin's innocent dark eyes seemed the bearers of this knowledge and of my own perdition. He turned back to his bedroom just as Dinah, downstairs, angrily slammed down the phone, and from that moment a deeper silence reigned in the house, suggesting the loss of all human connections.

V

Am I remembering this—any of this—at the moment Avery, his eyes fixed on mine, lifts his small body and begins pedaling across the highway? He has time, of course; that ancient wheezing farm truck is at least a quarter-mile distant, there's no other vehicle in sight, so naturally I'm gesturing him forward, of course I'm yelling out friendly taunts and boyish encouragement as Avery, his bike wobbling, starts across the highway. What I hadn't predicted, of course, is the dreamlike slowness with which Avery weaves across, not even glancing aside at the oncoming truck, his enlarged eyes in all their innocent dark fury fixed upon me. It's then I raise my hand, a half-completed gesture, to cry out, "Wait, Avery, go back!— there isn't time, look out for that truck, *look out!*" But he continues forward with perverse slowness, wobbling from side to side, not even reacting to the truck's blaring horn and its dramatic noisy skid as the driver, trying to avoid Avery, spins the truck over sideways and buries my cousin beneath several tons of braying livestock and crashing metal. From under the shuddering mess something flies out and lands near my sneakers—Avery's glasses, crushed and blood-spattered. It's then that a horrified cry tears from my throat and I mount the bike and begin pedaling wildly, madly. In less than ten minutes I'm back at Aunt Dinah's.

It turns out that my behavior will be excused as the result of panic, understandable in one so young. Even the truck driver, emerging shaken but unhurt from the wreck, will report to police how I had motioned frantically for my cousin to get back, how I had appeared to be shrieking in horror as Avery continued— obstinately, perversely—into the truck's path. At the time, of course, the opinions of these others mean nothing. During that desperate ten-minute ride, all my thought and energy are focused upon Aunt Dinah, whom I want to reach before all the fuss begins, before she has even heard the news. This is so important. This is so crucial. Once I hit the driveway and begin shrieking her name at the top of my voice, and by the time I throw my bike underneath the old water oak and turn toward the porch she is there, opening the screen door, blinking curiously as she squints out at the sunlight and at me. "Gary, honey?" she says, a tremulous catch in her throat. She comes out onto the porch, to the topmost edge of the steps. She looks youthful but worried, her dark hair gleaming in the sunlight, her hands splayed down the front of her pale-yellow dress. She leans out, fondly. "Honey, is something—" she begins, but doesn't finish. I see her face sag, her eyes darken, but already I am bounding up the porch steps, panting, weeping, ready to be enfolded in her arms.

III

from *I Am Dangerous*

Hemingway's Cats

I

When, on the first morning of their honeymoon, Antonia opened their door to let in some fresh air, an enormous cat sprang into the room. Mottled orange and gold, very quick despite its size, the cat leapt onto a chair beside the dresser and then toward Antonia, who recoiled and nearly fell backward, crying out in alarm. Next it went for the bed, bounding onto Antonia's dented pillow and into Robbie's lap, where it curled promptly into a ball and closed its eyes. Propped against his own pillow, half-sitting so he could see Antonia better—watching her dress, watching her move gracefully about the room—Robbie laughed hysterically at the sight of his wife crying out, jumping back into the room's dimmest corner. "Hey—hey, it's only a cat," he managed, but he could hardly speak for laughing, and certainly Antonia could not speak. In fact, Antonia could not move. For what seemed half an hour but was probably only two or three minutes, she stayed back, trembling, while her husband laughed and the cat slept.

Yet Robbie looked guilty, climbing out of the bed. The cat made a small disgruntled noise, then rearranged itself on Antonia's pillow.

"Honey, you're all right, aren't you?" Robbie said, in the solicitous bridegroom's voice he'd tried all during the night. Naked, he came toward her with arms outstretched. "I didn't mean to laugh, it's just that you looked so—so damn *funny*," he said, and he dropped his arms and started laughing again. "I'm sorry," he said. "It's just that squeal you let out, and that little jump backward—"

"I've got the picture," she said, though not bitterly, for seeing the incident through Robbie somehow helped. She felt her body loosen, and when Robbie embraced her, she felt again the wave of pleasurable emotion—gratitude? relief?—that had swept her into this marriage and changed her life so profoundly, in a dreamlike swift few months; had changed *her*, as she liked to think. (For she had lived a meager life, cramped and embarrassed and afraid. It was like her, she thought, to be afraid of an ordinary cat.)

"Don't be mad," Robbie said, rubbing her shoulders.

"I'm not mad," she said carefully. "I'm embarrassed, that's all. For acting like such a fool."

"You were just startled," Robbie said, "it's nothing to be embarrassed about," and he turned back toward the bed, clapping his hands. "Shoo!" he cried, and the cat's tail stiffened with alarm, and in an instant it had leapt off the bed and out the door. The room was still.

"I don't like surprises," Antonia said, from her place in the corner.

"Don't worry about it, it's nothing," Robbie said cheerfully, heading for the bathroom. "It's something to tell Dad—you know, an anecdote. When we get home."

Robbie's father, Vincent, was paying for this honeymoon in Key West. He'd spent his own honeymoon here, in the mid-sixties, and every few years he went back again, telling his wife and children and friends that the island was "another world"—not exactly paradise, he'd say, but as close as *he'd* ever get. Vincent was a large, bearish man with a blunt, square face and quick-moving eyes, ice-blue. Antonia had met him only a few times, and he frightened her in a pleasant way; from the beginning she'd felt that Vincent liked her— which was, of course, very important to Robbie—and on the flight down from Atlanta, her husband had delivered the final judgment, in the off-hand manner Antonia knew he had copied from Vincent.

"By the way," he'd said, turning a page of his magazine, "at the reception Dad drew me aside. He thinks you're terrific—that you're 'perfect' for me, in fact." He'd given a brief laugh; Antonia had felt that anything she said might sound tactless, so she murmured agreeably, gazing out the small blurry window. Down her arms and back went that shiver of apprehension she felt whenever Vincent's name was mentioned. She knew that he was, in his son's eyes, a colossus—a decorated Vietnam vet, a self-made businessman, an autodidact who knew several languages and liked to quote Nietzsche, an expert sailor and marksman. In short, any boy's hero. Learning that he thought well of her, Antonia had felt the permanence of her marriage far more acutely than at the moment she and Robbie had said, both of them quite meekly, "I do."

By the time Robbie came out of the bathroom, she'd made the bed and opened their drapes to a flood of sunlight. As she expected, Robbie kidded her for straightening the room—they were on vacation, for heaven's sake, the maid would be arriving any minute!—but she liked to keep busy; she'd never been the type to just sit. Nor did she enjoy waiting around for slower people, though of course she hadn't mentioned that to Robbie. Her mind worked quickly, her senses were keen, but if Robbie was a bit lethargic and had not quite mastered the details of everyday life, maybe that was an advantage: Antonia would have that much more to do, her days would be filled to bursting. Robbie was Vincent's oldest son but the last to get married, and had there been some tacit hope on Vincent's part that Antonia would assume the role of looking after him, keeping him on track? If so, maybe that only meant that Antonia had found herself; or, at the very least, had found a sort of refuge.

Man and wife, they went out into the cool morning air. Vincent had made a list of things they must not miss—not only tourist attractions, but restaurants and bars Vincent liked, little shops where they were to be sure to give the proprietor Vincent's best regards—and now, out in the sunlight, Robbie unfolded the list and stared at it, bewildered. "Dad's handwriting," he said, apologetically. "Somehow I've never been able to..." Antonia felt that he wasn't really talking to her, but she said pleasantly: "Here, let me try." Robbie gave her the list and immediately began fiddling with his camera. Antonia felt an obscure pleasure that she could read, and quite easily, Vincent's tiny, crabbed handwriting, which looked at first glance like some other language. Now her eye paused over one of the items on the list—"the Hemingway house." The address was across the street from their guest cottage, and looking up Antonia saw an enormous yellow-painted house, complete with columns and verandas, several outbuildings, a yard shaded by lime and banyan trees, and a red-brick wall separating the compound, in its dim-shaded serenity, from the sunlit noisy street. Squinting, Antonia saw that there were several cats perched along the wall, as though standing guard.

"Look, it's where Hemingway lived," she told Robbie. "We're right across the street." She didn't know why the fact should please her—she had never read a word of Hemingway—but somehow it did. She felt it might have been some clever signal from Vincent, who had arranged their Key West accommodations.

"Is that right? Hemingway?" Robbie said vaguely, pushing his glasses up his nose, lifting his camera. He snapped a picture of the house.

When they reached the front gate, Antonia thought she saw their intruder on the corner gatepost, stretched indolently on his side, eyes half-closed in the sun. Tawny-gold, tawny-orange, and really quite fat. Antonia had the impulse to lunge toward the cat, to frighten it, but perhaps the cat would not be startled. Perhaps it would not even move, and she would look foolish once again, and Robbie would start laughing uncontrollably. In any case, she resisted the impulse and followed her husband toward the house.

The cats, it turned out, had actually belonged to Hemingway. Every half hour there was a tour of the writer's house; and their guide—a tiny, angry-looking black woman in her forties—paused before one of the dining room windows, where a dainty tan-and-black kitten had perched on the sill. All the forty-odd cats on the property, she said, were descendants of Hemingway's own cats, and if anyone looked closely he would see that each cat's paw had six toes. They're all related, the woman repeated, all descended from Hemingway's cats. She spoke in a bored, precise voice. A man near Antonia and Robbie raised his hand to ask a question, but the woman was already leading them upstairs. Here they saw the writer's bedroom, though the bed itself had been roped off and could not be touched. The room had a musty, oaken smell. Spread out on the bed were several rare books and manuscripts of Hemingway's. The woman was reciting an anecdote about the friendship between Hemingway and Fidel Castro, but Antonia only half-listened—she had glimpsed something under the bed, a slender black cat hunkered down as though ready to spring, its huge gleaming eyes fastened on Antonia. Once again, Antonia froze. Now the other tourists were shuffling out, the guide's voice was fading down the stairs, and Robbie touched her arm: "This is pretty interesting, huh? The room where Hemingway slept, somebody famous like that?" Antonia smiled thinly. She could not take her eyes from the cat, which had not moved, had not even blinked.... But Robbie took her forearm and pulled her away, mumbling something about lunch. Downstairs, it occurred to Antonia that she had actually become involved in a staring contest with a cat—a little black orphan of a cat that no one else in the room had even seen. Even worse, the cat had won.

Yet somehow the incident cleared the air between her and Robbie, or perhaps cleared a space in her own mind. She laughed to herself about the cat under Hemingway's bed, and then she could laugh about the first cat, which had frightened her so badly. One o'clock of her first full day as Mrs. Robert Kendall, and a great tension had been relieved in her. She and Robbie found an outdoor café right on Duval Street, they had margaritas and sandwiches made with pita bread, they talked and laughed for more than an hour. When their food arrived, Robbie had continued the theme that everyone in his family loved Antonia— literally everyone, and Vincent above all.

"The others take their lead from Dad," Robbie said comfortably. "If he likes you, then everyone does."

"But you just found out yesterday?" Antonia asked. She kept her tone light, flirtatious. "Before the reception, you didn't know—"

"If he hadn't liked you, I'd have known," Robbie said. "In fact, there wouldn't have been any reception."

Antonia sat for a moment, not eating or speaking.

"But wait, I didn't mean—" Robbie dropped his sandwich on the plate, swallowed his mouthful without chewing. "What I meant is, Dad wouldn't have sprung for everything if he hadn't approved. So it would have been a much smaller affair."

"The wedding, you mean."

"Of course I mean the wedding. What else would I mean?"

Smiling, Antonia took a tiny bite of her sandwich, her jaws nearly motionless as she chewed. Abruptly, Robbie laughed. He lunged for the camera, snapping the shutter before Antonia could duck away.

"I never know when you're kidding!" he cried, delighted.

"I told you," Antonia said, fixing him with a keen, motionless gaze, "*no* pictures. Not today, not ever. Now give me the camera."

Antonia's hand darted out, but Robbie had lunged again, pulling the camera onto his lap; she swatted him several times, making little grabs for the camera, and Robbie hunched over, giggling and jerking from side to side, almost upsetting the table. From the other tables, several older couples looked over and smiled. A pair of young, playful newlyweds, they might have thought. Lighthearted. Carefree.

"Dad *did* mention that," Robbie said, facetiously protecting the camera with both his arms. "'She won't allow a single photograph?' he wanted to know. 'On her wedding day?' ...He seemed suspicious," her husband laughed, "but I told him to send the photographer home. I said"—and Robbie doubled over, nearly hysterical—"I said that you were wanted dead or alive in twelve states, and to forget about the society page."

"The society page?" Antonia said faintly. "But I thought Vincent—I thought your father scorned that kind of thing." She pawed at Robbie's lap a few more times, but half-heartedly; she didn't really want the camera. If she decided to destroy the film later, she could.

"Oh, that's just a line of his. Actually, he gets quite a kick out of it. They plastered Tod's wedding all over the *Journal-Constitution*," and here his voice lowered, "but then he and Karen had twice the wedding we did. Not that I'm complaining, of course. It makes sense when you consider that Karen's parents—"

Robbie broke off, perhaps catching the implied comparison of Antonia to Karen, perhaps censoring what might sound like criticism—however mild, however indirect—of his father. Stuffing the rest of the pita bread into his mouth, he chewed somberly for a while. Quite often he went into these boyish reveries, as though bewildered by the sinuous windings and sudden pitfalls of even the most ordinary conversations. Delicately Antonia licked the salt around the rim of her margarita, not really alarmed. During these past months she had negotiated her way among the Kendalls as best she could, generally steering clear of Vincent, sending him from a distance the kind of demure but enigmatic smiles that appealed to such men. Brusque and theatrical, with a braying voice meant for whole rooms to overhear, Vincent had few enough occasions to draw her aside, and she'd been careful not to create any real opening. His shrewd and watchful true self, she knew, was in many ways a slave to his persona, and after his booming queries received answers that were intelligent but so mild as to lead nowhere, he'd had little choice but to move along, or else to begin one of his monologues that soon had many others gathered around. The other Kendall wives were also intelligent, beautiful, and mild, though naturally rather than carefully so; and she lacked their sleek blond beauty, not to mention their patrician carelessness. Yet gradually she had felt that she'd won Vincent over; Robbie's comments on the plane hadn't really been much of a surprise. Antonia's eerie containment, her expressionless dark eyes and the dark fine hair that curved along her jaw identically on either side, and of course the graceful but alert silence, if not vigilance, that she had developed throughout her adult years and that had charmed more than a few men—all this had snagged Vincent's interest, perhaps even more than his interest. She discounted Robbie's remark about the society page, after all. The real energies of such men lay elsewhere.

After the waitress brought their Key lime pie, Robbie blurted out, this time not bothering to swallow, "I'm sorry, honey, I mean about suggesting that Karen— You know I don't *care* about that."

Antonia detested sweets, but she forked off a bite of her own pie. "I know," she said. "I don't care, either." As Antonia well knew, Karen had descended from Atlanta's higher social echelons to marry that upstart Vincent Kendall's youngest boy; soon enough, of course, he'd be far richer than any of Karen's family. "Actually," she said, "I sort of like Karen."

"I don't want to live like that," Robbie went on, not hearing. "I can't stand all the parties, and the pretentious house, and all the talk about their last vacation, their next vacation... I want something simpler, I really do."

Antonia laughed. "You've made a fine start, haven't you?" she said.

They spent most of the day following Vincent's list, checking off the items one by one. They bought T-shirts at Fast Buck Freddie's, stopped for a drink at Sloppy Joe's ("Hemingway's favorite bar," Vincent had scrawled), and rented bicycles and pedaled down to the beach, stopping at "the Southernmost tip of the United States," as a sign proclaimed, and gazing out at the calm, rather colorless sea. "Now I know why people love this place—why Dad does," Robbie said, shading his eyes against the sun-dazzled water, his mouth opened in delight. "It's so peaceful here, don't you think? So quiet and relaxed, with the palm trees and the warm weather, and nobody dressed up, nobody in a hurry..." Antonia had looked down, a bit self-conscious in her white linen dress and matching low-heeled shoes. Already she'd perceived that she was overdressed for this place, at least for the daytime, and vowed that tomorrow she would wear the T-shirt and pair of blue jeans she'd brought for lounging in their room. She didn't want to stand out, after all. She wanted to be part of all this. As they rode about the island, she'd paid less attention to the scenery than to her husband, watching him from the corner of her eye. Amazing that he seemed so comfortable, she thought, that *he* didn't notice if his wife were overdressed, her white straw purse dangling awkwardly from the handlebars; that *he* didn't keep checking to see was this real, was she really there, were they man and wife forever. He rode with his eyes squinted happily, tongue darting out the side of his mouth, pointing to a lighthouse in one direction—*look, Antonia!*—and a baroque church steeple in the other, *look at that!* Yet he didn't glance at her, and she felt that, yes, they were married, they were irrevocably bound together. Her calves had tensed with a sudden bright energy, and all at once she didn't care how she looked. "Try and catch me!" she cried, pulling her weight hard against the handlebars, and Robbie let out a whoop and began the chase, a wild, laughing pursuit, not of Antonia but of his wife.

She led him all the way to the bike shop and looked over her shoulder, head cocked, as he coasted into the shade where she had stopped, near the entrance. He was panting heavily, shaking his head from side to side; Antonia saw droplets of sweat flying off all around him. "You're amazing," he said. "I'm practically worn out, and you haven't even broken a sweat. Your legs must be—your legs are great," he got out, still panting. "Thank you," she said, with a little mock bow, but in truth she *had* begun sweating; a thin film coated her face and neck, even her slender pale arms. For some reason she lifted her wrist and touched her tongue to it, remembering instantly the salt around her margarita at lunch, and she said, "Hey, what does a girl do to get a drink around here," and Robbie raised his eyebrows in a villainous leer.

"Look," Antonia said, "they're selling fruit drinks across the street—go get us one, will you?"

Her husband trotted off, while Antonia carefully parked the bikes, then took her compact out of the purse. Startled, she saw a mussed version of herself in the tiny mirror, her hair plastered against her throat on one side, sweat glistening along her upper lip like delicate whiskers. Quickly she daubed at her face with Kleenex, freshened her tawny-orange lipstick, brushed her hair in place with a few deft strokes. Then Robbie appeared beside her, panting, bearing two Styrofoam cups with *Fruit Smoothie* printed diagonally along their sides; the cups held a frozen ruby-colored substance, ruby-colored straws. "Hey, there's a tour bus right down the street," he said excitedly, "it's just loading up. Let's go, Antonia! That way, we're sure to see everything!"

"A tour bus?" she said, and her first thought was how Vincent would disapprove—why follow the herd, why not strike out on your own? But Robbie looked so eager, shifting his weight back and forth like an overgrown kid, smiling. Her husband was past thirty, but Antonia knew he would always look boyish and that Vincent never had: his army pictures showed a stalwart, glaring youth of nineteen, ready to do battle with life. She could imagine him spitting the words out the side of his mouth—"oh, by all means, *a tour bus*"—and then grinning or even laughing, but his eyes staying cold, contemptuous. After only four months, could it be that she knew Vincent better than his oldest son ever had?

But she said, "Good idea," and as they boarded the bus—
which was actually an open-air trolley, several cars long, crowded
with chattering, brightly dressed tourists—Antonia felt glad to do
anything; that energy she'd felt when they were on the bikes
kept returning in great ecstatic waves. She could hardly sit still,
and when the tour guide maneuvered their attention from one
side of the street to the other, Antonia moved her head quickly,
obediently, as though watching a tennis match. Though really she
could not have remembered what she saw. Much of the route she
and Robbie had already covered on their bikes, and when they
turned into a quiet, tree-shaded street, her legs tensed before
she quite understood where they were. Then, just as she'd spotted
the compound of detached cottages where they were staying, the
tour guide reported through the microphone, with histrionic
enthusiasm, "And here on our right is Ernest Hemingway's house,
where he lived during the years 1931 to 1938, writing such works
as *For Whom the Bell Tolls* and *Death in the Afternoon*. At that time
Hemingway was married to Pauline Pfeiffer, a wealthy woman who
enjoyed gracious living and who…" But Antonia stopped listening,
her eyes narrowed as they surveyed the house, the spreading
banyan trees, the red-bricked wall. As usual, several of the cats had
placed themselves along the wall at random, cats of varying colors
in varying positions. None was looking at Antonia. As the trolley
passed, one of the cats jumped off the wall abruptly, and in her seat
Antonia gave a little jump, too; but the cat had leapt in the other
direction, toward the house. Now the trolley was in the next block;
the tour guide was pointing out something else. Antonia sat back.

"Honey, is something wrong?" Robbie asked.

"No, nothing," said Antonia. "I'm just restless, that's all. I wish
we could get off."

"Then we *will* get off," and before she could stop him Robbie
was moving up the aisle, bending to the tour guide's ear. The
trolley stopped at the next corner, and on the sidewalk Robbie
said, bowing gallantly, "What now?"

She had to laugh. "I hope we didn't offend him," she said,
sorting through her purse for Vincent's list. "But it occurred to me
that Vincent wouldn't have approved—" The words were out before
she could stop herself. She saw the flash of hurt in Robbie's eyes.

"But I thought—"

"Never mind," she said, looking from the scrap of paper to her watch. "Look, it's after six. Let's walk around a bit more, then go down to the Pier House for the sunset. Your father says it's not to be missed. Then we'll have dinner somewhere."

Briefly he'd lapsed into one of his daydreams, but he recovered quickly and soon they were back on Duval Street, pausing at art galleries and souvenir shops and open-air bars where folk musicians were playing. Already the air was cooler, the street atmosphere changing slowly from afternoon to evening. Now there were fewer children, fewer dogs; there were more young couples like Antonia and Robbie, some of them dressed casually for dinner after a day at the beach. Antonia felt relieved, her spirits lightened, and once again Robbie had the eager, slavish energy of a spaniel, loping inside a café to get ice water when Antonia said the fruit drink had made her thirsty, fetching a newspaper and postcards from a corner Rexall, then going back again when Antonia discovered she hadn't brought a pen or stamps. She wanted to send a card to the Lassiters, she told Robbie, and of course to Robbie's parents. Though perhaps *he* should write that card...? And what about Robbie's brothers, and his grandmother out in Scottsdale? Since she hadn't been able to make the wedding, perhaps they should—

"Hold on!" Robbie laughed. "I only bought a couple of cards." He reached out and pinched her cheek, lightly. "Let's just write to our parents," he said. "That's enough, don't you think?"

So they went to the Pier House, finding a table at the edge of the sunset deck; they sat to write their cards. Or rather, Robbie studied his for a moment, then thrust it at Antonia and asked if she didn't mind. "Your wifely duty, after all," he said happily, sitting back and opening the newspaper. Antonia stared down at the cards. She sipped at the milky-looking drink Robbie had ordered her—a piña colada?—and addressed the cards in her girlish, rounded handwriting. *Mr. and Mrs. Vincent Kendall. Dr. and Mrs. William Lassiter.* Though her adoptive parents had missed the wedding— her father had pleaded an important medical convention, her mother refused to travel alone—she knew they would want to hear from her. After she'd left Birmingham seven years ago, only weeks after her eighteenth birthday, there had been a good deal of friction over Antonia's disinclination to write, to let them know where she had settled. Yet she never *had* settled, really, moving from Birmingham to New Orleans to Dallas; then back to New Orleans; then to Atlanta; then to Nashville and back to Atlanta again—working for a series of powerful men. "Assistant" to a state senator, "staff coordinator" for an agribusiness tycoon... She'd done well in these jobs, even if she'd been little more, really, than a glorified secretary. A punctual, attractive presence in the morning; close-mouthed but alert all during the day, which her employers seemed greatly to appreciate without taking *her* very seriously; on occasion, a sympathetic listener at night, non-judging, non-committal. Yet she seldom stayed anywhere for more than a year, having a keen sense of when she was wanted, when she was not— the orphan's legacy. She did not want anyone saying she'd out-stayed her welcome; there was always another city, another man who needed her. Another opportunity, as she liked to think.

Once her mother had shouted after her, *Go on, then! I guess you can take care of yourself!* Mrs. Lassiter was sickly, a professional invalid; in a rare loss of temper, Antonia had remarked how much sense it made, her having married a doctor. The Lassiters had been a childless couple in their forties when they adopted the six-year-old Antonia; and now she thought, staring at the postcard, that she might never—was it possible?—see them again. When Dr. Lassiter had not been too busy, he had sometimes smiled at Antonia as though from a great distance, a rueful smile as though to apologize, to acknowledge that a mistake had been made, he hoped she would forgive them...? When she turned eighteen, he informed her that there would be little money, perhaps no money; it would all be channeled into a research foundation, established in the Lassiter name. This time he *had* apologized, not quite meeting her eyes. By now, his daughter being a very mature eighteen, his wife's shouted accusation must have seemed the one absolute truth about Antonia—that she could take care of herself; that she would always "land on her feet," as one of her bosses would later remark.

I understand, of course, she'd said, lowering her eyes. You've given me so much already.

Now she wrote, in letters a bit larger than usual, *Having a wonderful time!* and then wrote the same message on the card to the Kendalls. She signed both her and Robbie's names and quickly stamped the cards and thrust them in her purse.

"Done?" Robbie asked, not looking up from the paper.

"Done," she said.

She tried to pay attention to the lowering sun—an enormous orange ball, poised above the watery dark horizon—but her gaze had returned to her husband's bent head. It intrigued her, the way her attention kept snagging on Robbie; the way she kept thinking *husband*, rubbing the word along her tongue as though testing its meaning, its relevance to herself. As though feeling her attention—for how closely, how strangely she was watching him!—Robbie looked up, giving her a quick boyish smile, both happy and fearful.

He stretched his arm across the table, the hand upturned. "Antonia?" he said. "Is something—?"

Her heart had filled, and she felt a sudden catch in her throat, a loss of poise. Confused, she put out her own hand and Robbie grasped it, hard.

Off to the side, there was a burst of applause and the clicking of cameras.

Startled, Antonia and Robbie looked over. A crowd of perhaps forty or fifty, many of them photographers, had gathered along the deck; the couple followed the crowd's attention out to sea, where the sun had just dipped below the horizon, sending brilliant orange and pink trails into the sky.

"The sunset," Robbie said, and quickly he and Antonia exchanged glances, and just as quickly broke into laughter.

"And I thought—" But Antonia didn't dare finish: the idea was so absurd.

"Me too," Robbie said, and they laughed again.

When the waiter approached and asked if they cared for another drink, Antonia was remembering the cat that had bounded into their room that morning: so quick, insistent, full of life. She remembered how fearful she had been, her cartoonish alarm that Robbie had found so hilarious. Evidently the cat was one of Hemingway's, and evidently its paws had six toes; but the cat, after all, did not understand. The cat had not meant to frighten anyone. She remembered the way it had curled into Robbie's lap and gone to sleep, uncaring, as Antonia cringed against the wall.

I don't like surprises, Antonia had said.

Now the table was jostled, nearly upsetting Antonia's drink. When she looked up, she saw that Robbie had leapt toward the waiter and begun embracing him. "Hold on! Hold on!" the waiter laughed, pulling back from Robbie's ecstatic greeting. As Antonia watched, her husband kissed the waiter's cheek, the side of his neck; good-naturedly, the waiter kept pushing him away.

Then Antonia saw that the "waiter" was Vincent.

He had commandeered an empty tray, and one of the little red aprons; had approached their table with his head lowered and voice disguised, was there anything they needed, would they care for another drink…?

An elaborate, funny ruse: very typical. His skill in making himself the center of attention, delighting his sons, disarming criticism: very typical indeed. Antonia felt light-headed, though she was hardly surprised. Now Vincent winked at her, slyly, over Robbie's bobbing shoulder, as if they were conspirators. Oh yes, very typical: funny and charming, mischievous, certainly beyond criticism.

For Robbie, of course, this was the high point of the trip.

"Dad, you joker!" he cried in delight, falling back into his chair as Vincent took the seat next to Antonia. "When did you get here, anyway? Were you here for the sunset? We've been following that list you made out, all day long, but we never dreamed— Gosh, this is great! Isn't this great, Antonia!"

She gazed across at Vincent, her head lighter than air, feeling dazed in a half-pleasant way; but no, she felt no surprise, no alarm. She felt nothing. "Yes, this is great," she said without irony, not that Robbie was listening. He kept reaching across to cuff his father on the shoulder; he kept hitting the table happily, so that the glasses and silverware rattled.

"Now settle down, everybody," Vincent laughed, watching Antonia. He looked sunburnt, authoritative, his eyes a bright, sharp blue; he wore a tan polo shirt that stretched tight across his massive chest, and a tan nylon windbreaker, and white tennis shoes without socks. Dressed so casually, boyishly, he looked like a sportsman of some kind—an amateur sailor, perhaps. Out in the water, a few minutes ago, Antonia had glimpsed a sailboat going past, the sail billowing, tinted pink by the lowering sun. Now she glanced out to the horizon, but the sailboat was gone and the water had turned dark, choppy; dusk had fallen quickly, she thought, and craning her neck she saw that the crowd had dispersed from along the deck; most everyone had gone off to dinner, to their plans for the evening…. Antonia remembered that burst of applause, how it had startled both her and Robbie—the newlyweds, the lovers—and how they had laughed, embarrassed and pleased to discover that no one had noticed, after all; that really no one cared. They were part of the world, she thought, and why should anyone mind if they loved, or failed to love?

Watching Vincent and Robbie, their heads bent close in conversation, Antonia understood that her life was over.

II

There are no surprises, she thought. After all.

The next few hours passed swiftly, or very slowly—she could not be sure. It was true, she thought, that in dying you flung open a door to your past life, your past lives; and again you lived them, quickly. Or slowly. There are no surprises, she thought, because everything is connected, leading in a zigzag chain back from the present moment; leading back, finally, rather than forward. Attuned very lightly to "the present moment," her expression blank, stunned, neutral—vaguely she heard the scraping of chairs, vaguely she understood that Robbie and Vincent were leaving, Vincent's arm across his son's shoulders, their heads bent close together—she sat remembering the cat from that morning, understanding how everything was connected, knowing with a pitiless thrill of certainty that there were no surprises, after all. Only errors in perception.

Though the knowledge arrived, as knowledge usually did, too late.

When someone spoke, using the name "Antonia," she looked up. She fixed her eyes on Vincent settling back in his chair, Vincent drawing something from the pocket of his windbreaker—

a yellowed newspaper clipping, a bulky white envelope—and Vincent finally gazing back at her, his eyes a cold blue but not unfriendly, not really, just frank and forthright. Now that Robbie was gone.

Instantly she knew the contents of both the clipping and the envelope.

"Another drink?" Vincent asked, almost gently.

She shook her head, *no*.

"I sent Robbie back to the room, Antonia."

And she nodded, *yes*.

She said, "But the key—I have the key, here in my purse...."

"Don't worry, Antonia, he'll get the key from the manager. He can handle that much, don't you think?"

Vincent smiled, though his eyes didn't smile.

"Yes. Yes, of course."

But someone else was speaking in Antonia's place; someone else sat here prim and pale, hands folded around the icy drink as though anchoring her body to this table, this world.

"How did—how did you find out," she said, faintly.

She'd been afraid, for a while, that somehow her boss had found out, but he was a pathetic man, gossipy and embittered, and soon enough she'd dismissed him as a meddler. Those were satisfying days, after all, with the eldest Kendall son paying her such lavish attention, sending roses to her desk each morning, taking her to the same exclusive restaurants where her own boss took his clients. The owner of an accounting firm that had seen better days, her boss had two-thirds of his office space leased out from under him by the Kendalls and he spent much of his time gossiping about Vincent—that "heartless opportunist"—within hearing range of Antonia's desk, never failing to mention the two younger sons who were "sharks, just like their father," and that oldest boy who did well to find his desk in the morning.... Hearing this, Antonia smiled thinly; she signed for her flowers, she blocked two hours off her calendar for lunch. Why should she be afraid, after all? She'd never enjoyed such self-possession, such eerie poise. She'd never held such power.

Powerless, she sat watching Vincent as he examined the palms of his hands.

"I almost didn't," he said, trying to sound casual, trying to spare her, "and the man I had, um, looking into you, I'd paid him off the day before the wedding. He's an old gumshoe type, a real digger, and he seemed disappointed that he hadn't found anything. So he kept on, without my knowing—I guess he'd figured there'd be quite a bonus, if he could uncover..." Vincent was almost whispering.

He pushed the newspaper clipping to the middle of the table.

So she let her eyelids fall, let her eyes skim across the headline, ONE OF 'DAWSON'S GIRLS' KILLS SELF, Daughter Found in Locked Closet, but she said nothing. She felt nothing.

She remembered her own closet, back home. A locked closet.

She remembered how Mrs. Lassiter complained all during Antonia's high school years, why wouldn't she go out, why wouldn't she come downstairs when one of those nice young men dropped by, didn't she want to be popular, did she want people to think she was *odd?* There was no reason for this, absolutely no reason—she was so pretty, after all! Sometimes Antonia locked the door against her, she turned up the stereo or buried her head in a book, she felt her skin drawing tight along her bones, *no, no,* and soon enough the boys stopped coming around. Soon enough, her mother stopped worrying that Antonia would not go out at night, would not accept dates, would not lead the "normal" life of a high school girl. Dr. Lassiter took her side, saying to leave her alone; he'd always despised the slavish conformity of most teenagers; why shouldn't they admire Antonia's independence? Occasionally he would give her a twenty-dollar bill, or a fifty, which Antonia stored away. For the future. By her eighteenth birthday she had nearly three thousand dollars locked in her closet, in a shoebox thrust back into the closet's dimmest corner. Possibly the money would come in handy someday, for who knew what the future held, who knew?

"This is very awkward, of course, for someone like me," Vincent told her, "someone who has been brought up to respect women, to understand their needs...." He nudged the envelope a bit further in her direction, and obligingly she picked it up, gauging its thickness with her sensitive fingers, as though taking the measure of Vincent's grief, or embarrassment, or pride.

"Yes, of course," she whispered.

"I want the best for my family, I really insist on that," Vincent said mournfully. "It's more than just money, you know. It's a name they can be proud of, proud to give their own children, and their grandchildren.... If there were some kind of blight, at this early stage—" Out of tact, he stopped himself. He gave her a pleading look.

"I understand," she told him.

Do you understand? Father Callahan kept asking, and Antonia knew she must say yes, always yes, and especially to this tall silver-haired priest to whom Mrs. Lassiter had presented her new child, her dark-haired lovely child, for instruction in the faith. Eventually the Lassiters had become "lapsed Catholics," and when they stopped attending mass, Antonia stopped; but at six she had received the sacrament of baptism, followed the next year by her First Holy Communion, Antonia only one of a giggling horde of little girls in white dresses and veils, interchangeable. She remembered feeling happy, that day. She remembered feeling a vague sort of joy.

"Mrs. Kendall is very devout, of course," Vincent was saying, "but an annulment won't be difficult, I'm told, and we have a story—a rather carefully detailed story—which it would help a great deal if you didn't contradict. Not to anyone. Not ever. I'd be very grateful, Antonia. If you'll send your new address to my office, preferably an out-of-state address, I'll see that you're taken care of. This is my mistake as much as anyone's, and I don't intend for you to suffer for—" Again, he stopped himself. He nudged the envelope a little closer. "This," he said, "is only for now. I think you know that I'm a responsible man. You know that, don't you? So there's no reason for you to be angry or to feel—well, vengeful."

"Yes," she said, mechanically. "I mean, no."

And finally she'd answered Mama's question—What do you say to Mr. Jones, sweetie, what do you say?—and Antonia stammered Yes, I mean no, and while Mama and Mr. Jones laughed—she hadn't known him as "Mr. Dawson" then, much less as "Senator Dawson"—while they laughed she gripped her mother's leg, pressed her flaming cheeks against the warm fleshy thigh. What, you don't like me? Mr. Jones said again, grabbing Antonia's sides and hauling her into the air. Is that it, huh?—but the question confused her, she didn't understand, she winced at the smell of his cologne and his breath reeking of cigars and his eyes a bright hard blue in the fatty ridges of his face. Is that it, Antonia? Well, next time I'll have to bring you something, won't I? Maybe some jelly babies, how about that?—or a doll, one of those new-fangled dolls that wets and everything? Or I could take your picture, eh?—why should your Mama get all the attention? Thinking yes, I mean no, she'd only nodded, and Mr. Jones and Mama laughed again, and again they hugged each other in that slow way, and Mama said in her husky voice, She'd rather have money, she's just like me, and they laughed once more before he left. Mama was so pretty then! And after he left they always hugged in the real way, tight and wild and crazy, and Antonia said, What do I say, Mama, I never know what to say, and Mama said, Honey, it doesn't matter. They don't listen anyhow.

"Antonia, I wish you would say something," Vincent went on, returning the clipping to his pocket. Ready to leave, but wanting something more. "Listen," he said, "if it's any comfort, I think it's a shame what they did, letting that Dawson off, sending him back to Washington with a slap on the wrist.... I was a young man then, and I remember thinking how unfair it was, how badly the system had failed.... What could be more sickening, all those girls stashed here and there, half of them on drugs, and just because some oversexed buffoon.... Well, I shouldn't be bringing this up, but I wanted you to know—"

She reached across and took his hand; squeezed her fingers along his wrist, his forearm.

"Maybe it's not too late?" she said, hoarsely, her eyes vacant. "Maybe we can work out some kind of...arrangement?" she said. She smiled, thinly. "You like me, don't you? Robbie said you did."

"Yes—I mean, no," Vincent said, the first time she'd ever seen him stammering and confused; his eyes swerved away. "I'm sorry, but no," he said, taking a deep breath. He recovered. "...You look a little pale, why don't you sit here by the water, have a nice dinner," he said, and quickly enough the waiter was summoned, the order given; her food arrived only minutes after Vincent left.

Calmly, Antonia picked at the red snapper.

She picked at the roll and butter.

You're so pale, Mr. Jones said, taking off the seersucker jacket.
Doesn't your Mama ever let you play outside? Not waiting for an
answer he stalked around the little trailer, identical to the one on
the other side of the park where Mama's friend Rita lived, Rita
who hung around all the time after Daddy left, bragging about
how she never had to work, how modern these little trailers
were, complete with little stoves and little bathrooms and even
a closet for your clothes! And a TV. And a stereo. Rita hung
around her trailer all day reading magazines and smoking Kools
and taking little pills Mr. Jones gave her that made her feel airy
and weightless, and happier than she'd ever felt in her life.
C'mon, you've got to meet him, Rita said, and later Mama had
bent to Antonia and said, It's only for a little while, honey, till we
get back on our feet, OK? There was a little curtain to pull across
Antonia's sofa-bed, for when Mr. Jones came to visit, or Rita came
with a bottle of Early Times to sit gossiping half the night with
Mama, or even when Mama was home and Antonia just wanted to
shut out everything: she could draw the curtain, pretend she
wasn't there. But she couldn't pretend with Mr. Jones's heavy
presence in the room, his weight jostling the trailer as he stalked
up and down, looking into drawers, rifling through Mama's little
closet. Where is your Mama, anyway? he asked. Does she always go
out when she's not expecting me?—I'll bet she does, I'll bet she
does, but Antonia remembered not to answer; she just sat on the
sofa-bed with hands folded in her lap and waited, waited. When
he got close enough she could smell his breath, the same as Rita's
when she brought the Early Times, and he sat beside her and gave
her a wobbly smile and said, How old are you, anyway? Eight or
nine by now, eh? Antonia waited. She stared at the camera Mr.
Jones had brought out of the closet. What's the matter, kid, cat got
your tongue? he said, and something in his voice told her to
answer and so she said, No sir—I'm six, and for some reason Mr.
Jones found that funny and asked how long her mother would be
gone, and Antonia said she didn't know.

"Dessert, ma'am?"

"No," she said. "Nothing else."

Calmly she opened the envelope, extracted a twenty and put it
beside the check. Touched her napkin to one corner of her mouth,

then the other. Outside the Pier House she headed toward a taxi but then hesitated, turned, moved out along the street instead. A mild, fragrant night. All the shops and restaurants and bars were still open; music drifted onto the air; people were strolling, laughing, in no hurry. Antonia herself walked slowly, in no hurry. When she did reach the cottage, the door was unlocked, and first she checked the closet to see that Robbie's clothes were gone but hers were not. She went to the window.

She heard someone opening the door, she heard footsteps just behind her, and she tried to ignore her heart—it had begun to beat fast, as though she had raced all the way home. Willing herself to stay calm, she gazed out the window. She gazed across the street.

The windows in the trailer were too high, and she could not get to them; Mr. Jones was holding her down. In any case, there were no streets outside, no lights, nothing at all to help her. Only a few darkened trailers, placed about at random. It was quite late, Mama had gone with Rita and another friend to the movies, a double-feature, she had made Antonia promise not to go outside and *not* to answer the door, and to get in bed before ten o'clock. Of course, Mr. Jones had his own key. Of course, Mr. Jones had the habit of doing whatever he wanted, and now Antonia simply lay on her mother's bed, her legs twitching despite herself, pretending she was behind that curtain and fast asleep in her own bed, and then pretending she was outside, running, running, darting this way, that way! She did not feel the probing fingers, she did not hear the camera's clicking or see the dazzling flashes. She wasn't there, exactly, so how could she make a noise? But when she heard Mama's key in the lock (they decided not to stay for the second feature, Rita would say later: thank God for that, at least), she screamed and screamed. The other woman ran off, and then Mama started screaming, and Mr. Jones struck her across the mouth, but she kept screaming, and then she was crying, and by the time the police arrived Mr. Jones was crying, on his knees and crying, begging forgiveness. He came toward Antonia on his knees, begging, pleading, where she lay very still on the bed. And later, when her mother started screaming again, taking handfuls of pills and screaming at people not in the room at all, Antonia did not object when she opened the closet and said, Just for a little while,

I promise—till Mama feels a little better. She went out for a moment—to the phone at the corner, it turned out—and rushed back in, sobbing, and Antonia heard more pills rattling out, and all was still until the giant yellow-haired policeman unlocked the closet door and said, Good Lord—

Motionless, she stared out the window and across the street. Her heart had calmed. Her legs had relaxed. Every minute or two she touched her cheeks with the palm of her hand. Robbie had spoken a few times, but had fallen quiet at last. He sat on the bed, behind her; or on the chair. He didn't know what to do, he'd wept—whether to go or stay. "Antonia, what should I do? I feel like I'm nothing inside, like I'm dead, I don't know…. Can't you speak, Antonia? Honey?" Outside, a car had honked: several quick impatient beeps.

She didn't answer. She would like to comfort him, she thought, but it was not in her nature; she hated emotional displays. In any case, she couldn't pay attention to Robbie. Her eye was drawn out of this room, to the house nestled in darkness across the street. She stared, stared. Yes, it was Hemingway's house, and along the brick wall she could make out soft dark clumps in the moonlight, the cats perched at random, vigilant, eternal. They were everywhere, she thought, covering the walls and the grounds and the house itself, guarding everything that was not theirs.

Robbie tried again. "Antonia," he wept, "I'll die if I lose you, don't you understand? Already I feel like I'm dying, like I'm nothing inside…you understand, don't you? Antonia?"

Outside, the car horn blared. Or was it one of those cats, sending its wail into the night?

"I don't mean to be cruel," she said at last, "but Robbie you really won't. You really *won't* die."

Evening at Home

When the accident happened, June stood in the middle of her garden kitchen thinking that she looked like one of those newspaper ads the subdivision had been running. A happy homemaker at Windrover Estates, the caption might read, never mind that she had a good job—she made more money than Roy—and never mind that their sparkling beige stucco four-bedroom, with its sleek surfaces of cool white tile and glaring chrome, still felt nothing like home. Returning after work she sometimes felt that she'd stumbled onto a TV sound-stage; that Bill Cosby might appear in a doorway, in one of his ugly expensive sweaters. Nonetheless here she stood, at her "convenience island," making a garden salad—chopping at radishes with one of the ultrasharp knives her parents had sent from Fort Worth, knives in graduated sizes all tamed and nestled into a red-velvet-lined case like some sort of valentine. The knives had arrived UPS three days ago. June was thinking (because of her name, she had a lifelong sensitivity to months of the year), *But this is September, not February,* and wondering at the sudden pump-pump of anger from her heart. That's when she sliced open the tip of her thumb.

She wailed, holding her left hand aloft and grabbing a dishtowel off the refrigerator handle. Roy heard her—he was sitting out by the opened garage door, whittling, a boyhood activity that soothed him when he was nervous—and came running in.

"June?" he cried. "What on earth?"

She'd returned to the island and now leaned against it, holding her thumb straight up like one of those movie critics she couldn't stand; she felt ridiculous. She'd wrapped the towel around it three or four times, so it appeared to wear a grotesque green-and-white striped turban. June stared at the towel, waiting for blood to begin staining the cloth like some insidious blossom. She didn't look at Roy, but she'd heard the distress in his voice.

"It's okay, hon—I just cut myself. Run up to the medicine cabinet and get me a bandage, would you? One of those thick gauze ones—the lower left-hand side, I think."

While he was gone—she heard his clomping footsteps above her head—June gingerly unwrapped the towel. No blood had seeped through, and she felt a peculiar breathless curiosity about the wound. She lifted the last layer of towel just long enough to see the plush-white ball of her thumb, contoured by a neat rounded slit so exiguous and perfectly shaped that it might have been a surgical incision. Then the slit gaped open, as though emitting a small cry of outrage. The dead-white skin became empurpled and swollen, giving way to a little geyser of blood before June, her breath coming in quick pants, wound the towel back around the thumb. It began to throb, with an oddly moist and pleasant sort of pain. But she'd done the wrapping less neatly this time and now the turban looked comically disheveled. June felt tears springing to her eyes just as Roy came back in, undoing the bandage.

"Poor baby," he murmured, but when she saw that he wasn't having much luck with the little red string along the bandage wrapper, June grabbed one edge with her right hand—fortunately she'd wounded her left—and held it while he tore the string. Together they unwound the towel—"Have the bandage ready," she said, "it's a real bleeder"—and then Roy slapped on the bandage before that mean little slit had the chance to reopen. June had glimpsed the skin around it, though—all stained with blood. She had seen the whorls of her reddened thumb and thought of her thumbprint in red instead of black, her unique print, hers, *her*. She felt lightheaded, as though she'd lost a quart of blood instead of a spoonful. When he finished the bandaging Roy kissed her cheek and smiled as though she were a child, which struck June because he was seven years younger than she and in many ways a childlike type of man.

"Clumsy," he said.

Then he noticed the tears—one had started out from her left eye-corner and began following the bony contour of her cheek— and he wiped at the tears gently, with the sides of his own healthy thumbs.

"Hey, are you okay?" he said.

"Sure—I'm just a little nervous." But she couldn't look up. Roy had a large open childlike face—artless blue eyes, ruddy cheeks— and the sight of him might set her to bawling.

"Want me to finish this?" he said. She looked with him around the kitchen—pans on the stove, water measured into them for rice and steamed beans, casserole dish Pammed and ready beside the fridge; all the dessert makings, cooking chocolate and sugar and cream, stacked neatly next to her biggest mixing bowl; the four salad bowls in a rectangle on the island, alongside the separate little plates heaped with the vegetables she'd been chopping. She loved Roy to death, but he couldn't finish all this if you gave him three days.

"I'm okay," she said. Now she did glance over, smiling with one side of her mouth. "You could set the table, though."

"Sure thing," Roy said, turning aside. He'd given one last look at the bandaged thumb, as at a piece of handiwork done well. Now the thumb looked, to June, like a tiny doll's pillow, so thick and white that no pinprick of blood—still less the billowing red blossom that filled June's imagination—had much of a chance.

Her parents, driving in from Fort Worth, were due in an hour. They were on their way to Florida, where June's mother had a great aunt dying slowly of pancreatic cancer. "It's our last chance to see poor Bitsy," her mother had said last week, calling with her alarming news about the visit. June had lived in Atlanta for more than a decade, ever since coming here to college, but her parents had never visited together before. June's father wouldn't fly and her mother, a gregarious woman, claimed she couldn't sit still for long car trips. Several times her mother had flown out alone, and they'd done some mother-daughter things—shopping and matinees and expensive lunches out—but even she hadn't visited since June and Roy's surprise elopement three years ago. "Don't want to butt in," her mother would say brightly into the phone. She was the one who'd kept using that word, *elopement.* To June and Roy, what they'd done was just go down to the courthouse and get married, with Roy's widowed mother and June's best friend Sherry as witnesses. Both Roy and June went back to work the next day as though nothing had happened. They'd been living together for eight months, though they hadn't mentioned this to June's parents. Soon after the marriage they'd taken a quick trip out to Fort Worth so her parents could meet Roy, and the visit went well enough. June's mother had bought a paperback book on the etymology of names, and had told Roy that his name meant "king." June's mother had laughed, "So that means you're king of the castle." Though Roy had glanced nervously at June's father (but June had not), he'd blushed with pleasure. That night in their room, June's childhood room, Roy had said what a nice lady June's mother was.

During the past week Roy had repeated this compliment several times, as if reminding himself. He kept telling June that he looked forward to her parents' visit, but she could hear the boyish anxiety in his voice. She knew it wasn't her mother who concerned Roy, but her father, who'd said very little during their visit in Fort Worth and who, unlike Roy, never picked up an extension during one of June's phone conversations with her mother. One time Roy had made the mistake, near the end of one of these three-way chats, of asking about Mr. Caldwell. "Is he home?" Roy had said, with his country boy's friendly forthrightness. "Can he get on the phone, too?" June had lapsed instantly into silence, her breath coming fast. The question had reminded her that Roy was still an outsider, with minimal knowledge of her family's habits—for June's father was always home—and even her mother had succumbed to an awkward pause. "Oh, he's...out in his workroom, doing *some*thing," she'd said, with even more strenuous good cheer than usual. June had tried to breathe quietly, evenly, counting the breaths. Roy had said, puzzled, "Well, tell him hello, okay?" And June's mother had said quickly, "Sure will, sweetie," and then had changed the subject.

When the doorbell rang, Roy wiped his palms on the side of his jeans and grinned across the table at June. "C'mon," he said, "let's answer it together." He stood, looming above her, and for a moment June felt that he would bend down to help her, as though she were an invalid. She knew she must look fragile, drained. She held her good hand cupped around the wounded thumb as though concealing or protecting it. Above her, Roy looked impossibly large and healthy in his starched white linen shirt and new Levi's; they'd had a glass of wine together, waiting, and now Roy seemed eager rather than anxious, his ruddy face a bit flushed, blue eyes crinkled at their corners. June's friend Sherry had claimed for years not to understand why June preferred the boyish type—I like *men*, not boys, Sherry would say with a wink—but now Roy seemed formidable as any man, his body solidly muscled under the new clothes, his skin exuding a fleshy male heat. When he did bend down, not to lift her but to take the wounded hand with exaggerated tenderness and bring it toward his lips—"Kiss it and make it better?" he murmured, smiling—she jerked the hand back before she understood what she was doing. "I—I'm sorry," she said, "I'm just—"

The doorbell's second ring interrupted her.

"It'll be okay," Roy said huskily, not quite meeting her eyes. She could see the hurt and perplexity in that sideways glance. "Guess we'd better get the door," he said, turning away, and June had no choice but to follow.

There had been the typical exclamations from June's mother: how pretty the house was! how beautiful Junie looked! what an exhausting drive it had been, and how she could *kill* for a glass of that wine! From the foyer, Mrs. Caldwell had glimpsed the dining room table, neatly set for four, with candles and flowers, and the two half-empty wine glasses where June and Roy had been sitting.

"Coming right up," Roy said jovially. He hesitated for a second, but then said, "The same for you, Mr. Caldwell? Or I've got some Bud. And some of the hard stuff, too."

June's father had waited outside the doorway, in the shadowy September dusk, while his wife exchanged greetings and hugs under the small cone of light cast down by the foyer chandelier.

Now, as Roy's question echoed awkwardly in silence, he and June stepped forward at the same moment, pressed their cheeks together briefly, then parted. "Hi Dad," June said. "Come on back to the kitchen, both of you, and we'll get you something to drink." Roy was already headed that way, followed by Mrs. Caldwell, who exclaimed over the table as she passed. "Junie, I told you not to make any fuss!" she cried, but it was just something to say, not requiring any answer. Standing in the foyer with her father June felt lost, stranded. Yet she wasn't afraid. She looked at him and smiled, and as if by reflex he smiled back. People had always said they looked alike: the same deep-set eyes, stubborn jaw, slender build. Once their hair had been the same shade of tawny-red, too, but when June started perming hers out a few years ago, she'd had it lightened, while her father's had turned a deep auburn, tinged at the crown and sides with gray. In the past few years he'd filled out a bit—his cheeks less gaunt, a roll of fat above his belt. Though he looked tired, and clearly hadn't shaved in a few days, his smile seemed sincere, though it held nothing of guilt or apology.

"I guess I could use something," he said. "It's been a long drive. Your mother…"

But he stopped, presumably out of tact. June felt her own smile aching at the corners and said quickly, "I made you some veal—that's still your favorite, isn't it?"

His eyes had grazed down her body, slowly, and now he was staring at her hand. "What happened?" he said.

She lifted her thumb quickly, holding it up as if to ridicule it; at once it began throbbing with pain. "Oh, just a stupid accident," she laughed. "I was cutting some vegetables—it's nothing."

Her father smiled woefully. "Well, accidents happen," he said.

Dinner proceeded with a predictable but bearable awkwardness. After some preliminary chatting in the kitchen—more of Mrs. Caldwell's enthused observations about the house, along with her anecdotes (which she called "horror stories") about some renovations they were doing to their home in Fort Worth—June eased the others, drinks in hand, into the dining room. Roy took his usual place at the head of the table, but at the last minute, with a loud-voiced bonhomie that touched June, he insisted that he and her father should switch chairs. "You're the man of the house, now," Roy said, winking, taking hold of Mr. Caldwell's chair back, so that her father had no choice but to smile wanly, get up, and shuffle over to Roy's vacated chair. June saw that Roy's face had flushed a darker red; he'd finished a second glass of wine and had poured himself a third. Again June understood that he was anxious, since excepting a few beers during Sunday football games on television, Roy seldom drank. Of the four of them, only June's mother drank much; alcohol was part of her various activities—the weekly poker games and bowling league and her Friday nights out "with the girls." Roy had poured her a fresh glass of wine, too, and had offered a second drink to Mr. Caldwell, who had merely pointed to his still-full glass and smiled. Like June, her father was a sparing drinker.

Meanwhile June's mother was exclaiming over the lovely appearance and delicious aromas of the platters and bowls of food June had placed on the table. Once June had sat down, and had seen with relief her family's heads bent appreciatively over their first bites, she told herself again that all would be well. Her mother and Roy were both talkers, after all, and the extra glasses of wine would lubricate the conversation nicely. After dessert, when her mother would announce that she was exhausted, June would show them to the guest bedroom—at the opposite end of the house from the master suite—and in the morning there would be a quick breakfast before Roy went to work and her parents left for Florida. On the phone, her mother had insisted that they wouldn't be "in her hair" any longer than that; they needed to get down to Bitsy as quickly as they could, and anyway she knew that Roy and June were both very busy with their jobs.

And that's what they talked about first: their jobs. Soon after their marriage, June had learned through her mother that Roy's line of work—he was a construction foreman—was a sore point with Mr. Caldwell, who reportedly worried that some young stranger (he hadn't known Roy, then) might be trying to take advantage of June. For June, focused on work rather than romance all through her twenties, had risen swiftly through the ranks of her consulting firm; the year before she and Roy married, she'd been promoted to manager at the unprecedented age (for this company, for a woman) of twenty-eight, and now, four years later, she was the prime candidate for a vice-president's slot that would soon come open. Though Roy was doing well, too, she still made more than twice what he did. Mr. Caldwell had also been unhappy (so her mother had reported, in a quick embarrassed voice) that this new husband was seven years younger than his daughter. Yet June, in her quietly determined way, had managed the conflict well—it was her profession to manage things well, after all—and her father had never expressed any disapproval directly to her. By now, she sensed that he actually liked Roy, though of course he would never say that, either. He'd always been a silent man, but now in his quietness she sensed resignation, not anger. While the others talked, he listened to each of them in turn with the same studied, polite attention, but then turned back to his food, as if he were alone, whenever an awkward silence fell.

Thanks to June's mother, the silences were few. "We always knew Junie'd do well," she said to Roy, touching his forearm. June had always liked this about her mother: she had to touch, especially when she addressed you. "Why, on parent-teacher nights at school, the teachers were constantly drawing me aside. 'Mrs. Caldwell,' they'd say, 'we wish the other kids were *half* as serious and hardworking as your daughter. She's so grown up for her age.'"

June remembered those parent-teacher nights: her mother went alone, while her father stayed home with June. By the time June was eleven, both her brothers were already off at college; she was still too young, her parents said, to stay home by herself.

"How old was she, then?" Roy asked. "I mean, when they said that?" He'd reddened with pleasure at Mrs. Caldwell's words, as though June's childhood industry reflected well on him. Taking a deep breath, June had to smile, for she understood what was behind Roy's question: he was forever trying to synchronize the events of his and June's lives before they'd met. Early in their marriage, after much calculation, he'd deduced that when he'd caught the glorious winning pass at his high school football championship, one Friday night in 1985, June was alone in her apartment, watching the 11:00 news, and she *could* have seen the tape of the winning pass during the sports segment, a tape that had been played on all the Atlanta channels. (June hadn't the heart to tell him that she always flicked off the set when the sports began.) He'd discovered, too, that he'd starred in his fifth-grade operetta on *the same day* (for they'd both saved memorabilia from their school years) that June, a high school senior, had played Margot in her school's production of *The Diary of Anne Frank*. These synchronicities tickled Roy as much as they secretly depressed June.

"How old?" Mrs. Caldwell said, perplexed. "Why, they *always* said it. All the way through school."

"Oh," Roy said, crestfallen.

"But what about you, sweetie?" Mrs. Caldwell asked him. "How does it feel to be a *fore*man?"

"Well, it's been six months now," Roy said, his voice deepening. He'd sat back, squaring his shoulders as he did when feeling self-conscious or embarrassed. June had often noticed how natural modesty and a boyish pride in his accomplishments contended in her husband; such private observations were among her delights in living with Roy.

"But it's going okay," he added. "We're framing up a big place now, over in Sandy Springs. Eight thousand feet. And we're pouring slab on a couple of others next week, if the weather holds up."

"Eight thousand feet!" Mrs. Caldwell cried. "It must be a huge family."

"Nope," Roy said, "just a doctor and his wife, and one grown daughter. Retarded," he added somberly.

Mrs. Caldwell swallowed her mouthful of salad and then clicked her tongue. "Goodness, that's sad," she murmured. June glimpsed the sheen of moisture in her mother's eyes and quickly dropped her own. Her mother had always been one to empathize instantly with the plights of strangers. She couldn't pass a street person without digging in her purse for change; she ran the Christmas food drive every year at her church, and was always dunning her poker and bowling girlfriends to donate canned goods and bake holiday cookies. Still staring at her plate, June felt a blurring in her vision, as in some helpless mockery of her mother's quick tears. Her bandaged thumb, held carefully out of sight in her lap, throbbed mildly but persistently, as though the pain were a mockery, too.

"The odd thing is," Roy went on, "their plan is set up like three separate houses. There's one side for the daughter, with its own separate kitchen and sitting room, and a room for the live-in nurse. And on the other side of the house, there are *two* master suites, and they both have a sitting room, too. It's the weirdest plan I've ever seen. They'll never be able to resell it."

"Well—a doctor," Mrs. Caldwell said. "He probably doesn't care."

Now June's father spoke, for the first time since they'd sat down. "Sounds like they're hoping not to run into each other," he said, with a short laugh.

June looked up, startled.

"Goodness, it's really sad," her mother said again.

June glanced around at the plates and asked if anyone wanted seconds. That's when she noticed that her mother hadn't touched the veal: she was eating all around it. June's tasted all right, and she saw with relief that Roy and her father were both eating theirs, but still… June remembered that her mother had praised the salad, and the homemade hollandaise covering the broccoli, but she'd said nothing about the veal. Mrs. Caldwell, from a working-class Louisiana family, nonetheless had the Southern gentlewoman's aversion to rudeness, and June knew that at one of her friends' houses she'd have eaten the veal, oohing and aahing, even if it were rancid. Her mother had that gift: she could keep her high spirits if anything went wrong. As June watched, her mother moved back and forth eagerly between the salad and the new potatoes, talking busily, stopping long enough to chew and give vehement nods to Roy as he replied to her incessant questions. June marveled at how well her mother looked. Tonight she'd worn a red-and-blue plaid "peasant" dress, with gathered short sleeves and a full skirt; large plastic teardrops, a bright blood-red, dangled from her ears and swung manically as she chatted and ate. June knew that for a car trip her mother would have preferred blue jeans and an old oxford cloth shirt of her husband's, but she'd dressed up for this visit, and June supposed she should feel touched and mildly grateful. Instead, she had lost her appetite altogether. She could not stop staring at her mother's large but thin-lipped mouth, painted a blaring red that matched the earrings.

Mrs. Caldwell had worked through the retarded daughter's sadness quickly enough.

"She's lucky, really," she said to Roy. Occasionally Mrs. Caldwell would glance at her husband and June, politely including them, but it was clear that she preferred to address her son-in-law. "Her parents are keeping a nice roof over her head, after all, when they could have shipped her off to an institution. And a live-in companion! Heck, I wouldn't mind trading places with her!" Mrs. Caldwell threw her head back for a raucous laugh, hollandaise gleaming at one side of her mouth, and Roy laughed along. June felt her father glance up, sharply, but at once he bent his head back to his plate. Nervously June eyed her mother's empty wine glass.

"And I'll bet if you asked that doctor, he'd say that he's thankful for *any* daughter. I mean, what would they have without her? Anything is better than nothing, right?"

That's when Roy said an unexpected thing. What most soothed June about her husband was his good-natured predictability, but after all he'd had a bit of wine, too, and this "special occasion" had enlivened him.

He murmured, glancing at June, "I hope *we'll* have a daughter someday, or a son—I don't care which." His smile faltered when he saw June's strained expression. "That is, if June wants to."

Mrs. Caldwell glanced her way, too, but with a mischievous grimace.

"These career women don't know what they're missing, if you ask me," she said. "Now honey, don't mind your loud-mouthed old mother"—for Mrs. Caldwell had seen June's expression, too—"but that biological clock isn't going to slow down, you know. Granted you're just thirty-two, but for a first baby that's already kind of late."

June tried to smile, glancing down, cutting her veal methodically into tiny bites even though her stomach was writhing.

"Well, we've got plenty of time," Roy said, in a worried voice.

"One of these days," her mother said, "you'll have to sabotage her pill box—put in sugar pills or something." She was stage-whispering, in a throaty conspiratorial voice. "After all, accidents do happen!" she added cheerfully. "Why, our boys were half-grown when Junie came along. We wouldn't have missed you for the world, Junie

Moon," and her mother touched June's forearm, "but we certainly didn't expect you! Did we, hon?" she asked her husband.

Mr. Caldwell glanced up, smiling wanly, but didn't reply.

"We're not quite ready yet," Roy said uneasily. "But one of these days…"

June knew she should come to Roy's aid, but somehow she couldn't speak. She inhaled, exhaled; she had finished cutting the veal and now moved onto the broccoli. She tried to make all the bites the same size, exactly, as though she were cutting the food for a very small child. As she worked, her mother moved along to another topic while June kept hearing that phrase, *Junie Moon*, echoing again and again in her head. It had been years since her mother had used June's childhood nickname, one which sounded innocuous enough but whose open rhyming vowels were like hammer-blows against June's heart. *Why the moony little face, Miss Junie Moon*, came her mother's sing-song voice. *Poor little Junie Moon…* She remembered that in grade school she'd felt such relief when the kids played their own word games—*Loony June, June the Baboon*—and even laughed along with them; compared to the other, the taunts of her classmates were like mere insect bites, like a sharp sandy wind against her skin, the outermost surface of her being by which they identified her as *Junie Caldwell* and by which she fooled them into believing that's who she was. In her high school years, Junie had become June, and she corrected her occasional date if he tried using her little-girl's name. Now, at the office, her oversized pink-marble desk plate ("It looks like a grave marker," her friend Sherry had laughed) read *June C. Bynum, Manager*. If she got the vice president's job, she imagined having her marker read *J. C. Bynum*, but she supposed that would be ostentatious. Whenever a salesman visited her office and asked, in that new defensive way of younger men, "Should I call you—is it Mrs. Bynum? Or—?" she tried to put him at ease. "Mrs. Bynum, or June," she would say. "Whatever makes you comfortable."

For that was June's way, wasn't it? she thought in scorn. Make everyone comfortable. Keep things running smoothly. *Manage* things—schedules, other people, above all herself. Cut up your food efficiently, she thought, even when reaching a perilous stage of nausea.

June put down her knife and fork; her hands were trembling, but she noticed that her wounded thumb no longer hurt. She put the bandaged hand back in her lap, but then brought it out, placed it on the table as though for display. What difference did it make? she thought. Her father had already noticed the hand and her mother would refuse to notice.

"Mom," June said, as evenly as she could, "is something wrong with your veal?"

By now, Mrs. Caldwell had almost finished her salad, vegetables, bread; the untouched piece of meat sat on her plate like a little pale-brown island. Both men glanced at the plate—they'd finished their veal some time ago—and Mrs. Caldwell, caught off guard, flushed a crimson almost as lurid as her lipstick. She pushed the plate forward and laid her napkin on top, smiling awkwardly. "I'm sorry, honey, I hoped you wouldn't notice, but—"

She gazed plaintively across the table to her husband, who, of all people, tried to lighten the moment. He glanced at June, with a doleful smile.

"It's another of her 'causes,' I'm afraid."

"Not eating meat?" Roy said anxiously, looking from June to her mother. "You mean you're a vegetarian, Mrs. Caldwell? Shoot, you should have just told us and we'd have been glad to—"

"Not exactly," June's mother said. Her flush had died away, and now she gave a crinkly sad-eyed look to her daughter. "It's just—it's just that I can't eat veal," she said. "I'm sure you don't know about it, honey, but the reason veal is so tender, what they do to those poor baby calves—"

She stopped, a catch in her throat.

"She read a magazine article," June's father said dryly. "One article."

"Not only that, I've seen pictures," Mrs. Caldwell said. She seemed near the point of tears, yet June watched her coldly. "They force these little calves to live *standing up*, and to make them fat and tender they give them a diet that causes diarrhea, and there the little things are, trapped for their short lives and hardly able to move, and then while they're still babies they're led off to the slaughter. It's just—well, I don't believe in torturing animals," she said summarily, with a quick sniff. She grabbed her napkin and poked briefly at each of her eyes.

"It's okay, Mrs. Caldwell," Roy murmured.

But June's mother had recovered rapidly from her distress and now glanced around at all of them. "Sorry, folks," she said. "I don't believe in imposing my beliefs on others, please understand that. You can't control what other people do. And Junie, honey, I *do* appreciate all the work that went into this meal. I'm afraid your old mom is just one of those bleeding hearts...." She laughed, thinly. Again she picked up her napkin and dabbed at her eyes.

By now, June had pushed her plate away, too, discreetly covering the tiny uneaten bites with her own napkin. Her hands had stopped trembling. Her breathing had calmed.

"Don't worry, Mom," she said. "I don't know why I decided to cook, anyway. Roy offered to take us all out to dinner, and I should have let him. You could have seen a bit more of the city."

"Nonsense!" Mrs. Caldwell cried. "Why, we can eat out anytime, Junie. What we wanted was to see the house, visit with you and Roy, just have an old-fashioned evening at home. Isn't that right, Wilton?" she asked her husband.

"That's what you told me," Mr. Caldwell said. "Although it's not much like you—wanting to stay home."

He looked at June, winking. This was an old joke in the family, especially when June's two older brothers were around. When June was small and her brothers were in high school, they would kid their dad for staying home on weekend nights while their mother, as she herself phrased it, went "gallivanting around." Even back then she'd had her poker and bowling nights, her Friday nights of bar-hopping with her friends from her old job at the phone company—a job she'd had to quit when June was born. Mr. Caldwell, on the other hand, had few friends; he put in his eight hours and came home. June's own evenings at home, at ages ten, eleven, twelve, had been punctuated by the arrivals and leave-takings of her parents. Her brothers were almost always gone (they had jobs, girlfriends), and after her father arrived home from work Mrs. Caldwell would put together a quick supper before bathing, putting on her pedal-pushers, her colorful blouses and jewelry, and her slightly excessive makeup—the rouge in particular was too heavy, June had thought as a child, observing the reddish smears along the tops of her mother's sharp-boned cheeks. Then her mother, smelling of Chanel No. 5, would give June a peck on each cheek and blow a kiss to her husband. Already jangling her keys, already snapping her spearmint gum between her back teeth. She was out the door by seven o'clock, and June and her father would be left alone.

And then while they're still babies they're led off to the slaughter....

June pushed back her chair, just a few inches, but this was the signal they'd all been awaiting. Roy, rising, said something about brandy to June's father, and her mother asked for directions to the powder room. "But don't *touch* those plates," she said chidingly, as June reached down to the table. "I want to help with the cleaning up, honey. It's the least I can do."

Only June's father stayed at the table, while June followed Roy into the kitchen. As soon as her mother had left the room, they'd both gathered up an armful of dishes. June took hers immediately to the sink and stood there, gripping the edge of the counter. Behind her, Roy was scraping plates into the trash—she still hadn't trained him to use the garbage disposal—and talking idly about how good the food had been. When, after a minute or two, he noticed that June wasn't answering, he came over and eased his arms around her waist.

"June, are you—" He stopped, peering around at her. "What's wrong, baby, why are you crying?"

She could scarcely bear the tenderness in his voice, yet she didn't want to pull away; his arms seemed impossibly strong and pleasurable, applying just the right amount of pressure, not confining her but gently anchoring her in place. Tears leaked of their own volition from her eyes. Without moving or thinking, she held up the bandaged hand.

"It hurts," she told him.

"My goodness, why didn't you—it must be infected or something. Maybe we should—"

"No, listen, I'll just go into the bathroom and get some ointment. That, plus a fresh bandage, and I should be good as new." She wiped her eyes with a dishtowel, giving him the same sad wet-eyed expression (as she was uncomfortably aware) that her mother had used in the dining room. Now she did turn around, gently pushing him away.

"Well, if you're sure," Roy said.

"I'm sure," she said. "Just help Mom, get the clean-up started, and I'll be back in a flash."

"Use that new stuff we bought," Roy called after her. "It's got some painkiller in it."

Avoiding the dining room, where she could hear her mother chattering, clanking dishes together, June went down a short hallway that led from the laundry area to the powder room her mother had used. From the doorway, she stared down the darkened longer hall to the dining room door, the sliver of light beneath it showing the quick shadowy movement of her mother's footsteps. The movement seemed miles away, she thought. Years away. In the bathroom, once she'd locked herself in, she could smell traces of her mother's perfume, a thick sweetish scent that resembled honeysuckle. She flipped on the fan, thinking it would help kill the smell and also cover her noise if she needed to cry again, and then she opened the medicine cabinet above the sink. She was looking for the ointment Roy had mentioned, but then she remembered it was in the other bathroom, the one adjoining their master suite. Here in the powder room, she stored supplies that she sometimes bought in quantities on sale: economy bottles of aspirin, boxes of toothpaste, packets of Roy's razor blades. Roy disdained cartridge blades, preferring the old-fashioned kind of blades and shaver his father had used, and now June, wanting for something to do, took a little tin packet and slipped one of the blades out the side; she closed the medicine cabinet door and stared into the mirror.

It occurred to her that she no longer needed to cry. Instead she wanted to take this razor blade and slice a tip off her other thumb and each of her eight fingers. She decided to do this, and her hands became slender pale faucets of blood. With a dazed happy smile she drew them down along the medicine cabinet mirror, trailing wavy stripes of blood and leaving her pale triumphant face to stare outward from what looked like a prison cell enclosed by jagged red bars.

No, she would never do this—melodrama wasn't June C. Bynum's style—but it felt good to think about it. Her heart had begun racing, as if feeding that imaginary flow of blood and her own bitter joy. She blinked her eyes, as though to make that vision of the red bars reappear. She took a deep breath. Fortunately there was also a supply of gauze bandages and Band-Aids in the medicine cabinet and now she opened the mirrored door again, quickly removing her old bandage and replaced it with a new one, dispensing with the ointment. She didn't need it, for she had lied to Roy; the wound had stayed numb, there was no pain at all.

She told herself that the rest of the evening would be predictable enough, manageable enough, but when she opened the bathroom door she cried out when she saw her father's pale haggard-looking face looming out of the darkened hall. "Oh, it's you," June gasped, "—you startled me—" He stood there, gazing back at her. "Sorry," he said. "I didn't mean to." Again her breath came in quick shallow pants. She moved to one side and he moved to the other, in the awkwardness of such moments, and finally he was in the doorway and she stood in the hall. "No, it's all right," she said, "I just didn't expect—" Again his steady gaze broke off her words. She stood mesmerized, helpless, but he decided to be merciful, giving that practiced wan smile. "I'll just be a minute," he said, "then I'll come out and help." She shrugged quickly and said, "Oh, don't hurry, I'll just—" but then he closed the door and she stood there alone.

If it hadn't been for that thin crack of light beneath the dining room door, she might not have known which way to move—the house was still new, she still found herself making wrong turns when she came out of a room—but she saw the light and she heard Roy's voice, just on the other side of it. "I think she'll be fine," he was saying. "She's just a little…" but she didn't need to hear any more. She focused on the voice—its kind and virile certainty, its innocence of pain—and followed it out of the darkness.

Scene of the Crime

"You know how Daddy feels about shopping, don't you?" Mrs. Goodman says.

She fans her red-nailed fingers above the wheel, awaiting her daughter's reply. They're stopped at a traffic light, not far from the mall entrance.

Edie knows her next line, of course; it's just a matter of her delivery. She stares out her window and for some reason presses her nose to the glass, like a child.

She says, but not hearing herself, "No, how does Daddy *feel*."

Mrs. Goodman says rapidly, "He feels that shopping is our privilege and our right. Nay, our solemn duty."

Edie knows that her mother isn't smiling. It's part of Mrs. Goodman's humorous persona—the Marsha Goodman whom her bridge-party acquaintances consider "outrageous," "hysterical," etc.—that she almost never smiles.

It's a technique, of sorts.

"Is that so," Edie says back. "My, my."

Her father: the last person on earth she cares to think about.

Thank God, there's a parking place right in front of Saks. Mrs. Goodman complains mightily if she has to park more than a few steps from the stores. Lately Edie has noticed that Phipps Plaza—always Atlanta's ritziest mall, and now renovated and expanded—

has begun attracting larger and larger crowds. The mall has a Lord & Taylor, Tiffany's, Gucci, and Mrs. Goodman's favorite, the deliciously expensive Saks with its salmon-carpeted, curving staircase and unctuous sales clerks; and there are assorted smaller stores like Skippy Musket (antique jewelry) and La Bottega (imported handbags), which are equally expensive. Mrs. Goodman approves all the stores in Phipps Plaza and is a familiar sight in here: busy, prepossessing, overdressed, a heavily made-up blond Jewish lady, one eyebrow arched, her blank-looking daughter in tow. But most people can't afford this kind of shopping, after all. Not long ago Edie suggested, just for a change, that they go to Lenox Square, the much larger mall just across Peachtree Road. "You know," Edie had said, in a mock-petulant voice, "where the people are—the *normal* people?" But Mrs. Goodman had pretended to be shocked, her red-glossed lips forming a horrified *O*.

"Are you my daughter, truly?" she'd asked. "You know that Daddy prefers the better stores. You know that Daddy is very particular about our shopping."

Now mother and daughter maneuver themselves out of Mrs. Goodman's year-old burgundy Seville, a challenging task because both are rather plump inside their bulky fur-trimmed coats. The Cadillac's velvet upholstery is so luxuriously thick that it seems to retard their progress, urging them to stay seated, stay inside this beautiful car forever…. So Edie's sardonic thoughts run, in any case, as she opens the heavy car door, with a grunt of resigned effort, then stands and pushes it shut. She glares over the car's roof at Mrs. Goodman—a petite woman in her ash-blond wig (only one of her several dozen wigs), her thick powder and makeup that today include bold black eyeliner and violet shadow, and her famous wet-looking cherry-red lipstick. As she often does, Edie imagines that her mother is another woman, a stranger. Watching Mrs. Goodman gather her dark-red coat around her, fluffing the ranch mink collar along her jaw, Edie thinks yes, oh yes definitely: a stranger.

At such moments does Edie drift gently into lurid fantasies of escape and betrayal. Shall she simply turn and walk in the opposite direction from Mrs. Goodman, heading for Peachtree Road and Lenox Square instead of Saks, while her mother gapes after her?

Or, inside Mrs. Goodman's favorite store, should Edie pick a fight over nothing, over a necklace or a pair of gloves, screaming shrill obscenities in front of the clerks and well-dressed customers while Mrs. Goodman stares in disbelief? Or, more covertly, will Edie scrutinize the other middle-aged women in the store as though shopping for a replacement mother? And when she finds a likely prospect, does she simply walk off with her, taking hold of the woman's arm, chatter in her ear of inconsequential things?

Yes, Edie supposes dreamily that she might do any of these things—or all of them!—but instead she follows her mother into the mall.

It's eleven o'clock, a weekday in early January: out of the thin frothy sunlight, and into the open luxurious spaces of Phipps Plaza. Mrs. Goodman heads for the escalator, talking and gesturing, while Edie tries vainly to keep up. Inevitably she falls a few paces behind, her eyes downcast, and at such moments the fantasies intrude again: for what if she stopped, abruptly, and allowed her mother to continue up the moving stairs, chattering busily to herself? What if she ducked into a store and strode purposefully toward one of the outside exits? What then, what then? But, getting off the escalator, Mrs. Goodman pauses, waiting as Edie trudges up to her mother's side.

Her eyes blank as a statue's, Edie thinks, *Maybe we should start off with....*

"Maybe we should start off with a little drinkie," Mrs. Goodman says, eyeing the entrance to the Peasant Uptown, her favorite restaurant. "After all, it's almost lunchtime," she adds, as if convincing herself.

Edie thinks, *Then we'll be fortified, won't we ...*

"Then we'll be fortified, won't we, for a bit of shopping. And then we can get ourselves a bite of lunch."

Edie stays silent, so Mrs. Goodman stares at her.

"Right, honey?" she says.

"By all means, let's fortify ourselves," Edie mutters, following her mother inside. An effusive, hectically smiling hostess leads them to their table and, not needing to ask, a deft young waiter quickly brings a double martini with two olives for Mrs. Goodman and a diet cola for Edie.

"Good morning, ladies," he says with a little bow.

But it's almost...

"But it's almost afternoon, so we're allowed," Mrs. Goodman says primly, and now it's Edie's turn to stare.

"Honey, is something wrong?" her mother asks, when the waiter is gone. "You look so—so—" She gives a little shudder.

Edie ponders the ultimate sacrilege, then decides against it, then thinks why not, just why the hell not?

She settles her level, hard look upon Mrs. Goodman's eyes (which are really quite tiny and frightened-looking, inside all the mess of paint and goop), and says in her best droll manner: "Mother, I've been meaning to ask you something. What is the point—could you tell me, please—of all this shopping?"

Of course, her mother's beak is already inserted into the martini, her small eyes darting busily around the restaurant. Of course, her mother hasn't heard.

"Ah, thank you," Edie says under her breath. And she takes up her own glass. She drinks.

My goodness, there aren't many...

"My goodness, there aren't many people out this morning," her mother says, in her fake-disappointed voice.

"Oh, but *we* are," Edie replies.

During that busy, hectic time between Thanksgiving and Christmas, Dr. Goodman had finally left them.

Or, as Mrs. Goodman prefers to say, airily, he had "decamped," leaving them the big house on Haversham Road and all the furnishings—including some priceless antiques and paintings inherited from his parents—and both Cadillacs and the bulk, by far, of his stock and bond holdings. And his bank accounts. And those big chunks of Buckhead real estate he'd been quietly acquiring through the years. Two sets of lawyers had been in the house during those last weeks—Edie would pause at the base of the stairway, listening to their dark murmurous voices from the library-den where Dr. and Mrs. Goodman conducted their business—and the upshot had been that Mrs. Goodman could have everything, or almost everything. Dr. Goodman had kept the small stone-and-redwood house up at Lake Lanier, and his beloved little Porsche Carrera, and perhaps half a million in cash and securities: he wouldn't need any more, he told Mrs. Goodman, for the kind of modest retirement he wanted. As for the rest—worth four million? six million?—Mrs. Goodman could do her worst: she could fling wads of bills from the top of the IBM building, she could slurp Dom Perignon from morning to night, she could shop till her plump little legs wore down to nubs.

Or rather, Edie imagined that *she* might have said such things, in her father's position.

In truth, she could not put herself in her father's position, for she no longer knew him, really. Dr. Goodman no longer came home early from the office to take Edie on meandering strolls around the neighborhood, as he'd done when she was nine or ten. (Mrs. Goodman never accompanied them: she had her headaches, she was "indisposed." Mrs. Goodman hated any kind of exercise unrelated to shopping.) No longer did he take his "little girl" on impulsive Saturday trips to Six Flags, or to the lake house where they fished from the motorboat or tramped gaily through the woods, Dr. Goodman looking funny and boisterous in his short pants and sneakers, his portly frame moving nimbly over tree roots and puddles, his plump womanish legs gleaming mushroom-white in the dank gloom of the woods.... Yes, Edie had adored her father. People said they looked alike, which at that time Edie hadn't yet heard as a veiled rebuke or a sorrowful prediction. She and her father were short, squat, pale-complected, and both moved along with a "duck's waddle," as Mrs. Goodman laughingly said. (Rather heavy herself, Mrs. Goodman nonetheless walked with the bold and purposeful strides of a huntress. Following along, waddling along, Edie did her best to keep up, feeling by comparison that she was hardly "walking" at all.) Nonetheless Edie and her father had been inseparable, back then. Whenever Edie was taunted at school about her weight, or called "frog legs" by the prettier girls, she'd simply close her eyes and think of Daddy who called her his "little princess," his "little ballerina," and even (somehow, this was Edie's favorite nickname) his "little whatchamacallit."

But that had changed. By the time Edie was twelve or thirteen, her father spent much less time at home. Sometimes, late at night, they'd bump into each other in the upstairs hall, and he'd say "Oops, sorry" in the oddly formal voice one uses with a stranger, an adult stranger, or else he'd say nothing at all, just cup her face for a moment in his hands, as if she were one of his plastic surgery patients and he were asking himself was there hope, was there anything he could do. On one such night he bent down to kiss her forehead before shuffling down the hall to his room—by now, he slept in the spare room alone while Mrs. Goodman stayed in the master suite with a black sleeping mask over her eyes—and Edie would be left to return to her own room, where she had the habit of standing before a full-length mirror (stolid, dour-faced, her eyes dark and sad and impenetrable) for long silent minutes before climbing into bed. That time, a Friday night about six months ago, she'd felt her father's kiss still moist and clammy on her forehead, but she thought: Nope, not a little princess, still a frog. She thought: And tomorrow I'll get dragged to the mall by Mother, to shop for some frog clothes. She was tempted to give herself a little frog-croak in the mirror, but these days she'd begun losing even her humor, no longer quite seeing the point.

So she didn't respond to her mother's occasional late-night tirades about "that other woman"; she didn't look twice when, some mornings, Mrs. Goodman came down to breakfast without makeup, her face doughy-pale and unformed, and sometimes even without a wig, her colorless hair floating in thin dry wisps about her head. But Edie noticed that the woman's eyes were pink, like a rabbit's eyes, and she thought: The rabbit and the frog, having breakfast together. She thought: I hope she croaks, too, ha ha. But she said nothing.

So the weeks passed and the divorce happened and Mrs. Goodman has seemingly become obsessed with spending every penny of her ex-husband's money before she finally does croak, but Edie still follows along numbly—waddling, friendless, doomed—and knowing she still looks like a smaller version of her father, even with her chunky body wrapped in this bulky wool coat with its fur collar. But unlike him, she isn't able to cut herself off, get free, simply turn and waddle away. Unlike him, she's only fifteen years old.

* * *

Half an hour for her mother's two martinis, then an hour for their lunch—lobster crepes plus a third martini for Mrs. Goodman, Caesar salad and a club soda for Edie—so it's past one o'clock before their shopping really begins. Today, Edie has been thinking, as her mother chatters endlessly over her lunch about the divorce of one of her bridge partners ("Poor Brenda," Mrs. Goodman said, "everyone saw it coming but *her*"), today there is one good thing: Mrs. Goodman is shopping for herself instead of for Edie. One of her mother's New Year's resolutions, repeated endlessly to Edie around the house, was her plan to become more sociable: to accept invitations when they came her way, whether invitations of "the male or female persuasion." Yesterday she received one of the male persuasion—oddly, he was one of Dr. Goodman's divorce lawyers, a man likewise divorced, portly, good-natured—so it's important that Mrs. Goodman find a dress. Tonight they're going to the ballet, or the symphony—Mrs. Goodman can't remember which, she was so flustered and pleased by the offer. "Your father never took me anywhere," Mrs. Goodman told Edie, "so I've got to find something new—maybe a lovely white winter wool? Or should I get a new black frock, something sleek and 'slimming,' as they say? What do *you* think, Edie?" But of course she didn't wait for a reply. Of course she wouldn't have appreciated the reply, had her daughter dared to utter it.

So today Edie's merely a sidekick, a tag-along. She has no particular function, except as the receiver of her mother's queries, complaints, exclamations. First they go to Lord & Taylor, since it's closest to the restaurant, but this is just a warm-up, Edie knows. Recently Mrs. Goodman informed her that she doesn't "take Lord & Taylor seriously, not any more," since she no longer considers the store stylish enough. Nonetheless she tries on a bright gold silk jacket, with shoulder pads, and a matching skirt, then a burgundy velvet dress that shows Mrs. Goodman's pot belly so clearly that she shrieks the instant she steps before the triple mirrors, then a blue-and-black sequined jacket with black chiffon harem pants, an outfit that makes her look even shorter and dumpier than she is. "Oh well," she sighs, standing before the mirrors in this last outfit—she appears almost to be kneeling, Edie thinks cruelly— "I'm afraid that Lord & Taylor has failed us, once again."

The saleswoman who has been helping them comes up with two more outfits draped over her arm, asking would Mrs. Goodman care to try to these, but Edie's mother says brusquely, "No, I certainly would *not.*" And, winking at Edie, hurries back behind the curtains.

Edie hasn't winked back, but now the saleswoman stands gaping at her, as if awaiting an explanation. Edie feels the words forming on her tongue: Don't mind my mother, she's just your garden-variety psychotic, but of course Edie doesn't say these words. Or any words. She gives her best blank look until the woman, smiling feebly, shrugs and gives up and goes away.

At last, they're headed toward Saks, where her mother is sure to buy something: where her mother has never *not* bought something. Ah, the lovely muted colors and delicious aromas of Saks!—even Edie likes coming here, knowing that nothing really bad can happen, that even the most profound embarrassments are here diffused by the lilting background music and the perfumed, gently circulating air and by the smiles of the saleswomen, who are so impeccably groomed and dressed that at first glance Edie will often mistake one of them for a mannequin.... Now, as Mrs. Goodman veers toward an alcove marked "After 5," already talking to the woman who has hurried forth to greet her, Edie dawdles nearby at the glove counter. She picks up some soft brown gloves, brushing the fragrant cool leather against her cheek—the price tag reads $75—then drops them and picks up another pair, an irresistible vanilla suede so incredibly soft and supple that suddenly she is moved to gather up several pairs and thrust her face into them, inhaling with her eyes closed, and for a moment she's transported somewhere else altogether.... Then a woman behind the counter approaches: "Help you, dear...?" She is smiling indulgently, knowing well the power of those exquisite gloves, but quickly Edie straightens, drops all but one pair, and asks, "How much are these?" The price tag is plainly visible, attached to a small plastic security device that would trigger an alarm if Edie tried to shoplift the gloves; nonetheless the woman bends over the tag, frowning. "Let's see, those are $125. And so lovely, aren't they? Shall I check for a pair in your size?"

Edie hears herself say: "Yes, please. Size seven."

When the woman hands the gloves across the counter, Edie takes them reverently, works her plump fingers into them one by one.

"May I take them over there? Show them to my mother?" Edie says, not quite meeting the woman's eyes.

"Of course, of course!" the woman says, with a pleased glance in the direction of Mrs. Goodman. "I'm sure she'll want you to have them."

"Yes, um—thank you," Edie says, contorting her mouth into a feeble approximation of the woman's relentless smile, and then she backs off, in that dreamy, slow-motion way of experienced shoppers, her eye still grazing the glass shelves heaped with gloves. Then she steps across the aisle and joins her mother.

"Well, what do you think?" Mrs. Goodman says at once, holding up a black beaded cocktail dress with a deep-cut bodice and flaring skirt. When Edie stares at the dress but doesn't answer—she is picturing her mother's pale, dimpled cleavage, shoved upwards by that bodice—the saleswoman says quickly, "That one's so versatile—a perfect foil for your lovely skin, or a special piece of jewelry. Would you like to try it on...?"

"Yeah, maybe," Mrs. Goodman mutters, still plowing through the rack. She snaps each dress into view with an expert flick of her hand, stares for several seconds, goes to the next one. She pauses at a yellow silk with puffed sleeves, then slowly lifts it from the rack.

"*That* one's lovely, too," the saleswoman says. "With your hair color, especially, it would be simply—"

"Edie, what do you think?" Mrs. Goodman says. Her daughter stands there looking doleful, the suede gloves drooping from her clenched fist. With her other hand, she touches the shoulder of the dress—a meaningless gesture. "It's nice, I guess," she says neutrally. "The color is...I guess yellow would be..."

"Okay, I'll try these," Mrs. Goodman tells the woman.

While her mother is changing, Edie sits in the waiting area in a big overstuffed chair and endures the saleswoman's small talk. Helplessly Edie is remembering one Christmas day, many years ago, when Mrs. Goodman had given her husband a beautiful fawn-colored suede jacket. Though they were Jewish, Dr. Goodman had thrown a large "open house" every Christmas during Edie's childhood, declaring that the spirit of Christmas was available to everyone—and it was the spirit that counted, after all, not anyone's particular religious beliefs. Edie recalls that the year he'd gotten the jacket—she must have been five or six—her father wore it around the house proudly all during the party. *That's* why she remembered the smell, why she picked up those gloves, for she could still feel the thrilling luxury of riding in her father's arms, borne from room to room as he greeted their guests—his medical associates, his pals from the neighborhood and the club, aunts and cousins and other family members whom they saw only once a year, at this huge catered party. Edie was still young enough, that year, that she could ignore the guests, look away shyly when they proclaimed (speaking to her father, not to her) how "cute" she was, though even at that age when all children are cute Edie was, as she now knows, a borderline case: her body chunky and graceless, her face already lumpish, sallow, the same mushroom-white as her legs. But she didn't know, then. She didn't care, then. She felt so protected and privileged in her father's arms!—carried like a princess through the rooms. And didn't he sometimes say, laughing, that "his home was his castle"? He knew it was a cliché, he admitted, but he didn't care—like most clichés it was *so true*. And who had invented the majority of clichés, after all? Shakespeare!

Even that claim, which he repeated often, became something of a cliché for Dr. Goodman. He loved to say things like "Beauty is only skin deep, you know!" Or, pointing his stubby finger at Edie, "Money can't buy happiness, sweetie—it can't buy *love*." Even that Christmas Day as he carried her among the guests, looking pleased and prosperous in his new suede jacket, he told everyone, "It's days like this when we remember what's important in life, am I right?" And he jiggled Edie in his arms, up and down, and people would say with their eyes crinkled half-shut how *cute* she was, and Edie would feel the delicious thrill of ignoring them, simply putting her face to her father's big shoulder and inhaling the expensive fresh aroma of that suede jacket. Surely this was happiness, surely this was the happiest moment of her childhood—though she couldn't know it, then, and indeed its glory lay in not needing to "know" it, or to know anything. In any case, it's a moment Edie must now recall with jealous longing, with an emotion akin to dread. Sitting in this plush overstuffed armchair, in Saks. Waiting for her mother, eternally waiting, the saleswoman chattering brightly into her ear.

Finally her mother emerges, wearing one of the dresses. And minutes later reemerges, wearing another. After trying on six or seven outfits—asking Edie her opinion on each, not listening as Edie mumbles her noncommittal replies—Mrs. Goodman finally decides on two of them. One of which she prefers, but only slightly, the second as a "spare," in case she changes her mind.

Sometimes, when you get them home...

All the while Edie sits watching glumly from her chair. She hasn't even unbuttoned her heavy wool coat with its thick mink collar, and she supposes she must be getting warm, overwarm; but really she feels nothing. She imagines that she is a beached whale, enormous, numbed, immovable...and she recalls another cliché her father loved. "It's not a person's appearance that matters—it's what's on the *in*side." Edie wonders if her father repeated this particular cliché to his women patients, who came to his office shopping for expensive new faces. She wonders how he would react if *she* showed up one day and gave him her best impenetrable dull-eyed glare and said, "What about me, Dr. Goodman? Is there anything you can do for *me*?"

Now her mother says emphatically to the saleswoman, handing her both the dresses, "Sometimes, when you get them home, they don't look right after all. Yes, I'd better take them both. I can always use a spare."

So the matter is decided, and now there are shoes to buy, and some new earrings, and perhaps a scarf to drape across one shoulder, that's become such a fashionable look.... As her mother makes these various purchases she hands the boxes and sacks to Edie, who has become expert these past few months at shuffling packages from arm to arm, putting smaller sacks inside larger ones, and all the while giving her opinion—"Yeah, well, I guess so"—whenever her mother requires it. In this way do the hours pass. In this way does Edie's life pass. Once or twice she glances at her watch, adjusting the packages so that she can tilt her arm sideways, and she sees that it's past two o'clock—and then it's a quarter to three—and yes this day of shopping is passing quickly like all the others. For, as her father used to say, during their

Saturday father-daughter outings together, years ago, "Time does pass quickly doesn't it?—when you're having fun."

As if reading her mind, Mrs. Goodman now says, "Isn't this fun?" Edie can't tell if she's being ironic or not. They're at the jewelry counter, where Edie's mother has tried on perhaps three thousand pairs of earrings while Edie stands holding the half-dozen packages, long-suffering Edie in her heavy wool coat that's still buttoned up to her throat. Countless bright lights shine down on this counter, to give the gold and diamonds an added sparkle, and Edie is very hot. Yes, she *does* feel the heat, she *does* have a heavy lardish perspiring body, and as she confronts this knowledge she stares down, as if from a great distance, at one of her hands—it doesn't seem to be Edie's hand, quite—and watches it dart inside one of the sacks and then out again. When it comes out, the hand is empty. The palm is sweating, and itching almost unbearably.

"Okay, I guess I'll take these," Mrs. Goodman says, when Edie doesn't answer. Edie feels a gleam of sweat along her forehead and now, as her mother signs the slip, she says, "Mother, would you carry a couple of these? They're getting heavy."

"Sure thing, hon," her mother says, taking the sacks Edie hands her, and Edie feels a glow of satisfaction already pervading her chest, her stomach and limbs…oh yes, she definitely feels it.

Well, I guess we've done enough damage…

The jewelry salesman thanks Mrs. Goodman profusely, and so here they are, in the middle of a wide aisle on the main floor of Saks, looking unmoored and disconsolate. Edie feels her mother's tiny dark-gleaming eyes brush past hers.

"Well," Mrs. Goodman says, "I guess we've done enough damage for one day."

"Yes," Edie says mildly. "I guess we have."

Her mother turns and heads for the exit—not the mall exit but the one leading directly from the store into the lot where their Seville is parked. As though observing the scene in a dream Edie watches her mother getting farther and farther away, moving with her usual bold strides, confident that her daughter is behind her, that her daughter's legs have not turned gelatinous, then leaden, and then stopped altogether like two pillars of stone. Now Mrs. Goodman is out of sight, and within another five seconds Edie hears it—the security alarm, though in Saks even that sound is muted and almost pleasant, a low static humming—and now she sees a man, wearing a jacket and tie, headed in the direction her mother has gone. Her mother, who has just stolen an expensive pair of gloves.

Already the glow of satisfaction in Edie's belly is fading, dissolving, and in its place there is nothing. A blank sensation. An emptiness. *Not a person's appearance that matters—it's what's on the inside...* So she returns to the glove counter, the scene of the crime, and to the pile of beautiful vanilla-suede gloves still heaped on the counter, and again Edie takes two enormous handfuls and presses them to her face. She inhales deeply, greedily. When the saleswoman approaches again from behind the counter, asking her something, Edie smiles invisibly into the gloves and doesn't respond: doesn't even hear.

I Am Dangerous

O r was. This happened in a movie theater, 1973. I know the year because I'd just broken up with the love of my life, had my heart broken, etc., you give the cliché and I suffered it, blood and bone, skinless heart, and you don't forget such things.

I'd gone to the movie to do just that. Forget. This was the Silver Screen, an Atlanta theater that showed old movies, "classics" from the '30s, '40s, and early '50s. Two in the afternoon, a weekday, I'd cut one of my classes since grad school now seemed meaningless, even laughable when I pondered the notion of "Dr. Knowlton" leading his own graduate seminars one day. (I'd been wild for the Civil War since I was a kid and wanted to talk about it, talk about it forever, but otherwise I really had little interest in history, a fact that would become clear a year later when I flunked my prelims and moved back home to Augusta: but at least my heart was mended by then.) The fantasy had included Sheila, of course, the dazzling faculty wife, the prize on my arm, Sheila who had informed me the week before that she was moving to Asheville, North Carolina, she wanted to develop her talent, not our relationship, she was rethinking her life, she was rethinking *me*, I was too intense I didn't give her space I just gave lip service to feminist ideas, etc., but the upshot was I'd been dumped, just like that, so the idea of "Dr. Knowlton" seemed ridiculous enough when I felt like walking scum, I almost said an amoeba but that's an insult to amoebae, walking scum will do, so as usual when everything turned shitty I went off to the movies.

I hadn't even checked what was playing, but it turned out to be *The Heiress* with Montgomery Clift and Olivia de Havilland, which was perfect because there the woman gets it for a change. Olivia's the plain-Jane daughter of a rich doctor who disapproves of her new boyfriend, the too-handsome Monty, but Olivia believes he's *not* a gold-digger and even the audience isn't sure unless you've already read the Henry James story it's based on, anyway he proposes and she accepts but makes a fatal error, telling him she's giving up her inheritance, who cares if Daddy approves, all we need is each other, etc., so naturally on the night of their elopement he never shows up. It's a painful scene when poor dumb Olivia finally gets the picture, but I knew it would make me feel better, I guess I'd lucked out that it wasn't *Of Human Bondage* or something like that, so I bought the ticket and a large popcorn and headed inside.

The opening credits were rolling, white letters on a black background, and the theater was very dark. I couldn't see a thing and literally had to feel my way down the aisle. When I got to my preferred area, right-hand side about ten rows from the back, I waved my hand sideways toward the aisle seat and it seemed to be empty. So I sat, started munching popcorn, and was already feeling better. As the credits wound up and the opening scene began, my eyes started adjusting to the darkness, and to my left I saw that the theater was deserted—just rows and rows of vacant seats. I'd been here before when there were only ten or fifteen people, but had never seen the place completely empty. After a minute, though, I became aware that I wasn't alone, that in fact I had sat down next to someone—an auburn-haired girl, it was, who sat frozen (or so I imagined) in the seat to my right. Tasting panic, I swung my head around, quickly scanning the theater, and realized that, yes indeed, we were the only two people there.

I felt embarrassed. No, I felt mortified. She probably thought I was making a move or something, otherwise why would I choose the one seat next to her, when I had my pick of five hundred others? I thought I would explain, telling her I hadn't been able to see, I didn't mean to violate her space, and probably it would be best if I made some little joke, like "You keep the right half of the theater, I'll take the left," and then got up and changed my seat. But something stopped me. She did seem frightened, sitting there motionless, scrunched about as far away from me as she could get, and of course her arm nowhere near our common armrest. Did she think I was dangerous? Some sex-starved wacko wandered in from the street? What kind of man goes to the movies at two o'clock on a weekday? And *The Heiress* wasn't exactly a male sort of picture—I must have ulterior motives. All this ran through my head but by now, of course, it was too late to say anything. I'd made a show of stretching out, and digging into my popcorn, and giving every possible sign of being sanely involved in watching the movie.

Which meant, of course, that the movie was ruined for both of us. We were both pretending to watch but were distracted out of our minds by our sitting there together, two strangers, alone in this big theater, neither of us willing or able to change our seats without making, I guess, some sort of unwholesome admission about ourselves. She was probably imagining, "He'll think I'm some weak scared female if I get up and move, or leave, and he's probably just an ordinary guy, maybe he didn't even *mean* to sit by me." And I was thinking, "If I move now, she'll think she ran me off, that I really *was* coming on to her but got discouraged because of the way she's sitting there with the coat wrapped around her, her arms folded tight over her chest, like she has gold bricks under there." Every few seconds I glanced over from the corner of my eye and she did look attractive, small-framed with reddish curly hair and glasses, not dorky glasses but little round rimless ones, she might even be pretty but this frozen posture of hers was so annoying, so unnecessary. I didn't think she'd even blinked or breathed since I sat down.

By the time Olivia had gotten infatuated with Monty, though, I'd given up all hope of following the movie. In fact, something odd happened: I'd started enjoying this bizarre situation, sitting next to this paralyzed girl, more than I'd have enjoyed the movie itself. I couldn't deny it: her fear had caused me to swell with a sense of power. Now I was glad I hadn't changed my seat during that first minute or two, when I had the chance. I sat there with a little smirk on my face—the expression a dangerous man would wear, I guess—and had fantasies of turning casually to her and saying, "We've got to stop meeting like this." Or, "I always take this seat—always. *But I guess you knew that.*" Or more, suggestively, "I almost wore my raincoat, too. If I'd known you would be here…"

But of course I didn't speak, just sat there snickering to myself, feeling crafty and superior. During those minutes Sheila left my thoughts for the first time since our loud, lacerating argument the previous weekend.

The fight had started after Sheila gave me the shock of my life. People break up every day, so why was I shocked?—it was the very weekend, such is my luck, when I'd planned to suggest that we move in together. This was April and since Christmas everything had been perfect, we'd spent nearly every hour together when we weren't in class or working our grad student jobs (mine in the library, hers at a woman's clothing "boutique" half a mile from campus) and almost every night together, too, alternating her place and mine. I preferred my own surroundings, my own bed, but Sheila liked everything to appear *equal.* Fifty-fifty. A two-way street. Exactly half the time, she said, I should adapt to *her* reality. She wasn't going to become my appendage. She wasn't a stick of furniture. Nor was she a dishwasher: we shared all such chores. If we were running late and I had to leave for class before the dishes were done, she'd stop washing, too—she wouldn't finish without me. Two days later when I came back they'd still be there, in six inches of scummy gray water, and we'd pick up where we let off, Sheila acting like it was the most natural thing in the world instead of this stingy, obsessive game.

"Hey, let's don't keep score," I said once, when she complained that lately I'd been having three orgasms to her one, but that remark got me frozen out for nearly a week.

Sheila was a petite, dark-haired girl with big glowing eyes that could shine with tears one moment and turn to black ice the next. Her tiny white shoulder, with its lovely curve inward to her fragile collarbone and perfect small breasts, could suggest the heft of an iceberg when it shifted away from me in bed, the smooth expanse of her back an untouchable white negative to my warm, aching fingers. Okay, I'd say snidely, but not out loud, we'll buy a ledger book and have running tallies of money spent, dishes washed, and orgasms owed, just please don't leave me here drifting on my side of the bed.

Except for such incidents, though, our life both in bed and out had made Sheila, for the past few months, seem the one safe haven in a world I sensed as increasingly fraught with peril. Already I knew, though I hadn't admitted it to myself, that grad school wasn't going to work out, and my parents' acrimonious divorce when I was a teenager hadn't held out a great deal of hope for the consolations of domestic life. Yet with Sheila, who had seemed when I met her so glamorous and turbulent—she was, after all, an actress—it seemed that I had calmed and won over some element of life that had always seemed threatening and untameable, and far more power-ful than I could ever be. This was the reason, I guess, for the stranglehold of emotion I experienced whenever I saw her on stage. Never did I love her more passionately, more recklessly, than when she was playing someone else. These were drama department productions, edged with the self-consciousness of apprentices straining for greatness, but Sheila (the department's acknowledged "star") always outshone her surroundings. The role itself didn't matter. The angry befuddlement of Hedda Gabler, the serene altruism of Cordelia, the dazed self-immolation of O'Neill's mother as she journeyed into night—no matter whom she played, Sheila's hot glistening eyes and wavering flutelike voice brought all her characters to the same fever of incandescent passion, whether of rage or love or soul-destroying hatred, the words or situation mattering so much less than Sheila's tiny flamelike radiance on the stage, pulsing with energy, irresistible. Like everyone else in the audience, I watched her every move. At times it seemed Sheila fed on the inconsequent energies of the nameless crowd huddled invisible beyond the footlights, our power willingly sacrificed to hers, so that she might express the bold words we dared not imagine, the frightening passions we dared not feel.

It was after one of her performances (as Nora in *A Doll's House,* the slam of that infernal door still ringing in my ears) that I decided the time had come: I wanted her to move in with me, I wanted to buy her a ring if she didn't think it was too bourgeois, I wanted us to start thinking about getting married. I knew what she would say—that I was trying to "trap" her—but I would point out this wasn't a final commitment, we weren't saying "I do" but only "maybe I will," and if she wasn't happy she could always move out. But before I could even pose the question, she turned her small pert head and gazed off into the distance (we were in a crowded Italian place, red tablecloths and glowing candles, one of our favorites because it was both cheap and atmospheric) and paused a beat, two beats, before saying in a soft, rueful voice, "Chet, I've decided to move—I'm moving to Asheville."

It didn't help that I knew she was acting, even now—that her timing had been flawless, both the pause and the tone of her delivery precisely calibrated, the script improvised but self-conscious, the taut face she now turned toward me (still flushed from that night's performance) ready for its close-up as I sat there chumpy and nameless, expected to make the best of a thankless bit part. I could feel the blood draining out of my head, and I think my mouth was open.

"But—but what—" I stammered. "Why would…"

Sheila's phantom director had decided she ought now to take pity, let her eyes fill with the generous, fond remembrance of our shared but insufficient love, maybe reach across the table and squeeze my hand. Sensing this, I withdrew my hands to my lap where they curled abruptly into fists.

"Come on, don't look so grumpy," Sheila said. "You know what this means, don't you?—it's a chance that won't come again. It's only for a year, Chet, and it doesn't have to change anything. It's not even that far from here—you can come up on weekends. We'll have a great time! The managing director called last night—he's the *nicest* guy—"

And she went on to tell me about this experimental theater company that offered a fellowship each year to a promising young actor. She'd get to do a broad range of work, cutting-edge people came down from New York every season to check out the company's new productions, it was all so exciting so fantastic and I was happy for her, wasn't I? I didn't want to hold her back, did I?

These weren't answerable questions so I just said, dully, "You didn't even tell me you'd applied. Did you."

"Chet, I apply for all kinds of things—all of us do. The competition is so fierce that you don't really expect—" She stopped herself. She moved back slightly in her chair—just an inch or two. "You don't take me seriously, do you?" she said. The corners of her eyes slanted upward when she was angry, as though pulled by strings. Or when she was pretending to be angry. Her cheekbones seemed to sharpen. "Did you think acting was just a hobby, just a college 'major,' and that once I graduated I'd take some ordinary job and get married to some—" She broke off. "Didn't you think I was *serious* about my work? Chet?"

I stared at her. Despite the ache in my chest, I offered my line with an understated drollery. "I guess I was too ordinary. To understand such things."

She rolled her eyes; she grinned, as though I were being a difficult child. "Come on," she said again, "don't act this way. This has nothing to do with *us*—it doesn't have to change anything."

"Right," I said mildly. "You mentioned that."

I went home that night in the kind of raving, wild-eyed despair you can feel only in your twenties. Back in my cramped apartment, dustballs in the corners and the usual pile of dishes in the sink, I felt like a student out of Dostoyevsky, ready to murder the next old lady I came across. Instead I cleaned the apartment, slowly and methodically, and for the rest of the weekend stared at a half-written paper on the tricky relationship between the last Russian Czar, Nicholas II, and his cousin George VI, who refused the Czar and his family sanctuary in England. They were massacred a short while later, of course, and so much for family feeling. In my own misery I felt strangely attracted to the topic, but the words wouldn't come.

Monday rolled around, and though I had an appointment with my graduate adviser I spent the day in bed. I tried calling Sheila until past midnight, growing more jealous and desperate with each call, but no answer. Fortunately, these were the days before answering machines, for no telling what message I might have left. The next day I tried calling my older brother in Tampa, but his wife said he'd just left for a business trip and would be back Thursday night. (I didn't know his wife very well, so I couldn't dump on her.) My two best friends in Atlanta, roommates who lived in my building, were also out of town, on a camping trip with their girlfriends. Since I had no taste for solitary drinking, the only escape I could imagine for my Tuesday afternoon was a trip to the Silver Screen, where I found myself sitting beside that poor woman, both of us alone and in the dark, both frozen into roles we hadn't chosen and didn't quite know how to play.

The surge of adrenaline I'd experienced, that primitive sense of power you feel when someone else is afraid of you, was short-lived. As the movie plodded forward, the painful throbbing of my heart had reasserted itself, my mind's eye assaulted by lurid images of Sheila with someone else ("the managing director called last night—he's the *nicest* guy"), though I was trying hard to follow the movie. Even when I succeeded, Olivia's trials brought no relief. It didn't matter, of course, that she was a woman: we were going through the same thing, we were both romantic fools, we both deserved our fate. But as the movie wound up, I knew that Olivia had quickly outpaced me in hardening herself, as she finally succeeded in doing, to the likes of dimpled Monty. By now, Olivia's rich father had died, and though the two never reconciled he didn't disinherit her, after all. She was now a rich woman, possessed of a mansion on Washington Square and a mountain of cash, but alone. After Monty, no other man had come along. In the final scenes, Monty comes back to town, claiming he'd gone away to seek his fortune, wanting to be worthy of her, though by now we have to assume he's just the same opportunist as before, returning only because Olivia now has the money and no hawk-eyed father to mess things up. That's when it dawns on you: why shouldn't she marry him? Wouldn't that be better than living alone in that hulking mausoleum of a house? Isn't a late-arriving, imperfect love better than none at all? And it seems Olivia decides that's the case, for she agrees to see Monty and then accepts his ardent proposal, telling him to come back for her later that night. They're going to elope! That wild, passionate honeymoon of Olivia's long-ago dreams is going to happen after all! But the movie ends with Monty knocking frantically on the bolted door, and Olivia ascending the staircase alone, a candle in one hand, her eyes glazed with a look of suicidal determination. Now that her heart had died, Olivia had closed up shop. She didn't want Monty and she didn't want anybody else, either. She couldn't trust or love anyone again, so her life was over. The movie was over, too.

Slowly the lights came up, and I shook myself out of the foggy mixed emotions that had descended during those last scenes of *The Heiress*. Despite myself, I'd finally gotten involved in the movie and had forgotten about the poor scared girl sitting next to me. I sat forward in my seat, ready to bolt out of there, but something held me back. Though we were strangers, it seemed rude to just get up and walk out, especially since the girl still sat there, staring at the screen, arms crossed, making no gesture toward leaving. Whether I liked it or not, our being there alone in the theater, just the two of us watching the movie, had created a bond between us. I had to say something.

So I decided to explain, finally, about sitting next to her—just to be sure she understood.

"When I first came in," I said, turning stiffly in her direction, "I couldn't see—" But I stopped. The girl still hadn't moved, but there was something I hadn't realized: she was crying. Not sobbing, not shaking, just staring motionless at the now-blank screen with tears streaking down her face. She didn't look at me or acknowledge me in any way.

If I'd had any sense, I guess, I'd just have mumbled "Sorry," and quietly gotten up and walked out. But again something held me back. Though I wasn't thinking this at the time, not in so many words, I could plainly see—any idiot could have—that she'd been badly hurt, that here was another human being, suffering. Maybe her situation even resembled mine, maybe she'd gotten her heart smashed to bits. Now that the lights were up, I could see that she *was* fairly attractive, her reddish hair done in a sort of Orphan Annie cut, her skin milky-pale with freckles, her body underneath the raincoat graceful-seeming, slender. Not beautiful, but cute. Maybe a cheerleader in high school, perky and popular, with a name like Cindy, or Susie. But now her damp blue eyes looked almost deadened by pain. The tears kept coming, but she didn't wipe at them and still hadn't acknowledged me.

"Um, I guess the movie really got to you—yes?"

No answer.

"I hope I didn't—I mean, I didn't mean to violate your space, or to bother you—"

I broke off, understanding that I was bothering her now. But I couldn't stop.

"See, I guess it sort of got to me, too, because I've been going with this girl, her name is Sheila..." And I kept talking, though the girl gave no indication that she was listening at all. She just kept staring at the blank screen, quietly weeping. But for some reason the situation no longer felt awkward. I sat there and in a calm, reasonable voice told the girl everything that had happened between me and Sheila.

It didn't take long—maybe three minutes, five minutes. It must have been a relief, it must have felt wonderful, otherwise why would I have done it?—though I can't quite remember what I felt. It must have been the kind of emotion peculiar to one moment, urgent and essential and deeply strange, never to be experienced or even remembered again. The romantics among you, at this point, listening to this in the same way I was watching *The Heiress*, might be supposing, or hoping, that I invited that girl in the theater out for coffee, and we hit it off and eventually got together, happily ever after, etc. But I'm afraid not. Once I got to the part where Sheila told me about moving to Asheville a big lump rose in my throat, surprising the hell out of me, and I realized I was about to cry, too. So I got up and ran out of the theater. I went home and called Sheila, tried to talk her out of moving, failed, asked if there was another man involved in all this, was told there wasn't, and decided I would try to make the best of a long-distance relationship. She moved a few weeks later, and the situation gradually unraveled. I drove up every weekend, of course, but then she insisted on every other weekend—she needed space, I was smothering her—and by the middle of the summer the visits were worse than the time I spent alone in Atlanta. Each time we made love, it became for me a desperate effort to reclaim her, while for Sheila it just seemed a chore. On that Sunday afternoon in August when she finally said, "Chet, we've really got to talk," I was almost relieved.

Romantics are said to be incurable, so I did go back to that theater, sometimes several times a week, but I never saw the girl again. She'd never spoken a word or acknowledged me, but still I knew that I'd failed her. Or maybe I'd spared her? Who knows but that we might have fallen in love, that I craved the treasures of kindness, sympathy, understanding she kept so well-protected under her raincoat, and that once I'd taken my fill I might have skipped out, no less treacherous than Monty Clift, just one more of the random dangers you find in the world's every corner, even in an empty movie theater on a weekday afternoon? Instead I got married, had kids, became reasonably happy teaching history to bored middle-schoolers, though I know by now that the history books are nothing but lies and I can't teach the kids anything worth knowing. I'll never know their private histories and they'll never know mine, and what other kind of history is there?

Even my wife, a self-confident woman famous for her loud, bracing laugh, has no idea that late at night, on the rare occasion when she cries in my arms, I'm sometimes holding an actress I once loved, at other times consoling a nameless red-haired orphan I found stranded that day at the movies and with whom I shared an intimate couple of hours unequaled in my life before or since. We're playing our own parts, that girl and I, struggling through our own lines as well as anybody, but neither of us, I hope, can quite give up that moment in 1973, when our hearts stop as we watch Olivia de Havilland mounting that darkened staircase, alone. Her face has become ours: eerily bright in the candle's flame, fronting the darkness as she ascends implacably, ignoring that faint but dangerous knocking from the terrible world downstairs.

And we ignore it, too. We stay with Olivia. We watch her every step of the way.

Alliances of Youth

They were in league against me: I felt that from the moment I arrived.

Aunt Veronica, whom I could never call "Ronnie," so ample of bosom and leg, swathed in layers of heavy, stifling black despite the September heat.

Carole Ann, Barrie's "long-time fiancée," as the local newspaper had it (this far south, a small-town paper could still employ such a euphemism), a woman who, strung along by my cousin for more than two decades, now had a sallow, absent look, as though the years of waiting had cast a glaze upon her features.

We stood in baggage claim, three entirely dissimilar women unrelated to one another except through Barrie, who had died unexpectedly of heart failure three days before, at the age of thirty-eight. Yet almost at once I did sense a relation. When I left the South, twenty years ago, Veronica had been a grim, commanding woman who felt that no one—and certainly not the slight, rather fey Carole Ann—was good enough for her darling Barrie, while Carole Ann, thinking very mistakenly that Veronica's inelastic will alone stood between herself and connubial bliss, had played the miffed and ill-used heroine to the hilt. (Barrie, mischievous as always, loved telling me of their latest contretemps—a snide remark at the dinner table, for instance, from his mother, followed by Carole Ann's swift, disdainful exit from the room. At that time,

I was hardly an unwilling confidante.) Encased in her heavy mourning, Veronica now looked stolid but rather pitiable, like a fallen idol, while Carole Ann, still pretty in her way, gave the impression that Barrie's death had not really surprised her, but had only confirmed a long-acknowledged fate. It was a static quality, I suppose, that somehow united them; something in their empty, fish-eyed stares.

"You both—you both look wonderful."

They didn't respond, at first; and I stood rooted, a bit shocked that I'd spoken insincerely.

A long moment, then a wan smile from Carole Ann.

"We're glad you could come. We decided to invite you, if we invited anyone."

"It's going to be small, mostly family," Veronica added, as if issuing a pronouncement.

I wasn't really "family," of course, since Veronica already had Barrie when she married my Uncle Rex; in fact, Barrie once said that his mother had warned him of me. "Warned you? What do you mean?" I asked. Barrie glanced away, slyly. "*You* know," he said.

"Really, I think it's just us three," said Carole Ann.

I spotted my bags, slowly approaching on the conveyor belt, and used the moment to ponder their invitation once again. At best, I'd felt they acted out of some dim, vestigial notion of Southern propriety; at worst, out of a long-cherished and perhaps unconscious malevolence. Their apparent collusion edged me toward the latter. (Although the question I should have been pondering, of course, was why I had accepted, and so eagerly.)

During the long drive into the hilly, parched-looking countryside, we tried to make pleasant conversation. They asked about my teaching, of course, and I launched into a glowing description of the private girls' academy in Bucks County, Pennsylvania, where I'd spent most of the years since my rather abrupt departure—though I deliberately did not tell them that I'd become headmistress more than three years ago (perhaps because this connoted a certain prim, fussy self-sufficiency, along with a hopeless spinsterhood). They seemed impressed and interested, though I felt that Veronica saw through me. She drove in her cold, efficient style, her profile etched in steel as she listened, the large diamond Barrie had given her on his eighteenth birthday (one of his eccentricities, of which he was so vain, was the habit of buying Veronica a present for his own birthday: "a compensatory gesture," he'd said one year, bowing gallantly) glinting near the top of the steering wheel. Carole Ann sat crushed between us, slump-shouldered, fiddling with a kerchief in her lap. I kept putting fingertips to my brow, to the back of my hairline: the humidity and heat were nearly overpowering. Veronica kept the windows of her late-model Cadillac rolled up, but had not turned on the air conditioner.

"It must be strange, coming back home," said Veronica in a still, even voice. "Things must be quite different up there."

"Yes indeed," echoed Carole Ann. "I remember that winter, after Barrie went up—why, the stories he told! The terrible snowstorms, and all the traffic. And the people being so unpleasant."

"Except for Ruth, of course," said Veronica, indulgently. She smiled across at me. "Of course, he didn't mean you."

Carole Ann wrinkled her brow, as if dimly aware that her meaning had been distorted.

"No, of course not," she said. "Heaven knows, Ruth is one of us."

"Though he did express his fears, Ruth, that you'd been 'converted.'" Veronica gave her dry, croaking laugh.

"Well, I have my work," I said, with calculated brevity. Had they brought me here simply to find out, at last, what had transpired during Barrie's month-long stay in Philadelphia, nearly two decades before? I'd received letters from both Carole Ann and Veronica shortly after Barrie returned home, Carole Ann's wondering coyly and Veronica's demanding outright to know what was the matter with him, what happened to the charming Barrie they'd known and loved, had I gotten some kind of power over him? I hadn't answered the letters.

"Yes, you have that," Carole Ann said philosophically.

A thin film of sweat had covered my face; I felt that I could scarcely breathe.

"One thing we don't have up north," I said, trying to sound polite and offhand, "is this terrible heat. It's a sweltering day, isn't it?"

An interminable two hours passed before we reached the house. Carole Ann remarked that she didn't mind the heat, though she spoke absently, as if her thoughts were elsewhere. Veronica raised her eyebrows, sympathetically, but didn't reply. Nor did she offer to start the air conditioner.

The house, more than a century old, had been in the family for less than thirty years, my late Uncle Rex having been prompted by his new wife and a cynical, precocious, eleven-year-old Barrie to set them up in proper style, with all the trappings of Southern gothicism. Shading the sinuous front drive (full of potholes, and threatened on both sides by thick crabgrass and kudzu) were a number of stately, decayed-looking trees; there was an imposing front veranda, complete with white columns and a creaking swing; from the third story, turrets jutted out like gaping, disconsolate eyes. There was even, dear God, a tight-lipped housekeeper, her black hair parted severely down the middle and plastered against her skull, whose every gesture seemed distinct with menace. Before leaving school for the airport, I'd joked with one of my colleagues that I'd be staying in a "mouldering mansion" while down South, and had even given a mock shudder. In truth, I'd carefully prepared myself for the dispiriting atmosphere of this house that Barrie somehow could never leave. I was not prepared, however, for the nature of what Veronica, with uncharacteristic vagueness, termed "the arrangements."

Quite simply, they had arranged that Barrie's remains should be displayed in the front parlor. To an outside observer, this might seem merely old-fashioned; or, at the worst, fantastically distasteful. I felt confirmed, however, in suspecting that the two women were somehow ranged against me, for neither of them told me that Barrie's open casket waited in the house. This might have been merely stupid of Carole Ann, but it was certainly disingenuous of Veronica. I could imagine her playing and replaying in her mind the rather embarrassed, unsavory scene that did in fact occur.

It was later that evening, some four or five hours after I arrived. I'd wandered downstairs after my nap, hoping for some sign of dinner, for I'd awakened ravenously hungry. Near the base of the stairs, the main hall had entrances on either side to a pair of great front rooms, identical in size and shape (at the time this house was built, symmetry had been the chief criterion of good taste), both high-ceilinged, stiffish, cool. Before proceeding back toward the kitchen, I peered expectantly into the dining room with its magnificent cherrywood hutch and table, its stately chairs poised upon ball and claw, its heavy draperies. Though the room looked well-maintained, I felt that no meals had been taken here for a very long time. (Even ages ago, when I was a mere girl who felt herself a shadow in the house, all except holiday meals were in the big breakfast room off the kitchen. But Barrie and I, occasionally alone in the house, would hold elaborate mock-formal dinners in here, Barrie got up in his dead stepfather's old tux, in which he looked astonishingly handsome, while I wore some jeweled and high-necked thing of Veronica's, laughable because it was several sizes too large. Though her dresses, I supposed, would fit well enough now.) Unsettled, I stepped back into the hall, but could not resist the other room, either; the ancient, sumptuously decorated "parlor" where infrequent guests of the family were entertained, where Carole Ann for long years had tortured the grand piano with her tinkling melodies, and where Barrie and I, though nearly out of our teens, had played hide-and-seek among the hulking furniture, the ornately carved screens, the window seats so capacious that their drawn curtains might conceal a dozen men. It was in this room, as imposing now as when I was a girl, that I saw flanking one wall a plain low table that supported, unmistakably, a large and dully gleaming coffin with its lid opened wide.

Before I had time to think, to react with my customary caution or mistrust, I was standing above the coffin, staring balefully down. Nearly twenty years had passed since his visit to Philadelphia; after that we had exchanged no letters, not even a card or photograph at Christmas. Yet here he was, my Barrie, unchanged but for a few silver streaks in the dark, well-cut hair, a couple of shallow creases in the broad forehead, and a slight puffiness to the cheeks and sealed eyelids. The severe, midnight-blue suit only enhanced his youthfulness. He might be a boy, temporarily well-behaved, dressed for a birthday party; he might be the same lovable, prankish Barrie, lying so utterly still only to open his sparkling cornflower-blue eyes to shout "Boo!" and release an impish laugh.

My Barrie.

Behind me came a soft footfall, but I didn't move my damp eyes even when I heard Carole Ann whisper, in a reverent tone, "He looks wonderful, doesn't he, Ruth?"

I'd been about to reach down, stroke the side of his cheek or the lovely dark hair; but now I breathed deeply. I cleared my throat.

"Of course," I said, with sudden bitterness. "But why wasn't I told?"

"Told?"

"That he was—that he—"

A tiny, sharp exclamation escaped Carole Ann: "Oh!"

I shook my head, uncaring that two or three tears had streaked across my cheekbones, deriving a morose pleasure from Carole Ann's apparent shock. Did she think me incapable of tears?

"Never mind," I said, wiping roughly at my face. "I just didn't expect it."

"Oh, Ruth, I just assumed that Ronnie had told you. I mean, when she telephoned—"

"She said the arrangements were made. She didn't specify."

I tried to keep the rancor from my voice, for I felt a grudging conviction that Carole Ann was innocent in this; that she could be charged, at the worst, with an unthinking complicity. It had always been the dragon Veronica who ran this house and the lives of its tenants.

Carole Ann had begun to whimper, almost noiselessly. A dry, desperate sound, not unlike a hiccough. Stiffly, I turned and took her small ringless hand. She was gazing woefully down at Barrie.

"He's so—so beautiful, isn't he?" she said, in a kind of disconsolate rapture. "Even now?"

"Yes," I said, uncomfortably. I wanted to release her hand, but now I felt trapped in the gesture, as though committed to some unspoken bond. I felt the need to keep talking.

"He never aged, somehow," I added. "He looks twenty-five, twenty-six at the most. He looks like a college kid."

If my tone had become sardonic, it didn't faze Carole Ann. "Oh, I know," she whispered. "Whenever people met us, they'd always ask if Barrie was a college student—and of course he'd say yes. On the spot, he'd invent some fictional college and go into all kinds of detail, saying with a straight face that he majored in astrology, or sexology, or that he'd gone out for cheerleader this past spring but had lost. And he'd look so downcast. And the poor guest would just stand there, gaping."

Despite herself, Carole Ann wore a faraway smile. She reached down, lightly touching Barrie's fingers with her own.

"That sounds like Barrie," I said. "But what *did* he do with himself, all these years?"

Carole Ann frowned, as if this were an odd question. "Do? Well, you know, Ruth, just what he always did, even when you lived here. Supervised the house and the landscaping, helped Veronica with her finances, her investments…. Played master of the house when anyone came to visit—friends of Ronnie's, you know, or old cronies of your uncle."

Her voice had tightened, as though she felt the need to defend Barrie.

"He stayed very busy, really," she said. "Toward the end of the week he'd usually go into Atlanta, to meet with Ronnie's broker, or her lawyers…sometimes he'd be gone until Sunday night."

"Big cities fascinated him, didn't they?" I said, but I confined my sarcasm to a curling lower lip, which Carole Ann couldn't see. After all, she'd been hurt enough. I added, gently, "He loved Philadelphia, too. For the brief time he was there."

It was then that Carole Ann, still gazing down at Barrie with her eyes misted over, almost casually said, "Yes, he talked about that all the time, and about *you*. He truly admired you, Ruth. Your independence, I think. And your being so smart."

I laughed, sharply. I dropped her hand.

"Oh, now don't act so surprised," she said, and I could not help but recognize that particular asperity in her voice: the familiar, brittle jealousy that Carole Ann had suffered almost from the moment she met Barrie.

"Carole Ann, I really don't think—"

"No, I know that he worshiped you," said Carole Ann, giving me a look of rueful honesty. "I always felt that I had to measure up to you, somehow. And that I'd always fail."

"Carole Ann, please don't cry," I said tightly.

"It was always 'Ruth this, Ruth that.' Always 'the time I visited Ruth, in Philadelphia.' There were days when I wanted to say, Go on back up there, then! Go live with your wonderful cousin!" She sobbed for a moment; then her voice came low and penitent. "But I was afraid he'd do it. And guilty, too, because I could never make him happy."

My gaze fell again to Barrie, in whose stilled features I no longer saw the bright, high-spirited child I'd known. I wanted to slap the waxen cheek, demand an explanation as I've done so many times with especially sullen or willful students back at school.

"But I guess—I guess Barrie was already happy," said Carole Ann, sadly.

And I replied, sharply, "Maybe not."

In any case, neither of us was really listening to the other. Carole Ann kept touching Barrie's fingers with an insipid, forlorn look of pity.

"Listen, it's nearly seven," I said, irritated. "Where is Veronica? What time do you people eat dinner?"

My appetite is the one thing I can depend on, for it carries on efficiently, not to say relentlessly, regardless of the state of my mind or health. It has proved equally impervious to depression, stressful conditions, sudden shifts of environment, or poorly cooked food. All these appetite-suppressing elements were present during my visit, and still I ate. That first night, an underdone roast beef. The following day, just before the two o'clock funeral, a luncheon of inexplicably greasy fried chicken, charred black in places, served with large helpings of tepid and watery black-eyed peas. Coffee that no amount of cream could lighten, leaving a bitter residue near the back of the tongue that lingered for hours. Since several guests had been invited for the funeral baked meats later that afternoon, I dared to suppose that the housekeeper, Mrs. Hodges, might make a special effort to see that the ham was served hot, the fruit salad and butter kept cold; but this witless assumption quickly died when she issued from the kitchen, wearing a fearsome scowl and a filthy apron, carrying a platter of ham that might have been sliced with a hacksaw. No one dared to comment, not even Veronica; we took the large, oddly shaped hunks of meat with an air of deference and gentle thanks. After the ham came an unexpectedly festive dish of sweet potatoes covered with marshmallows, though the marshmallows unfortunately had not melted and proved to be quite stale. Then the warm fruit salad. Then the black-eyed peas, again, even more watery than at lunch. Finally, more of the coffee into which one poured cream as into a bottomless well.

Yet I sampled everything, and even had seconds of the peas. Since my arrival, I'd begun to experience a peculiar lack of self-consciousness: appraising my naked, rather bloated frame in the bedroom mirror that morning, I'd thought only in passing of how radically this image of middle-aged complacency, which would soon present itself for the last time to Barrie, differed from the thin, nervous, laughing girl who'd once chased him about this house. Nor had I cared to present any but my rather abrupt, moody self to those long-suffering partners of his existence, Veronica and Carole Ann. And now, surrounded by strangers, having just seen my life's single bright object of passion dropped into black earth, I contentedly ate. It was mostly an awkward, stiff company, so there was little to do but eat. There were people like myself, who knew no one, and others who seemed to know each other all too well. So there were two kinds of silence, uneasily blended. Veronica tried to maintain a semblance of conversation, but the results were brittle and uncertain, like the notes of a child struggling through his first piece on the piano.

"He looked lovely, don't you think?" she said for the third or fourth time, though "lovely" had no place in her usual vocabulary.

"Oh yes!" breathed Carole Ann, whose fork, bearing three black-eyed peas, trembled aloft.

The local minister, a young, full-faced, rather wistful and hapless young man named Reverend Cray, vehemently nodded. "A fine-looking young man," he agreed. "So pleasant and well-mannered."

He gave a benign, avuncular smile, though he appeared at least a decade younger than Barrie had been.

"And so talented, too," said a neighbor (the nearest house was three miles away) who'd been introduced as Mrs. Nesbitt. She was a bony, perky woman in her sixties; her black cloche sported a plum-colored feather. "Bursting with talent, really."

This boundless hyperbole distracted my attention from the sweet potatoes. Innocent and ignorant, "family" flown in for the funeral, I could ask: "Really? What talents were those?"

Mrs. Nesbitt, it was clear, owned an intractable faith in her own observations; she smiled brilliantly. "Oh, all sorts of things," she said. "He could do—well, anything he wanted. We always said that."

Mr. Nesbitt was a quiet, silver-haired man who resembled a rabbit. "A right nice boy," he said, looking melancholy. "And in the flower of his youth."

Even his wife seemed startled by this unexpected poetry. "Yes," she said, her eyes bulging. "He could have done anything."

"He was always so helpful," someone else said.

"And such a good sense of humor!"

"Very selfless, too. Especially for such a young man."

"Oh yes—so sweet and thoughtful. Why, one day, for no reason at all, he came over with some flowers—a bright bunch of zinnias."

"So charming. Quick-witted, too."

"And handsome—let's not forget that! Those big blue eyes."

"Always smiling, always humming a gay tune."

"And never a cross word. Not in all the years I knew him."

"Never!"—the word came like a chorus, an emphatic *amen.*

Then Mrs. Nesbitt, who still looked a bit dazed by the bright bunch of zinnias, said rushingly to me: "And you were terribly close, weren't you? Despite your having moved so far away?"

This was not a question of course but rhetoric, another item in the litany of Barrie's praise, but as my appetite became sated so had my indulgence proved short-lived. "Close?" I said. "Hardly. We hadn't communicated in many years."

All seemed to slump a little in their chairs—all but Mrs. Nesbitt. "But I know you were!" she cried. She wagged her finger, as though I were being naughty, and performed her favorite gesture of ducking her head, as one ducks when laughing uncontrollably. With each duck, the purple feather came closer to her untouched cup of coffee.

And now Veronica, unexpectedly, took my side. "It *has* been quite a few years," she said, "since we lost Ruth."

"Oh yes, it's been *too* many years!" echoed Carole Ann.

I looked at them, the familiar pang of suspicion—of jealousy—smarting no less keenly now that Barrie was gone. They'd never forgiven me for leaving, of course; for nearly succeeding in drawing him out of their lives forever. Against only one of them I might have succeeded, but as an alliance they were unbeatable, as through these long years of mutual dislike and mistrust they had doubtless come bleakly to know. I had crawled out on my limb, had played my long shot, and had crashed. Now, of course, they were mocking me, indulging their sweet privilege; why else had I come?

"But it's true that Barrie and I were close, long ago," I said to Mrs. Nesbitt. "That's why I'm here."

Reverend Cray bobbed his head. "Family feeling," he said, sagely. "It doesn't fade away."

Both Veronica and Carole Ann glanced in my direction.

"But you knew, Reverend Cray," I said politely, "that we weren't blood relatives?"

"Well, I suppose—I mean, I had always gathered—" Flustered, he broke off.

"See, what did I tell you?" Mrs. Nesbitt said gaily, if somewhat cryptically, to the company at large.

"But they were just like brother and sister," Carole Ann said. "They grew up together, sort of."

Reverend Cray, who had recovered himself, smiled at me. "I didn't know," he said.

Didn't know that we weren't blood relatives, or that we had grown up together, sort of? I frowned at him.

"Ever since then, she's been a schoolteacher," Carole Ann said. She had assumed the knowledgeable, slightly pompous air of a tour guide through the family's history.

"We've certainly missed her," Veronica sighed. "And so did Barrie."

"Oh yes!" added Carole Ann.

There was a scattered murmuring of agreement, but the group's attention had wandered. Reverend Cray was downing the last of his coffee, and Mrs. Nesbitt delicately patted her mouth with her napkin. The meal was over. Mrs. Hodges had entered from the kitchen, bringing along her air of intense disapproval, and had begun clearing the dishes.

My heart pounded. Various rebukes, sarcasms, and imprecations rose in my throat, but I could not choose among them. The moment passed. All at once I felt Barrie's presence—blithe spirit extraordinaire, prankish poltergeist, presiding genius over this comedy of errors. That drizzly morning in Philadelphia, outside the train station, he had indeed said to me: "I'll miss you, Ruthie. God knows I will." A tear had gleamed in his eye, and I'd wanted desperately to lash out—to say something witty and devastating, something unanswerable. But the opportunity passed, and I'd watched his fawn-colored raincoat recede, with a swarm of fellow travelers, into the cavelike recesses of the station. Shakily, I had walked away. Shakily, I now stood up, and before hurrying from the room I said, in a quavering voice, "Excuse me, I'm going to be sick."

But I was not sick; I didn't take the time. I left by the main entrance and began striding rapidly along the winding front drive. I didn't care that Veronica, Carole Ann and the others might be peering out the windows, clicking their tongues. I rushed along, at once bold and furtive. The graveyard was less than a mile down the main road.

The day was sultry, the reddish-brown earth seemed to radiate waves of moist heat, and my stomach did feel queasy. I took deep breaths as I walked; with one palm I wiped the sweat from my cheeks, my forehead. They had lowered Barrie's silver-toned casket into the cool, deep-delved earth, six or eight feet down, and now I saw him lying in that utter dark, crisply attired in the midnight-blue suit, imperturbable. Reverend Cray had mumbled a few words, reading from a damp, much worked-over sheet of legal paper crushed in his hands. Veronica's head was bowed. Carole Ann had groaned, like a wounded animal. Oh Barrie, how cleverly you have escaped us all!

Reaching the main road, I slowed my pace; I even considered turning back. A quick, murmured explanation, and everyone saying that *of course* they understood. But no. Something I preach to my girls, endlessly: Follow through. There is no awkwardness, no indignity like a half-completed gesture. Halfway along a tightrope, one doesn't hesitate or look down; one doesn't pause to reconsider—! Not even if there's a net, which there isn't.

When Barrie and I were young, we used to play a game that Barrie called "Trust." It was the simple game of standing perfectly straight with your eyes closed, the other person behind you, and letting yourself fall backward, freely, trusting him to catch you in his arms. In truth, I disliked this game. Not because Barrie delighted in teasing me—shouting happily that I was a coward on those days when, unable to entrust myself even to Barrie, an insuperable reflex made my arms spring out behind me during the free-fall; or, when I was more reckless or brave, waiting until the *very last* moment, when I had fallen within inches of the ground, before scooping me in his arms and lifting me, shaky and pale, into a standing position. I'd considered it a given, I suppose, that I was cowardly, and that my salvation depended on the unearned beneficence of my cousin—which he might justifiably withdraw, at a moment's notice. Rather it was Barrie's turn that made me uncomfortable. He would accept the vulnerable role with alacrity, often clasping his hands behind his head, or stretching them forward like a somnambulist. Or he would stand with his arms crossed upon his breast, like Queequeg in his coffin. Miserably I watched his stiffened spine, and the dark-haired, vulnerable-looking back of his head. Sometimes, as he fell backward, he would let out a mock-scream, or would yell out, "Geronimo-o-o-o!" He never showed the slightest hesitation or fear, and afterward, his head cradled in my arms, I would see his great blue eyes, upside-down, opened wide in delighted laughter, for evidently I looked even more pale and terrified than when I'd taken the fall myself.

Invariably, when Barrie began to fall, two things would happen. First, I would feel suddenly incapable of catching him, sensing that my arms were not quick or strong enough to prevent his crashing to the ground. Second, I would feel a sudden reflexive twitching in my arm muscles, an unexplainable urge to *withdraw* my protection and deliberately allow him to fall. This never happened, of course, but on several occasions the impulse was quite strong. Hopelessly in love with him even then, I nonetheless disliked the free, unblinking way he entrusted himself to my care. Though he never allowed me to fall, either, I could never attain this certitude, this abnegation of control. When for no particular reason Barrie abandoned this game, never to mention it again, I felt an immense relief.

It was this same relief, I suppose, that I would experience years later, after that terrible winter of my nineteenth year, and for which

I now had such a dire, unappeasable longing. Having reached the top of the next hill, I looked back; I could just glimpse the house, glimmering whitely through the tangled mass of trees. A few steps down the other side, and it was out of view. Over the next hill, I knew, lay the scattering of gravestones—too small, really, to be called a cemetery—adjacent to a now-defunct Baptist church, its paint peeling, the wood itself rotting away. The same church on which, in his extreme youth, Barrie had heaped such open, cheerful scorn. One evening, just at twilight, we had been riding along this road with Veronica, in her stately, slow-moving car, on our way to a restaurant in the next town. Passing the church, we saw a gathering of some thirty or forty people having a cook-out, on the small strip of ground that divided the old building and the graveyard. Barrie, who despised organized religion, made some typically scathing remark—"Wouldn't it be nice" (I think it was) "if some sort of concentration camp could be set up, where they could truly flock together. Like sheep." And I giggled, nervously. "Remember, we have to live among these people," Veronica had said, sternly. "Why Mummy," Barrie said, with his best mock-aghast expression, "those weren't people—those were *Christians*." And our laughter had drifted out the back windows of Veronica's car, into the bluish twilit air.

The innocent, conspiring laughter of children, ringing out into some clear, long-past, irrecoverable evening—that sound for two decades has accompanied my heart's convulsing, blended surreally with images of his wide, ingenuous, matinee-idol face, lit with tenderness, mischief, or the slightly aggrieved look of bewilderment that was Barrie's response to the vast and hostile world surrounding us; or with his fine alto voice singing "Clementine" as we tramped together through the woods on midsummer mornings, a voice that cracked sentimentally on the refrain, "You are lost and—gone—forever—oh, my darlin'—Clementine—" and brought hot stinging tears to my eyes.

My Barrie.

I heard only vaguely the singing of tires on the main road as I turned to face the graveyard. It looked smaller now, emptied of the preacher and the mourners and the inevitable small-town gawkers and hangers-on. The old church building, mostly denuded of paint, seemed to sag in the moist late-summer's heat. Atop the reddish mound of Barrie's grave were the several dozen sprays of flowers, exotic and somehow minatory, as if they might be carnivorous; and arched over them the undertaker's canopy, a bright unnatural green, with gleaming aluminum stakes and a fringe of gold tassels. It all had a look of misplaced festivity—some lost gypsy caravan, stranded amid ruin. Around it the older graves (each decorated meagerly with its own clutch of flowers, fresh or sun-weathered) had a pathetic stoicism as the red earth received their slow deliquescence. I stared, disconsolate, remembering a visit we'd once made to a farm in the next county, where one of our school friends lived, and Barrie had turned to me and said, with a grave flourish, "Behold our Ruth, amid the alien corn!" By then we were in high school, though, and I didn't laugh. For a moment Barrie's face had that bruised, sagging look that came whenever I stepped back, primly, and let him crash to the ground—as I'd begun doing, so often. Less than two years would pass before I fled the South.

Still at the roadside, blinded, I could move forward only with an awkward, jerking motion. With flat open palms I wiped my eyes. The warm air felt heavy, gelatinous. Each step took a conscious effort as I picked my way through the maze of stones and flowers.

From behind came a solid, whacking sound: a car's door, slamming.

"Ruth— Please wait—"

I half-turned; I didn't want to face Veronica.

"Are you all right? Ruth?"

"Yes," I said coldly.

We stood a few yards from Barrie's grave, two women who had been violently weeping. For when I allowed my hot glance to brush hers, I saw that her eyes, too, were red and swollen.

I distrusted this. Even though her shoulders sagged; even though one of her brown-mottled hands reached out, in a half-imploring gesture.

"Everyone—they're all quite concerned, back at the house," she said, in a queer, ingratiating tone.

"Are they?" I answered.

"Ruth, you mustn't be angry with us," she said, so pathetically that a sudden chill passed along my arms.

"I'm not angry," I said, trying to sound casual, but it was hopeless. "All right, I'm angry. But not really with you."

She took a step forward, then reached out and let her fingers lightly brush my knuckles on one hand. Her face had the awkward, near-desperate look of one who seldom resorts to touching another person.

"Thank you," she said. "That's what Barrie would have wanted."

We both looked back to the canopy, the mound of earth and flowers.

"I mean—he would have liked to see us here, together like this," I heard Veronica say.

What had been Barrie's power, I thought, whose passing could reduce his strong and coldly disposed mother, whom even he called "the dragon," into this grief-stricken, ordinary woman?

"Yes," I said.

"I—I hope we'll become closer, you and I," she whispered.

"Yes," I said, absently.

She opened her purse, extracted a couple of tissues, and handed me one. She blew her nose.

"You know, he never got over you, not really," she said. "In the last year or two, his heart condition slowed him down quite a bit; he stayed home a great deal. And he spoke of you even more frequently than in the past. Sincerely, too. Not with that odd sense of humor."

Something of the old Veronica surfaced as she spoke that word, "odd," but then she wiped her nose again and went on, her voice hoarse with emotion.

"I knew then that I'd never reach him," she said. "It was always you."

My eyes had fastened, mesmerized, on a clutch of white roses near the center of Barrie's mound—about where his heart would be. When Veronica had phoned to report his death by heart failure, I'd thought with quick, malicious zest: Of course, his heart! That little-used organ! I stared at the white roses, stricken.

"I hope you'll understand, try to—to forgive me," Veronica said, faltering. "I was always very attached to Barrie, you know, particularly after his father died and I married your uncle. I—I didn't love your uncle, Ruth, but he loved me, and I knew he would take good care of us, and I didn't know what else to do. But when he brought us back here, back to—to this kind of life—well, I wasn't used to it. I was accustomed to city life, you know, and so was Barrie."

She paused, swallowing hard. I wanted to stop her, say it was all right, but I couldn't resist her uncharacteristic meekness, her air of penitence. She resumed:

"Try to understand, Ruth. Everything went so well, for a year or so, but then Rex got that telephone call about his brother and sister-in-law, dying in an auto crash somewhere in Texas. I'd never even met them, or seen pictures. And one day Rex comes home with this young girl, thirteen years old—exactly Barrie's age—and announces that she'll be living here, too. Barrie's cousin, he said. Another member of the family." She paused, perhaps aware that an ancient rancor had crept into her voice. "It was quite a shock," she said, subdued. "Particularly when Barrie took to you that way, seemed to come alive in your presence. I'd stand at my bedroom window and watch the two of you, out back, sitting under a tree and reading poetry to each other, or chasing through the woods, laughing, or playing some silly game or other. Children, I kept saying. They're just children. But it did no good. My—my hatred," she said, groping, "it grew like a cancer." A bleak satisfaction had filled her voice. "Yes. A cancer."

"Veronica, you don't need to—"

"No, Ruth, it's all true. You know it is. He adored you, he preferred you even to me, and certainly to Carole Ann, but by then something had happened—I didn't know what, and I don't mean to pry—but you seemed to lose interest, to be nourishing some secret disappointment of your own, and within weeks after finishing school you were gone, just like that. *Gone.* You were eighteen, your trust fund had come due, you suddenly decided to go to college, to move far away...." She spoke dazedly, as if still not quite believing this had happened. "And you were at your very prettiest then, too, as Barrie mentioned more than once. But after you left, of course, I didn't get him back, and of course Carole Ann never got him. No one did. He stayed the way he was, that willful attractive teenaged boy, and I was left to hate you, that's all I could do, and then, as the years passed, even that hatred grew abstract and lifeless, unsatisfying. I didn't even have *that*—"

Weeping, she'd lifted the tissue to her eyes. The wattled flesh shook along her throat and jaw. I reached out and patted her shoulder, awkwardly, but then withdrew my hand.

I said, in a careful, measured way, "It hasn't been easy, I'm sure, for any of us." I had an almost irresistible urge to become, like Veronica, garrulous and self-pitying; to portray that plump, authoritative, bitterly isolated woman of recent years; to summon up that scene of parting, in Philadelphia, when I had been too weak and cowardly to do anything but send Barrie away. And soon after that, the schoolmarm. A bit later, the witch. Veronica might well sense a kinship, however distasteful.

She looked up, timidly. "Did you ever—I mean, in Philadelphia, were you eventually able to—"

"No," I said.

Why wouldn't she leave? How to get rid of her? I wanted to stand here, alone, mooning over those halcyon early days, paying homage only to *that* Barrie, sweetheart and brother, confidant, my soul's guide, who answered to my complex of girl-adolescent longings with just the right blend of love, foolishness, and glamour. I would forget those other Barries—the amiable idler who could never abandon the hothouse protection of his mother's possessiveness, of the South itself; the young man who flirted so openly (and so exotically, to my sheltered awareness) with other men, and who took off sometimes, alone, for Atlanta—"where the boys are," he said once to me, winking, leaving me too stunned to feel jealous; the inert, absurdly youthful figure I'd gazed upon yesterday, his eyelids sealed, dressed in midnight blue. No, I would not think of them.

"Veronica," I said. "If you don't mind, I'd like to be alone for a little while."

This confused her. "You want—you mean, *here*—?"

"Yes." And I turned again toward the grave, starting away from her.

Then I heard, from behind: "You'll never give up, will you?" A fierce, accusing voice.

"Veronica," I said sharply, turning, "you must understand that this picture you have—this vision of things—is greatly distorted. I mean, Barrie was fond of me at one time, yes, but he didn't—I mean, he never—"

I couldn't finish.

Veronica, her face taut with fury, stood her ground. "What *do* you mean?"

I breathed deeply. "We loved each other, in a strange way, but we were weaklings. *You* were the strong one. You deserved to win, and you did."

Her mouth twitched, as if she were choking on her own malice. "You're one to talk about distortion," she said, bitterly. "You've been gone for twenty years, and not so much as a letter, a phone call. What do *you* know about him? About me?"

Unconsciously she had clasped her hands together, as if she were strangling some invisible assailant.

"You didn't have to go through what I did, Ruth, right up until the end. Why, only last week I passed by his bedroom, he was lying fully clothed on top of the spread, even his shoes on, he didn't see me, he lay there staring upward at the ceiling and talking to himself, in a dreamy voice. It was a voice I'd never heard before, not ever; he'd never shown me that side. He was reciting a passage, I realized, from that Brontë novel—you're the English teacher, you should know—where the hero cries out, 'Oh, Cathy, be with me always—take any form—drive me mad! I *cannot* life without my life. I *cannot* live without my soul!'—you know how it goes, I'm sure. He lay there repeating it over and over, I'll never forget those words!"

Tears wandered down her face, a strange route of dried reptilian skin, puckered by grief. Her shoulders shook, her eyes were half shut, yet she looked imperious as ever with her clenched hands and her gritted teeth.

"Over and over," she said, "in that sad, dreamy, faraway voice. 'Oh, Cathy! Oh, Cathy!'"

Abruptly, I turned aside. I hurried to the grave. To my relief, she didn't follow; but neither did she go away. We could never escape each other, I thought, any more than that unholy alliance, love and death, might ever dissolve within the compass of idle passions, idle dreams. Not quite alone, I stood staring at a mound of dirt, in the middle of nowhere.

IV

from *Last Encounter with the Enemy*

Last Encounter with the Enemy

The boy knew her name, all right, but he liked to call her the peacock lady.

Ever since that article in the Sunday supplement, with the photographs of her propped on crutches and surrounded by peachickens pecking the dirt and her scowling hard as if she knew the callow young newspaper photographer was the devil himself and she wasn't fooled for a minute, the boy had thought of her that way. After he'd scampered off the Greyhound from Atlanta and found a taxi, he'd thought maybe even the illiterates in this godforsaken town might have heard of her, since she was famous and all their own, so he'd spoken her name to the driver and asked if he knew where she lived. But the driver, a dumb kid with Elvis sideburns, just wrinkled his nose and said, "Huh? You ain't got the *ad*dress?" So the boy had prompted him, "You know, dontcha? The famous lady writer? The peacock lady?" That last phrase had done it. Elvis smirked and said yup, he'd driven a couple of priests out there last week and the damn peahens had been stalking around all over the place—yeah, he remembered—and he'd rapped the meter and off they went.

The boy had sat back, mightily pleased.

By the time the cab slowed along the Eatonton highway, he'd gotten so deeply enmeshed in a fantasy scenario of what lay ahead that he hadn't understood the big moment was here. He'd read everything the woman had written, but because he was a puny little towhead fatally underestimated by adults, the peacock lady wouldn't guess at that. He planned to make an impression by casually dropping things into the conversation that would amaze her. Soon enough she would realize he was her equal if not better; and then, being a woman, she would probably start confiding in him. Though he was only eleven and small for his age, maybe she'd develop a crush on him, a little. Unmarried women were prone to that, he'd heard. He knew what probably lay underneath that exterior of the nunlike spectacles she wore, and the fearsome scowl; he wasn't fooled by the black going-to-church dress and string of pearls, or by the smart-alecky comments she made in interviews about "modern man" whenever she got off on one of her tangents about the Holy Apostolic Church and all the rest. He supposed she'd be vulnerable enough to a modern man if a real live one strolled right into her kitchen.

As for the Church, he went to parochial school, and his careful references to the nuns, especially his English teacher Sister Imelda for whom he was writing his extra-credit essay on the peacock lady's work, were probably the reason she'd agreed to see him. He'd tossed in a whopper about being an altar boy, too, though he'd long ago repudiated all that nonsense. At some point he'd spring on her the essay's brilliant first sentence that had come to him only yesterday: "Life itself is the peacock lady's wound, and the Church is her Band-Aid." He'd written down the line and read over it maybe three hundred times and thought it was about the cleverest thing he'd done yet. He couldn't wait to see the look on her face.

The driver stopped the cab beside the road and jerked around. "You wanna get out here, or you want me to pull on up that driveway?"

The boy squinted toward the white clapboard house, maybe a quarter mile down a rutted lane, and then to the dark ridge of trees he recognized at once from the fiction. It had rained yesterday and the lane was muddy, full of potholes with standing reddish brown water. He supposed Elvis was worried about his shiny hubcaps.

"If I'd wanted to walk, I don't reckon I'd have hired a taxi, now would I?" the boy said.

His heart pounded queerly in his excitement. For two or three years he had been scribbling odd little stories in his school notebooks, and he'd started typing them up and giving them to Sister Imelda, who would read them aloud to the class. "It seems we have an aspiring *writer* in our midst," she said the first time, a comment that had made him squirm with pleasure, and he didn't care that later he got shoved around at recess for sucking up to the teacher. His stories were about people drowning in floods and people kidnapped and tortured by ruthless thugs and babies born with such hideous deformities that their mothers plotted to kill them but none of this fazed Sister Imelda, who said the boy had "a real flair for language." So when he'd read the Sunday supplement article about the peacock lady he'd gotten wildly excited that there was somebody else who not only wrote odd things, but got paid for them and got her picture in the paper; he'd read the article countless times and knew it was only a matter of time before they would meet.

Then he'd read her stories, which he thought were pretty good (he knew his were better) and he'd gone to the school library and let old Sister Blanche look up things other people wrote about the peacock lady, and some interviews she'd given; that's when his stomach had begun to turn. All that palaver about the Church. The Church this, the Church that. He was disappointed, but guessed he shouldn't have been surprised. A lady writer, after all. Probably would have joined the convent if she hadn't lucked into publishing a book.

As they pulled in sight of the screened-in porch, he caught a glimpse of her inside, waiting, in one of those ordinary metal porch chairs; the aluminum crutches were propped against a second, empty chair, and a third had been placed opposite the woman, across from a rickety old table. All this for him, he thought. He pulled out his billfold and gave the driver one of the tens he'd been lifting these past few days from his mother's purse—he could always go to confession, he'd thought, smirking—and strode forthrightly toward the back door, which stood propped open to the cool spring morning with a gigantic milk can.

"Come back in two hours," he spat over his shoulder at Elvis. "And don't be late."

The peacock lady had turned in her chair and was smiling as he climbed the brick steps and entered the porch. "Hello there," she said. "You must be—"

"Nice to meetcha!" the boy cried, rushing forward. "I been looking forward to this all week long!"

He pumped her hand, noticing how white and pasty her upper arm looked in the sleeveless black dress. His heart glowed with pride. It was the same dress she'd worn for the Atlanta paper, that day they came out to take her picture! He'd debated whether to dress up or not, and now was glad he'd picked the long navy pants he wore on Sundays when his mother dragged him to mass, and the white Ban-Lon shirt an aunt had sent for his birthday. He'd thought even a lady writer might have appreciated his usual T-shirt and cutoffs, taking him for a youthful bohemian, but then he'd worried she might think that was improper for a meeting of two intellectuals and had opted for attire befitting a serious occasion.

"Glad you could come," she said, with her measured smile. He saw how intently her dark eyes fixed on him, behind those chunky-looking glasses. He glanced down, his gaze settling on the nicked wooden table that was stacked with books surrounding a glass-covered cake dish piled high with little white cookies. The powdered sugary disks made his mouth water instantly. The woman added, "Have a seat."

As he took the chair, pausing first over the books and nodding, as if he were intimately familiar with each volume, and glancing sideways at the pile of cookies, the woman kept giving him the same careful smile. When she'd first seen him emerge from the taxi, she'd worried for a moment about keeping a straight face. She knew she was dealing with a schoolboy—that was part of the reason she'd agreed to see him, though she tired easily these days and didn't welcome visitors so readily as she once did—but she'd expected a tall gangly high school boy, not this little blond child who looked as if he'd made his first communion the week before last. The letter he'd sent had been semiliterate, but she'd ascribed that to ignorance rather than extreme youth, and now she was glad indeed that she'd invited him down. She wished her mother hadn't gone into town for the afternoon; lately, Regina spoke the word "interviewers" in the same tone an old countryman might say "revenuers," and liked to disappear when one was coming out. But she'd have gotten a kick out of this.

"Your mama let you come all this way by yourself?" she said, kindly, but at once the boy frowned as if the question offended him. "I come on my own," he said cryptically, looking off. "It's Sareday, you know. I ain't got no school."

Maybe that's just as well, if that's how they teach you to speak, the woman thought, but she kept her smile going.

"She knows you're here, don't she?"

She had a bad habit of adopting the grammar of her interlocutor, whether a visiting theologian or a white-trash dairyman, but it was a habit she hadn't tried very hard to break. Somehow she felt it helped in her writing.

"I come on my own," the boy repeated, stubbornly. He reached into his pants pocket and pulled out a tiny spiral notebook with a cheap fountain pen clipped to its cover; she'd already noted, approvingly, the boy's ink-splotched fingers. He added, "Like I said, it's nice to meet you and all. I reckon we can get started, if it's all right by you."

She bent forward and set aside the glass top of the cake dish. "Would you care for some of these cookies? I'd planned to give you chocolate chip, but we're out. My mother's at the store right now."

The boy reached out for one of the wedding cookies—she saw that his hand was shaking—and popped it into his mouth. "That's OK, my mama buys these too," he said. "I like them all right."

"I'd fetch you some sweet tea, but you'd probably get it quicker if you went into the kitchen yourself." She glanced toward the crutches.

The boy shook his head. "Nope, ain't thirsty," he said. "Had me a Coke on the bus."

She sat back, already feeling a little tired. But this was certainly an interesting specimen. Last week it had been a couple of Jesuits who'd droned for more than two hours about doctrinal niceties she considered about as important as hen droppings, and a few days before that a pop-eyed woman historical novelist who sold more books in one day than she'd sold in her whole life but who'd come to "pay her respects" and get an "expert opinion" on character development. The woman had said she was tired of writing historical bestsellers and wanted to write what was in her heart, and when the expert opined that if characters didn't develop on their own there wasn't much you could do for them, and anyway that what was in her heart probably would be much less interesting to most people than lively, made-up history, the woman had left in a huff. That visit was shorter yet had made her more tired than her strenuous afternoon with the Jesuits.

But this child sitting here, his legs crossed at the ankles and swinging about a foot above the porch floor, was something else altogether.

"All right then," she said, in what she hoped was an encouraging voice, "I reckon whatever you aim to ask, you can ask." Hoping to break the ice a little, she added, "Just don't ask me about none of my boyfriends, now."

At that the boy's eyes—a pretty but veiled soft blue—met hers directly. He even gave her a little smile. "I wasn't gonna ask you nothing personal," he said.

She laughed out loud. "That's good," she told him. "Then shoot."

For a few minutes he lobbed the usual questions at her, and she batted the memorized answers back. To her surprise the boy kept flipping open the little notebook, which was filled with page after page of his large, left-slanting, childish handwriting. He'd written all the questions out! Lately she'd come to believe that no one could surprise her anymore but just when you dared think your wisdom was complete, along came a new twist in human nature you couldn't have anticipated. Several of the questions she recognized from recent interviews she'd given and it occurred to her that a little speech about plagiarism might be in order, but each time she looked into his fresh pink-cheeked face and virginal blue eyes she had to remember how young this child was, for all his prematurely mannish, even old-mannish pride. Now he asked a question that was so ridiculous—"Please give me your observation on the issue of point of view in today's fiction"—that again she laughed aloud.

"Come on, boy, ain't you thought up any better questions than that?"

He met her smile with a challenging look. "There's some says you got a problem with thisyer point of view," he observed.

She gazed out into the yard, where one of the hens had paused to admire herself in a rain puddle.

"That may be, but I've got bigger problems than that," she said. He kept staring.

"All right," she relented, "the fact is, you're not supposed to switch it around while you're telling a story, but I do it all the time."

Though the boy supposed this was an evasive answer, he decided to let it pass. Everything was going according to plan; he was just biding his time while she warmed to him. One of the newspapers had suggested that she was "defensive" about her work and so he thought a few routine, boring questions for which she had pat answers would help catch her off guard. He glanced at his Timex and saw that half an hour had passed; he guessed it was time to turn up the pressure. He rubbed one forearm across his brow, for the late-morning sun had shifted and he now sat bisected by a plane of light that had warmed him uncomfortably even though this was March and the air wafting inside from the propped-open door was cool. Already he'd scooted his chair as far into the shade as he could but the sun kept sliding sideways upon him, implacably, while the peacock lady sat unbothered in her patch of shade, observing him. He thought to change his mind about the iced tea but decided that would show weakness so he plunged ahead, flipping another page in his notebook.

"Okay, religion," he said, as if ticking items off a list. "What is the religious sig—sig—" Damn, he couldn't read his own words he'd copied from one of Sister Blanche's articles.

"—of yer stories!" he shouted.

She sat quietly for a moment. An almost melancholy look came over her face.

"That's a tall order," she pointed out.

He smiled; when they got sad, it was time for you to turn up the charm.

"Well, I didn't come here to ask you no silly questions," he said.

Her answer came quick. "Son, I really can't figure out why you did come here. This seems like a mighty big project for somebody your age. They assign things like this in parochial school these days?" Behind the thick glasses her eyes seemed to narrow. "By the way, you ain't told me your name. You didn't even sign that letter you sent me."

He tried not to smile too broadly; she'd fallen right into his trap. He gazed off through the screen enclosing them to the woods, uncomfortably aware of the beads of sweat along his upper lip. It had even collected on his eyelids. Out in the yard a couple of the peachickens were indulging in a grooming ritual, and on the opposite side of a fence in the middle distance a few cows stood picturesquely, their tails swishing. One of the peacocks sat sunning himself on a fence post, his long tail feathers almost reaching the ground. Beyond the fence loomed the dark woods and he thought about everything that was going on out there, the dead bodies oozing blood and the kids leaning against trees getting beaten within an inch of their lives and the strange violations so dark and perverted even he couldn't imagine them. Maybe if there was time before Elvis came back he'd take a stroll through the pines and have a peek at the blood and the mayhem.

"Well?" she asked, adjusting her glasses. He caught her checking her watch, just a flick of her pasty-white wrist. "What's your name, boy?"

He looked her full in the face. "I'm Jesus," he said.

She did a good job of hiding her shock, he'd give her that; a couple of faint lines scored her forehead but that was all. "Is that a fact? Are you part Mexican, child? You sure don't look it."

"Nome, I'm Swedish on my daddy's side—he's dead and you don't want to ast where is he now—and my mama's folks came from over in Switzerland. But that ain't got nothing to do with who *I* am."

"Is that a fact," the peacock lady said. She looked pleased, but whether pleased with him or herself he couldn't quite tell. Her lips had flattened in an amused little smile. "I guess it's a relief, Jesus," she said, "to know that you're a Catholic."

Another trap. For the second time he reached across and grabbed one of the sugary white cookies. He longed for something to drink, for now he was bathed in sunlight except for his right elbow, and the cookie was stale and dry. He chewed rapidly, hacking up the spit to swallow it down.

"Just because I go to school where they's penguin teachers don't mean I'm Cathlick," he said. "My mama's Church of God and I'm the same. We believe the Church of Rome is an out-and-out fraud and that the pope aims to take over the govvermint!"

All this was a lie—of course his mother was Catholic, and until he'd wised up he'd been one, too—but he wanted to erase that little smile off the woman's face.

"You sure have lots of opinions for a youngster!" the peacock lady said. She leaned forward, her dark eyes enlarged behind the glasses. "Now why don't you tell me. Who are you, really?"

"I believe I'm the one s'post to be asking things, but I'll answer you. I reckon I'm a temple of the Holy Ghost," he said, narrowing his eyes as he checked her reaction, "and I'm that good man you think's so hard to find, and I'm sure enough good country people, too! So put that in your pipe and smoke it."

Her eyes blazed, but with pleasure rather than anger. She stayed bent forward, as if daring him to peek down her dress. But the neck was too high, and the old-lady pearls were in the way.

"That's a heap of erudition you just displayed," she said. "I'm mighty impressed."

He'd worked on the line for days and was proud of himself for getting it out; sometimes, practicing, he'd stumbled a little. He should know better than to doubt himself.

"I thank you," he said.

"But really, Jesus, I wish you'd tell me what I did to deserve an audience this morning."

He jerked his head around, supposing a crowd had gathered behind him, but then he understood: she'd meant that *he* was the audience. He'd worried all week that she might start talking over his head, which she could probably do just because she'd read a lot of books he knew better than to bother with, so he decided to cut her off at the pass by changing the subject.

"I got my reasons," he said, "but you listen to this. Now s'pose I told you that on the one hand, I'm eleven years old and I go to this school where the penguin ladies teach, and I write down little stories that would make your glasses flip backwards if you read them. But on the other hand, I'm something else again. Okay, I ain't Jesus, I just said that to get your attention. But I'll tell you what I really am—a *prophet.*"

He folded his arms and waited for that to impress her. She was cagey, all right, but his words had set her back in her chair. She grasped its metal arms as tightly as she would have gripped her crutches.

"A prophet!" she marveled.

He couldn't tell if she was ridiculing him but decided it didn't matter. He'd get the last laugh. He continued in a solemn voice, as if she hadn't spoken: "Had my first vision come along last weekend—hit me right between the eyes just like a bullet. The future done come to me in a blaze of light and glory, and this is what I seen. Now picture this: it ain't 1964 no more. Nope, and it ain't 1970, and not 1980, neither. Why, it ain't even this dang century any more!" He paused a beat, just for the effect. "No ma'am, it's the year *two thousand!* And guess what: you're dead as a doornail and I'm all growed up and somebody done ast me to write down something about *you!*"

The peacock lady's gaze had drifted off, not as if she were troubled by this outlandish scenario but as if it bored her. She said, "If you agreed to such a thing, you'd be mighty hard up for writing assignments."

The boy smiled grimly. From inside the house, a door slammed. She looked aside, briefly. "That must be Louise…" she murmured.

The boy's heart leapt: what an opportunity. She was a tough nut to crack but this ought to split the shell wide open.

He leaned forward and said, with a little flutter of his eyelids, "Or maybe it's Parker. Maybe Parker's back."

That got her attention; she straightened abruptly and no longer pretended to smile.

"All right, boy, this was fun, but I get tired awful easily these days. Now that story about Parker ain't been printed yet, and there's only five or six people in America who've read it. Who put you up to this? Was it Betty? Was it Cecil?"

The boy made his eyes round and puzzled. "Betty who? Cecil who?" he said innocently.

"You didn't come here for any school assignment, child. Now who are you? I'm all tired out and I don't have time to waste."

He was feeling overheated, but he stood and held his pen aloft as though displaying a sacred relic. "I told you, I'm a prophet, and

I come with a pen instead of a sword. I'm here from the next century to tell you that God is dead and so are you!"

She gave him a stony look. "If He was dead, then I might as well be."

"And as for these stories of yourn, they done been analyzed, psychologized, feminized, disconstructed, put in their historical *con*test, and hung on out to dry!" He lowered his voice. "Why, they's some even thinks you're gay—that you like wimmin!"

The peacock lady blinked, as though impressed by this idea. "I'm happy enough when I ain't sick," she said, "and I like women fine. After all, my mother's one, and I'm one. But I—"

"And one more thing," the boy said impatiently, tired of her stalling. This might have been the moment to lay that brilliant sentence from his essay on her: *Life itself is the peacock lady's wound....* But no, there was no time for that. Instead he shouted: "Ain't nobody believes that God claptrap but you!"

From behind, as he struggled to his feet and stood triumphant against her steely glare, he could hear the cries of those stupid peachickens. He glanced around and saw a couple of gray females regarding him from the lane, and from another direction several males dragged their long tails out of the flower beds (dollops of bedraggled chrysanthemums, roses) alongside the house. Some fluttered down from the roof, while others scurried out from the crepe myrtle. He glanced around and saw more descending from the oaks and cedars, from the fig trees.

The peacock lady bent forward in her chair, her eyes narrowed to slits.

"You're mighty young to be so—so hard," she said, almost as if talking to herself and not to him. "But not too old to be saved, that's for sure."

He slapped his knee and let out a loud guffaw. "Lady, your head must be hard as a rock!" he cried. He demonstrated by knocking a fist against his own head, then he reached down in a cavalier gesture and swiped another little white cookie off the plate. As soon as he popped it inside his mouth, he knew his error. His mouth was dry as sand, and now the chalky mess of cookie and powdered sugar kept expanding the more he chewed, like a fistful of ashes he could neither swallow nor spit out. His very throat seemed paralyzed.

"You got something more you want to say, boy?" the woman asked. She reached for the crutches, deciding she'd had enough. This poor deluded child had angered her, yes, and she had no idea who'd told him about "Parker's Back," which she'd been writing and rewriting for several years and wasn't done with yet; but entertaining infantile blasphemy hadn't been part of her plans this morning. After all, shortly before this boy arrived she'd gotten home from a ten o'clock funeral—one of Regina's old friends— and hanging there on her crutches at the cemetery while the minister droned his consolations, she'd wondered how soon she'd be returning here. In a horizontal position, most likely. After she and Regina drove home in silence she'd been too tired even to change her clothes, and now here was this maddening child sent to try her patience. Sent as a joke, she supposed, but it wasn't funny anymore. .

Struggling with the crutches, she got to her feet, watching as the boy clutched at his throat, his eyes locked onto hers in an outraged, pleading look.

She said gently, "Just turn around, boy. Believe. God is watching you—in the present and in the future, too. Anyone can be a prophet, son. Anyone can live forever. Just turn around and behold the Lord!"

His face was turning blue, a few shades darker than his eyes, but he turned as if helpless to do anything but obey. Just outside the opened screen door the peacocks were approaching the brick steps, their cawing sound risen now to a chorus of screams: *Eee-ooo-ii! Eee-ooo-ii!* Gathering close, the hens in front and the cocks arrayed behind them, the birds resembled an audience of outraged, elderly citizens prepared to tell the boy just what they thought of his pretensions. As though following some divine choreography the peacocks had begun strutting forward and back, heads pecking the air, their blue necks and crested heads jerking in majestic spasms, their screams growing louder and more urgent as the seconds passed. The boy, gripping his throat, writhed on his feet as though performing some doomed parody of the peacocks' dance. The birds shrieked so that even her own ears hurt: *Eee-ooo-ii! Ee-ooo-ii!* Their distinctively sour, peppery scent wafted inside the porch on the morning air. And now, as if obeying a summons, all the birds went silent and the peacocks in rustling grandeur lifted and spread their tails—each a shimmering aureole of bright blue-green and bronze, each tipped with a tiny sunlike burst of light.

She pointed with one of her crutches. "Observe and fall to your knees, boy! You are face-to-face with God's revelation! Don't dare to deny him! Don't dare to turn away!"

The boy glanced back at her, his face a swollen bruised purple, his mouth stubbornly clamped shut. He glared as if to say that he would die refusing to accept her obscene visions, he would stand here as a prophet of unbelief and a martyr to the future! Soon enough she would be dead, and he'd have the last word and the last goddamn laugh! She read all this in his desperate squinted eyes, while the majestic peacocks circled the porch in their full, brilliant display that after all these years could still rend her heart.

She lifted one of her crutches and slammed it with all her might against the side of the boy's head. Then, aiming carefully with the other crutch, she struck him across the back, observing with satisfaction the mass of whitish glop shooting from his mouth just as he stumbled down the steps and fell into the grass. The chickens went running. The peacocks' tails descended quickly as they rushed off, their wild screams lowering to ordinary squeals and squabbles.

Exhausted, she dragged herself to the edge of the porch and observed him lying there in the yard, his little hands fallen from his throat, the flushed pink of innocence returning to his cheeks. His eyes were open and blinking but emptied of all that rage, all that horror.

He stared up at her, wondering.

"Vengeance is mine, saith the Lord," she allowed herself with an angry smile.

She turned and hobbled back inside the house.

He couldn't remember much about Elvis helping him inside the car or the ride back to the station. Numbed as though stumbling through a dream, he found a seat at the back of the bus. He spoke to no one and no one spoke to him. Half an hour later, he sat with his head leaned back against the seat and watched as the desiccated fields, still beaten down by winter, streamed along his window in a colorless blur. Eventually his gaze fell to his lap and he understood that he held something between his folded hands—it was a single, brightly colored feather, a thing of such singular beauty and perfection that it seemed to match this new, shy, peaceful emotion inside him, something not of this earth.

He kept holding and staring at the feather, all the way home.

To the Madhouse

No, the birds didn't sing in Greek: I made that up.

And the King shouted no obscenities from the hedge: another lie.

Oddly, biographers don't seem to understand: I'm a novelist. I make things up. I lie.

Nor was I raving, or frothing at the mouth; nor did my eyes roll up inside my head.

Truly, I did not thrash about.

One feels apologetic, dispelling this nonsense. Certainly one has difficult times, and the summer of 1904 was one, but a few made-up (that is, metaphorical) incidents one dropped into an obscure essay have mushroomed—through the heightening, the intensification of passing time—into "madness." And so easily! So thoroughly!

To continue. In truth, I read the morning paper: no ripping it to shreds. I merely lay in my bed: no chomping at the bedpost. I heard voices, yes, but not from the birds outside my window (almost, one wishes one had; it sounds rather amusing) and certainly not in Greek but in quite intelligible English prose, albeit lowered to malevolent hissing. And I spoke, behaved in an unaccustomed way (admittedly!) but certainly I wasn't mad, even if I allowed myself to be installed for a couple of brief, ignoble sojourns into bedlam-like accommodations. Where I'd met, at least once, what might be termed faery company along the way.

I daresay a large number of certifiably sane people—even biographers!—have known one or two such interludes.

All that summer she was mad.

Dear, foolish Quentin. One becomes famous—let this serve as fair warning—and younger male relatives begin swarming you like mayflies. Even Vita's youngest boy, Nigel; I saw that same lust glinting in his eyes by age thirteen. Dotty old Virginia, who produces books; who gets written up; who tires one with her ceaseless questions, her intrepid fancy. "Insane" at times, surely. One of "the great English novelists"—oh dear. Most boys their age are mussing themselves in cricket matches or mooning over young ladies, but not these ink-stained wretches; they're making notes on poor Virginia that might accrue to their future glory. *All that summer she was mad*, indeed.

All that summer, truth be told, she tired of the gray prose of what her Victorian forebears called "reality," rather, and she put on something of a show.

And time passed. Decades passed. One grew famous, and one grew wretched. There were voices, it's true; once or twice there were visions. Yet oddly, the day in 1936 I succumbed to Leonard's plea that a rest cure and kind doctors might be advisable—the same "logic" they'd used on me in '04—I grew directly worse, as if to justify such a step. Pulled down the walls, as it were, and let my fancy gallop free. In the motor-car, our handsome Lanchester that I refused to drive—that is, learn to drive—and that even Leonard, always grumpy and preoccupied, didn't drive particularly well: in our car, as I say, I chattered nonsense all the way to Twickenham.

Wondering had it changed, after twenty-odd years. Consulting my dim memory of dimmer rooms, ghostly nurses passing to and fro, bearing trays piled with food which one "must eat" but which, of course, one could not possibly eat. Much rest, much food. "The cure." These days, surely, one suffers instead some young disciple of Freud at bedtime, murmuring incomprehensible nothings into the shell of one's deadened ear.

Somehow I'd agreed to three weeks of this, and from my passenger's vantage I watched as Leonard fiercely drove, his sharp beak of a nose pointing the way.

I'd a ticket to bedlam, if it pleased. One-way?—that remained to be seen. But first class, of course, and few distractions; and little motive for second thoughts along our journey.

We were halfway there before I heard him: that young male voice, from the rumble seat behind us.

My first thought: "Dear God, Quentin has stowed away, determined to record this juicy bit." But no, it wasn't Quentin's voice; nor was it Nigel's. It wasn't any voice I knew. Clearly an American accent, from one of the southernmost regions of that country. Raw, plaintive, yet charged with a suppressed excitement, too, as he addressed me.

"Mrs. Woolf? May I have—I mean, would you mind—"

I turned around; having been pronounced "mad," like a stamp upon my forehead, I considered it no breach of etiquette to ignore my eminently sane husband with the same diligence he used in ignoring me. (He sat hunched—amusingly, it must be noted—in his peculiar driving posture, both hands on the upper part of the wheel, his trowel of a nose jutted forward in opposition to that direst enemy, the open road.) Instead I began to converse with my phantom interlocutor.

Yes, I had turned round; I was half-smiling (a bit of froth at my lips, no doubt): and there he was. Aged twenty-four or -five; his blondish hair tousled, rather longer than was fashionable (but it was fashionable, perhaps, in the wilds of America's nether parts?); and dressed in that odd, segmented way young Americans seemed to favor. A white shirt, wrinkled but clean; tightly belted khaki slacks. The shirt was peculiar: crisply starched, with a tiny, crimson-red mammal sewed onto the chest like an ornament. A pony, evidently? A polo pony?... He wore no jacket, though the day was windy. His shirt sleeves were precisely rolled up, two folds on each side.

Unexpected, his sudden appearance might have been; but I had my suspicions.

"Are you here to interview me?" I asked, for I saw the notebook in his hands.

"Oh, no ma'am—I mean, Mrs. Woolf. I'm just here to witness. To remember."

I stared. "'To witness, to remember'—is that right? For three shillings a page, perhaps?"

He looked offended at this, but then his face resumed its round-eyed, slack-jawed approximation of unashamed awe.

Since this particular kind of admirer makes me uncomfortable above all others, I took a breath and reasoned that it shouldn't surprise me, my mind tossing this particular fancy in my path: almost as if I wished to conspire with my husband, with Nessa, with my dear friends: to confirm my lunacy on my own.

"No, ma'am," he drawled, in his quiet way. "I haven't published anything. Not yet."

My eye dropped to the notebook. "And what's that for?" I asked. "Taking notes on the flora and fauna?"

He smiled. "They all said you were witty. They all acknowledged that."

"'They?'"

He bit his lip, as though conscious of an indiscretion; his chalky-looking face turned a creamy pink. I reminded myself of his extreme youth and added, more gently, "It's just that I'm surprised, you see, to find you stowed away in our motor-car."

We'd come to a crossing; Leonard took advantage of the pause to glance in my direction.

"Easy does it, Virginia," he said. "We haven't much further."

He'd been listening to my prattle, but only to decide it was prattle; not troubling to make out the words. My habit of conducting dialogues independent of Leonard, when the two of us sat alone, was hardly a novelty for him. My dear Leonard inhabited another mental zone in recent days: thinking of Hitler; thinking his manly war-thoughts. Often I retaliated by making up my anti-war book aloud, rolling its fanciful periods off my tongue like accomplished facts so that, by now, the very words *Three Guineas* brought a deepened scowl to my husband's ever-scowling face.

Male war-monger and woman pacifist: portrait of a marriage, circa 1936.

Of course this oddly dressed, shiny-faced young man, this abrupt and bewildering product of my fancy, could know nothing of this.

"Not much further, then? Will we arrive in time for tea?" I asked Leonard, with what I considered the right blend of responsiveness and irrelevancy. "Shall the King be there, with his lewd remarks?" My husband smiled grimly; kept at his driving.

Now I turned full round in my seat (stolid Leonard never glanced back there, smugly aware that he'd see nothing) and fixed my sharp gaze on this awkward, fair-haired boy. My comment on his stowing away had perplexed him; he seemed at quite a loss. Now he squirmed a little, in a boyish way. He'd tossed aside the notebook as if to dramatise his innocence of mercenary intentions.

"Well...of course, I'm not really here," he began. "I *am* one of your fancies, I suppose. Yet now that I'm here, I'm immensely curious, and pleased."

"Curious about what?" I rapped out. "Pleased about what?" I added, a bit cruelly, "And why would I fancy *you?*"

He smiled as though I'd kissed his cheek.

"A tendency to malice," he said. "I've read about that, as well."

This sounded unpleasant indeed. "Read? Read where? I subscribe to everything and I haven't—"

"Oh, Mrs. Woolf, you've hallucinated one of your *future* readers, not a present one."

I gaped. "A future reader?" The phrase had an agreeable sound but I'd no idea what the boy meant.

"Yes, I—I mean, I wasn't even born until 1953."

Now I understood *he* was mad. Leonard hadn't bargained for a carload, I suppose, so he'd kept determinedly at his driving. Had my remark about the King offended him? My husband now seemed almost strenuously oblivious to my fanciful colloquy and could not be aware, of course, of my interlocutor's preposterous claim.

"Is that so?" I said, for once at a loss for words.

"Yes, that's not until twelve years after—" Again he bit his lip.

"After what?"

He said, rather hurriedly, "In college, I began reading your novels. First *To the Lighthouse* and *Mrs. Dalloway*, which the professor assigned in Modern British Lit, and now that I'm in grad school I've gone back and read the more obscure titles. I love *Orlando*," he added, fervently. "I love *Jacob's Room*."

"I'm not sure what you mean by 'obscure,'" I said, pretending to be miffed but secretly pleased, of course, that someone so young had read my books.

"Oh, only that the others are acknowledged classics." He'd dropped his gaze, as though suddenly viewing me—gangly, ill-dressed Virginia, being carted off to the madhouse—as a monument of some sort; akin to the Elgin Marbles, or Stonehenge.

A dreamy, faraway look had entered the young man's eyes.

"I took a seminar, you see, in the gender politics of your novels, and for my dissertation I'm deconstructing the phallic imagery in *To the Lighthouse.*"

I sat there, agape; my throbbing brain trying to close round that odd word, "deconstructing." I had visions of the boy taking my poor lovely novel apart, page by page, and then…doing what with it, precisely? Making paper aeroplanes (German, no doubt) to terrorize the English skies?

Of the "phallic imagery" I didn't care to think, at all.

As the young man delivered the dread news about Quentin's book, and Nigel's, I glanced back to the driver's seat, observing my husband's taciturn features in the slanting light of mid-afternoon; we'd happen upon some village or other before long, and of course we'd stop for tea. We'd have the daily harangue over whether Virginia will eat something, or will not eat something. Since he'd soon be rid of me, perhaps he'd overlook my ruse of tearing a scone to pieces, making small nibbling motions (I cribbed them from our marmoset, Mitzi) but swallowing not a morsel. He'd hide himself behind a paper, no doubt; behind the war news. Since Hitler invaded the Rhineland my husband had taken the war as a personal affront, interpreting my pacifism as another symptom of madness.

But tea would be conducted properly, as tea must be. I should take a sip, perhaps two; I'd take monkeyish bites at my scone but swallow nothing. The maidservant would address me as "Ma'am"; she'd ask me reasonable questions and get unreasonable answers, for which the uxorious Leonard would apologize gruffly.

When we returned to the car, surely my blond-haired hallucination should have vanished.

From the rumble seat, I now heard a polite cough; instinctively I turned round again, gathering my defences.

"Mrs. Woolf, I hope—I hope it isn't distressing, learning such things."

"Such things?" I said, more timorously than I intended.

"About your work, and your reputation," he said. "I thought you'd be tickled to know, well"—he dropped his eyes, shyly—"that you're the century's greatest woman novelist."

"My dear boy! It's only 1936, after all." I bit my lip, but too late.

Politely, he ignored my error. "There was a big Woolf boom in the seventies," he said, informatively, "and nowadays you're a virtual industry. My adviser says I've got a chance of publishing *Woolf at the Closet Door: The Pillaging Phallus and Lesbian Logocentrism in 'To the Lighthouse.'*"

"Indeed?" I said. (Entirely lacking any other response.)

"Yes, ma'am. She feels my chapter on the 'Time Passes' section needs some work, though. We don't agree about the poetics of gendered space—I mean whether it valorizes the narrator or the absent author—and she can't stomach my characterization of Mr. Ramsay as an erotic marauder. The word 'rapist' should be used, she feels, since the novel privileges sexual politics as an ontological arena of desire and disavowal. But I stuck to my guns until just lately."

He flushed.

"Oops, that was a sexist metaphor, wasn't it. I apologize. And of course she's right. After all, she *is* my adviser."

Though my head had begun to ache: though my stomach, empty these past three days, had become a cauldron of molten lead: though my nights of sleepless misery over *The Years* had left me in a state of exhaustion so profound that I felt dissociated from my own body and thus could not really be surprised that the voices and hallucinations had returned, and so could hardly object to Leonard's farming me out to Twickenham yet again: despite all this, a kernel of sanity asserted itself, at this moment; goaded me into speech.

"Young man—I'm sorry, but you haven't given your name—are you really talking about my novel *To the Lighthouse?* It's more than a decade behind me, I grant, but I *do* still remember—"

He leaned forward, eyes alight; the same posture he might assume, I thought, when attending a professional conference and discovering someone else who had read my novel.

"Yes!" he fairly shouted. "And ma'am, if you'll allow me to compliment the way you employ phallic mediation to deconstruct patriarchal linguistic paradigms, validating Irigaray's notion of *Etablir un genealogie des femmes* and supporting Foucault's analysis of the delusive textuality inherent in male pretexts!"

The boy's cheeks had reddened with delight.

"I just can't imagine how you did it," he added.

"Nor can I," I responded, though my voice must have sounded mechanical, if not fearful. Clearly, the boy was mad.

My anticipated village had materialized about us, but I saw through a perceptual blur; Leonard had slowed the Lanchester, and from the way his head poked to and fro—I knew him so well— I gathered he'd started thinking of his tea. I remained fixed in that awkward, half-turned posture, my eyes darting between this youthful chimera with his shining, smiling face and my frowning, all-too-real husband.

Leonard said: "A spot of tea might be nice, then?"

The question was rhetorical; we'd be stopping soon, of course. A heaviness in my lap forced my gaze downward, where I saw the grievous evidence of my recent life: namely, the proofs of *The Years*. I'd brought them along, hoping to correct a page or two during our journey. Kindly, Leonard had pretended the novel was good; I'd experienced a false, momentary elation; but now they weighed, indeed, like the deadest of dead cats on the exiguous shelf of my knees. What bizarre optimism led me to believe I might "correct" this lumpen prose I'd spent years bludgeoning into place—I, the mad Virginia, on her way to the "nursing home" where, of course, one was not allowed to read, much less to write. (Leonard, again kindly, had said not to trouble further with the proofs, for now; the book wouldn't appear in America until '37, so we needn't hurry. I needed time away from the novel; from my work; from life itself. I'd thought quietly, gently, "It's *you* who needs time away, perhaps.")

I said, "Yes, tea would be lovely. And I'm rather hungry."

He looked over, startled. *I'm rather hungry* wasn't the kind of thing Virginia said. Nor had my tone sounded uncertain, or refractory.

"Lovely," he repeated. The scowl giving way, almost, to a collegial smile.

I turned back to the boy, a notion entering my head.

"And what of *The Years?*" I asked.

His smile faltered; he glanced to one side. "Yes, well, of course I've read—I've read all your novels, Mrs. Woolf."

"But what of that one?" I insisted. "Is it not an 'acknowledged classic,' to use your handsome term?"

His lips had begun to twitch; he chewed the inside of one cheek; again his choirboy's face had paled.

"Well, ma'am, in the process of—of canon-making—I mean, there's a historical process that occurs, almost Darwinian in nature, so that even with the greatest writers there are certain works—I mean, if you think of Melville's novel *Pierre*, or Forster's *Maurice*," he said quickly, plunging ahead, "to mention a novelist you know personally—"

"*Maurice?*" I said, irritated. "I'm not aware that Morgan has written anything called *Maurice.*"

"Published posthumously, in 1972," the boy said pedantically, as if answering a question for his oral exam. "You're right, that's stupid of me not to remember, but the idea is that even great novelists falter, sometimes, when they—"

"So I've faltered with *The Years?* Is this your verdict?"

"Oh, not *my* verdict, it's just that the novel is generally considered a reversion—well, the unexpected return to realism, to conventional storytelling after the brilliant experimentation of—"

I raised my palm; he stopped at once.

"No need to continue," I said. "I see. I do see."

What the boy could not have imagined was the welling-up of joy that flooded my being. It warmed my limbs; it unclenched my heart. My eyes cleared, and I saw the village where we were stopping, wherever we were, was lovely.

Of course, I'd been right all along—*The Years* was far from my best novel; perhaps it was a wretched novel. Had my own beneficent madness thrown up this vision from the future simply to liberate me, at last, from this incubus now turned negligible and weightless in my glowing lap?

I looked down. The pages no longer seemed malevolent; they were simply...pages. Sheets of paper. Yes, I would correct them; and we would publish the book; and it would have its fate with reviewers and the public, with posterity. But my part was done. And it didn't matter. After all, I had written *Mrs. Dalloway*. I had written *To the Lighthouse* and *The Waves*.

No one else had written them. *I* had.

But I'd forgotten something, hadn't I. My sultan of the future must know, mustn't he, what *To the Lighthouse* was about. I must tell him about my parents, and my wish to recapture them; I must describe Cornwall, and my effulgent girlhood memories; and I must tell him, while I'm about it, what novels are for. It was clear he had no idea. His commentary seemed sheer madness— sounding very like Greek, in fact!

On that day, as we traveled to Twickenham, a young man from the future appeared in our motor-car, chattering in Greek.

I might have put *those* words in an essay, and let Quentin or Nigel make of them what they would.

When I turn round, of course the rumble seat is empty.

I can't say I'm not relieved. For he wouldn't have listened; something about the beatific certainty with which he spoke had assured me of that. In any case, now I'm free of the need to talk "insanely," as Leonard might think. As he pulls up to the little inn, I turn to him and smile.

"Leonard? Leonard, dear, please look at me."

He looks, fearfully; then looks again. He must see the radiant health in my face; my untroubled eyes; my unlined brow. I can see all these, certainly, mirrored in his grimace of profound surprise.

"After tea, you know," I tell him, "I think we might go back to Monk's House. After all."

Poor Leonard stares: but he isn't scowling.

"But are you…"

"Yes, yes—quite well. Something overcame me—I couldn't possibly describe it. But I'm quite capable of dispatching these proofs"—I flick at the dead cat with one hand—"by the weekend. And I want to start a new book directly." I smile, in the old way. "You know, that book *Three Guineas* we've argued about. I must make you and Clive understand why you're so wrong about the war."

He sits there, astonished. I can glimpse the passing emotions in his fierce dark eyes—uncertainty, relief, pleasure. A kind of pride.

His Ginia is back. His old Goat.

"Are we wrong, then?" he asks, half-seriously.

"Yes," I inform him, tartly, "you patriarchal pillagers are always wrong. You can't help it."

I give my bright, metallic laugh. Leonard wrinkles his eyes, ironically.

"Shall we have our tea, then?" he asks.

"Indeed," I agree, grasping for the door handle. "Indeed we must have our tea."

Double Exposure

Her hair smelled bad.

The day we came to visit Mr. Thomas, that awful February, she happened to come downstairs—"just checking the mail," she said, with a half-apologetic smile—and after collecting a few envelopes she stalled a moment. That's when I noticed the smell, and focused my attention on the oily mane of darkish blond hair through which, I imagined, she had splayed her fingers many times. Though ten years old, I was an observant child, and passing my gaze downward I saw that her clothes looked cheap and not very clean. Her fingers had stains on them as of dark ink, or ashes.

My mother, with her middle-class American politeness, shook the woman's dirty hand without hesitation. From the smile she gave, she might have been meeting the queen. The woman kept looking back and forth between us, smiling eagerly, as my mother launched into a needlessly detailed explanation of our presence outside Mr. Thomas's door. He was the great-uncle of a pilot's wife my mother had befriended while we still lived on the base, and Mrs. Fellowes had insisted we stop and meet the old man, since we were going to be his neighbors. The day before, my mother and I had moved into our own flat in the next block of Fitzroy Road, and though we hadn't finished unpacking she'd resolved that morning to fulfill her obligation promptly. She called it an "obligation," but I knew my mother was hungry to meet people—even a British woman's elderly uncle.

While my mother explained all this I stared at the woman, whose name was Sylvia. It struck me that Sylvia was just the kind of person my mother needed at that moment, for she was an intense, compassionate listener, expressing no impatience with my mother's volubility. That was the first time I guessed that Sylvia was lonely, too.

My mother kept talking. Within minutes she had told Sylvia the story she'd been giving everyone we met (our new landlord, neighbors she encountered in the hallway, even the elderly woman who owned the greengrocer's shop on the corner). The main details were these. Her husband, my father, was in the air force—which was true. He was stationed in London for another six months, at which time his term of service would end—also true. Though we'd been living on the base in quarters provided for married airmen, the U.S. government instead had provided a tiny flat in the Fitzroy Road for my father's dependents—a disappointing but temporary arrange-ment, my mother added quickly, for we'd all be returning home together in six months' time.

This last part was not true. The truth was my parents had split up, and my father had told us both, in separate, difficult conversations, that when we returned to America he planned to file for a divorce. My mother had moved us to the Fitzroy Road flat supposedly because she wanted, now that we were here, to "experience a different culture." It would be a fine learning experience for me, she said. We could stay in London (where I would follow a reading list sent by my fourth-grade teacher back in Atlanta) until August, when we'd have to return to America and my school. But the real reason we'd stayed in London, of course, was that my mother couldn't accept the separation—my father had met another woman—and was lingering in the hope that she'd get him back.

She hadn't told me this, in so many words, but I'd known what would happen in the way intelligent children know such dismal things. Perhaps I knew before she did, months earlier when my mother was still pretending to herself we were a happy little family about to conclude its British adventure.

Standing there in the freezing entryway with my mother and Sylvia, I'd begun fidgeting. I wanted to return to our flat, which at least was well-heated, and help my mother unpack, then read until dark and in that way make an end to another day against the time when we could finally return to America and a semblance of normalcy. But I fidgeted quietly; I was a polite boy. There was a baby's pram, empty, there in the vestibule, and I held the bar and moved the pram forward and back, forward and back, as though soothing an invisible child.

When my mother finally stopped talking, Sylvia related in a few, efficient sentences how she'd come to be here, occupying the two floors above Mr. Thomas's flat. He was such a nice and helpful man, she said; she knew we'd like him very much. By now, however, Sylvia had told us that Mr. Thomas had gone out for the day. He worked for an art museum, she said, and was an artist himself.

"Oh, really?" my mother exclaimed, as though delighted by this news.

Sylvia, ducking her head mischievously, cupped her mouth and stage-whispered, "But ringing the bell won't do, you know. He's deaf as a corpse."

"Oh, is he?" my mother said, sympathetically.

Sylvia laughed. "You have to bang and bang," she said, miming the action against Mr. Thomas's door. "Like you're trying to wake the dead. Literally."

My mother gave her most forced and gracious smile. "Really, I'll have to remember that."

Neither my mother nor Sylvia seemed to sense any awkwardness in their eager, serendipitous conversation here in this foyer—I saw that Sylvia was cold, too, the tips of her nose and ears a waxen pink—and now Sylvia was exclaiming over her "luck" in meeting another American woman living just a block away. They were about the same age, weren't they? She hoped they'd become good friends. Her babies were napping, or she'd have invited us upstairs to meet them, and make us a cup of tea.

"I've taken up all the British customs," Sylvia said, in her nasally half-Boston, half-British drawl. "I imagine you have, as well?"

My mother agreed because she was always agreeable, though she disliked tea. She swerved onto another subject, a tactic she often used just after committing a lie, then feeling her insincere, polite guilt about it. She latched onto another bit of information the woman had offered.

"You know, we've never met a real poet before," she said, admiringly. "Have we, honey?" she added, glancing down at me.

Uncomfortable beneath the gaze of the malodorous, poorly dressed Sylvia and my genteel-looking, perfumed mother—whom no one would recognize as a woman plunged into raving despair—I glanced away. I kept playing with the pram.

"No," I said quickly, fearing what would come next, as it did.

"You know, my son has written quite a few poems at school, back in the states," she said. "He goes to Catholic school, and the nuns read them aloud to the class."

"Is that so?" Sylvia said, staring down with renewed curiosity, her lips edging upwards in a smile.

I imagine that, to Sylvia, I looked much too well-fed and well-scrubbed to suggest a budding poet. Though I can't recall what I wore, I must have been nicely dressed, since my mother took great care with my clothes and grooming, knowing that my appearance reflected on her. In the coming days, after meeting Sylvia's children, she would exclaim privately how she couldn't imagine a woman not keeping her babies' nightgowns clean, their faces shining. Especially now when the weather had turned so brutally cold and almost everyone you met had the flu.

The woman asked, "And what do you write about? You can't have had any *deep* experiences." She gave her throaty laugh.

I shrugged; probably I blushed. "Just about...old houses and forests, and sometimes ghosts. Things like that." I shouldn't have been so specific, but unlike my mother I instinctively told the truth when anyone asked a question.

Sylvia laughed again. "A budding Gothicist, are you?"

Neither my mother nor I knew what that meant, not then; but we smiled as though she'd paid an extravagant compliment.

"I guess so," I mumbled.

My mother asked, blinking, "And how many poems have *you* written?"

Sylvia's eyes chilled briefly at this gauche question. I saw the disdain a "real poet" assumes in the face of someone ignorant of poetry. But instantly her American cheerfulness returned.

"Oh, far too many!" she exclaimed. "I've been writing like a fiend, these past few months."

Then came a silence. The awareness had grown, I suppose, that here we stood in this frigid, dank-smelling entryway, talking pointlessly, when my mother and I should return to our unpacking and Sylvia should get back to her children. It was Sylvia who broke the silence, her own politeness a bit forced, this time.

"I'd offer to help you get settled in, but I can't leave with the babies napping. The cabin fever I get inside here, though!—it gets tiresome. But why don't the two of you stop over tomorrow, around four? We'll have our tea then, and get acquainted."

I knew this invitation would not please my mother; for all her loneliness, I could sense her dislike of Sylvia, with her shabby clothes and intimidating vocabulary.

After my father left her, my mother seldom befriended any women, since it was a woman, after all, who'd broken up her marriage; she gravitated toward men, especially fatherly, even grandfatherly men. (Perhaps that was part of her eagerness to meet Mr. Thomas.) And I'm sure she was thinking tomorrow was too soon. After settling into our flat, no doubt she wanted to luxuriate in her misery, to weep for hours in her darkened bedroom with the door partway closed, and to make brief, anguished phone calls to my father, begging him to reconsider. Each time she did this, I hurried to my room, closed the door, and snapped on the radio. I didn't want to hear.

"I'd love that!" my mother cried. "Are you sure it's not too much trouble?"

Again that throaty laugh. "My version of 'tea' is pretty meager, I warn you. Just a few sweet rolls, but I *did* find a shop round the corner that sells the most wonderful Darjeeling. I think you'll like it." Another glance at me. "And there'll be an orangeade, of course, for our young Mr. Poe."

My mother smiled as if Darjeeling and Poe were part of her everyday discourse. "Thanks so much," she said, and then she looked at me, too. She added, in her shrilly polite voice, "Isn't it nice, honey, that we've met one of our neighbors?"

I gave a vague smile but could think of nothing to say.

"There aren't many Americans around here, I'm afraid," Sylvia said. "The people you see out in the streets—well, I love the British, but there's that intense reserve, you know, and eccentricity. Plenty of old widows with ill-tempered pugs, or retired bachelors who spend their evenings reading Kipling, drinking brandy until they pass out for the night."

My mother laughed. "Oh, dear," she said.

Sylvia bit her lower lip. "I shouldn't say that. I'm known to take a brandy myself, after my work's done in the evening and the children are in bed. I suppose it's my poetic license, enjoying a drink alone once in a while?"

There was something strange in her tone, as though my mother or I might contest this. But my mother simply repeated, touching my shoulder, "We've never met a *real* poet before, have we, honey?"

I started backing away, toward the glass-paned entrance door; someone must bring this overlong encounter to an end. My mother was too insanely polite and Sylvia, I sensed, too lonely; she'd be willing to stand out here for a long time, talking of anything at all.

"Well, I don't know how *real* a poet I am," she said, rolling her eyes.

I'd begun to appreciate the irony in her rich, throaty voice, and in the serious attention she gave to every inane remark my mother made. There was a kind of generosity there, I thought; or perhaps the loneliness was simply that desperate.

"I'm sure you're quite talented," my mother said.

"Well, my first collection came out not long ago—I'll be happy to give you an inscribed copy tomorrow, if you care for such things. And I've done some talks and things for the BBC, and an interview." She bit her lip. "I hope that doesn't sound pompous, but poets don't get much attention in this world—so we savor what little we get!"

"Interviewed on the BBC! Imagine that!" my mother said. She reached aside to touch my arm, only then realizing I'd retreated toward the door.

Sylvia made a quick, dismissive gesture with her hand. "Oh, it's nothing. Just a bunch of unanswerable questions to which I was obliged to give intelligent, long-winded answers."

My mother laughed. Sylvia laughed.

"Mommy, we'd better finish the unpacking," I said, in a plaintive tone. I sounded six rather than ten.

My mother nodded. Sylvia nodded. They said their good-byes quickly and reiterated their pleasure over finding each other, and their pleased anticipation of the next day's tea.

"But really, don't go to any trouble," my mother said, as she turned away. "And I do hope we'll hear some of your poems. I'd love that, and so would my son. "We've never met—"

I'd winced, thinking surely she wouldn't repeat that phrase yet another time; fortunately, she'd caught herself.

"Don't worry, the tea will be modest. As for the poems, I don't think you'd care to hear them."

"Oh, but we *would*," my mother said.

"Oh, but you wouldn't," Sylvia said. "Believe me."

It was the only disagreeable thing she'd said—if to say something with a private reference may be called disagreeable— and it left my mother stranded in an awkward silence. The three of us stood there a few seconds longer, my nostrils twitching at the smell of Sylvia's hair, which reminded me of spoiled food, littered alleyways, the hamper of dirty laundry my mother sorted each Monday. Why didn't Sylvia shampoo her hair? I wondered. My mother still used the large green bottle of Prell she'd brought from home.

"Until tomorrow, then," my mother said, finally. "Shall I bring anything?"

Sylvia paused and lowered her eyes, in a way I recall as girlish. "No, just yourselves," she said. "Just the company."

She turned and vanished up the dark flight of stairs.

My mother whispered, angrily, "This is just our luck, isn't it."

I nodded. It surely was.

II

Her hair smelled worse.

And her face seemed discolored, the nostrils reddish-pink and raw, plum-dark shadows beneath her eyes. Even so, she gave that bright American smile when she greeted us. She wore a nicer outfit, I recall, some tight-fitting black Capri pants and a red velour sweater that looked new, but the hair had that same oily, much-fingered look, and ink stains still streaked her hands. I remember the side of her left hand, a large blotch as though it had rested on wet ink. I wondered why she didn't scrub them, why a grown woman wouldn't want her hair and hands clean. I confess I was in a foul mood—the kind children get when dragged some-where they don't want to go—as I was fearful of my mother's embarrassing me. Otherwise I might not have minded, as Sylvia's being a poet had snagged my interest.

There were books and papers everywhere. After Sylvia let us in, she took my mother upstairs to see the babies, who'd been put down for their nap. But Sylvia said they were still awake and she wanted my mother to see them. She knew I had no interest in babies—she said this with the droll smirk she often gave me—so she invited me to "dig into" the pastries heaped on the tea table, arranged neatly on a ceramic plate. In retrospect it seems that Sylvia, too, no less than my mother, was trying to maintain an appearance of normalcy, even a determined conventionality, but in my boyishly harsh judgment her efforts had failed.

While they were upstairs, I shambled around the room, hands plunged into my pockets. My mother had insisted I wear my navy blazer; she'd also dug out my red bow tie from the preceding Easter. I passed my gaze along the desks and tables, pausing over each item like a miniature curator. There were so many heaps of papers, some an unsettling bright pink. So many books, too, stacked haphazardly: I stopped and glanced with my head turned sideways, reading titles before moving to another. I seem to remember books on history, including some on Napoleon (which struck me as odd). Memory is notoriously unreliable; it would be easy to claim that I recall reading, in Sylvia's spiky but legible hand, now-famous phrases like *White Godiva, I unpeel* or *I eat men like air.* I do remember seeing manu-script poems, neatly typed with many cross-outs and additions in the same spiky hand, but the only recollection I trust is my thinking that Sylvia had been right: my mother wouldn't like these poems.

Hearing them descend the stairs, I hurried to the table and sat down, examining the pastries as if I'd spent the entire time deciding which to eat. Sylvia had been modest in apologizing for the tea: the pastries were quite elaborate, some with fruit and cheese fillings, and it occurred to me that she'd spent a considerable sum on this little meal. Her furniture and belongings suggested she didn't have much money. The walls had been painted a stark white, and the sparse furniture included some plain bookcases and two uncomfortable-looking, vaguely Oriental chairs made of straw. I wondered if she couldn't afford to furnish the apartment properly or simply liked this spare, inhuman style. This thought, combined with the shadowy, chilly atmosphere of the rooms, made me wonder again if she was lonely.

Cheerfully, Sylvia approached the table, gesturing my mother toward an empty chair. "Don't they strike your fancy?" she asked me, smiling, "or are you just being polite?"

"I was just...waiting," I said.

My mother said, "He's never been one for sweets, actually. He's not like other children, that way."

"Oh?" Sylvia cocked her head, regarding me. "Try one of the cheese ones, then," she said, pointing an ink-stained finger at the very one, in fact, I'd planned to take. Delicately I lifted the pastry, took a small bite, and set the remainder on my plate. Both Sylvia and my mother stood watching me with anxious smiles, making me long to rise from my chair and rush back down Fitzroy Road to our own apartment. Of course, I did no such thing, and after pouring tea and getting settled in her chair Sylvia directed her attention to my mother, sending a volley of questions her way as if her guest— an ordinary-looking woman in a pale-blue dress with pleated skirt, and a conventional string of fake pearls—were the most fascinating person in England.

Since her separation from my father, my mother had mastered the art of giving courteous answers to people while providing very little concrete information. This was one skill of hers that I admired and soon enough deployed on my own (especially the next fall, back in Atlanta, when I returned to school). One thing I noticed was that neither Sylvia nor my mother talked about their husbands, as if honoring some tacit compact that such a disagreeable subject wouldn't do for polite teatime conversation. Once or twice Sylvia did refer to "my ex-husband," but only in a casual, glancing way, as you'd mention a pet now deceased, or a piece of furniture you'd thrown out; clearly, she no more wanted to talk about her marital disaster than did my mother—who now, perhaps fearing such a turn in the conversation, inevitably raised the subject I most dreaded.

"So, have you been writing poetry today, Mrs. Hughes?" she asked.

Sylvia reached out, playfully, and gave my mother a pretend slap on the arm. "Now really, do call me Sylvia," she said, for perhaps the third time. She withdrew the hand. Her smile vanished, her eyes seemed to retreat into shadow. "No, no—I really think I'm done writing poetry, for now."

My mother and I glanced up from our plates, surprised.

"But why is that?" my mother said. "If you've published a book, and been on the BBC—"

"I'm working on a novel," Sylvia said quickly. "It's called *Double Exposure*—at least at the moment!—and I'm enjoying it quite a lot. As for the poems, they—they seemed to come to a natural end, a few days ago. I put them together into a sequence, you see, so I suppose there'll be a new collection...."

Her voice trailed off, as though she didn't quite believe this.

"*Double Exposure!*" my mother exclaimed, as I'd known she would. "What an excellent title. Are you interested in photography, Mrs.—oh, I'm sorry. Sylvia..."

Sylvia gave a deep, disdainful laugh. "No, no, it's about marriage—but especially about betrayal, infidelity. It's something else you wouldn't want to read!"

This silenced my mother; even she wouldn't deny the truth of this. Sylvia, chewing the last bite of her raspberry-filled scone, licked her stained fingers and shot a look at me.

"And how about you?" she asked. "Are you writing poetry these days?" I heard an ironic lilt to her voice, as though we shared a poets' complicity that excluded my mother.

I said, "No ma'am, not really. Only during school."

This was a lie, as I'd been writing small things here and there for weeks, late at night, after my mother had taken her sleeping pills;

but I feared any questions from Sylvia about my writing. I kept the poems hidden in a drawer so my mother couldn't read them.

"Oh, but he reads a great deal," she said, recovering her ladylike smile. "Novels, mostly, but poetry as well—don't you, honey?"

I lowered my eyes. "Sometimes. At night," I said.

"When I was little," Sylvia said, in a gentler, nostalgic voice, "I'd memorize my favorite poems. They were short ones by Emily Dickinson, Edna St. Vincent Millay, and I loved walking round the house and saying them aloud—much to the consternation of my father. He was a college professor who mostly worked at home, and he did not like to be disturbed." She laughed angrily. "But poetry is such a *force* in my little world that I couldn't contain myself, at times."

My mother and I stared. Sylvia sounded as though she were talking to herself, not to us.

"In fact, I was about your age!" she said brightly, as if discovering a remarkable fact. Again she settled her red-rimmed gaze on me. "And you? Do you memorize poems, ever? Do you enjoy doing that?"

I winced, for I knew what my mother would say next.

"Oh yes, they had an assignment just last spring," she broke in. "They were each given a poem, and the next week they'd stand before the class and recite it. The teacher said *his* was the longest and he recited it beautifully, not only getting the words right but even the right pauses and rhythms, and so forth."

Sylvia's eyes were alight. "Do you still remember the poem? Would you recite it for us?"

"Oh, I couldn't now," I murmured.

"You little silly, of course you can!" my mother cried. "Remember, the other night at dinner I asked you?—and you recited it beautifully."

Sylvia's eyes had softened. She had sensed my embarrassment and regretted pursuing the topic. But my mother was adamant.

"Come on, now, recite the poem for Sylvia. And stand up, just like you did in the class. That should help you remember."

I did a quick mental calculation and reasoned it was easier simply to recite the poem than to refuse. I did remember it, so the ordeal would be over soon enough. Then I'd ask Sylvia to read some of her poetry and my mother would insist on that, too. They'd leave me alone for a while.

I stood, my legs wobbly as a newborn fawn's. Only then did I understand I was nervous. This woman, Sylvia, had published a book; she was an authentic poet; and what had seemed an excellent recital to my English teacher back in Atlanta might sound foolish and incompetent to her.

These anxieties mounted quickly; I felt my skittering heartbeat and tasted dry panic in my throat.

"Come *on*, honey," my mother prodded. "Don't keep us waiting all afternoon."

Sylvia's compassionate, pained stare is an image I'll never forget. It was the moment I first began to like her.

I swallowed; I licked my dry lips. I began: "'Joyce,' by Trees Kilmer..."

A moment passed before I caught the mistake. I noticed Sylvia's bent head, my mother rolling her eyes, and only then heard the quivering echo of my words. But doggedly I stumbled through the poem, transposing who knows how many words and lines, until I'd reached the end. I sat down.

Sylvia smiled. "I read that poem in school, too."

"You recited it much better the other night," my mother complained.

I saw that Sylvia was shivering. To change the subject I said, "Are you cold?" It wasn't the brightest question, for we all sat huddled around the table, hands in our pockets when we weren't eating. A small portable heater, glowing a faint orange in the room's corner, was the only source of warmth.

Sylvia looked rueful. "I've been cold ever since we moved to London. That's why the children and I have been sick so much— I'm sorry it's cold in here, but I keep the good heater in Nick and Frieda's room. You know, I was so thrilled to find a flat in this building, since Yeats lived here and I thought it would...inspire me, I suppose. But then this awful weather descended. There hasn't been a single day when I or the children—sometimes all three— haven't been sick. The flu, bronchitis, sinusitis, plain vanilla colds— you name it!"

My mother said, conversationally, "I read it's the coldest winter in London in more than a century. We didn't know what to expect, since it's our first trip abroad, but the snow, especially, *has* been awful."

"The frozen pipes are the worst," Sylvia said, answering my mother but still regarding me. "When I finally got plumbers to come out, they stood shaking their heads and said to pour hot water on the outdoor pipes. They said they'd come back the next day, and of course I'm still waiting. Everyone's pipes are frozen. Everything is paralyzed."

My mother frowned. "Really? I guess we're a bit luckier, in our building. We get the afternoon sun, and I suppose that helps."

"Yes," Sylvia said, absently. "I suppose it does."

During this brief impasse in the conversation, I sat remembering a poem by Yeats another student had memorized for her recitation. "The Folly of Being Comforted" was the title. I knew that my mother had no idea who Yeats was, and I also thought that our visit was providing no comfort to Sylvia.

When she offered my mother a second cup of tea, my mother placed her palm over the cup and exclaimed, "Oh, no, we've really got to be running! We're still living out of boxes, and I'm the type who can't rest until everything is put away. I like things neat and tidy."

I didn't think she intended a reference to the cluttered state of Sylvia's rooms—my mother was a frivolous, dishonest woman, but she wasn't mean-spirited—yet I saw Sylvia glance dolefully around.

"For us writers, nothing is ever tidy," she said, and added one of her throaty, enigmatic laughs. "Except," she said, turning to me and tweaking my bow tie, "for certain tidy young poets, perhaps. I'm sure you'll grow up to write flawlessly rhymed sonnets and immaculate sestinas."

I dropped my eyes, embarrassed and pleased.

Laughing, my mother got to her feet. "For now, I'll be happy if he keeps his room straight." She held out her hand. "It was lovely meeting you, Sylvia. When we get our place in order, we'd love to have you over. But you *must* promise to read us some poems."

Walking us to the door, Sylvia seemed unexpectedly shy and girlish. "This went by so quickly," she said, and as I passed her slender form, which she seemed to drape along the edge of the open door, I caught again a whiff of her rank, unwashed hair. Since I'd grown to like her, I remembered that her pipes were burst and excused her on that account. During our tea she'd mentioned that she gave the babies sponge baths with water she carried several blocks from a store near Primrose Park.

Head bent, my mother adjusted her coat, pulled her gloves tight; we said good-bye.

That was my last glimpse of Sylvia: standing behind her door, almost as if hiding, with her face and a shank of that dark blond hair hanging against the whitish gray light from inside her apartment. I can't remember if we stopped downstairs and spoke to Mr. Thomas, but it was he who gave us the news, several weeks later, that Sylvia was dead. My mother had thought to reciprocate Sylvia's hospitality and invite her for tea; she'd called Mr. Thomas because Sylvia had mentioned, with an air of apology, that she had no phone, but that Mr. Thomas occasionally would bring her messages upstairs.

I recall very clearly that phone conversation: as I stood listening, a cold lump of sorrow settled in my chest. After much talk of days and times, my mother and Mr. Thomas calculated that Sylvia had killed herself only a few days after our visit. He told her about the flurry of activity that had followed—the father coming to retrieve the children, the police coming and going, and their questioning Mr. Thomas about what he might have seen or heard. I got these details later, from my mother, for her side of the conversation that day was mostly, "Oh dear, oh dear! *Killed* herself? Really? But how did she— *Really?*" She was shouting, since Thomas was indeed partly deaf. Her tone was an odd mixture of dismay and quite audible relish. Another woman, she must have been thinking, had died because her husband had abandoned her, but she had survived. She still wept at night, she wrote and telephoned my father after drinking two or three gins to steady her nerves, but she hadn't killed herself.

"I suppose we all think of that at times, don't we," I remember her shouting to Mr. Thomas, as they were about to hang up. "The poor woman," she said, "and those poor, lovely children!" She put down the phone, then stared for a long moment at me.

"Tell me what happened," I said.

Almost a year passed before my mother's own suicide. We were back in Atlanta, the divorce had become final, and my father was sending monthly checks from England. He'd continued his affair and finally married the other woman—my stepmother to this day—and had returned to her in London, which he'd decided he preferred to the American Southwest where he'd grown up. But my mother stayed frozen in her grief, her rage, her self-pity. I remembered Sylvia's words, *Everything is paralyzed.*

I'd gone back to school, of course, and I remember dreading the bus trip home, knowing she'd still be wearing her housecoat, her eyes puffy from crying. The day I found her face down on the living room sofa, an empty container of pills and a coffee mug half-filled with gin on the table beside her, I wasn't really surprised. She'd left no note; unlike Sylvia, she lacked the consolations of language, much less of poetry. I shed a few tears and called my aunt Ruth, whose house was two blocks away and with whom I would live until I graduated high school.

Sylvia's prediction was correct, at least partly. I did try my hand at sonnets and sestinas, feeling drawn to fixed forms, but I suppose they weren't "immaculate" since magazines always rejected them and finally I gave up. In college, studying library science, I met a quiet girl who shared some of my classes and shortly after graduation we were married. We stayed in Atlanta and both got jobs in a major university library, sharing the same shift so we could spend our time at home together as well. Too late I discovered that I'd married my mother, for the girl had nothing of her own— nothing, that is, but me. Soon enough I felt stifled and began an affair with my wife's opposite number—a graduate student who did modeling on the side. I'd become, I suppose, a reasonably handsome young man, and my mistress was the catalyst for my trying to write poetry again. I remember reading Shakespeare's sonnets and trying to imitate them, including specific references to my mistress that delighted her. I asked my wife for a divorce, and after a few predictable scenes she agreed and moved back to rural Alabama to live with her mother.

Around the time of my second marriage, my new wife quit graduate school to start modeling full-time, and I stopped writing the poetry that nobody wanted to publish. I enjoyed—and still enjoy—being a librarian, and I always experience a small frisson of delight when a new book about Sylvia comes into the library. By now, there are many dozens, perhaps hundreds. My name has never appeared in the index of these books, though I've always been fearful that some intrepid biographer might track me down—as they did Mr. Thomas, who sometimes gave them interviews. (Recently Mr. Thomas, the only person who knew of my brief connection with Sylvia, passed away, forcing me to recall that in the mid-seventies, alarmed by the way Sylvia's legend was growing, I'd phoned him. During that awkward, staticky, trans-Atlantic call, shouting so that he could hear, I'd extracted a promise that he'd never mention my name.) Nor did I tell anyone else, not even my wife, about my two encounters with Sylvia, though my wife occasionally mentions her in passing. She studied Sylvia's poetry at school.

All this has come to haunt me, I suppose, especially since I've understood that my second marriage, too, will soon come to an end. My wife, well past forty, no longer gets modeling assignments, and our intimate life together has shriveled to nothing. She's what people call a "well-preserved" woman, but no man can help the way he feels, after all. The difficulty, of course, will be telling her, going through the inevitable arguments with their tears and recriminations, and then finding a new place to live, a new life altogether. A first-year graduate student, who teases me about the "distinguished" streaks of gray in my hair, seems to find me attractive, but I'm not yet ready, I know, to marry again. That will take some time.

Yes, I do feel haunted by the ghosts of my past. Poor Sylvia, and my mother, and my first wife, and even my elegant second wife who seems already in my imagination part of the past though we still live together. (We never had children; I feel fortunate in that.) Sometimes at my desk, in an idle moment, I'll recall that image of Sylvia, peering around the door at me, bidding me good-bye. Or my first wife's moony, tear-stained face the night I turned my back on her forever. Or that famous television commercial in which my second wife appeared, shortly after we were married, a memory with a peculiar resonance I don't quite understand.

This was the mid-eighties, and we were particularly thrilled because it was her first commercial to go national. We would cuddle together under a quilt in our big four-poster, before or after making love, and replay the tape over and over.

I haven't seen the tape in years, but I remember it as clearly as I recall Sylvia's ink-stained fingers. It was an ad for a feminine product and my wife appears on horseback, first at a distance. She wears an elegant yellow sweater, brown jodhpurs and boots, her thick blond hair flying behind her; her body and the spectacular chestnut-colored mare are one, rippling through the sunlight and shadow. As the camera moves closer, we see her galloping along a dry, rutted lane overarched by the foliage of a spectacular New England autumn.

I have not cried since childhood but I did cry, or came close to crying, during the final seconds of that stupid commercial. The camera zooms in, showing my wife canted forward eagerly as she rides. My heart beats quickly, guiltily. For somehow, in that moment, she metamorphoses into the epitome of confident, glamorous womanhood, glorying in a fierce moment of power and vision with her hands clenching the bridle and her lovely hair flowing, springing behind her, wild and free.

First Surmise

I

I told him, politely, that I hadn't expected him—or anyone. I told him that I simply hadn't time.

His expression, though kindly, held an obdurate indifference to my wishes that I recognized quite well. Father had been dead a dozen years, but his firm, awe-inspiring countenance had sprung at once to my mind. Sometimes I saw that set, masculine, "I'll-brook-no-opposition" grimace in my brother's milder features as well, especially about the eyes. Neither Vinnie nor I could deal with him, then. Long ago we'd learned when to yield, when not.

I suppose that's why Vinnie had interrupted me in the conservatory with an announcement which, for years now, she would not have troubled to make.

"There's a gentleman to see you," she said from the door, glancing off, and thus avoiding my gape of profound surprise.

Yet into the parlor I'd gone—unthinking, disconcerted. And still grasping the watering can.

Having left my sickbed for the first time in many days—and feeling unaccountably at peace, and free of discomfort this morning—I'd thought while still dressing of my day-lilies. In mid-May, they needed special tending, and I knew that with me confined upstairs they'd have suffered neglect, since the busy but distracted Vinnie did not enter the conservatory for days or weeks at a time. Maggie would do the watering, if instructed; but lately there had been no one to instruct her.

I'd been far too ill. Perhaps that's why Vinnie had given me such a questioning look (for here I was, dressed, and perhaps looking as well as I felt) as she ushered me into the parlor. But she quickly retreated, putting her head down as she closed the parlor doors.

Left alone with my visitor, I was the one who looked down. I stood there silent and, as I thought, prepared, in the very center of the parlor rug. Only after the gentleman spoke did I feel the watering can, still clutched in my benumbed fingers.

"Oh, I'm—I'm sorry," I whispered, in a rapid, wayward voice. "I hardly know what to say."

That's when he offered his kindly bow, this magisterial-looking gentleman in his black waistcoat and breeches, and his formal top hat with its look of a shiny, miniature smokestack, its wide black brim.

When he proposed our outing and I told him, in my faltering way, that I simply hadn't time, he made no reply; but he seemed prepared to wait there—or so his erect and unyielding posture suggested—until I found the time. By now, the weight of the watering can had set my arm to trembling, so I was forced to place it on a nearby table. I used the gesture to cast my eyes downward, and this time I kept them there.

He knew, somehow, that I was ready. He offered me his arm.

Outside the day was brilliant, and fairly warm. Spring chuckled and gurgled all around us, in that way I'd always loved to hear. I thought with longing of my pencils and paper, on my table upstairs, and I supposed that might be a word, *chuckled,* I could put to some use.

Did I dare yield to the urge to flee? Scurry back up the sidewalk, and bolt the door? Lift my white skirt efficiently as I made quick progress up the stairs, then close my bedroom door and turn, with a sharp twist of my fingers, an imaginary lock?

No, I dared not. I followed the gentleman to the waiting carriage, pulling my shawl close about me. Already the chuckling seemed fainter to my ears.

The carriage top was down, and only after the gentleman opened my passenger door did I notice, from the corner of my eye, another gentleman waiting in the back. I stood there docile and reticent as I was introduced, but I wasn't sure I'd caught the name—"Tim Moriarty," it might have been? I hardly dared ask my dignified-looking caller to repeat himself.

So I said, simply, "I'm pleased to make your acquaintance."

To my astonishment, Tim Moriarty seemed eager, almost urgent as he pumped my proffered hand. (I watched the hand being shaken, and so briskly, yet felt nothing. Was this where my decades-long fear had led me? Into non-feeling altogether?) I detected a Southern accent, I thought. Virginia, I supposed, or Georgia. I'd met so few Southerners in my day.

"Oh, boy, I'm the one who's pleased to meet *you*," Tim Moriarty said with a wide and ingenuous smile. "I'm one of your most enthusiastic readers!"

"One of my—my readers?" I whispered.

Had someone told on me, yet again? But Mr. Bowles, my false confederate of earlier years, was gone; and my brother, who in high-spirited youth might have committed such a sly misdeed, had become too overwhelmed with adult concerns to notice what I did. Possibly the culprit was Mrs. Todd, in some mix of the reverence she felt for my work and the vengeance she perhaps desired after I'd denied her, more than once, a face-to-face interview. Or was it Vinnie herself, perhaps? It was impossible to know. I supposed it didn't matter.

Tim Moriarty arrested me still with his fresh-faced look of awe. A fair-haired, hatless gentleman: his dressy black attire (the coat, trousers, and shoes all more youthful-looking than those worn by his older, more solemn companion) contrasted notably with his shining face. He might have been fifteen or thirty-five, I thought, puzzled; he had an ageless look as though somehow freed from the lineaments of care, or passing time.

Yet there he sat, awaiting my reply.

"You are—you like to read?" I asked, carefully shifting the focus of attention.

To no avail. "I like to read *you*," this brash youth replied, all but grinning in his pleasure. His face was overbright, like a miniature sun. I looked away and said, confused, "I'd always assumed that readers—that they'd be the death of me."

He laughed, as though I'd intended to be witty. But I bit my lower lip, instantly regretting the words. Why had I confessed giving thought to the preposterous notion of "readers"? The small handful of verses I'd let slip from my control had appeared with no attribution, and I'd instructed Vinnie firmly (especially as this recent illness had worsened, and I contemplated the disposition of my private things) that everything should be *burned*. Naturally Vinnie, being Vinnie, had reacted with a measure of stubborn recalcitrance, failing to offer the forthright promise I would have preferred; she had even wondered aloud, indulging herself, why didn't *I* burn them, if I wanted them burned. But Vinnie could not understand that while I had life, the papers and packets crammed into my cherry-wood bureau were part of that life: indeed, they were almost all.

Burning them was as impossible as sharing them.

The young man, taking note of my response, had stopped laughing, and seemed now to take my remark seriously.

"Oh, Miss," he said, in a solemn tone. "The opposite is true, believe me."

Since I did not respond, and since my gentleman yet stood there holding the opened door, there was nothing left but to step upwards, yielding to his grip of manly insistence under my arm. Once I was seated, I took in the familiar sights of Main Street from this unfamiliar vantage. This was my first carriage ride, it now struck me, in more than two decades; my first glimpse of the brick mansion my father built—seeing from the outside, I mean, like any common observer—since I was barely more than a girl. From one of the downstairs windows, I glimpsed Vinnie's pale, doleful face; perhaps she'd been watching all the while, but she backed away too quickly to allow a parting wave. I kept staring, hungrily, but the windowpane was empty.

A knot of emotion had seized my throat.

As my top-hatted companion settled into the driver's cushion, I felt the need to break our awful silence.

"It's just the three of us, I gather?" I murmured.

But I must have spoken too softly, a failing common to those who pass much time in solitude. I risked a sideways glance, but he

gave no sign that he'd heard. He lifted the crop, and with a brief
whinny of protest from the horses, we began our journey.

II

We drove.

In the past, from my bedroom window, I'd glimpsed young
men galloping along with their carriages at alarming speeds, so
that when their cargo was a young lady she'd be forced, literally,
to hold onto her bonnet. Both would be laughing, but the sight
troubled me. So easily they could hit a rut, or a stone left
carelessly in the road, which might tilt the carriage sideways and
send them flying. Some of these young men, aged eighteen or
nineteen, I recognized as the small boys to whom I once lowered
baskets of sweets and muffins, on a slender rope, from that same
window. Some accident befalling one of them would be more than
I could bear.

Yet my gentleman drove in a slow, stately manner that befitted
his dignified appearance and bearing. He seemed, indeed, to have
all the time in the world, and I noticed another carriage or two
passing along at much faster rates, their drivers not so much as
acknowledging us, or seeming bothered by our slower progress.
This reassured me. I settled into my seat, adjusting my white skirts
and leaning down to check the hem for traces of dust, or pollen;
but there was none. We might have been traveling, moreover,
along a road layered in satin or velvet, so smooth was the ride. I
thought with puzzlement of those bumpy, jolting carriage rides of
my youth. Perhaps the wheels, the roads themselves were made
more skillfully now? And certainly my companion drove with
consummate skill, as though he'd passed along this street
hundreds of times and knew precisely what he was about.

Occasionally he glanced aside, as though to assure himself of
my comfort; once or twice he allowed himself a smile—a rather
grave one—and when our eyes met, he gave a just-perceptible bow,
touching the brim of his hat. He demonstrated such a degree of
civility, indeed, that I no longer felt the alarm, nor even the sorrow,
of that last glimpse of my father's house, or the lunge of grief when
I knew that Vinnie had departed from my sight.

It seemed agreeable, in fact, to have left paper and pencil, and even the pulsing thought that required them, behind me, in exchange for the gentlemanly grace with which my top-hatted caller had dealt with me, thus far. I'd had a fleeting thought, too, that I might have brought a book, or one of my favored journals, but even such leisurely pursuits (that is, my recollection of them) had an air of the superfluous, considered here. I felt it might have been a rudeness, in such company, to have occupied my time in any way not entirely passive, and docile, and un-questioning—behavior that my gentleman seemed to take for granted. I recalled that my initial response ("I have no time"— how foolish the words now seemed!) was something he'd politely but definitively ignored.

The younger gentleman in the rear of the carriage was a different case altogether. Once or twice I glanced around, and each time he seemed eagerly to await my notice: not wishing to intrude on my silence, or my thoughts, but readily speaking when my eyes met his.

He said, in his shy but suggestive way, "I suppose anybody in his right mind, given this chance, would want to ask you all sorts of questions."

I offered a perplexed, fleeting smile.

"There are few questions I could answer, sir—of that I'm certain. But it's kind of you to think otherwise."

He said rushingly, as though I had not spoken, "For instance, the way you use punctuation. Or the habit of capitalizing certain words. And what about titles? And what made you decide to renounce—"

But he stopped himself; his blue-green eyes held a look of alarm, as though he'd glimpsed the hurt in my own.

"I'm sorry, I don't mean to be forward," he said quickly.

I thought it best to change the subject.

"Amherst is at its best during this season, don't you think? I haven't been able to enjoy the spring, this year, as much as previously." I gave a polite cough, avoiding his hungry gaze. "Whatever glimpse my window offered, from my bed-ridden vantage, has been the sum total of my springtime enjoyment, I'm afraid."

He smiled and looked off, as if yet ashamed by his attempted inquisition. That provided me the opportunity to turn back around, and to notice the spring day myself. We had stopped at Pleasant Street, and we made no turn; but in the distance, at the far end of the Common, I thought I glimpsed the rotund Mrs. Tuckerman taking her constitutional, dressed in mourning, tapping along the thick grass with her cane. Birds chirped merrily from the trees; a squirrel, on urgent business, traversed the road in seconds and began ascending one of the full-leafed oaks near the corner where Amity Street stretched to the west.

Again that bothersome lump entered my throat. Springtime. Amherst. Home. Such a flood of memories came reeling through my head! Girlhood rides with Father, as he took me along—the eldest and thus "special," just as Austin was sometimes taken as the only boy and thus "special," or Vinnie as the youngest and thus "special"—on some errand in town; or playing with Vinnie and Abby out in the same field where poor Mrs. Tuckerman (her husband only two months dead) now took her walk; or being escorted up the muddy, darkened margins of our street (for in my youth there was no lighting or sidewalk, and getting home from anywhere with clean hems an impossible challenge) by Mr. Newton, from a lecture at the College or a social evening at church. Lines from my own verses came rushing back, too, as though written by someone else and permitted me, now, to enjoy; their rhythmic verve capturing all the spring-inspired fervor of my sentient life; their select words restoring a few unforgotten ecstasies from my splendid menagerie of recollections, reveries.

Almost, it was too much to bear.

I glanced aside to my gentleman, hoping he had not noticed the sheen of moisture that had blurred my vision. But his attention remained fixed ahead of him, his posture and the set of his jaw looking stern with purpose, though not a purpose lacking in kindliness or, as I have said, in a grave civility commensurate with his bearing. I considered that I should stay idle, contenting myself that I had retired the fripperies of my daily life in deference to his gentlemanly deportment. Since our brief, embarrassing verbal exchange, I'd heard nothing more from Mr. Moriarty, and I had not glanced back there again.

I allowed my hands to rest quietly, idly, in my lap. My companions were quiet, too.

We drove.

III

Though my gentleman had called in the forenoon, I can't say precisely when, as we rode along, a quality of darkness began to invade my perceptions.

Having put aside my lexicon, my papers, and even my habit of ceaseless thought, I sensed that words, from this moment forward, would fail me; and though I tried to formulate a more precise phrase, only "a quality of darkness" came to mind. It must have been half past nine, or ten at the latest, and uneasily I was aware that beyond our sphere of quiet, dignified motion there was an ordinary day in bustling Amherst, in springtime. Yet we were not part of this, my companions and I. Any familiar structure or stand of trees we passed seemed increasingly tinged with this sense of apartness. And despite my heightened sense of alarm I remained passive, my hands motionless in my lap.

Silence enwrapped our carriage like invisible gauze.

Proceeding down Amity Street, we passed the public school, which had been erected on the same lot that once held my beloved Amherst Academy, where as a girl I'd spent so many happy years. Just as we approached I saw, to my right, the school door opening and a gaggle of children, all vivid colors and scissoring limbs, bursting out the doorway for recess. They were shouting and laughing, yet somehow I could not hear them. A few took their places in a dusty, cleared-out circle in the playing yard, and they began a game that involved much running and chasing, one child after another. I could see a peculiar look, not really a childlike look, in their faces, which seemed contorted with the effort of their play. So physical and incessant was their activity, so intense was the strain of their effort, that within seconds I'd begun viewing their play as a semblance of some prolonged and inescapable labor. Their faces had reddened with strain; veins stood out at their foreheads, their throats.

I shifted in my seat, uneasily. Somehow the sight had become disagreeable to me; this was not the kind of play that I remembered, from my long-ago days at the Academy. I looked in the other direction, past the bony profile of my resolute gentleman, and resolved not to glance rightward again until we should have passed beyond sight of the school.

To the left, however, another unsettling sight awaited me. We passed an empty field, a little beyond Professor Warner's homestead, but though we rode along through this brimming sunlit morning at the height of spring, the field lacked entirely the effulgent green clover and thick grass of the Common, where I'd seen Mrs. Tuckerman taking her constitutional. I felt my nostrils widen, instinctively, for the smell of clover, of spring iris and roses, but quickly they pinched shut again, disappointed.

For this field, against all probability, seemed to exist in its own sphere of weather, its own season, where the time appeared to be *autumn* rather than spring!

I stared, scarcely believing my eyes. It was a field of ripe grain, ready for harvest, and I was so taken aback by this impossible sight that I felt the grain, too, gazed with similar shock and discomfiture back at *me*. As if I were the unnatural sight, and not itself.

I shook myself, thinking I had entered some disagreeable waking dream. Not only did I withdraw my gaze and shrink back into my habitual quietude—which, for a considerable time now, both my gentleman and Mr. Moriarty had consented to share—but to dispel myself of that disturbing autumnal vision I closed my eyes altogether, as though a few moments' of resting them, of allowing myself to be lulled by the somnolent rhythms of the carriage ride, might put everything to rights. Only when I felt that, as with the school, we must have passed by the field did I allow myself to open them again. Such was my caution, this time, that I chose to follow my gentleman's wise example and gaze implacably forward, vowing to glance neither to the left nor to the right.

Yet there was no escape, it appeared, from the dreadful change of my fortunes. For straight ahead was a sight far more discomfiting than the other two.

I had left my father's house, as I say, at roughly half past nine, and I estimated that our carriage ride, to this point, had lasted no more than half an hour—three quarters at the outside. It was, I insist, a brilliant morning in Amherst. It was, I insist, springtime in Amherst.

Yet directly ahead of me, as we drove westward on Amity, what did I see on the far horizon but, to my fearful astonishment, the setting sun!

Even as I sat there, agape, mute, and distressed beyond all measure, my gentleman turned the carriage again, this time onto Lincoln Street, so that the western horizon with its sun perched above the Pelham Hills like a bloodied egg yolk stretched along my right-hand side. As we drove, it seemed we were leaving the sunset itself behind—passing beyond it, as it were. Still paralyzed with unhappy wonder, I kept staring at the red-orange disc, now so far descended that one could gaze directly upon it with no visual discomfort, and soon enough I was forced to crane my head backwards, seized with the idea that we were abandoning the sunset to another sphere, another realm of being altogether. I thought clearly that it belonged to a darkening world which, though we drove so slowly, we were nonetheless quickly passing by. That aura of darkness I described earlier, not to mention its attendant silence, its chill air of permanence and its fog-like, unearthly smell, seemed an ever-widening scrim dividing our carriage from the sunset, as though we were being drawn inescapably into the fearful gloaming that had begun to thicken all around us, pulling us away from that familiar world now bathed unaccountably in the reddish light of a premature sunset.

Nonetheless I kept craning my head, in a parody of extreme desperation, or extreme stubbornness, until a new vision of our progress, and of our very journey, finally released my perception from its fruitless adherence to what I believed I'd seen. For we had not passed the setting sun at all, of course, any more than we had passed that unaccountable field of grain, or that ring of striving, grimacing children at their awful play. For a moment, I thought to glance aside at my gentleman, or even—such was my sudden loneliness and despair—to the rear of the carriage, to engage Mr. Moriarty in some distracting bit of talk. Yet this would be pointless, I reasoned, now that I'd seen what I had seen.

Or, more to the point: now that I knew the terrible thing I knew.

IV

What I knew, of course, was that we had not passed any strange vision of a sunset descending around ten o'clock of a fair New England morning.

I'd had the profound awareness, indeed, that we had not passed anything; and that the reason our progress seemed so slow, and so lacking in the customary jolts and rattles of a carriage ride, was that despite my belief that we had passed the various sights I have recounted, and despite my unhappy visions of the school, the field, and the sunset, in fact *the carriage had not been moving at all, for the entire length of our journey.*

Rather, I understood, with a sudden lurch of perception, it was the sunset that had *passed us*; the field and the school that had *passed us*; Professor Warner's house and old Mrs. Tuckerman on her walk that had *passed us*. All these things had been more than passing, indeed. They had been fleeing us, rather, and steadily darkening as they fled. It was we, not they, who were disappearing. And as I suffered this terrible new perception, I saw gathering about me something far more portentous, vast, and fearful than anything the innocuous phrase "quality of darkness" can begin to convey.

Quite simply, we'd entered another world. I'd begun to shiver, feeling the air growing damp, or dank, with a chill moisture that made my body tremble; I felt myself physically shrinking inside the ordinary dress and shawl I'd happened to wear this morning. Though I had seen, dimly, that we had turned onto Northampton Street and then onto Pleasant Street, where we'd lived until we moved permanently back to the homestead, I could barely make out the ground, the trees, the sky itself through the quivering veil of dusky unreality that had descended around our carriage. Shaking with cold, I glanced down to pull my skirts and shawl more tightly about my body, and was astonished to see that my dress, a solid white gingham an hour ago, had become a filmy gossamer, an envelope that seemed fully transparent even as it revealed nothing at all. My worsted shawl, too, had changed magically to a white, tulle-like mist, so that as I tried to gather it about me, my chilled hands pressed through to nothing, or almost nothing. Rather, my shawl now seemed a phosphorescent shimmer of the air, a substanceless mockery of solidity or warmth. As my gentleman, undaunted, pressed the horses forward, I felt I'd become an uncertain, whitish blur inside the carriage.

Rather than face my sternly erect gentleman—for somehow I could not raise my eyes to his—I looked behind me, wondering how Mr. Moriarty had dealt with this profound change in our surroundings. How amazed I felt, though not at all reassured, to see that he sat there still fresh-faced and smiling, looking about him quite as if he saw nothing that I was seeing. For him, it was a beautiful day in May, surely. For him, the world had not descended into this chill, preternatural dusk.

He tipped his hat and gave a pleasant grin.

"You know," he said, "I don't blame you one bit for not answering those questions." He nodded, as though he'd satisfied himself on the matter. "Nope, you left us the poems and the letters. And that's all that matters."

"Left you—? But Mr. Mor— I mean, Tim—"

"Yes, Miss, and I'm not even going to ask about that wild year you had in '62, or about the good reverend or the good judge, or whoever it was you sent those letters to. No, Miss, I'm surely not. That's just too damned personal."

My head was reeling. "Left" him my poems?—my letters? I couldn't grasp what this man was saying. Had he known Reverend Wadsworth? Had he known Judge Lord? He seemed far too young, and neither of them had mentioned a Mr. Moriarty. And how painful to see him sitting there, in a pool of sunlight, while the rest of the carriage and everything about us had sunk into profoundest gloom! I felt, almost, like reaching out a hand to him, that he might pull me back into the springtime, back into the sun-dappled, fragrant world he was so clearly enjoying. If I could join him there, I thought, he might ask any questions he liked. If he might somehow return me to Main Street, to Vinnie, to home, I should be more than happy to tell him everything.

I felt an unexpected choking sensation that I could only describe as panic, compounded by extreme desperation and extreme fear. The young man had mentioned that dreadful year 1862, when I'd endured such emotional storms by the day, by the hour; was it possible he knew that I had suffered, furthermore—But I couldn't bear to think of that, even now.

It was essential, of course, that I face my gentleman and ask him to take me home at once. My desperation had provided courage. My fear had provided the necessary recklessness with which, shivering, holding my arms clasped tightly around a gauzy nothingness I could not feel, I now turned to face him.

Only to learn that he'd chosen this moment to stop the horses, and, ushering in a further horror, turn abruptly to face me, his helpless and bewildered passenger.

V

If I'd felt that any warm blood yet coursed through my veins, I might have said that last bit of coursing blood stopped at once, and became ice; I might have said the marrow in my bones had chilled, had it not already frozen in despair. Even as I looked upon his now-hideous countenance my vision itself seemed locked within a vault of cold, so that I had gone beyond trembling, or shivering, to become one with the gelid horror of what I saw.

My gentleman yet wore his black boots, his breeches, his handsome waistcoat; his top hat still shone in the weird half-light of the dusky world we had entered. Yet instead of the stern but handsome face he'd presented—such a short time ago, it seemed!—that face now was gone. All its flesh, tissue, and blood had utterly vanished as though they'd never been.

I sat staring, in short, into the gaping, grinning face of a naked skull, its look of cheerful horror only enhanced by the suit and top hat of my seemingly distinguished gentleman caller. Every shred of the intense emotion with which I'd planned to confront him, all the fear and desperation and sheer unbridled panic, shrunk at once to a ludicrous pinpoint and became part of the frozen absence I sensed, about equally, within and without that phenomenon once known as "myself." It took only a moment of the skull's mocking expression, its look of silent, cosmic laughter, for me to turn away. Clearly, my "gentleman" and his friend Mr. Moriarty had each departed to a different world, and neither of them could help me.

I vowed never to look at either of them again.

Glancing around me, I felt we had stopped at a place that seemed familiar and yet, in that paradoxical simultaneity I'd experienced from the moment our ride began, weirdly unfamiliar. I had the strange sensation of glimpsing a dreamscape in which one struggles to find the words for ordinary things but cannot, so that everything hovers eerily, in a present moment that seems potentially everlasting, in a hideous state of namelessness. Whether things had lost their names or I had lost the words attached to them, I cannot say: I can only make feeble attempts to describe the things I saw.

We had stopped at what looked, to my dimmed perception, like a house that had sunk gently, gracefully, into the ground. Peering down, I observed that the ground had a swollen look, as though it had engorged on a secret but blissfully satisfying aliment. At the far end of the swelling I could glimpse one corner of the roof, incompletely swallowed. As for the cornice, the walls, the porches, and all the rest of what might once have been some ordinary homestead, they had vanished entirely. Except for that hint of a roof, one might not know that a fine house, never mind its human inhabitants, had existed at all.

There was an air, moreover, of quietness; of satisfaction; of inevitability. The horror that I'd sensed in the darkening surround, in my own melting out of substance, and in the vision of my gentleman turned to a skeletal escort who seemed amused at the clever trick he had played—all this seemed only the painful procedure by which not only a painless, but even a peaceful, state of transcendent completeness had been reached.

Yet I remained puzzled. I recognized the swollen mound of earth, and the shard of roof, but I could not name them. Casting my looks out further, I could see other mounds, with other suggestions of a gable, perhaps, or a cement stoop where someone now silenced had once placed her foot, on any of a thousand ordinary spring mornings. But my eye kept returning to the ground, to the earth that seemed both humanly tended and fully indifferent to human wishes, human dreams. I kept staring at the ground for what seemed a long while but might have been a moment, my attention disturbed only when, with another switch of the crop, the horses resumed their canter, and we continued slowly forward.

Then I looked up, and received a shock that beggared everything else that had happened since Vinnie entered the conservatory, interrupting my colloquy with my beloved day-lilies.

VI

That last moment is more than I can describe.

That last moment is more than I care to remember, though I do remember.

First I'd noticed there was no more cold, no more sense of my arms grasped tight around a chilled and shivering human frame with whose proportions and peculiarities I must once have been intimately familiar. I was no longer a whitish, ghostly blur in the carriage; whatever that vision had been, I had left it behind during our brief interlude in the field of buried houses.

Yet still I saw, and it might be said there was only that: my seeing. No longer did I care for my gentleman, or Mr. Moriarty, or even myself. I cared only for what I perceived, though my perception again was the source of a profound shock that even now, centuries agone, seems to mark that moment as the longest of my life.

I heard the horses' whinnying response to my gentleman's crop; I saw the familiar shake of their heads, the twitching of their small brownish ears, as they began drawing us forward. They were handsome, ordinary horses—that I could see. One had a white spot above his mane while the other, his body a darker nut-brown, had a solid, glossy sheen to his gently bouncing head which, on an ordinary day, would have made me yearn to pat him between the ears.

Then my gaze lengthened beyond the two horses and their glossy snouts tossing and swaying as they trotted. Perhaps I expected to see that we'd turned onto yet another Amherst street, that perhaps we were near the railroad tracks or, taking another direction, sauntering past the handsome College buildings with their grandfatherly air of pre-eminence and pride.

But no. The Amherst streets, along with Amherst itself, had vanished from my seeing.

The earth itself had vanished from my seeing.

I saw that which one can use only dissatisfying abstractions to describe—that is, I saw eternity itself. (I admit that I feel a ghostly memory of human shivering, a half-welcome recrudescence of human feeling, even as I speak the word.)

Eternity. How glibly I'd spoken the word in my tight, compacted verses! Now it spread before me, first into the predictable endlessness of skies and stars; and, beyond them, into vast spaces of night through which our carriage and our two innocent, healthy horses must also pass. Opening still beyond were further vistas of space, further provinces of night. And beyond those? The knowledge of so many layers of dark-shrouded reality, each multiplied endlessly, swept into my widened, feverish eyes in a single moment of disbelief. But of course I did believe. And, as I have said, it was the longest imaginable moment.

Its only reassurance, for me, lay in the knowledge that I might continue to travel, even though the journey should never end.

And its only reassurance for you—my readers, who have indeed been the death of me!—lies in the sound of my solitary voice, purely alone and purely itself.

A voice that shall never perish, so long as you are there.

V

New Stories

Women I've Known

23 April 2037

Dear Ms. Cather:

This inquiry may surprise you, but since I know that throughout your life you've striven to keep an open mind, and to respond in a forthright, honest way to those interested in your work, I hoped you would entertain an inquiry about one of your stories from an unlikely but most sincere and respectful source.

Though a professor emeritus from a state university in Georgia (I retired many years ago), I've lately been invited to teach at a private liberal arts college in your native state of Nebraska, a one-year post I'm enjoying very much. My syllabus includes your enigmatic short story "Paul's Case," and in the course of doing research I've become intensely fascinated not only by the story but also by your life. There are dozens of biographies, of course, and I've read several of the best ones. As for the story, its gay themes have been explored ad infinitum during the last few decades, but there is surprisingly little material relating its own vision of hegemonic, heterosexist intimidation and the covert realities of your own relationships with women, not to mention such tangential issues as cross-dressing and vivisection as deconstructions of the female body.

Most artists are disinclined to analyze their own work; I know this is true of you, and certainly I respect your position. However, if you might enlighten me to some degree regarding your intentions in writing "Paul's Case," and especially in relating Paul's experiences as a gay, sensitive music-lover to your own struggles as a gay woman and artist, I would be most appreciative.

I felt sanguine about writing you at this time because you have reached the point in your career when, as I hope you'll agree, "a backward glance" might yield a valuable perspective; and a point at which you have attained a status enabling you to speak as forthrightly as you wish, even on sensitive matters, without caring what anyone thinks. I understand your decision not to allow publication of your letters, and I will pledge not to publish any reply you'd deign to send my way. At most, I would paraphrase salient passages for the purposes of my research.

I hoped you might be sympathetic to my position, as well, as a long-retired critic who yet feels he might have one more good article in him. I don't ask for special consideration due to my advanced age, or even because we are, as the young people like to say, "members of the club"; rather I address you as one writer to another, divided by time but united by sensibility. After a young colleague—a handsome young man I think you'd like very much—offered to assist me with the technological difficulties of this correspondence, I found I could not resist. Without him, I would be reduced merely to composing this letter in my head, since I remain something of a Luddite where technology is concerned. According to my friend, this letter will have appeared on your front porch, genie-like, inside a silver-toned "cyberspace envelope," which will likewise bear your response back to me. You need only re-tuck the envelope and leave it just where you found it; my friend's state-of-the-art computer software does the rest. I wish I could explain further, but I'm unaccustomed to dealing in cyberspace or writing through the space-time continuum.

In any case, this is all beside the main point, and perhaps uninteresting to you. You cannot imagine the interest with which, Ms. Cather, I await your kind reply.

> Yours sincerely,
> Georgina Johnstone, Ph.D.

P.S. I've forgotten to mention that I've been involved in gay studies throughout my long career.

April 24, 1937

Dear Professor Johnstone:

I must tell you frankly that I found your letter long and puzzling in about equal measures. (In addition to other typographical errors, I noted with amusement that you mis-typed "2037" for "1937." Again to be frank, I'm sure neither of us would care to live that long, considering the "progress" our world is making.)

As to your specific inquiry, "Paul's Case" is a story written in my youth and though I remember it well and fondly, I think a story should stand or fall on its own merits, regardless of what the author might say about it.

I wish you good luck in your research and hope you'll understand the brevity of my response.

Sincerely,
(Miss) Willa Cather

P.S. I'm very glad to hear that you enjoy your studies.

April 30, 2037

Dear Willa Cather:

Thanks for your prompt reply. Of course, in my first letter I did not account for inevitable misunderstandings regarding the date of my letter and other "typographical errors." Although I could explain these, I'm afraid we would get sidetracked from my queries about "Paul's Case," which is considered the finest of your stories. According to the biographies, we are in agreement there.

It occurred to me that instead of rambling on about theoretical matters, I might have a better chance of a detailed reply from a straightforward, no-nonsense woman such as yourself (I like to think I'm the same kind of woman) if I simply sent you a list of questions that get to the heart of my critical inquiries. This strikes me as a compromise that we could both "live with," as the saying goes. So here are the questions, which I might want to follow up briefly after receiving your replies.

1. "Paul's Case" is a riddling story in some ways. On the one hand, it deals with a sensitive and artistic young person who lives in Pittsburgh and longs for a life filled with beauty and art. Also, as the incident with the "boy from Yale" makes clear, he is gay and yet, this being the nineteenth century, he must hide his gayness. In all these respects, the story seems highly autobiographical. But on the other hand, Paul is clearly immature and self-destructive: he has internalized his society's homophobia, as his suicide makes clear. His theft of a large sum of money, which he uses to treat himself to a "last fling" in New York—staying at a suite in the Waldorf, surrounding himself with flowers and champagne, etc.—suggests also a complete lack of morality (in the larger, more generous meaning of that term). Did you feel this seeming discrepancy in his characterization, as you wrote the story? Did you project onto Paul the personal qualities you most admired in yourself, but also the qualities you most loathed? Did this inner conflict, as you wrote the story, account for the virtues that have made it live as a work of art—namely, the vividness and energy of its prose? Did the story thus serve as a vehicle through which you worked out personal issues regarding your own character?

2. At the time you wrote the story, you were living with Isabelle McClung and her family. Now Ms. McClung, if I may say so, was your first great, gay love; and her wealthy family provided an elegant atmosphere that featured not only art and beauty, but also a stable atmosphere in which you could, and did, produce some of your best fiction. Was the bedroom into which you and Ms. McClung repaired after dinner in some ways your personal equivalent of Paul's suite at the Waldorf? Was Ms. McClung the equivalent of Paul's

"boy from Yale"? (This seems to make sense, given, of
course, the biological reality that women naturally prefer long-term, nesting relationships, while men, especially very young men, prefer fleeting liaisons of the
kind that Paul enjoys.)

3. Was Paul's suicide a fictional analogue to your feeling,
during this happy and productive period of your
youth, that you had, as the saying goes, "burned your
bridges," and that you were determined to escape the
philistine realities you'd suffered earlier in your life
(on the plains of Nebraska, in the high school class-
rooms of industrialized Pittsburgh) into Ms.
McClung's world of love and beauty? And regardless
of the personal cost?

4. Alternatively, it has also struck me that Paul might
resemble an even more youthful self: namely, the
Willa Cather of your undergraduate years at the
University of Nebraska, a girl who dressed and
groomed herself as a boy and who called herself, vari-
ously, "William," "Willie," or "Bill." That Willa Cather,
of course, loved her beautiful and feminine young fel-
low-student Louise Pound with the same kind of wayward passion that Paul exhibits toward everything he
loves but cannot have. In this reading, perhaps, Paul's
suicide could be viewed as a working-out of those
undergraduate suicidal impulses you clearly entertained (you wouldn't allow publication of your letters
to Ms. Pound or to anyone, Ms. Cather, but I have
seen them) and that you gratified figuratively by
"killing," as it were, William/Willie/Billy, resuming
female dress and hair styles for the rest of your life. Do
you find that this reading has any merit?

5. You based "Paul's Case," of course, on a former student of yours who'd come under disciplinary review at
the high school where you taught, and on the case of
two other boys who had stolen money and left town
for a wild spending spree not unlike Paul's. Did you
realize that as you used this source material, the story

had a kind of hidden, even taboo subtext? Were you consciously hiding the latter beneath the surface respectability of the former?

I hope you will not find these questions either too tedious or too intrusive. I have run them by the young man I mentioned in my previous letter—he's a huge Willa Cather fan, by the way—and though naturally he is more concerned with the technological minutiae of getting my letters to you than with their literary content, he seems to find them not lacking in substance and relevance.

Thank you again for your patience, and I patiently await your kind reply.

> Yours sincerely,
> Georgina Johnstone, Ph.D.

P.S. If I might add a personal query, I've always been uncertain of exactly how to pronounce your last name: should the consonants "th" be spoken as in "rather" or as in "wrath"?

May 5, 1937

Dear Professor Johnstone:

Again I'll be frank and say that I was surprised to get another those unusual "silver-toned" envelopes from you. (My postman says the letters have not arrived through him. Have you employed some nocturnal delivery boy, who deposits and removes your envelopes, under cover of night? It's rather disconcerting.)

I can't say I enjoyed this second letter any more than the first, especially since I'm confounded as to how you know so much about me. By "biographies" I presume you mean those newspaper interviews I once gave, but no longer do. And my instincts are correct, it would seem.

Regarding the personal matters, I think I'll just say that yes, Miss McClung (now Mrs. Hambourg) was my "first great, gay love," in a sense. (I must admit that I rather like the phrase.) In fact, she was the happiest, most carefree person I've ever had the privilege of loving, if truth be known.

I tell you this against my better judgment, particularly since I find your numbered questions all but incomprehensible. As I said before, the story had better stand on its own or not at all. I will remark, however, that Paul may exude a kind of surface "gaiety," but that happy people do not normally throw themselves in front of speeding trains.

Though I certainly wish you the best in your research, I wouldn't be the forthright person you take me for if I didn't say that I don't think I can be of any further help to you. Good luck.

Sincerely,
(Miss) Willa Cather

P.S. It rhymes with "blather."

May 10, 2037

Dear Willa,

I do understand. Really I do. In my scholarly zeal, I failed to account for the fact that to you, I am a complete stranger, whereas you have been, for these many decades, a vividly real and powerful personality in my life. Having read and reread your books so many times, having read every scrap of secondary material ever produced about you, I'm not exaggerating if I suggest I know you better—or feel that I do—than I know any of my colleagues or even my closest friends.

I was discussing this with my new friend, Jeff Pentland, the other day. (He's the youthful computer buff I told you about.) He has a "thing," if I may use such a colloquial term, for two or three screen actresses of the 1940s and 50s; his collections of material about them, and his formidable depth of knowledge about all facets of their lives, testify to his scholarly passion. Like Paul, who waited so patiently outside the stage door to glimpse his favorite opera star as she left the theater, gay boys to this day suffer extremes of "heroine-worship." As we were saying the other day, this may be pleasurable to the fan, but disconcerting or even annoying to the heroine. So, I hope you will forgive my persistence in writing you again; certainly I do not mean to be obnoxious, or intrusive.

It occurred to us that perhaps I should share a few more details of my life, so that you might feel that you know me a little, and thus slightly rectify the imbalance. I don't mean to try and curry favor by stressing, first, that I am no longer a young person, and that my article on "Paul's Case" may well be my last publication of what has been, if I may say so, a long and fairly productive scholarly career. In fact, some of my colleagues are amazed that at my advanced age, I continue to teach and write at all. I suppose they think I should be sitting on my front-porch rocker, an idea that does sound appealing when you're 34, but when the time to start rocking actually arrives, seems instead profoundly boring, and a little sad. So I hope to die "with my boots on," as people say.

Second, I am somewhat isolated here. Except for Jeff Pentland, who is one of those gay boys who enjoys befriending elderly people (thank God for them!), I really have no friends, unless the occasional busy colleague who asks me to coffee, or to lunch, can be counted as such. The condition of the "visiting professor" has always been solitary, since everyone knows this time next year you'll be gone, and there's no reason to invest time in you. There's not even anyone, much, to talk with on the telephone. I've outlived all my family, and virtually all my close friends (including my "great, gay loves," Willa; if there's anything more melancholy than outliving people, I hope I die before I find it out). So, I teach my two classes of colorful, energetic undergraduates, I hold my office hours (the students almost never drop by), and the rest of my time is devoted to researching my article on "Paul's Case," and on you.

It's my reason for being, I might say, without exaggeration.

I've heard you speak (yes, in those old interviews) about how central and all-consuming a book becomes, once you've begun it.

Everything else recedes in importance. So I feel certain that you can understand what I'm saying, and sympathize.

All that said, I hoped you might entertain a few somewhat briefer, and I hope not "incomprehensible," questions that are less cumbersome and that are, I hope, nothing at all like "blather." (I suppose I was hurt by that, a little. Literary critics do have feelings, too, Willa.)

Anyway, here are the questions. Thanks in advance for whatever input you might wish to give an elderly person who is simply doing his best to add a soupçon of insight into the great art of the great Willa Cather.

1. In the context of "Paul's Case," which ends with a gay character's suicide, please discuss his feelings as they relate to feelings you had about any of the following women: Louise Pound, Isabelle McClung, Dorothy Canfield Fisher, Zoe Akins, or Edith Lewis. Am I leaving anyone out?

2. Paul worships opera stars because they are great artists, but he is doomed to remain on the periphery as one of the faceless audience; the woman he idolizes never so much as acknowledges him. Is this a common attitude, do you think, among artists—among writers, for instance—once they become well known? Can they not be bothered to interact with the hoi polloi, once *they* are securely rich and famous? Is that the way it works, Willa?

3. Why did you make the neurotic and self-destructive Paul a male character, whereas in most of your fiction you idealize female characters (I need only mention Antonia, I think) beyond all semblance of reality? Is there a reverse sexism at work here, do you think?

4. Do you know that without scholars and professors, your work probably would be unknown today? People under thirty only want to read what was written in the last two weeks. Are you aware of that, Willa?

5. Paul is entirely friendless. Aren't *you*, in 1937, entirely friendless as well? Can the entrance of a well-meaning

admirer of your work into your life really mean so little
to you?

As before, I look forward to your answer, which I know will be
ample and generous and will contain not one iota of blather.

Most sincerely,
Georgina Johnstone

May 17, 1937

Dear Georgina (if I may),

I'm sorry if my previous letters made you angry. That wasn't my
objective. You might consider that there is material in all your
letters to make their recipient angry ("great artist" or not), but I
don't think you're in a position to perceive that.

No, I wouldn't have guessed you were "elderly." If I ever
reach that status, I hope I'm half as energetic and feisty as
you seem to be. Your letters, including your pose as a critic of
the future, testify to a lively and fertile imagination, among
other qualities.

Now, Georgina, I'll try to answer your questions. (By the way,
is "Georgina" your real name? I thought I detected a slip, in your
most recent letter. I don't know what ever gave you the idea that
I like women to the exclusion of men. If you know so much about
me, you should know also how much I revere my former
employer, Mr. McClure, and my present publisher, Mr. Knopf,
among many other fine gentlemen it has been my pleasure
to know.)

Now I don't care to number the answers, but here they are.

First, as to your uncanny knowledge of women who have been
important in my life. Yes, Georgina, of all the women I've known,
these five are perhaps the most important, but there are many
others with whom I've enjoyed close and confiding friendships.
These friendships, however, are something of a personal matter,

and I don't really think any details would help you or anyone to understand "Paul's Case." And no, his suicide has only to do with what happens to him in the story. Possibly I wrote some intemperate letters to Louise when I was nineteen or twenty, but perhaps everyone writes intemperate letters when they are nineteen or twenty. Perhaps even you did, if you can remember back that far.

As for writing to, or "acknowledging," people who write to say they like my work, I used to answer such letters faithfully, and sometimes at great length, but after a while, frankly, I found that I began to repeat myself, and my letters got shorter and shorter. Nor did the letters I received become either more respectful or more intelligent as I became well known; quite the opposite, in fact. At some point, I decided that I needed to save my writing energies for my novels, or otherwise they wouldn't get written. But the last thing I ever want to appear is snobbish, or big-headed.

I already answered your question about my liking women and not men, so I'll move ahead to the one about readers. We'll just have to agree to disagree about whether "scholars and professors" keep my work alive. I don't think they do. Though I was thrilled and grateful to get the Pulitzer, and a few honorary degrees here and there, those wouldn't have come my way, I'm convinced, if ordinary people hadn't bought my books in large numbers. I'm happy to report that is still the case, and that I make a comfortable living from my novels. If only a few academics were reading me, I'd probably have to go back to journalism or high school teaching. Now I could be wrongheaded about this, but that's my take on the matter.

I can't imagine where you got the idea that I'm "entirely friendless," since I have many close friends of both sexes, and I enjoy them very much. Even when I travel to Europe (with my close friend Edith, usually) there are friends in almost every capital whom I'm pleased to visit.

I admit I was affected, however, by your description of your own life, and wonder if you aren't just presuming that my position is similar to yours. You sound like you have much to offer your friend Mr. Pentland, however, and I'm sure that you could find other worthwhile colleagues who'd befriend you if you'd give them a chance. When I think back over a long lifetime of friendships, Georgina, I must tell you that my heart fills and I get a little teary-eyed. True, most of the closest friends have been women, and I find that all the women I've known, especially those with whom I've shared many hours of intimate talks, frank discussions on many topics, mutual sharing of emotions and personal matters that have helped me escape the essential isolation that all of us, as human beings, have as our condition throughout life—well, without the women, I couldn't have been the writer I am, or even the person I am. It makes me feel very lucky that I have experienced such wonderful friendships and to be honest, Georgina, I'm grateful that you have forced me to sit down and acknowledge this fact, in writing. (Even though, as you say, I do not allow my letters to be published, and I know you will respect my privacy in this regard.)

By the way, I'm not familiar with the college where you teach, but I'd be happy to send letters of introduction to my many friends at the University over in Lincoln, if that would please you. I also have many non-academic friends there. Just let me know.

Well, I feel I've rattled on too long. Though I've been little help in your scholarly project, perhaps I've enabled you to understand my point of view. Your last letter certainly helped me to understand yours. If you ever find yourself in New York, I would be pleased if you would call on me.

Sincerely,
Willa

P.S. Loneliness is nothing to be ashamed of, Georgina.

10 June 2037

Dear Willa,

What a wise woman you are. Though decades younger than me, you have a generosity and understanding I simply don't possess, at least not without the urging of a great soul or mentor like yourself. Thank you.

I apologize for my previous letter. It was written out of loneliness and bitterness and all the other plaints that bedevil both my stage in life and my profession. How willingly an elderly critic would trade places with a middle-aged novelist! Oh, in an instant, Willa.

One sentence in your letter, intended so kindly, brought instead a reaction of such frustrated longing that several weeks have passed before I was able to write again. I'm speaking of your invitation to visit you in New York. You can scarcely imagine how that affected me. It forced me to recognize my actual motivation in writing you. I'd wanted to discuss "Paul's Case," I thought. I wanted to discuss "biographical issues," I thought. But intuitively you've understood the ordinary, pathetic truth: I simply want to be your friend! Yet we are separated by such a barrier as not all the generous feelings in the world, combined with the most sophisticated form of travel now available, could overcome. My friend Jeff Pentland says that the new technology enabling me to write you through the warping time-waves of a century will some day, almost certainly, allow actual time travel for human beings. Oh, if only I could live long enough to experience this! But Jeff tells me frankly it will be another hundred years, at least, before that comes to pass. (Jeff is such a sweet boy, by the way. As you might have gathered, I've developed quite a "crush" on him, and though the emotions are unrequited, his friendship remains steadfast.) I hardly know what to do, now that the spring term has concluded and my teaching duties are over. Move back South, to Atlanta, where I have outlived everyone? Linger on here in Nebraska, rather pathetically, because of my crush on a young technology professor? How odd that I, at my age, should feel so homeless and adrift.

But I've decided to visit New York, after all, and if he consents, I will bring Jeff Pentland with me. (If, of course, he will allow me to pay his expenses.) We will, in spirit, accept your kind invitation: we will come to the address printed on that last, lovely letter you've sent, and we'll hope the house is still standing. If the occupants will not let us glance inside, into the parlor where you would have received us, then we'll be bold and peer in at windows (an odd couple indeed, this elderly person accompanied by a tall, well-knit companion!) and try to imagine the scene.

"I'm pleased you could come," you might say, offering us tea, and perhaps a wedge of spice cake.

"You can't imagine how pleased I am," I would say, quickly adding: "I guess you can see, that you correctly guessed my secret."

And we would both laugh, cordially, and settle into overstuffed chairs arranged companionably around the fireplace.

But I should spare you my fantasy, Willa, of this meeting that will never happen. In any case, now I'm the one who writes with a sore heart, and tears filling my eyes.

I should close, Willa, by promising not to bother you any more. Though I live in the value-free year of 2037, I do try to keep my promises. I'm old-fashioned, that way. I can't say how much your letters mean to me, and I will treasure them always.

Sincerely,
"Georgina"

P.S. Thanks for your care in re-tucking the special envelope, but Jeff Pentland asks that you refrain from using white paste to seal the letter. Evidently that mucks up the works.

June 11, 1937

Dear Georgina,

Your letter does concern me, a little. That you persist in using the date "2037," which I now see is not a typing error but an error of another kind, I am especially concerned.

If you do visit Lincoln, I also know a wonderful doctor there, whose card I'd be happy to send along if you think that would be useful. And as for your "fantasy," I can promise you that I'd more than welcome a visit from you, which probably would be much as you describe it! (But then, you have read my interviews, so I guess you know my domestic procedures quite well.)

Above all, I wish you good health. I wish you clarity of mind, and a peaceful heart. These are the important things, as we grow older.

Your friend,
Willa

P.S. Thank you for being such a loyal reader.

12 June 2037

Dear Willa,

We're fated to misunderstand one another, it seems. (I quail at the fantasy that you might be writing a new story entitled "Georgina's Case.")

Can any one person know another? For all these weeks I've subsisted on the idea that I might know you, Willa Cather! That somehow I might build a bridge back through your fictional character Paul, back to the mind and heart that created him! But I've abandoned my article, finally. All I'd managed was a frail and spurious linkage of words, words, words. Perhaps even your great story "Paul's Case" is merely that? Perhaps you, like me, sit spinning your words outward in the fiction that they mean something, when actually they're only a colorful distraction from the silent abyss of space and time that surrounds us all?

For any kind of writer, even a literary critic, such an insight can mean only that the rest is silence. Without words, a critic cannot exist, nor can the hopeful correspondent. (Even though my friend Jeff Pentland and I have promised to write, following his imminent departure for graduate school in Wisconsin, it's difficult to imagine that we really will—that such a tissue of mere words could sustain itself.)

Will you try to think of me as a friend, dear Willa? As an eccentric footnote, perhaps, added to that distinguished list of women you've known? That's a consoling thought, at least.

There's no point in your answering this letter, I'm afraid. By the time it reaches you, both Jeff and I will have left Nebraska. And instead of signing the letter, I'll leave poor Georgina in the fictional ash-heap where she belongs. But I wanted you to know that I appreciated your "P.S." and would have liked to respond *You're welcome. And I'll keep reading you, too.*

Shameless

She remembered their voices clearly, all too clearly. Her cheeks flamed red.

"Oh Liddie, how could you!" they'd cried, laughing. "You're just awful—you're shameless!"

Back then, she hadn't blushed at all to reveal her secret crime, which she hadn't considered "criminal" at all but merely a bold prank, a bit of girlish mischief. She'd felt rather proud, in fact, for hadn't she achieved her goal? Her college friends, two or three of whom she'd known since grade school, were only pretending to be scandalized and shocked. She'd thought: they wished *they* had such daring, such pure brainless guts. Even two decades later the flush-faced Lydia could recall a certain begrudging admiration in their shrill cries, as they'd put their hands to their cheeks: "Oh Liddie, how could you! That's so funny! I mean, that's so *wrong*!"

She'd kept up with these friends over the years and of course all were married with almost-grown children and here Lydia was, at thirty-nine, impenetrably single and living alone in a plush high-rise condominium off Peachtree Road, not far from the private Catholic high school where she'd first learned the meaning of shame. She paced her hushed carpeted living room with the sound of Aaron's husky whisper, unchanged after all these years, almost drowning out—but not quite—the bright incredulous chorus of her friends' youthful voices.

"I've got a conference this weekend, and I know this is short notice but"—that old, familiar clutch of guilt in his tone, likewise unchanged—"but I wondered if maybe we could get together, maybe at my hotel? I mean, whatever's good for you."

Whatever's good for you—she'd stopped herself from laughing in derision.

Instead: "Sure, why not?" she'd said jauntily. "It'll be good to see you."

So they'd set the date and time, her place on Friday night at eight. Vainly, she wanted him to see how well she'd done for herself, knowing the museum-like order of her rooms bespoke an achieved elegance and clarity that might surprise him, well-versed as he was in the messiness of her youthful emotions. Not that Aaron hadn't done well, too—he was that strange anomaly, a male professor of women's studies on a tony New England campus, and he'd published well-received volumes on Charlotte Perkins Gilman and Edith Wharton that with their mix of biographical and New Historicist criticism had won him a solid if still "promising" reputation. The second book, after all, had appeared more than a decade ago, and Lydia (who had kept up with him sporadically via e-mail and assiduous Google searches on his activity) knew he had become mired in family life, the father of four children by three different wives. By contrast, Lydia had settled into a quiet routine enabling her to produce six books and a steady stream of articles that had vaulted her to the forefront of American studies in this country; some of her work had appeared in England and France as well. Because of her subject matter—her most celebrated book dealt with abortion and suicide among prairie wives of the mid-nineteenth century—she'd been dubbed "The Dark Lady of American Criticism" in a favorable essay-review published in *TLS*. The review had been accompanied by a witty caricature of her familiar publicity photograph: the dark helmet of hair pulled back into a tidy chignon; the dark, protuberant eyes; the severe line of her mouth cemented into a grim smile. That was the famous Lydia Reynolds, a woman her students worshipped and her colleagues feared; even her old college pals, writing her admiring letters now and then, no longer seemed to remember the girl Liddie who had been so reckless in her passion for Aaron Summers. That shameless girl, this flush-faced woman awaiting her first encounter with him in almost two decades: what was the connection between them? Who was it, Liddie or Lydia, who awaited his arrival at her door in less than an hour?

Reckless in her passion, indeed. The phrase was painfully and literally true. Yet she'd been calculating as well. Even at age nineteen she'd possessed a certain patient cunning where her goals were concerned. She adapted to circumstances. With her father, a corporate attorney who was seldom home (her mother had died when Liddie was five), she had developed just the right mix of wheedling and flirtatiousness to get whatever she wanted. To her Emory professors she was the diligent, "mature" Miss Reynolds who faithfully stopped by during office hours several times each semester to discuss an issue brought up in class or to seek out additional work for extra credit. With her friends she adopted a kind of ironic bravado, the notion being that Liddie would do or say virtually anything, a daring that her friends found outrageous but that for Liddie was merely pragmatic, the way to achieve a desired result. For hadn't she succeeded in meeting Aaron Summers, after all, and hadn't she slept with him almost as often, in the ensuing weeks and months, as even the needy and appetitive Liddie could have desired?

It was the fall of her sophomore year. She'd first sighted him at registration, drawn at once to his startling good looks—Aaron was tall with a wrestler's build, shaggy dark hair, a strong nose and dazzling blue eyes—but he'd given the impression, even before she knew him, of bearing a burden of unacknowledged guilt. His posture, the only flaw in his appearance, sagged a little as if this load of guilt were almost too much for him. Yet the aura of needing to apologize for something had given Aaron a vulnerability that was undeniably appealing, especially to girls. That day in the registration line, when she'd pointed him out to her friends Amy and Susan, they'd immediately pronounced him a dreamboat and half-anxiously they'd asked Liddie what she was going to do. "What do you mean, 'do'?" Liddie had asked with an impish smile. "What makes you think I'm going to do anything?" And her friends had laughed, for certainly they knew better.

It hadn't surprised Liddie to learn that Aaron Summers was a campus star. He was president of his fraternity, a senior English major with a 4.0 average, and he was involved in several campus organizations in a leadership capacity. His picture appeared several times that semester in the student newspaper, and she'd learned even more through the English department grapevine. She had signed up for two advanced English courses that term, but Aaron Summers wasn't in either of them, nor did he spend time in the English lounge or anywhere else she looked for him. But one day in October she saw him exiting the library, and she'd cautiously followed him to his white BMW, jotting down his license plate number on the back of her paperback of *Sense and Sensibility*. She could imagine her friends' mocking sing-song as she did this: "Oh Liddie, what are you doing! Liddie, you're unbelievable!" Here she was, an attractive slender girl wearing a royal-blue windbreaker and designer jeans, her fine dark hair whipped by the wind as she watched Aaron Summers drive off, feeling not the slightest anxiety and dismay at the plan that had already sprung full-blown into her mind.

It happened two days later. She had reasoned that if he parked in the library parking lot on Tuesday, then he was likely to be parked there at the same time on Thursday; and of course he was. Liddie sat in her idling Pontiac Firebird just a few spaces away, pondering her options. Couldn't she simply wait for him, hop out of her car and introduce herself, not caring what he thought of her forwardness? What had she to lose, after all? But Liddie lacked that particular kind of daring. She was personally quite shy. Her favored methods were more covert or, as Amy had once put it, "passive-aggressive." She could no more have introduced herself to Aaron Summers than she could have stripped off her clothes and run naked and screaming through the hushed reading rooms in Woodruff library. Instead she sat in the car, steeling herself for what she'd decided, after much contemplation, she *could* do. She craned her neck to make sure that no one was around, and then she backed out of her space, aimed her car directly at Aaron's BMW, and rammed the Firebird into the back of his car with her teeth gritted and her eyes shut tight.

The rest was accomplished in seconds. She backed up, noting with satisfaction the sizable dent in the BMW's rear left-hand side, jumped out and slipped the prepared note under Aaron's windshield. Then she sped off, her heart racing. She felt an aching dryness in the back of her throat, the taste of sheer panic, excitement. "Oh Liddie you *didn't.* I mean, how could you?" Now it was simply a matter of hurrying home to await his call.

In the note she'd written: "Hello, I'm sorry but I've accidentally hit your car. Please phone me and we can arrange for my insurance to take care of this. Again, I'm so very sorry!"

She'd signed the note and underlined her name once, her phone number twice.

Aaron called the next day, and at first her plan had seemed to backfire. She was so "nice" to leave the note, he'd said, most people would have just taken off and stuck him with the bill, so he'd decided to take care of it himself. A friend of his worked part-time at a body shop, and the repairs really wouldn't be that expensive. But Liddie had been insistent. She felt so bad, she felt so stupid, *of course* she must reimburse him for the damage. Would he care to stop by her apartment, so they could exchange information? Was he available that evening, in fact? She'd feel so much better if they could take care of this right away.

Aaron had paused, considering. She could hear his breath through the phone. She could hear the hammering of her heart.

She added, "I don't live far from the university. Just about a mile up Decatur Road."

And he'd said, "All right, I could do that. What time is good for you?"

Variations on that phrase would become a mantra over the next few weeks, for Aaron was the most considerate of lovers. *Whatever's good for you, if that suits you, are you sure it's convenient for you...?* He stopped by her place several times each week, usually around six o'clock. They'd have an hour together, maybe an hour and a half, and that was only because, as he'd told her frankly, his girlfriend was out of town. No, it hadn't troubled Liddie that he had a girlfriend. If she were honest she'd have admitted this was part of his allure, part of the challenge and the entire forbidden aura of their relations from the start. They spent much of their time discussing the girlfriend, in fact, Aaron complaining in his soft husky murmur how possessive she was, how subtly controlling, how insistent on monopolizing Aaron's time when he wasn't in class. Already he'd gotten into "trouble" over the few hours he'd managed to spend with Liddie, for it seemed that the girlfriend, whose name was Ruth (of course, Liddie's private nickname for her promptly became "Ruthless"), would call Aaron's apartment repeatedly in the hour before their almost nightly dates at 7:30 P.M., becoming enraged when she couldn't reach him. Where had he been at 6:30, at 6:45, Ruth would demand of him—what, he was in the shower? But she'd been calling for more than an hour, how long did a simple shower take, was he deliberately not answering the phone? Aaron had tried to placate her, making up excuses, claiming he must have been down in the laundry room or out running an errand but, Aaron said, rubbing Liddie's shoulder as they lay naked in bed, he feared she was becoming suspicious.

"Sometimes she'll want to have sex the minute I get there," he admitted, as though confiding in a male buddy, "and you know, I just won't be *ready*, I'm afraid she'll somehow figure it out."

Liddie said simply, "I'm sorry," her lips pursed in sympathy. For really she did feel sorry for him, in a way, and rather guilty, though not guilty enough to refrain from saying, each evening as they hugged good-bye at her front door, "Tomorrow, then? Maybe around the same time...?"

And he'd lower his heavy-lidded blue eyes and mumble, "Sure, Liddie. I mean, if that's okay with you."

Which it was. Which it certainly was.

She spent most of her time contemplating him, recalling each gesture and caress, thinking of his handsome strong-jawed face and his naked muscular body dappled by the late-afternoon sunlight that slowly faded each afternoon as they lay together. Of course, he would tire of Ruth, eventually, grow more resentful of her possessiveness and strong will; soon enough Aaron and Liddie would be able to go out on actual dates, be seen together, become boyfriend and girlfriend. She had no doubt of this. Oddly, she was not jealous of Ruth but simply regarded her as an impediment to her own happiness, someone who could slowly be maneuvered out of her position of control. Aaron claimed to find Liddie's company "soothing," which seemed definitively to oppose the anxiety and stress that Ruth caused him. Liddie had never had a boyfriend for any length of time but then she had never felt about anyone as she did about Aaron Summers: in delicious solitude, she feasted on her memories of his face, his voice, his touch. Someday, she would probably even tell him the truth about why they had met, and why not? For she was rather proud, she had to admit, of what she had accomplished. Liddie herself was a star English major who discussed feminism avidly in her classes and at nineteen already she thought of herself as the kind of woman who got what she wanted, a force of nature who did what she pleased and would not be denied.

Admittedly, the affair with Aaron had ended badly. After the Christmas break he had told her, shamefacedly, that he'd applied to a number of Ivy League schools for graduate study, and had been accepted by Penn; he'd be moving to Philadelphia as soon as the spring term ended, and Ruth was moving with him. Aaron sat on Liddie's rented sofa hunched forward, kneading his hands together in a repetitive, anxious rhythm and not daring to meet her eyes. Ruth had been admitted to Penn, too, he said, and was planning to get her Master's in sociology. Liddie had snorted, not knowing what to say or what she felt, "Sociology!" And Aaron glanced over with a wan smile.

He said, "She wants to teach. High school."

Within minutes Liddie had composed herself and led him back into the bedroom, where they made love with a robust ferocity, with something like desperation. Detached from her body, Liddie had stared past Aaron's bucking shoulder to the ceiling and came to understand during those feverish minutes exactly how she must behave. Despite her roiling emotions, despite the terror of abandonment clawing at her insides, she'd absorbed Aaron's news without any of the emotional fanfare he must have expected. She hadn't become enraged; she hadn't wept. Instead she plotted and planned, basing her next step on what she knew about Ruth Applewhite. For Ruth was Liddie's opposite number in almost every way. Ruth was an Atlanta debutante who wore frilly high-necked dresses and full makeup to class, whereas Liddie favored hip-hugging blue jeans and ordinary knitted tops that showed her full breasts to advantage.

Ruth's picture, which Aaron had reluctantly pulled from his wallet for Liddie's inspection, showed a fair-haired girl with a pretty moon face who would clearly, Liddie thought with satisfaction, become overweight by age thirty if not before, while Liddie was slender as a whippet with her dark hair pulled back severely from her face even then, her only makeup a little blush for her cheeks, which tended to sallowness, and a quick daubing of frosted lipstick. And Ruth, of course, was imperious, demanding, ever-vigilant, while Liddie was the poised, listening presence Aaron seemed to need. "I can really *talk* to you," he would say, in a quiet, marveling voice. "Ruth hardly ever listens. She asks questions but never hears my answers because she's always thinking of the next thing she's going to ask me."

Aaron had shaken his head, his eyes clouded with the self-pity they both allowed him.

At the door that evening, as she sent him off for his date with Ruth, Liddie had said, "We'll work it out, won't we? I can visit you in Philadelphia. You can come visit me here."

And Aaron had said, "If you want, Liddie. I want whatever is best for you, really I do."

Their affair had meandered on through the spring, though Aaron's visits became less frequent and less satisfying. They talked determinedly of everything but the future, their voices low, furtive, as though they were conspiring together. But Ruth remained a stubborn fact in Aaron's life, which came to trouble Liddie more and more. What was it in Aaron that commanded his allegiance to such a demanding, suspicious girlfriend? Liddie had taken her share of psychology courses and she supposed Aaron's mother, to whom he rarely referred, might be the same type of woman. Liddie had felt uncomfortably helpless and adrift, feeling that Aaron was slipping through her fingers. Even his passion seemed to be lessening, as though they were going through the steps of an old-fashioned dance that suited neither of them. But Liddie was determined. Liddie would not give up. By the time she had decided her course of action it was late April and Aaron was only weeks away from his move to Philadelphia. She might lose him one way or another, Liddie reasoned, but she wasn't going to simply sit doing nothing while he drifted out of her life altogether.

One muggy evening she reached into a drawer and pulled out the phone book with a sense of foreboding that was equaled only by the sense of inevitability she felt. The listing was "Applewhite, R," and the very sight of her rival's name gave her the energy she needed to punch the number.

Liddie began slowly. Unthreateningly. She was a friend of Aaron's, she said, and she hoped she wasn't calling at a bad time? Liddie stood in her tiny windowless kitchen, staring at the oven clock: it was 4:18, and well she knew that Aaron was in his afternoon Gothic novel class that ended at 5:00. By 5:30, she supposed, everything that mattered in her life would be decided.

"A friend of Aaron's?" Ruth was saying, her voice edged with mistrust. "Is there a problem? I mean, Aaron is in class right now."

And Liddie said, "I know Aaron is in class right now. But I suppose you always know where he is." Her breath came in short, quick pants. "Or you think you do."

The conversation had devolved quickly from there: didn't Ruth understand what she was doing to Aaron? she demanded. Couldn't she comprehend why Aaron had sought a refuge with someone else, and how would Ruth like it if someone tried to keep tabs on her at every hour of the day and night?

"I—I don't believe you," Ruth stammered. "But how do you know Aaron? Who *are* you?"

"You may as well believe me," Liddie said, in a faintly mocking voice. "I'm the person he's with in the hour before his dates with you every night. I'm the reason you can't get in touch with him at six-thirty, or seven o'clock. Believe me, I've heard all about the crazy messages you leave on his answering machine when he's with me. Oh, Ruth, I've heard all about *you* I want to hear."

And Liddie had known she'd said enough, if not more than enough. Ruth had sputtered a few angry disjointed words but Liddie wasn't listening; what she'd intended to do, she'd done; she simply replaced the receiver.

The next few hours were perhaps the longest of her life. Last night Aaron had promised to stop by after his class, but he always went to his apartment first for a shower and a quick change of clothes. He'd have heard from Ruth, of course; he'd have gotten an earful from Ruth. Liddie could imagine him rushing over to

Ruth's place, his attempts to placate her, his denials giving away to a tearful confession, profuse apologies, promises that something like this would never happen again. Liddie meant nothing to him!—Liddie was obviously crazy! Liddie's eyes worked darkly in their sockets, imagining the scene between Ruth and Aaron. She had wagered everything on her knowledge of the kind of person Ruth was; she was certain Ruth would never forgive him. Aaron would be angry with Liddie, of course, but soon enough he'd realize that what had happened was inevitable, that he and Ruth really weren't suited to one another, that Liddie and he belonged together. Liddie was nineteen. She had convinced herself that she would possess Aaron within days if not hours. She had convinced herself that her plan was a sensible plan.

It was almost midnight when Aaron phoned, but the angry confrontation she'd expected simply failed to happen. Aaron's voice was calm, logical, self-possessed; it was a voice she hadn't heard from him before.

"Liddie," he said simply, "I don't want you to call me, to write me, to contact me ever again. Ruth and I are working on our problems. I don't blame you for what you did, and I'm sorry if you had unrealistic expectations. Ruth and I are working through this, and we plan to be married one day. I hope that you wish us well."

Liddie had opened her mouth to respond, but no response was required, for she heard only a dial tone. With numbed fingers she'd replaced the receiver.

The days and weeks following were only a blur in her memory: she must have wept, she must have grieved, but she could not remember the pain. At some point during graduate school (Liddie had stayed at Emory) she had sent Aaron a brief, friendly note, to which he'd replied within a few weeks in a fairly long letter, written out neatly in his careful, left-leaning hand. He was doing well at Penn, he had a teaching assistantship, he'd met a girl named Marie who was getting her degree in library science and they planned to be married before the end of the year. There was no mention of Ruth Applewhite. There was no mention of any resentment toward Liddie. The letter was relentlessly upbeat and positive, the kind of letter Aaron might send, as Liddie thought, to a sister or female cousin. He hoped Liddie was doing well, he'd said, in closing. He hoped they might keep in touch, occasionally, and he thanked her very much for writing.

Liddie had read and reread the letter as if studying an abstruse text out of her Modern Poetry seminar. Deliberately she'd waited several months before contacting him again, this time to send a birthday card; to this, he hadn't responded. Liddie pressed on with her life, excelling in graduate school and, the year she completed her Ph.D., accepting a tenure-track appointment in Emory's Institute for the Liberal Arts. She had occasional romances during these years, but they were always brief in duration; in some cases she sought companionship, in others simply the sex, a welcome diversion from her immense professional discipline and her absorption in work. She did not think often of Aaron Summers but when she did, her emotions were a blend of sentimental nostalgia for a youthful indiscretion and a growing sense of shame that she, Lydia Reynolds, had ever behaved so recklessly, with such little regard for the feelings of others. Quite simply, Lydia supposed, she had matured, had become an accountable and responsible adult with a sterling reputation both personally and professionally. By the time she entered her thirties and had achieved a measure of success, even fame of a minor sort, her romantic life had tapered off, faded into virtual non-existence. It was unwise, of course, to become involved with male colleagues, and unethical to consort with her graduate students, though she'd been tempted once or twice. Instead, she worked; she enjoyed friendships with both men and women, virtually all of them part of her academic world; she indulged in her fondness for opera, fine dining, and collecting small antiques. But ironically enough, it was an office conference with a student of hers who bore a startling resemblance to the youthful Aaron Summers that had left her feeling unaccountably breathless and agitated, and that led her to contact Aaron after a lapse of so many years.

The era of e-mail had begun, and she'd simply sent him a short, clipped message through the campus website. (She knew where he taught, of course, for she had encountered several of his publications through the years.) Her e-mail had elicited a friendly reply, congratulating her on all her success, and they'd begun chatting back and forth, once every month or two, gradually filling one another in regarding their careers and, to a degree, their personal lives. Aaron was much more open and unguarded than was Lydia, freely offering intimate glimpses into his domestic arrangements, including the woes of alimony and strained relations with his ex-wives, Marie and Claire, and his fights for custody (both of which he lost) over a child he'd fathered with each of the women. Now, he insisted, he was happily married at last, to a former student named Rachel, and they had two children, ages five and three; life was good for him, and he certainly wished her well; he hoped their paths might cross one day, perhaps at some professional meeting or other. Lydia didn't inform him that she never attended professional meetings, being far too busy with her teaching, research, and writing; but then, she didn't inform him of many things. Including the fact that she was annoyed when he kept beginning his e-mails "Dear Liddie" even though she always, without exception, signed her own messages "Lydia." But this annoyance was minor and she told herself it didn't matter even though she felt, each time she saw that word "Liddie," a faint stinging warmth in her cheeks, the way one might feel after a literal slap in the face.

By seven-thirty on Friday evening, she wasn't sure what she felt. A sense of pleased anticipation, she supposed, though nothing like the pure, unbridled excitement she'd known as a young girl, awaiting his nightly visits to her shabby college-student apartment. She had passed through her rooms several times, using the hour before his arrival to make sure everything was in perfect order, pausing to adjust a clock or a knick-knack but really accomplishing nothing, since her housekeeper had visited that morning and in any case her condominium (with the exception of her pleasantly cluttered study, whose door she had firmly closed) was always well ordered. By eight-fifteen, she was virtually certain that Aaron wasn't coming, at all, and she told herself that was all right, that probably she deserved no better. That's when the doorbell rang.

There he stood, the Aaron Summers of old, a little heavier yet still well-built, his face handsomely chiseled by the passing years, his blue eyes seeming more deeply set in their sockets, perhaps more guarded. He stood in his familiar slouching posture, dressed in a navy jacket, open-collared white shirt, and blue jeans. He had both hands dug into the pockets of the jeans, just like the undergraduate Aaron. She thought she detected a faint odor of cologne, the scent of apples.

"Hey, Liddie." He smiled anxiously. "Sorry I'm late."

She welcomed him inside; they shook hands, chastely, Lydia feeling her small damp hand all but lost in his overlarge one. They stood awkwardly in the foyer for a moment, exchanging chitchat. No, he hadn't gotten lost, he'd had no trouble finding her building, but he'd promised Rachel a phone call when he arrived in town, and that had taken longer than he expected. He wore the same rueful expression Lydia remembered from years ago when he'd mention the demands of Ruth Applewhite.

"You're looking well, Liddie. Really well."

She thanked him. She supposed it was true, for other friends of hers, whose harried lives and childbearing had aged them prematurely, had often claimed that Liddie did not look her age. She didn't yet need glasses; her dark chignon had no hint of gray; her fine poreless skin, of which she was rather vain, was taut and unlined. Tonight she wore a plain black linen dress that accentuated her slim figure, and no jewelry but the pair of diamond studs her father had given her, the year before he died, to commemorate her first book publication. Since her living room, into which she now led Aaron with a ceremonious wave of her hand, was fairly crammed with colorful art objects, gilt-framed oils and bold lithographs, and bookcases lined with rare first editions, Lydia felt she appeared pleasantly spare and unpretentious by contrast, an effect she had calculated ahead of time. As they sat on her small, red-damask sofa, an antique into which Aaron settled himself gingerly as if fearing he might overload it, she saw him looking around almost sheepishly, like a small boy lost in a museum. He cocked his head in pleased awareness of Mario Lanza—one of her sentimental indulgences, though she had turned the volume low in deference to conversation—emanating from her speaker system. (She could imagine him mentally comparing her rooms to his own house, which must be strewn with children's books and rubber toys.) Then he turned back to her, seeming to regain his self-possession.

"I love it, Liddie," he said, with a bashful smile. "I love what you've done with your life."

This comment had an effect on Lydia, enabling her to relax; there had been such warmth and satisfaction in his voice. He'd truly meant that e-mail, she supposed, when he used a trite phrase, saying he'd "wished her well." Clearly there was no residual animosity in Aaron, no barrier between them of resentment or mistrust.

She said, sincerely, "Thank you, Aaron. That's kind of you to say."

He shrugged his shoulders, in a boyish-bearish gesture she remembered well. Charmed by this, Lydia quickly chastised herself for being a poor hostess and asked what Aaron would like to drink. She had a well-stocked wet bar—she gestured to a small alcove, behind them—and would be happy to give him whatever he liked. It was then she felt her first pang of dismay.

For he said, "No thanks, I really can't. I've got to get back to the hotel, I can only stay a few minutes."

"Back to the hotel?" she repeated, awkwardly. "But I thought—"

"I promised Rachel. She thinks I'm down in the hotel dining room, grabbing a bite to eat, and I told her I'd call again when I got back to the room. She's having problems getting the kids to bed, with me not there."

Lydia had hoped they might have dinner together, and had even made a reservation at an elegant Thai restaurant, just in case; but she supposed she was too proud to mention this. Instead she inquired after Rachel, the children. She inquired about his job, his teaching. Though he'd seemed rather tense when he arrived, he relaxed visibly as he spoke, especially as he described the antics of his small children, readily going into detail about their various quirks and small maladies. The youngest had been sick with a cold and tended generally to be fretful, especially when his father was out of town. Then Aaron brought himself back to the present, squaring his shoulders, smiling. "But I know this isn't interesting to you," he said. "Domestic life."

She wasn't offended by this and gave a demure little smile of her own, as if agreeing with him. Their conversation went on for another ten or fifteen minutes, Aaron asking reciprocal questions about Lydia's own life and especially her career, of which he claimed to be envious.

"I'm always reading about you," he said. "I'm amazed by the amount of work you get done. And its quality."

Whether this meant he'd actually read her books, Lydia didn't care to pursue. She was accustomed to vague rather than specific praise from well-meaning friends. Aaron went on to say how difficult it was for him to work at home, with Rachel and the kids wanting his attention, and how it was equally difficult at school, with students and colleagues always dropping by. He had roughly a hundred pages of a new manuscript—he was working on Emily Dickinson's "marriage poems"—but he supposed he was stuck; yes, he was blocked; it wasn't really his family or colleagues and students that were the problem. Immediately upon the mention of Dickinson the great lines began flitting through Lydia's head: *Mine—by the right of the White Election! Mine, long as ages steal!* What a contrast there was between these bold assertions and the rather droning, earthbound tone of her long-ago lover's voice.

As he spoke, however, Aaron glanced several times at his watch. Lydia felt how quickly they had run through their store of appropriate conversation, for each kept the focus relentlessly on their present lives, avoiding any venture into reminiscence or reflection. For Aaron, she supposed, this was a way of life, enabling him to face a mirror each day, while for Lydia it was simply the tactic she had adopted for this particular, much-anticipated encounter. For she was aware of a stupidly girlish flutter in her heart as she regarded Aaron's frank, pained blue eyes, his well-built frame, his fine strong hands. She was aware of a response tinged with desperation when she saw him glance at his watch yet another time and say, "I'm sorry, Liddie, but I've really got to go."

What happened next would be a cause for much reflection, indeed, on Lydia's part in future months and years; and accompanying it, yes, some emotion akin to shame. But these responses were well into the future as she sat there helplessly and watched, as if disembodied, one of her feet in its expensive Italian-leather shoe move decisively toward Aaron and begin gently, but firmly, stroking his well-muscled calf. This happened so spontaneously that she had no time to predict what his reaction might be; she simply watched her own foot stroking his leg repeatedly, even determinedly, as if to dare him not to react, after all. And it happened in just that way. He kept talking—he was recounting some argument he'd had with Rachel over their older son, whether or not he should be attending pre-school—and didn't so much as glance down, much less change the pained expression or pull his leg away from Lydia's bold unthinking gesture. Was her sudden demand such a feather's weight, after all, atop the burden of other people's general claims on his time and attention? Did Lydia's shamelessly flirtatious move, coming from a seeming nowhere in her soul, really take up so little space in his crowded awareness? These thoughts struck her with the force of a blow to the head.

Soon enough, she desisted, using the moment to sit up straight, take a deep breath, and square her own narrow shoulders as though she, rather than Aaron, were bringing their encounter to a close. They rose at the same moment and, moving out toward the foyer, began exchanging the banalities that must precede any final goodbye. At the door, Aaron performed an unexpected gesture of his own. He touched the curve of her pale cheek with the edge of one forefinger and said, "I'm sorry, Lydia."

For once, he had used her adult name, in the way one addresses a child in formal terms when wishing to encourage mature behavior. She was caught off-guard; instead of responding, she uttered another banal remark or two as he left her, and even as she watched his harried gait down the long corridor and out of her life, she lacked the presence of mind to say, nor even to think, "I'm sorry, too."

Who, What, When, Where

I

A good-looking man on his wobbling bike, in the rain. Heading east on Ponce de Leon Avenue.

"Good-looking" is a subjective opinion, admittedly, an error *no good journalist* would commit. Much better to find some witness to say he's good-looking but there is no witness, no living witness.

So here we are.

Good-looking, then. Fairly tall, though hunched forward against the rain, and clearly well-built, by which we mean muscular though not with the opulent muscularity acquired in gyms but lean, natural muscle, a man of whom one says *There's not an ounce of fat on him.* A pair of blue jeans, faded. Royal-blue windbreaker. It's important to sketch in the body type, the clothes, but in voyeuristic curiosity we keep going back to the face.

A pleasant yet anonymous face. Pleasant by the standards of TV commercials and billboards. Anonymous by the standards of TV commercials and billboards. Good looks, then, that might be called notable but not daunting; friendly, American good looks. Dark hair, clearly well-cut even when rain-plastered. Symmetrical face, strong jaw. A thin-lipped mouth of the kind termed "cruel" in dimestore detective novels of the 1940s but now merely congruent with the innocuous adjective *good-looking* and in that sense not congruent with contemporary notions of *the rapist,* which he is.

Is he approaching the woman? No, he hasn't seen her. For all we know, he's riding along innocently thinking about a cheeseburger for lunch, but nonetheless it's time to notice the woman.

To swerve the camera in her direction, so to speak.

This woman he's approaching/not-approaching doesn't see him, either. Heading west on Ponce, along the sidewalk. Head downcast, hurrying. Wearing a neon-green nylon poncho over a cable-knit sweater, a denim skirt. The poncho's hood, inexplicably, down. A thin woman, not good-looking but not unattractive but, admittedly, not a likely prospect for TV commercials or billboards, alas. An ordinary woman, we might say. Slender, mid-thirties. A longish face and long wheat-colored hair, past her shoulders, giving the impression of rain-whipped wheat as if glimpsed from a speeding car with a dampened windshield but what the hell does that mean, how could that be a fact? No one is looking at her hair and anyway there is nothing metaphorical about it and no one should give a thought to it, not even the man on the bicycle. In fact, he doesn't notice her at all until six seconds before she makes her crucial error, as women tend to do, stupidly failing to avoid a place in the sidewalk where the earth has swollen upward and left jagged shards of concrete just waiting to trip up an *innocent victim,* as a newspaper would phrase it, but how innocent is a woman walking along a famously unsafe and deserted street in the rain, alone and unarmed, her head uncovered?

There's no one to ask this question. No witnesses.

He's the only man on a bicycle, she's the only woman daring or stupid or guilty enough to be walking along here in the rain. One man, one woman. Without editorializing we might say that's the old story, isn't it? And this often-congested street *is* deserted except for an occasional rain-blurred, colorless car hissing along the pavement at thirty miles per hour, wipers beating the same indifferent rhythm. As if passing along robotically, without drivers, for the windows are fogged and the drivers' faces indistinct, anonymous. They don't count. It might be said they don't exist.

For nobody calls in, later. Nobody sees a thing.

II

It must have happened this way. It could have. It did.

Something in the way she moved—but isn't that a line from a song? We don't know where that came from, scratch that. After all, *no good journalist* would write that. As for "The man noticed the woman from ten yards away," that's awfully precise, how could we know that? We might take another stab with "The man noticed the woman from a distance of roughly thirty feet, sources said," which is better, but didn't we already admit that nobody saw? Who the hell are these "sources," the abandoned red-brick buildings with their narrow, shuttered windows (please don't compare them to eyes) or the handful of scabbed leafless oaks and magnolias (we haven't talked about *when* yet, but there's an early hint) somehow persisting along this stretch of urban blight?

All right, make it simple, so the toughest editor will glide along, unprotesting: "After seeing the woman, he—"

There we are. See how we avoided, that way, what prompted him to look up, what she might have done, whether he was somehow on the prowl or she was somehow flirting anonymously with her hips in a way no red-blooded American male could fail to notice, and anyway does it matter? Causality isn't our beat.

Truly, it must be something in her walk, her rhythm, her quick, awkward, yet unmistakably female progress up the street. Otherwise why would he glance up, preoccupied as he is? Preoccupied-looking as he is? Yet he catches sight of the woman six seconds before she falls. Not ten, not two: precisely six, just enough time to focus on her body, her walk, the womanly side-to-side of her slender hips as she half-walks half-trots through the rain, which is medium-heavy but not "pouring" rain, still less "driving" rain. Ordinary rain, an ordinary woman, yet she stumbles and, distracted, he loses control of the bike so its harmless wobbling becomes a dangerous, sideways lurch. He jerks the handlebars to the left, up against the curb. Instinctively drops his feet to the pavement, straddling the bike just as he'd have done at age eleven though he's thirty-six years old.

(Age thirty-six, on a rusted old bike in the rain? On a Sunday morning? We haven't yet mentioned it's Sunday, which accounts for the sparse traffic: but it is. We'll tell this story out of order if we want, we'll editorialize if we want. Take this as reported or go read some other fucking story.)

Some of his happiest memories in life have been on bicycles, he'll later confess. (To himself, that is, lying in bed that night: for he isn't caught, and won't be.) Some of his most innocent sky-blue memories. He hates the noise of engines, hates the stink of pollution in this city and refuses to add to it, *of course* he owns a car and drives one when necessary (in this city hostile to pedestrians and bikers, it's often necessary) but on weekends and after work and at other random times he's a familiar sight in midtown Atlanta (there's your *where*) though to whom he's a familiar sight remains an open question. For no one, it must be stressed, sees him on that day, there are no "police sketches" drawn from eyewitness accounts, no interviews with the sad-eyed buildings or desiccated trees overseeing this tawdry little crime. If there's no identifiable *who*, can it be said—in fact, in objective truth—there's any *what?*

Arguably, no. Quite convincingly, *no.*

So he thinks later that night as he reruns everything in his head. In sequence. In order. The way everything went down (no pun intended, that wouldn't be appropriate in serious reportage of this kind; and morbid, "sick" humor is certainly inappropriate in any context) it could be argued he doesn't exist. And if he doesn't exist, the crime didn't happen, never mind the physical reality of the woman's lumpish, chilled body lying toe-tagged in the morgue.

Yes, she's dead. That's a big what, granted; previously we'd stipulated the rape but not the murder. We weren't coyly delaying this information in the manner of those annoying "suspense" novelists (their tactics are so obvious!) but simply felt the reader should feel accustomed to the rape before getting socked with the murder. After all, sentimental readers occasionally get attached to characters, especially young women characters. Especially "innocent" young women characters preyed upon by modestly good-looking men in the cold rain in a "deserted alley"—as the moronic newspaper report phrased it, the next morning—just off Ponce de Leon Avenue.

But we are getting ahead of ourselves and a good reporter wouldn't do that, would he?

The man, fired from his newspaper job several days before the rape-murder for "inappropriate writing skills" (strange phrase!) and "insubordination," brought his wobbling bicycle to a stop against the curb. His manly, strong-fingered hands gripping the handlebars. Rain streaming along the raised healthy veins of his hands, his protruding knuckles. Rain dripping off the shelf of his brow, his strong nose, his well-cut chin. Amazingly the woman still hasn't noticed him though now she's fifteen, twelve, ten feet away. The six seconds are passing, slowly, his solemn gaze dipping to the undulant cracked sidewalk a mere instant before her low-heeled shoe catches on the upward-rearing shard of ancient concrete and sends her sprawling, *oof!* he hears, that one syllable and she's down, her cellophane bag of groceries from the corner market two blocks away (milk, tea bags, and the one souvenir he'll take with him, a copy of *Time* magazine, flipping the pages later that night like a man in a doctor's waiting room) slamming against the brick wall to her right. Then she's on all fours, as if panting, *what else* can he think about but the heat, the irresistible bitch-heat down in her crotch?

The thought pierces his brain like hot jagged glass.

He stands, lets the bike fall to the curb; he'll retrieve it later, waiting by the alley entrance for a moment until the nearest car is two blocks off. He rushes forward, grabs her bent arm, and crouches down. Looking no more threatening than a TV commercial actor who plays the friendly neighbor in a sweater, just come out to get the newspaper: "Miss, are you all right?"

Yes, that's what he says. You may quote him.

Miss, are you all right?

She's struggling to her feet. Her frightened glance meets his earnest pained grimace. She is not attractive enough to play the woman neighbor in a TV commercial, but she might play the neighbor's friend, her face slightly out of focus. Across that face now pass in quick succession emotions that might be labeled *embarrassment, chagrin, defensiveness, fear....* But is that true, really? Fear? What woman in her right mind would feel fear as she glances into the kindly, handsome face of this man coming to her aid? (Did we mention his mild blue eyes, the boyish dusting of all-American freckles across his nose and cheekbones?) She must be familiar with Ponce de Leon Avenue, after all, its littered sidewalks and alleys peopled with coke dealers, homeless psychotics, prostitutes, *the dregs of humanity.* (A phrase his editor would cut in an instant, but the man, the fired reporter, the rapist, might have used the phrase just to annoy him a little, and why not?) Now they're both standing, the woman glancing down, seeming to laugh in embarrassment, brushing at her denim skirt—already rain-soaked, so brushing at herself is a tactic, he's thinking, maybe a way to deflect attention from her heated cheeks, her general awkwardness and discombobulation. She reaches out, shyly, to take the cellophane bag the man patiently holds for her, waiting, does she think he has nothing better to do on a Sunday morning than stand here in the rain?

"You're okay?" he says, ducking his head in a gesture forcing her gaze to meet his. Her eyes are blue as well, but a bluish-gray, almost a slate color as though dulled by rain, or tears; her eyelids are half-shut over them (that's the "defensiveness" we spoke of) or perhaps her eyes are half-shut against the rain, or perhaps her eyes are always half-shut because she's dropsical or has an IQ of 45, we cannot know every fucking thing nor what is "appropriate" or "inappropriate" to report—such terms, we believe, don't have any meaning in any context relating to the complexity of human existence. The editor simply didn't like the man and wanted to fire him, so he came up with these ludicrous charges. No matter that he'd worked there four years under a previous editor with no problems, only an occasional mild-voiced suggestion that he remove the "personal touches" from his story, that he avoid fifty-dollar words, "fancy" vocabulary most readers out there might not understand. *That* editor would give a tilted smile, even poke him in the side in their complicity against the great unwashed, the huddled masses yearning to read free *without having to think.* When somebody gave you criticism in a nice way of course you didn't mind taking it! But the new editor was another matter. The new editor was a piece of shit, now how's that for fancy language.

The man isn't thinking of this as he hands the woman her cellophane bag and says, meeting her anxious grayish eyes with his steady bright-blue gaze, "You took quite a spill there, didn't you," and then as she steps aside he lurches forward, grabs her elbow, and yanks her toward him, hard. The alley is fifteen feet away.

The rest could be described in excruciating detail but this isn't an exploitative true-crime story. You know what "rape" means. You know what "murder" means. It's enough to say that the rape was a stand-up formality, three minutes against a cold brick wall with his knuckles jammed in her mouth because he didn't want to hear anything, not one word. His other hand and his half-hard dick did the rest. It's enough to know that he doesn't take pleasure in murder and in fact had never committed a murder before, though he had thought about it; no, he takes no pleasure at all, far from it, and certainly didn't enjoy her fear, her anguish, her terror, would actually have liked to send her on her way *(no harm done, OK?—we all get a little horny, sometimes)* but of course she'd have identified him.

Since his teenage years he has carried a small pocket knife at all times, as did his father before him, and his grandfather before him. (His grandfather used it to whittle! Carrying a pocket knife is a perfectly innocent, manly thing to do.) It was a matter of thirty seconds, or twenty-five seconds, to extricate the knife with one hand, open it one-handed, and slit the woman's throat with a very deep cut in the way the losers down at the newspaper would describe, with their faked air of apology and regret, "from ear to ear." The blood spurted onto his windbreaker but the jacket was made of shiny nylon and stepping back the man glanced down and saw the rain conveniently washing the blood away. (Not that he won't bury all the clothes he's wearing, eventually, in a deserted woods fifty miles outside of town.) Then he glanced up and down the alley and in both directions: there was no one, nothing. Another thirty seconds and he was back on Ponce de Leon, his bike wobbling in the rain, making a casual turn at the next cross street. Not to avoid being seen but because that's where he lived.

One more thing, in case you've wondered: when he'd set out on his aimless bike ride, around 9:15, it wasn't raining. He's not stupid.

III

For those attached sentimentally to facts, this was a Sunday morning in early February, in the year 2001. But what does that tell you, really?

Twenty years earlier, give or take, he'd understood he was two people. At least two people. The likable and nice-looking man you've met already, who wants very much to please. And another man, also likable and nice-looking, who has been fatally underestimated all his life by those individuals commonly known as *authority figures*. Parents who offered him that same loving kindness, certainly they did, they lavished on his two older sisters, but who treated him, he often felt before he could formulate the thought in language, as *an afterthought*; a family appendage; a mistake. (Had he been an "accident"? It's pointless to think in such terms!) It was clear to him they had wanted two, not three, children. It was clear to him that his father, unlike the vast majority of normal fathers, would have preferred a third daughter, being the kind of man who thrived in the company of women and who viewed other men, even drooling male toddlers, as potential competitors. It was clear that his mother thought and felt whatever his father thought and felt, and that in general she was mildly uncomfortable with a certain biological reality, that physical fact of male biological reality known as *the penis*. (She had gone to Catholic school in the 1940s.) Yes, there were grade school teachers who refused to assign him the grades he deserved, and priests who had no sympathy with his quavering teenage voice when he returned to the confessional week after week, confessing the same few sordid sins again and again. In college there were professors of journalism who complained his prose was too "artistic," professors of creative writing who regretted that his prose wasn't artistic enough. There were head-doctors who smiled heartily, encouraged by his agreeable looks and personal grooming, and said not to worry: he was normal, his worries were normal, everything about him including *the most primitive and alarming thoughts, fantasies, fears* were entirely normal for a young man in the United States, at this time.

And then the bosses. Don't get him started on the bosses. Passing him over for promotions, merit raises, "plum" assignments.

Passing him to other departments, other editors. Criticizing his work habits his "eccentric" use of language and punctuation his adoption of unconventional points of view his focus on irrelevant details his tendency toward purple prose and above all his subjective interpretation of news events *when all people wanted were the facts.*

Easy to see that *when* is mingled inextricably with *who.* Nothing to be done about that.

Really, he might have raped a woman five years earlier, when he was fired from his third newspaper job, but he had not. (In a midwestern city, that had been; he always moved to a new city after he was fired, armed with invariably glowing "recommendation" letters of the kind people write when they feel guilty for firing you.) He might have raped his woman journalism professor who gave him the only "C" he'd received in graduate school, but he did not. (He'd almost left the M.A. program, out of shame, but he knew and others in the seminar knew she'd gotten her panties in a wad because occasionally he'd make fun of the textbook they used, which she had written, an overpriced paperback called *Who, What, When, Where, and Why: Get the Facts. Get the Story!*) When he was seventeen he might have raped his sisters and mother while his bound-and-gagged father watched in horror, but he had not. (Though he thought about it. Often.) When he was twelve he might have poured kerosene on his mother's miniature wire-haired terrier, "Precious," one day when his family had gone to church and he'd stayed home feigning illness and the dog had sat in the corner staring at him (normally the little bitch pranced around his sisters and mother, craven in her constant bids for attention, affection), *but he had not.* He has been attractive and well-groomed and law-abiding all his life. Why wait until now? How did these past whens lead into the present of this story, that riddling word we call *now* as if we know what the fuck we're talking about? (It's always now. He took elective philosophy courses in college but he'd known that since he was ten.) Why wait until he's thirty-six and arguably arrived at what an untalented writer would call "the prime of life"? Why is now the time? (Now being the moment, what might be called the climactic moment, when his knife pierces the woman's pale slender throat.) Why this time and no other?

All right, enough. It was a rainy Sunday morning in early February, at 11:02 A.M. Home by 11:15.

IV

The city too busy to hate, as he'd heard *ad nauseam.* Like most people who live here, he's from somewhere else.

"The city that rose like a phoenix from the Old South," as one ludicrous commercial has it; but in fact rose in the form of sparkling midtown cones of steel and light, admittedly pretty after dark but drably gray, silent, and deserted on rainy Sunday mornings; the city that not only rose but spread outward like a fungus, like a stain. Absorbing once-autonomous smaller towns (some of which still maintained their picturesque but laughable "town squares"), oozing northward for twenty, twenty-five miles into the white-flight suburbs and their numberless subdivisions of brick and stucco houses, their oversized malls, their traffic-clogged interstates. (The south part of town is the black area, little-changed these past thirty years.)

He has the good taste to live in midtown, at least, where blacks and whites occupy the same blocks, the same buildings, even if he lacks the income to live in anything but a drafty high-ceilinged apartment that will soon be purchased and renovated, no doubt, converted into a condominium far out of his price range and landing him in the street. In fact, that same rainy street *Ponce de Leon Avenue*—which everybody here calls "Ponce" but he relishes the long, ludicrous name—with its liquor stores lit by garish neon tubing, its shabby restaurants and donut shops, its abandoned brick buildings, cracked and littered sidewalks, shambling pedestrians. Homeless people, crazy people. Drunks and loiterers. Young black men standing on the corner waiting either to rob you or perhaps to catch the bus to their minimum-wage jobs in Decatur or Stone Mountain. Middle-aged black women, waiting to catch the bus for their jobs cleaning houses in Buckhead. Prostitutes, crack-heads, gold-toothed pimps, rough-looking Vietnam vets in wheelchairs, tall malnourished kids with pierced eyebrows, noses, lips, all in ratty black clothing. And the traffic!—the endless traffic in both directions along the wide four-lane street. (Much lighter on Sunday mornings, though.) For some reason he loves it here, loves biking or walking along here though he's out of place, too ordinary-looking, too straight and nicely dressed though never once has he been harassed. Asked for money, yes, but not harassed. Asked if he wants a date, yes, but not harassed.

He is polite to everyone, always. Some of the street people know him, know that he will not give money but still they speak, nod, move on. He lives here. He belongs here. He might walk in front of a MARTA bus barreling along at forty miles per hour pleased with the knowledge that he might die here. First he'd throw away his wallet, so they couldn't identify him. Couldn't notify his next of kin. (His next of kin might not remember him, in any case; he hasn't phoned them in nearly a decade.) Couldn't give his former employers the pleasure of knowing they'd fucking killed him. City workers would scrape him off the street and that would be that, one morning in the near, possibly very near future. Above all he'd want to avoid a newspaper obituary that might hypocritically note in mournful tones the passing of *one of our former reporters* not mentioning they'd fired his ass.

He'd end up in the same morgue, that way. Toe-tagged just like that clumsy hapless woman he'd raped and killed. We all end up in the same place, don't we? Isn't that the only *where* that counts? It could be Boston or Detroit or Cleveland or Dallas as well as Atlanta, couldn't it? Or some small town? The demographics of random rape-murders is not a topic he cares to study or write about, really.

Though the only significant place, he supposes, is that tender indentation in her throat, between those bones frail as chickens' bones, that he'd slit with the little pocket knife (one of his pet possessions, that coincidentally he'd sharpened just last week). He'd tried not to hear but under the hiss of cars passing twenty feet away, outside the shadowy hidden confines of this alley, he'd detected the anguished gurgling of her blood as he cut deep, deeper, *there*, so that he might have come in his pants if her cunt-heat hadn't ceased to interest him, if his dick hadn't shriveled in frank embarrassment and dismay. *There*. Then wiping the knife against his jeans and backing off, letting her fall. Waiting a few seconds to be sure. Staring at the red crevice spurting blood, there, as if he'd found some secret destination, wellspring, origin, for which he'd been searching all his life.

Late that night, rising from the bed, he wondered if he'd be able to finish this story, but there is no *why* and he knew he could not. You just found some point, more likely random than not, at which you must make an ending.

Schadenfreude

Violet felt just terrible about what had happened to Mary Ann.

Through the family grapevine she'd heard, long before it happened, that Mary Ann's new husband had a history of scrapes with the law: a couple of DUIs, an arrest for petty theft, various traffic offenses for which he'd failed to appear in court. But, as Violet's older sister Rebecca had told her, the two of them clucking over their niece's dubious taste in men, this new charge surely took the cake, for evidently the man had been caught not only possessing methamphetamine but attempting to sell part of his stash to an undercover cop.

"I feel *so* sorry for her," Rebecca had said in her nasal, slightly cross voice, and Violet, who had essentially the same voice but did not realize it, said back, "Oh, and so do I."

"I really don't know what the poor girl is going to do," Rebecca said, and she'd gone on at some length about Mary Ann's uncertain future, Violet listening and making appropriate noises of assent now and then but otherwise keeping her counsel. For Violet knew exactly what Mary Ann was going to do, since Violet, late last night, when the girl had phoned her distraught and crying, had suggested that Mary Ann come and stay at her place for a while. Violet's quiet home out in a residential area of Decatur, miles away from the chaotic hubbub of midtown Atlanta where

Mary Ann and her husband had been living, would be an ideal "retreat" for her, Violet had argued, and the girl, after a polite demur or two, had gratefully accepted her aunt's offer. Violet told Rebecca none of this, however, partly because, since they were young girls, Rebecca had always been a know-it-all who liked to speak to her younger siblings as though issuing edicts from a great height, and so Violet enjoyed her private awareness that she, in this instance, knew more than her sister; and also because Violet didn't want Rebecca, who was impulsive as well as bossy, deciding to drive up here from Macon and start trying to run the show. Rebecca would find out soon enough, Violet reasoned, but not in time, she hoped, for Rebecca to engage in any serious meddling.

Finally Violet had gotten her sister off the phone: she needed some time to herself, after all, to enjoy the sheer anticipation of her niece's arrival. Since retiring from her decades-long position as a high school reference librarian, Violet had discovered, in her new and most welcome solitude, that the *looking forward* to a social engagement, or any encounter with another person, was in its way sweeter and more to be prized than the visit itself. (For actual people, after all, could be quite disappointing, at times!) She spent most of her time quite happily alone, often seeing or speaking to no one for days at a stretch, but Violet knew herself to be a resourceful, self-reliant person. She enjoyed reading, of course, and she did a little gardening, and a little crocheting, but the part of her daily routine of which she was most proud was her devotion of at least one hour, and often more, to the benefit of other people. This was a vow she had made when she retired: she didn't intend to become one of those sour, self-involved older women who could not see past their own personal interests and problems. No, at least one hour a day would be devoted to activities like visiting nursing homes, volunteering at the nearby branch library, helping out with other, less fortunate family members and friends around town. Though Violet had never married, she had seven siblings who had (if you counted poor Agatha, her youngest sister and Mary Ann's mother, who had died so tragically at age twenty-seven, in a car crash), and therefore much of Violet's daily selfless ritual was spent in writing to far-flung brothers and sisters, and nephews and nieces, and grand-nephews and grand-nieces, all of whose birthdays she remembered with a tastefully chosen card, and all of whom she wrote periodically, keeping up with all their little trials and tribulations as best she could, careful to end each letter (on her scented, pale purple stationery—Violet's trademark) on an upbeat, positive note. For Violet, who was not otherwise religious, believed fervently in the law of karma: what you sowed, you would eventually reap, and though many of her relatives never responded to her letters she continued to write, doggedly, knowing that by seeing to others she was, in the end, helping herself as well. To that form of self-interest Violet happily pleaded guilty—guilty as charged! Otherwise she considered herself a genuinely kind-hearted and selfless person.

As she waited for Mary Ann, she went busily from room to room doing small chores: folding laundry, adjusting pillows and doilies, tidying up the guest room though the entire house, as she well knew, was immaculate. She lived in a handsome one-level ranch only a mile from the old Decatur city square, and over the years she had managed to pay off the house in her prudent, methodical way. Her gleaming three-year-old Buick under the carport was paid for as well, and overall she considered that, when you took into account the modest salary she'd earned and her lack of any inheritance, she had done quite well for herself. She wished the same for Mary Ann but the girl, like other young relations of Violet's, had thus far lived a rash and improvident sort of life, she and her husband living on his motorcycle-mechanic's salary "from paycheck to paycheck," as the girl had confessed tearfully to her aunt during their phone conversation the night before.

"Carl never wanted me to work, or even finish college," the girl had complained, her voice raw and aggrieved, "he always said *he* would take care of things and not to worry, not to worry"—she repeated the phrase several times, senselessly—"and everything would work out. He was saving up to open his own garage, I guess he got in a hurry and that's why he started selling the drugs, but aunt Violet, I hope you believe me, I had *no knowledge* of that, none whatsoever!"

"Of course," Violet had murmured, a queer kind of excitement pinching her heart, "of course, dear, I have no reason to disbelieve you."

"—And his lawyer says, and this is the terrible part, that the best he can hope to do is take a plea, but even so he's looking at two to five years. Can you imagine, Aunt Violet, what that would do to Carl? *Five years* in the Georgia state prison? And for that matter, what it will do to *me?* Carl is such a sensitive soul at heart, he really is, I'm afraid prison will just destroy him, and as for me, I don't know how—"

And the girl had railed on, for twenty or thirty minutes, occasionally stopping to catch her breath, or let out a few ragged sobs, while all Violet could do was try to listen, try to console the girl as best she could. Violet, who knew a thing or two about human psychology, wouldn't dare to suggest that what had happened might actually be good for Mary Ann, in the long run; that the girl was well rid of the likes of Carl, whom Violet had met only twice but about whom she'd quickly developed a strong and definite opinion. No, it wasn't the time for that, Violet reasoned. Rather it was a time simply to listen, and to bite her tongue.

Yet she was unable, once Mary Ann finally appeared at her door looking disheveled and irresolute, as though she might have stopped accidentally at the wrong house, to keep from crying out, "Oh, you poor thing, what has that man *done* to you!" as she threw her arms around Mary Ann in a smothering hug and drew her inside.

For it was true that Mary Ann looked terrible. She'd always been a slight, delicate girl, with an almost translucently pale skin and pale-blue, protuberant eyes. Violet could remember well how Mary Ann had looked as a girl, and then a young teenager—how fragile-seeming she'd been, with her aureole of shimmering whitish-blond hair and her slender, slightly concave body that made her look as if a normal hug might crush her brittle bones, irreparably. But now the once-lovely hair was a stringy, darkish blond, as if unwashed for days; her cheeks were sunken, and her eyes stared out from their frail bone-sockets like those of a concentration camp survivor. Most disturbing was the shadowy bruise along her right jaw, all the more alarming to witness against the girl's otherwise chalk-white skin, with its delicate tracery of pale-blue veins at her throat, her temples. Violet tried to dissemble, but she felt horrified and was unable fully to disguise her true feelings. She felt tiny pinpricks of tears in her eyes along with the surge of a strange and terrible joy that convulsed her heart.

"I know, I must look awful," Mary Ann said, eyes downcast, adding in a barely audible murmur, "I'm sorry." In one hand she held a battered suitcase while the other fluttered upward to the one side of her face, as though to hide the bruise.

Violet didn't trouble to wonder how she might appear to the girl, who had some reason, perhaps, to feel intimidated if not apologetic. For at age sixty-four Violet Cummings was a formidable woman, with a sturdily built figure to which the years had added a discreet bulk, especially in her sloping, shelf-like bosom and her full hips. Today she wore an ordinary house dress of an indeterminate, greenish hue—it was now early May, and she considered this one of her spring dresses—and her face was dominated by her rather narrow, slit-like eyes that might have been lost amid the fatty ridges of her well-rouged cheeks but for their look of sharp and perpetual vigilance. They were a sterner blue than her niece's, and in times of duress or annoyance could darken to a silvery-gray, the color of nail heads. Violet didn't *feel* formidable, however, at least not at moments like this one, experiencing such a violent rush of joyous sympathy, or sympathetic joy, in beholding her bedraggled and trembling niece.

Finally, the initial shock of the girl's appearance wearing off, Violet (who was several inches taller than Mary Ann) bent to relieve her of the suitcase. With her other hand she took the girl's arm and led her into the dimly lit living room, where Violet hoped the overstuffed sofa and chairs, the dustless tables and vaguely Oriental lamps, might soothe and reassure Mary Ann.

"Please sit," she told the girl, unable to help noting how Mary Ann's faded blue jeans and red halter-top looked out of place in this prim, orderly room, "and I'll get us a nice cup of tea."

Mary Ann didn't respond, which Violet took as an assent, and by the time she returned with the tea things her niece had shrunk to one side of the sofa, looking about as pathetic, Violet thought, as an adult woman can look. Her thin shoulders were slumped, and she had wrapped her arms around her knees and begun moving forward and back in a slight rocking motion as though trying to soothe herself. Yet the girl's face was pale, stricken. Tears glistened in her eyes.

Violet's heart went out to her niece, but she decided to behave as if this were an ordinary social occasion. She poured the tea, she asked if Mary Ann preferred one lump of sugar or two. The girl said meekly, "One, please," but when Violet handed her the cup it happened that Mary Ann's hands were shaking too badly to accept it. So Violet set both cups down on the coffee table, then went over and sat by her niece on the sofa.

"Now, dear," she said, hesitantly touching Mary Ann's trembling shoulder, "I think you'd feel better if you just told me everything, don't you? From the start."

To Violet's great surprise this suggestion elicited a sudden, dramatic reaction, the girl all at once hurling herself into Violet's arms and managing to choke out, in her hoarse, rasping voice, "Oh, Aunt Violet, I hardly know where to *begin!*"

Yet begin she did, and over the next hour or two, and indeed over the next several days, the outlines of Mary Ann's story had emerged. It turned out, and Violet wasn't naïve enough to be surprised, that Mary Ann and Carl had met in a midtown bar. "A hook-up place," the girl had frankly called it. During the next few weeks, Carl had been so attentive and romantic, Mary Ann insisted, and really she knew that at heart he was a good person—"a sensitive soul," as the girl kept repeating. He loved motorcycles and racecars, yes, but he also played guitar and wrote poetry. Violet, all the time her niece was speaking, kept recalling the rather sullen, awkward impression Carl had made at family gatherings, but she watched enough Oprah and Dr. Phil (daytime TV was one of Violet's guilty pleasures) to know that people were complex beings with many sides to them, so she tried to imagine that rather scruffy young man she'd met, with his curly dark hair and frayed leather jacket, as a guitar-strumming poet. For the girl's sake, Violet could imagine it. But to Mary Ann's surprise, though hardly to Violet's, Carl had a different personality altogether whenever he'd been drinking. At such times, the girl admitted, her husband could be mean, and even—Violet happily supplied the word—"abusive." He would call her awful names—bar slut, stupid cunt, whore. He would threaten her, a little. He would slap her around, a little. Violet shrewdly noted how the girl, even now, bruised and weeping, had the tendency to minimize her husband's bad behavior. "But that's not really like him," she would say. "That's not really *him*, at all, it's just the alcohol," and she would add, solemnly, having perhaps watched her own share of Oprah and Dr. Phil, "it's a disease, you know. Just like the drugs, which I just found out about not long ago, it's the disease that's saying and doing these things."

Balderdash, Violet thought, though she was discreet enough not to voice her opinion. For now, the girl simply needed to be comforted, not to be confronted with the truth. Her facing the truth would take time, Violet thought. It would take a lot of time, and fortunately her niece had come to the right place, for Violet had all the time in the world.

That first night, she had simply let the girl talk herself out, and then she'd shown her to the guest room, where with motherly concern she'd drawn back the bedclothes, set out a fresh towel and washcloth in the adjoining bath, and helped Mary Ann unpack her things. Her clothes and personal items were modest enough, but the battered suitcase held one surprise: a compartment had come open and spilled out a dismayingly large number of amber-colored prescription containers across the bed. Seeing what Violet had discovered, the girl let out a small, embarrassed "Oh!" and quickly gathered up the pill bottles and refastened the suitcase compartment that had contained them. When Violet looked at her questioningly the girl said, in her soft, apologetic voice, and with the hint of a smile as though she'd like to make light of this, "Oh, Aunt Violet, I have such a collection of ailments!—bad nerves, insomnia, headaches, you name it." Though alarmed by all the prescription drugs, Violet had chosen not to query the girl any further, at least for now, and instead she simply gave what she hoped was a sorrowful but sympathetic look as if to say, Of course, of course, she understood. There was no one in the world, she hoped to convey, who could understand as Violet understood.

A few days passed, and the two women settled into a pleasant domestic routine. In the mornings, Violet cooked the girl a nutritious breakfast—scrambled eggs, oatmeal with cinnamon, dry toast smeared with blackberry jam—and then they would read the newspaper together, and vaguely talk about what was happening in the world, Violet trying to emphasize the pleasant things, scant as they were. It didn't matter what they discussed, Violet reasoned, so long as it was not depressing and did not encourage the girl's tendency to focus on her personal problems. Reaching the entertainment section of the paper, they would talk about movie and TV stars, and Violet tried to engage the girl about books, but it turned out that Mary Ann wasn't much of a reader. She read magazines, mostly, and when the two of them went grocery shopping in the afternoons the girl would even pick up one or two of those ghastly tabloid newspapers that Violet couldn't abide. Over time, she thought, she could gradually educate the girl: she would take her to the symphony, to the free lecture series Emory University was having, to book signings and readings over at Barnes & Noble. But those first few evenings they'd simply gone out to dinner each night, Violet quickly using up her knowledge of local restaurants—she'd gone out so little in recent years. And grateful as the girl seemed for all the attention being showered upon her, Violet admitted to herself that she was enjoying herself as well, for the girl was certainly pleasant and agreeable company. Violet liked to think that Mary Ann would slowly blossom, over time, under her aunt's tutelage and care, into the lovely, self-sufficient young woman Violet felt the girl had it in herself to become. As for the husband, that terrible man who would be locked away for years, Violet was confident that Mary Ann would simply forget him, over·time. That would certainly be best, Violet thought comfortably, for everyone involved.

Yet the girl, for no good reason, would often look so downcast, so depressed. One night they were having dinner at an Italian restaurant and Mary Ann, who had been picking at her food, had finally dropped her fork and covered her face with both hands.

"Oh, Aunt Violet," she moaned, "I miss him so much!"

Violet glanced around, embarrassed, and then she reached out and touched her niece hesitantly on the arm.

"There, there," she murmured, not knowing what else to say. The conventional wisdom, perhaps, was that the girl should be encouraged to vent her emotions, but Violet found emotional displays distasteful and besides that she felt the less Mary Ann thought about Carl, the better. Through one of her colleagues at the school where she'd worked Violet had already gotten the name and number of a divorce attorney, though she knew it wasn't yet the time to broach this sensitive subject with Mary Ann.

There was one good thing: her niece had had no contact with Carl since coming to Violet's house, and Violet would do everything in her power to keep it that way. Once or twice Mary Ann had spoken vaguely of wanting to visit him down at the jail, or at least phone him, but Violet had talked her out of this, arguing that Mary Ann needed to focus on herself and her own well-being. Violet would stare pointedly at the fading but still-visible bruise on Mary Ann's face and the girl would hang her head, just perceptibly nodding. "I know, you're right," she would say. "It's just that I get so depressed, when I try to imagine my life without him...I just don't know what I'm going to *do*. I mean, I have no job, I'm almost out of money, and I'm just such a mess right now...." Inevitably she would glance up at Violet, who was giving her a look of stern benevolence, and say, "I'm just so grateful to you, Aunt Violet. I don't know what I'd have done without you...." And yet again Violet would say something about time healing all wounds, and how Mary Ann needn't worry about the future—she could stay here with Violet as long as she wanted. Together they had driven back to the ramshackle duplex apartment Mary Ann and Carl had been renting, and the poor girl had so few possessions they'd managed to collect everything in a single trip. Mary Ann should consider Violet's place her home now, Violet kept telling her, for wasn't there plenty of room here for the two of them, and didn't they get along quite well together? Mary Ann had no choice but to agree.

Soon enough, as Violet might have predicted, her niece began to insist that she was "taking advantage" of her aunt, and she really ought to start looking for a job. Violet, though she'd grown pleasantly accustomed to having the girl about the house during the day, could hardly dispute this, for it would be therapeutic, surely, for Mary Ann to keep her mind occupied and to begin financially to pull her own weight. It so happened that an old acquaintance of Violet's from school now worked at a public library branch only a few blocks from Violet's house, and it turned out there was a clerical opening on the staff. Mary Ann had looked dubious at first, worrying that she wasn't qualified, but the position required only basic computer skills (a previous job as an administrative assistant had provided that) and an ability to deal with the general public, so one bright June morning Violet saw her niece off to the interview. It was a warm day and at first Mary Ann had put on a sleeveless pale-blue dress in which she looked quite pretty, Violet thought, especially since she had done a lovely job with her face, applying a modest amount of lipstick and mascara (the bruise was now completely gone) and brushing her freshly washed hair out in a becoming, "natural" style, the ends of her hair almost but not quite touching her shoulders. But Violet almost gasped when she saw, on one of the girl's pale upper arms, a heart-shaped tattoo bearing inside it, in Gothic script, the name "Carl." Violet shuddered, and quickly urged Mary Ann to put on something with sleeves. The only other "dressy" outfit the girl owned was a gray wool pantsuit, the jacket looking slightly too large as though Mary Ann had lost weight since buying it, but although the outfit seemed much too warm for late spring Violet smiled resolutely and told her niece that she looked lovely indeed.

"Are you sure it's okay?" Mary Ann asked, tugging awkwardly at the neck of her white silk blouse.

"Yes, yes, and don't worry, I've been meaning to take you shopping for some new clothes."

The girl smiled sheepishly, and though Violet offered to drive her, the girl insisted on walking. As it turned out, this was a stroke of luck, for no sooner had Violet shut the front door than the telephone rang.

For some time Violet had intended to get Caller I.D. service, but she hadn't done it and now she wished she had, for when she answered she heard a sour, suspicious male voice, asking for Mary Ann.

"She's not here," Violet said quickly, and then she added, inspired, "she's not here, anymore. She's moved—she's moved out of state."

Violet's heart was beating, fast; she lied so rarely, but in this instance it was so pleasurable, too, for wasn't she doing what was best for Mary Ann?

"Ma'am," Carl said slowly, and she could hear a sly, insinuating tone to his voice, "I've got people lined up behind me to use this phone. Now, I know my wife is staying with you, and I'd appreciate your putting her on the line."

Flummoxed, Violet hardly knew what to say. "Well, I—" she stammered. "I'm sorry, Carl, but she doesn't want to hear from you."

"Ma'am, please put my wife on the phone," Carl repeated. "Me and her, we've got things to work out. We—"

Violet hung up the phone, and immediately it rang again. She lifted the receiver several inches and then hung up a second time. Now there was silence, but still Violet was worried, for what would the man do next? Send one of his cohorts over here, to confront her and Mary Ann? Violet went to the front door and locked it; she drew the shutters of the living room windows closed. Her breathing had become shallow, and she could still feel the beating of her heart though the sensation was no longer pleasurable, not at all. She went to the sofa and sat, willing herself to stay calm. The house was completely silent. How had she lived in such a silent place, for so long? she wondered. She had become so pleasantly accustomed, these past weeks, to Mary Ann with her radio or the television blaring, and to their shopping expeditions and running errands together. One evening over dinner the girl had asked, apropos of nothing, "Aunt Violet, do you ever get...you know, lonely, living here all by yourself?" And Violet had said quickly, "No, of course not, dear, because I keep myself *busy*." The girl hadn't pursued the question, perhaps hearing the rather cross note in her aunt's voice, but Violet had known Mary Ann's words would become one of those small needling memories to plague her in the coming months and years. *Do you ever get—you know, lonely?* Certainly, she did not. "I do *not*," Violet said aloud to the empty room, and she was relieved that the plaintive echo of her voice was broken by the sound of Mary Ann's key scratching at the front door.

"Guess what?" the girl trilled, slamming the door shut in her exuberance. "They gave me the job!"

Mary Ann rushed forward and hugged her aunt and Violet hugged her back, awkwardly.

"That's wonderful," Violet said, sincerely. "That's excellent news, indeed."

That evening, Violet took her niece out to an elegant Thai restaurant, to celebrate, and she couldn't help noticing that Mary Ann's behavior was a little strange. Violet had ordered a bottle of champagne, and after the waiter had poured their glasses Mary Ann lifted her flute and said, her eyes glassy as if she were already drunk, "To my new life—my happy new life!"

Mary Ann's voice was so loud and exuberant that people at the next table glanced over, so Violet reached out and touched the girl's hand, hoping to calm her down. But there was no calming her. She tossed back her champagne in two or three swift gulps and reached for the bottle, pouring herself a second glass. "You know, Aunt Violet, I feel so much better about my prospects now, I really do! Walking back from the interview, I was thinking how badly Carl has been treating me, and how he's brought this new misfortune on himself. I really think it's best that I'm free of him—I mean, with him controlling my life I was really going nowhere, you know? But now I feel—well, I feel like the sky's the limit!"

She held up her glass for a toast, and though they had already done this Violet raised her own glass once again, giving the girl a small, measured smile.

"I'm glad you're feeling better, dear," she said. "I do hope you'll enjoy the new job."

"Enjoy it? I'm going to *love* it!" Mary Ann cried. "Everyone there was so nice, and they showed me around the library, of course, and everything was so calm and peaceful, you know? And orderly. That's what I really need right now," and here she nodded vehemently, her blond hair cascading into her face and Mary Ann flicking it backward, leaning excitedly toward her aunt—"do you know what I mean? Like at your house, where everything is so peaceful and quiet, everything in its proper place. I mean, that's what I really *need* right now, and Aunt Violet, I'm so grateful, as I have you to thank for—for everything!"

The girl laughed giddily and took another long swallow from her champagne.

This buoyant mood persisted for the next several days: Violet was an early riser, but Mary Ann was always up before her, busy in the kitchen. Now it was she who insisted on cooking for her aunt, and though Mary Ann wasn't particularly skillful in the kitchen Violet thought it best to indulge the girl's extraordinarily happy mood. Yet Violet was uncomfortable, somehow. She thought guiltily that she really enjoyed Mary Ann's company more when the girl was sad and dejected, for then Violet had something to do: namely, to console her. To give her advice, one older and hopefully wiser woman to a younger, somewhat rash and heedless one. Now, watching Mary Ann bounce around the kitchen, Violet could do nothing but look on helplessly, since she could not really share in the girl's happiness. For what was it based on, exactly? Violet somehow feared for her niece, without quite knowing why.

As it happened, her fears were well founded. Each afternoon, returning from work, Mary Ann appeared a bit less energetic; she was beginning to look tired and withdrawn. Over dinner she would complain vaguely about the repetitive nature of her work, checking books out and, when they were returned, helping to re-shelve them. Her work had no meaning, really. It was something any moron could do. And she had nothing in common with her co-workers, she added. They were ordinary people with dreary, ordinary lives. The other women she worked with did have husbands and children, at least, so maybe they got satisfaction from their families; yes, the girl said, nodding, giving her aunt a bleak look, they were always talking about their families and Mary Ann had nothing to say in return. Of course she couldn't tell them she had a husband in jail, so she'd simply said that she wasn't married and they hadn't questioned her further about her private life.

"People are so self-absorbed," Mary Ann said. "They all talk about themselves and don't seem to care about me, getting to know *me*."

"Well, you'll just have to give them time," Violet said, smiling inwardly at the irony in the girl's words. "I'm sure they're very nice."

"'Nice'," Mary Ann said, in a thoughtful and slightly contemptuous tone. She gave a hollow laugh. "That was a word

Carl hated. He was a poet, you know. Words like 'nice' annoyed him to no end."

Violet was offended but decided to say nothing. The girl was staring into space, a desolate look in her eyes. She said, "I've been thinking a lot about Carl, these past couple of days. He's probably upset that I haven't called him, or gone down to visit. Carl is so proud, I know he's waiting for me to make the first move. I suppose I *could* call him, at least, and see if he needs anything."

"Oh, I don't think that's a good idea," and Violet allowed a note of asperity into her voice. "Given all that's happened, I don't think that's a good idea, at all."

Mary Ann shrugged, laid down her fork, and said she was going to her room, to rest. While Violet was cleaning up the kitchen the telephone rang, and of course it was her niece's husband.

"I've told you, she does *not* want to speak with you," Violet said, cupping the mouthpiece with one hand. She added, not telling the truth but wishing that she were, "In fact, Mary Ann has already consulted with a divorce attorney."

There was a long pause on the other end. "A 'divorce attorney,' eh," Carl said, mockingly. "Well you can tell that bitch I said to go to hell!" He spoke so loudly that Violet had to hold the receiver away from her ear.

Violet said, in a satisfied voice, "I'll be sure to give her your best wishes." And she hung up the phone.

She thought, triumphant, that they'd never hear from that awful man again.

Over the next few days, however, Mary Ann seemed to feel worse instead of better. No longer did the girl seem concerned with her appearance, despite a Saturday afternoon shopping expedition during which Violet had bought her several attractive summer outfits at Macy's. The following week, the girl put on the new clothes for work but she'd begun rising later and later, no longer bothering to apply makeup or brush her hair. Violet even wondered if the girl were bathing properly, she looked so disheveled and forlorn. Violet would rush them through breakfast but still the girl dawdled, resting her head on one hand, and she ended up being late for work several days in a row.

"What's the point," she would say. "The job is so simple-minded I can do the work in a few hours. What's the point of being there *all day.*"

Because they're paying you for *all day*, Violet didn't say. Instead she tried to cheer the girl up by suggesting they take a little weekend trip together—to Savannah, maybe? One of Violet's brothers lived there, and the city would be so lovely this time of year.

But the girl said, morosely, "I don't want to visit anybody. I don't want to go anywhere."

Violet, for her part, had never felt happier. During the day she cleaned the house, and worked at her crocheting, and she'd begun rereading the novels of Dickens: she'd decided to read them all, from start to finish! When her niece returned home from work, Violet tried to interest her in watching television, or some new DVD that had come out, but the girl always made an excuse—she was tired, or she wasn't feeling well—and she'd go into her room and shut the door. Sometimes, late at night, Violet would hear her in there, weeping. Yet Violet wasn't worried. She told herself she wasn't worried, too much. It was only natural, wasn't it, that Mary Ann should go through a grieving process over the breakup of her marriage? Though Violet herself had never married, or even had a serious relationship with a man, she had to imagine this was so. It had become Violet's role in life, she felt, to serve as the girl's mother-figure, her counselor, her friend, and this was something Violet not only knew that she could do but was happy to do. Violet's only trouble was the slight guilt she felt over her own happiness at a time when Mary Ann was so dejected, so disconsolate. Nonetheless Violet knew that her niece would get better—the young were so resilient, after all. Soon enough, Violet was sure, they *would* be taking that trip together, and in the coming months and years, as the girl healed, the two women would become ideal companions for one another. Violet felt supremely confident this was so.

But: one morning the girl was even later than usual in getting up for breakfast. Anxiously Violet kept checking the time: it was nine-fifteen, it was nine-thirty, and already Mary Ann was half an hour late for work. Violet tiptoed to the girl's room and put her ear against the door, but she heard nothing. She said, softly, "Mary

Ann, dear, are you there? Are you almost ready...?" There was no response. Violet waited for a moment, uncertain. She checked her watch: it was nine-forty. The girl had never been this late before, and what if she lost her job? Then Violet thought she heard something: a soft moan. Without hesitation she flung open the door.

At first she could hardly process what she saw, for there was Mary Ann, unclothed except for her bra and panties, limbs splayed at an awkward angle across the bed. One arm rested over the girl's eyes, and her mouth—for Violet had rushed to the bed—appeared coated with a whitish, viscous substance. Again, her niece moaned, though this time the sound was barely audible.

Violet touched her shoulder, which felt cool and clammy. "Mary Ann?" she said, alarmed. "What's wrong, dear—are you sick?"

The girl did not respond. Her eyes were closed, the eyelids a pale, ghastly color; she showed no awareness of her aunt's presence.

Violet shook her, hard. "Mary Ann, are you—did you—" She broke off. She added, more to herself than to Mary Ann, "Did you take something...?"

For she had remembered: the pills. One day while Mary Ann was at work she had wandered into the girl's bathroom, had opened the medicine cabinet and looked at the amber prescription vials that were lined up neatly in a row: Xanax, Ambien, Percodan, Vicodin, Lithium.... Violet's heart had gone out to the girl, but she'd wondered, did she really *need* all these medications? Violet was one who fervently believed in minding her own business yet still she'd resolved to talk to Mary Ann one day about her health, to try and wean her off the pills, somehow. Violet, for her part, took only one medicine daily, to lower her cholesterol, and she couldn't imagine why Mary Ann, at her young age, should need so many pills. Yet somehow Violet had never broached the topic, and now she berated herself, for what if it was too late?

Hurrying, unsteady on her feet, Violet went into the girl's bathroom and what she'd most feared, she saw: for there in the sink, in a little heap, were all the prescription vials, all of them empty. Pointlessly Violet picked them up, then dropped them again. They clattered into the sink with a flat, mocking sound.

"Oh, God," Violet murmured. "Oh, my God...."

The next few hours passed in a blur. There was the frantic phone call to 911, of course, and the terrible wait until they came, though they came within minutes; there was a brief, equally frantic call to her sister Rebecca, in which Violet blurted out "Becca, the poor girl has tried to commit suicide," and Rebecca had said she was on her way; and then there was the commotion of the EMT workers who came barging into Mary Ann's bedroom armed with medical equipment, one of them telling Violet to please wait outside the room while they worked on the girl. Violet had no choice but to comply. She had never felt more helpless in her life.

Ten or twenty minutes passed, Violet could not be sure, before a young woman wearing latex gloves and a sorrowful expression on her face, came out to tell Violet the sorrowful news that it was too late: Mary Ann had evidently ingested a huge quantity of drugs, some hours before: they had not been able to save her.

"What?" Violet said, panicked. "Do you mean, she's—she's—"

The paramedic was looking down, shaking her head. "I'm sorry, ma'am," she said. "Very sorry."

Then came the awful time after they had taken Mary Ann's body away, and Violet was left alone to ponder what had happened. Afterwards, she would never understand how she had gotten through these hours, her only clear memory being that she kept wandering into the girl's bedroom and bathroom, looking for a note, for something, some clue to what exactly had happened. But there was nothing. The girl had left no note. Nothing at all. Violet kept walking around, wringing her hands together. "Oh, dear.... Oh dear, oh dear...." By the time Rebecca finally arrived at the house, around two o'clock, Violet felt utterly depleted. She had lain down on the living room sofa and had been simply staring at the ceiling when her sister blustered into the house.

"Violet, Violet? Oh, there you are..."

Violet stared up at her sister, helplessly. Rebecca was an imposing, big-boned woman who looked perfectly comfortable in her present role. Violet managed to communicate to her what had happened, that the girl was dead, but oddly Rebecca seemed more concerned with Violet herself.

"You don't look well, Violet," she said. "You don't look well, at all."

It was only then that the tears finally came springing into Violet's eyes. "Oh, my God, what will I do now?" she moaned. "What will I do with my life, how can I live, how can I—"

"There, there," Rebecca was saying. She had sat down awkwardly on the edge of the sofa, and she was patting Violet's cheeks and forehead. Her dark-gray eyes, the color of nail heads, were glittering with energy and purpose. "Just don't worry, Violet, for I'll take care of you, I'll take care of everything."

Violet said, helplessly, "But I—"

"Don't worry, dear," Rebecca said in her eager, peremptory voice, her eyes gleaming. "I've said I'll take care of you, and that's exactly what I'll do. I mean, haven't I always?"

His Parents, Naked

They gave his parents such an ebullient welcome—"What a surprise! Come on in!"—that Bobby wondered if his mother felt ashamed of what she'd said in the car.

"They don't want to see *us*," she'd insisted. "Let's don't stop, honey."

Bobby had hoped his father would relent, since Bobby didn't want to stop at his aunt and uncle's house, either. More particularly, he didn't want to hang around with his boisterous cousins, Connor and Gary, while the adults sat out by the pool and chatted. But Bobby knew that his father, fortified by the two beers he'd downed at the restaurant after twelve-o'clock mass, had driven out along Rock Springs Road—which wasn't the way home—with a visit to his sister and brother-in-law in mind. They'd dropped in on Bobby's aunt and uncle before, and though Bobby's father enjoyed these Sunday afternoon visits, Bobby's mother had always claimed to feel "out of place" in the Matsons' cavernous living room, or out by the sparkling kidney-shaped pool.

"Haven't you noticed," Bobby's mother had hissed, knowing she'd lost when her husband turned onto the Matsons' street, "how they never drop in on us?"

Bobby's father had winked at his son in the rearview mirror. "Well, it's obvious we should visit them, not vice versa. They're the ones with the pool."

He gave his jovial bark of a laugh; he was a man who often laughed after he spoke, whether his words were funny or not. Even from the backseat, Bobby could smell the beery fumes of his father's breath.

It had taken a while for his aunt and uncle to answer the door, and of course they were wearing swimsuits.

"Bill and Myrna! Bobby! I *told* Jack I heard the doorbell," his aunt Rhonda said. "Lucky thing, we'd just come into the kitchen to fix a batch of daiquiris. You're just in time!"

Rhonda was a buxom woman in her late thirties whose breasts and hips overflowed her bathing suit. Her mid-length blond hair with its dark inch-long roots was wet and stringy from the pool. After greeting Bobby's parents and hugging his father—"Hey, big brother," she said in her husky, playful voice—she bent to embrace Bobby, the bare and fragrant tops of her breasts pressing against him. "Hey, sweetie," Rhonda said. Bobby could only respond "Hey" in a quiet, choking voice. His senses were reeling.

Jack Matson was a fleshy, solid man with a sizable paunch hanging above his baggy bright-yellow swim trunks. He was a couple of decades older than his wife but, as even Bobby's mother once admitted, he was still a handsome man. He had a sharp, imposing profile and a full head of silver-gray hair. Smiling broadly, he shook his brother-in-law's hand, nodded to Bobby's mother, then put both hands on Bobby's shoulders and squeezed.

He repeated how glad he was to see them.

Silently Bobby and his parents followed Rhonda and Jack out to the kitchen, where Jack crossed to the blender and the two icy-looking drinks he'd been pouring. Rhonda told him to get down two extra glasses.

"Oh, none for me, thanks," Bobby's mother said. She'd stayed in the doorway, looking abashed and uneasy, whereas Bobby and his father had come into the kitchen and leaned back casually against the counter. His father made a playful grimace, tilting his head back toward his wife.

"She's a stick in the mud," he said. "Never a drop before five o'clock."

Rhonda nodded as though she agreed in spirit with Myrna. "I know, and it's not even two o'clock. We really ought to be ashamed, but these are so good"—her husband was handing her one of the foaming glasses—"on hot days like this."

"Can't argue with that!" Bobby's father said, accepting the glass from his sister.

Rhonda said, again bending down, "What'll you have, Bobby? A Coke, or some iced tea?"

"A Coke's fine," Bobby said. He wondered where Connor and Gary were. Maybe they weren't even home?

"You can just give him the can," Bobby's mother said quickly. "Don't bother with a glass and ice, we really can't stay very—"

"Is this a new refrigerator?" Bobby's father asked, running his free hand along the silver-toned door. "One of those—now what do you call it?"

"Sub-zero," Jack said. "Yeah, just got it last month. We've been grilling out so much, we sort of outgrew the other one."

"It's huge," Rhonda said, "but would you believe we've already filled all the extra space? We're right back where we started."

"It's—it's a lovely refrigerator," Bobby's mother murmured.

"Thanks," Rhonda said, handing Bobby his Coke. "Hey, Bobby, your two big bad cousins are in the pool, want to join them? There's a pile of extra swimsuits in the cabana."

Jack nodded, smiling as he took a sip of his daiquiri. "We should have suits to fit all of you, for that matter. Come on out and join us."

Bobby's mother began, "Oh, we can't—"

"Sure thing!" Bobby's father said. He'd already downed his daiquiri; Jack took back the empty glass and reached to pour another. "It's too hot to sit outside in our church clothes, that's for sure." Already he was pulling at his tie.

"Honey, I don't think we should," Bobby's mother said. "We shouldn't impose."

"Don't be silly," Rhonda said. "You sure I can't pour you a drink, Myrna? No? Well come on outside, then. We'll find suits for all of you. That's no problem at all."

"We really shouldn't stay," Bobby's mother repeated, a hint of reproach in her voice.

"Of course we can stay!" Bobby's father said. He was already following Jack and Rhonda out to the brick-floored den where glass doors opened onto the patio and pool.

It wasn't that Bobby disliked swimming; it wasn't even that he disliked his cousins, exactly. At thirteen, Connor was two years older than Bobby, while Gary was two years younger. Both were lean, athletic boys, their limbs tanned from many months—this was late in July—of swimming in the pool. Connor already had a teenager's aggressive physicality and Gary had a nine-year-old's crazed feistiness, a willingness to try anything his older brother proposed. It didn't surprise Bobby that the moment his uncle opened the glass door, they could hear Connor yelling "Geronimo!" as he flung himself into a deliberate belly flop that sent water splashing far outside the pool. "*Ow*, that was a wicked one!" Gary shouted in admiration. He was eagerly climbing the diving-board ladder with the idea, Bobby knew, of replicating his brother's comical feat. Flinging his skinny kid's body off the edge of the board, he even yelled "Geronimo!" in flawless mimicry of the tone his brother had used.

Rhonda was rearranging the patio chairs to accommodate her guests. She glanced toward the pool and cupped her mouth. "Hey, boys—not so *loud*," she pleaded.

Jack was sipping his daiquiri and smiling, Bobby saw, as though proud of having fathered such rambunctious boys.

It wasn't that Bobby disliked anything about his cousins or his aunt and uncle, exactly, but rather that he disliked the way he felt when he was around them. Unlike Connor and Gary with their sleek, darkly tanned bodies, Bobby had a redhead's milky complexion. Though he had inherited his skin tone and its propensity to sunburn from his mother, she liked to complain that Bobby was something of a "bookworm" so that even now, this late in the year, he was no less pale than he'd been last winter, and had none of the lean, supple musculature his cousins enjoyed as a natural birthright. But what most troubled Bobby was something else he'd gotten from his mother: the awkward timidity and general discomfiture he felt whenever they visited the Matsons. Accustomed to thinking himself superior to his cousins, since he knew they weren't very bright, he nonetheless felt intimidated and inadequate in their physical presence. So he'd dreaded the inevitable moment when his aunt gestured to the cabana—a redwood structure, enmeshed in wisteria, that dominated one side of the Matsons' back property—and said, "Don't you want to get a suit on, Bobby? You can hop into the pool with Connor and Gary."

What he really wanted was to stay here on the patio but he smiled vaguely and headed toward the cabana, eavesdropping out of habit on the adults' conversation.

"This is lovely outdoor furniture," his mother was saying. She had switched from her hesitant, reproachful voice to the polite voice she used once she'd decided to be agreeable. Bobby knew this was a bad sign, as it meant they might be in for a long visit.

"Thanks for noticing," Rhonda said. "We ordered it from Ethan Allen and it finally came in last month."

"Ethan Allen!" Bobby's mother said, admiringly.

"Their stuff's damn expensive," Bobby's father said. Without turning around, Bobby could see the approving look his father would be giving Jack, the kind of automatic obeisance one man gives to another, much richer man.

"We figure it's worth it," Jack said.

"Oh, I'm sure it is—it's beautiful!" Bobby's mother said.

Bobby was relieved to shut the cabana door and get rid of the adults' sing-songy voices. Inside, however, the close, dank smell of the cabana depressed him further. The single room, with a small bathroom off in one corner, had a warped floor covered in dirty greenish linoleum; Bobby's aunt and uncle had a full-time housekeeper but, the boy thought disapprovingly, it was obvious the woman never came in here. The cabana had one window with open Venetian blinds above an old rusted air-conditioning unit that looked as though it wouldn't work. Overhead a lone fly buzzed around the room like a demented thought. The air in here was not only smelly but overpoweringly hot. People dashed in to change clothes or use the bathroom and then hurried back out. Bobby went to an old chest of drawers placed next to the window and in the weak light he rummaged through an old assortment of swimsuits, looking for a faded-red pair of trunks he'd worn the last time he and his parents had visited, on Memorial Day weekend. He found the trunks, shot a glance at the doorknob to make sure he'd locked it—it would be just like his cousins to come barging in, whooping—and quickly took off his clothes and wiggled into the suit. He came outside with a sense of relief: out here the air was hot but fresh and sweet-smelling after the hellish stale heat inside the cabana.

At first, when he shyly stepped onto the skirt of concrete surrounding the pool, his heart leaped with pleasure, for his parents were standing as if about to leave. But, as it turned out, Rhonda and Jack had talked them into donning swimsuits and they were only on their way to the cabana. "Look, here's Bobby!" his aunt Rhonda said, gesturing vaguely toward Connor and Jack who were both floating on air mattresses in the deep end of the pool. Rhonda was applying suntan lotion to her shoulders in a dreamy, circular motion. "Why don't you boys play some kind of game or other?"

Connor glanced over at Bobby, lazily. "Want to play Marco Polo?" he said.

"C'mon, we already played that," Gary complained.

Bobby said quickly, "That's okay," and crossed to the shallow end and sat in one corner, above the stair-steps down into the pool, with his feet in the water. "I'll just sit here for a while."

"Connor and Gary have been in that pool all day long," Rhonda told Bobby. "They're getting dark as Indians. Here, honey, do you want some of this cream? Your chest is so white—I'm afraid you'll get burned."

"No, that's okay," Bobby said. "I don't think we're staying all that long."

"Sure you are!" Jack boomed, from the pool. He sat looking kingly in a webbed chair that floated close to his sons. "We've got the whole afternoon in front of us."

Fortunately for Bobby, this didn't turn out to be true.

He stayed in his corner of the pool, idly kicking his feet as he waited for his parents to return from the cabana. When they did, he felt a bit crestfallen—and yes, ashamed—by the way they looked. His pale-skinned father was slim at the waist, and his suit, obviously one of Jack's cast-offs, looked as if it might slip down to his ankles at any moment. Bobby's mother looked worse. Likewise slender, with small breasts and hips, she didn't come close to filling out the purple-and-white striped one-piece that Bobby remembered his aunt having worn for the Memorial Day cook-out. Still the ever-cheerful Rhonda called out, shading her eyes, "You two look great!"

As though wanting to deflect attention, Bobby's mother said, "That's a lovely suit you have on, Rhonda," as she and Bobby's father settled back into their chairs.

"Oh, this?" Rhonda said, glancing down. She was wearing a reddish-orange bikini, the same shade as her lipstick and her nails. "Thanks, it's a Donna Karan." She made a little face that Bobby couldn't interpret. "We went over to Lenox Square last weekend and I got it at Needless Mark-up. On sale!"

"Oh, I love Neiman-Marcus," his mother said, which Bobby supposed was a white lie. His parents could never afford to shop there.

"So Jack," Bobby's father said, "how does it feel to be *senior* vice president? How are they treating you?"

The Memorial Day cookout Bobby and his parents attended had been to celebrate his uncle's big promotion down at the insurance company where he'd worked for thirty-odd years. He'd started as a file clerk and had worked his way up. At home, Bobby's father had told his son more than once that Jack was a "self-made" man, as though this were the highest goal anybody could attain. Bobby knew, since his father had mentioned it often, that Jack and Rhonda had invested in real estate through the years and had done very well with that, too. Bobby's father told him that Rhonda had married Jack when he was a "nobody," but she'd stuck by him and here his little sister was, a millionaire, though she'd never had to work a day in her life. Bobby's mother had objected to this (she didn't have a job, either) and said that Rhonda was raising two active boys, besides handling all the books for the real estate investments, but Bobby's father had just laughed and said, "You women."

Bobby's parents were not self-made, and that had caused Bobby, more than once, to wonder how his father did think of himself, exactly. He worked a regular nine-to-five job at a paper-products company, as an industrial engineer, and though Bobby's family never wanted for anything, they lived in an ordinary ranch house out in Decatur that was nothing comparable to this sprawling two-story Jack and Rhonda had built here in Morningside, one of Atlanta's most prestigious neighborhoods. The lot itself, Bobby's father said, must have cost more than Bobby's family's entire house. Bobby noticed that his father spoke in a wistful, slightly aggrieved tone whenever he talked about his sister and her husband. Usually this was in the evenings, when Bobby's father would be drinking beer while his wife prepared dinner, all three of them in the kitchen where they tended to gather when everyone was home. Occasionally Bobby's mother would add some mild admonition, like "Money doesn't always buy happiness, you know," to which her husband would respond, annoyed, "No? Well, I sure wouldn't mind giving it a try."

Jack Matson just gave a shrug in answer to his brother-in-law's question. "Hey, it's a job," he said. He grinned, looking vaguely sinister, Bobby thought, in his mirrored sunglasses.

"The Strykers are just wonderful people," Rhonda said, gushingly. "They've become such good friends, you'd never think Phil Stryker is actually Jack's *boss.*"

"That's a good situation, it really is," Bobby's father said, leaning forward in his chair. Bobby noticed that he'd drained his daiquiri glass.

"They seemed very nice, when we met them," Bobby's mother murmured.

They had met the Strykers at the Memorial Day get-together. Bobby hadn't thought they seemed very nice, at all, and Bobby wondered if this was another white lie from his mother or if she really felt that way. The Strykers were a tall, imposing couple—the wife almost as tall as the husband, well over six feet—with prominent teeth and frosted-blond hair, though they must have been in their sixties. Bobby knew that Phil Stryker had taken his uncle "under his wing," as Bobby's father had told him, quite a few years ago, and that the man was worth "a cool thirty million." Jack had told Bobby's father this, and Bobby's father had no reason to disbelieve it. Phil Stryker was not only president and CEO of the Atlanta-based insurance company where Jack worked, but he had land development and real estate projects going all over northern Georgia. It was Phil who had gotten Bobby's uncle into real estate in the first place.

"Yeah, Phil Stryker is like a brother to me," Jack said. He took a handful of water and threw it at Connor, who merely looked up from his air mattress, frowning, and said nothing.

"Bobby, don't you want to float in the inner tube or something?" Rhonda said, gesturing toward the round white object lying on the cement.

Bobby kicked at the water a little harder, as if to show he was busy. "Oh, no ma'am, I'm fine," he said.

Rhonda looked over toward Bobby's parents, and cried out as if wounded, "Why Bill, you need another daiquiri!" Then she was out of her chair and headed toward the empty glass. "What about you, Myrna, can't I get you something?"

"Thanks, but no. I'd better not." She turned toward Bobby's father. "Are you sure you should have another one, honey? You're driving, remember."

Bobby's father grinned. He sat back comfortably in his chair. "One for the road won't hurt."

Rhonda crossed to where Bobby sat, her sandals clacking on the cement, and bent toward him. Her breasts hung swaying and pendulous in Bobby's face, and he had nowhere to look but directly at them. His aunt gave off a fragrant, fruity scent, like honeysuckle. She said, "How about you, buckaroo? Another Coke?"

Bobby shrugged and smiled. "No thanks," he said, picking up his can. "I've still got some."

Rhonda drifted off toward the house, and the conversation lagged a little. Connor and Gary were evidently worn out from their long hours in the pool, and simply floated around on their air mattresses, occasionally pushing away from their father's chair. Bobby's mother sat with her ankles demurely crossed, pulling at the straps of her swimsuit, while her husband bent forward eagerly, twirling his empty glass in his hands.

He glanced upwards and said, to no one in particular, "Sure is a beautiful day." Reflexively Bobby glanced up, too, his eyes singed by the blaring sun surrounded by a cloudless whitish-blue sky.

For some reason, Jack laughed. "Sure is, Bill. It surely is."

Then they were quiet for a while. Bobby noticed his mother fidgeting in her chair, and despite the new drink Rhonda would be bringing his father, Bobby hoped his mother might be about to suggest that they should leave. Somehow, the silence around the pool felt ominous to Bobby. But then they heard the glass door sliding open and there was Rhonda, leaning out.

"Hon, guess who just got here!" she called. "The Strykers!"

As though jolted by electricity Bobby's uncle began kicking his legs to the side of the pool, then he pulled himself up onto the concrete. He said, "C'mon, boys. Come say hello to Mr. and Mrs. Stryker."

Somehow Bobby knew that the "boys" did not include him.

Gary and Connor got out of the pool and followed their father back toward the house. Jack called over his shoulder, "Be right back," and they were gone.

So Bobby and his parents were left alone out by the pool. Bobby felt anxious, fearing that the Strykers would be coming out to the pool, too, and a whole new phase of the afternoon would begin, with endless small talk among the adults while Bobby sat there awkwardly not knowing what to do or say.

But this didn't happen. When he thought back on it later, he reasoned that it might be better if this *had* happened, after all, but it did not.

Instead Bobby and his parents continued sitting out by the pool, alone. The minutes that passed seemed very long ones to Bobby. He could feel the tip of his nose and the tops of his shoulders burning in the sun. He could imagine his aunt Rhonda in the kitchen, busily preparing a fresh batch of daiquiris for her important new guests, while Jack chatted with them in his loud, gregarious way. Bobby was thankful, at least, that he and his parents hadn't been invited inside to join them.

It was then that Bobby's father said, holding up his glass, "Sure could use that daiquiri." But he sounded doubtful.

Bobby's mother said quickly, "You don't need one."

And his father said, "If I'd known Rhonda and Jack were expecting company…"

"They weren't expecting anybody," his mother snapped. "The Strykers just happened to stop by, like we did. Uninvited."

Bobby wished his parents would be quiet. Beneath their words he knew that other things were being communicated that his parents didn't want to say, or maybe didn't want to think. Bobby felt an ache of pity for them, and even for himself. The three of them were the shabby, unwanted relatives out by the pool, and Jack and Rhonda had simply forgotten about them—or worse, they hadn't forgotten.

Another tense few minutes passed before Bobby's father muttered, "I suppose we could go inside."

"We certainly will *not*," his mother said, vehemently. She stood and called over to Bobby, "C'mon, honey, we're leaving."

To Bobby's surprise, his father didn't object. He stood, too, putting his daiquiri glass upside down on the glass-topped table beside his chair.

The three of them headed toward the cabana to change back into their clothes, not even glancing toward the house or the glass sliding door. Bobby entered the cabana first, assuming his parents would wait outside while he changed, but now that they'd decided on a course of action, they were hurrying and all modesty was brushed aside. Before Bobby had time to react, much less object, his parents were out of their swimsuits. They stood with their backs to Bobby in the furthest, dimmest corner of the cabana, both of them completely naked and fumbling with their clothes. He couldn't remember the last time he'd seen his parents naked—he must have been four or five. The moment passed quickly enough but it would stick in Bobby's head for a long time. His parents, naked. Humiliated. In a few quick seconds Bobby wriggled out of his swimsuit and got his clothes on, and within seconds after that Bobby's parents were finished dressing, too. They all tossed their discarded swimsuits back into the drawer and then Bobby's mother touched his shoulder, saying in a hurt, angry voice, "Come on, honey, we're getting out of here."

His father said, "Listen here, Myrna, don't be upset," but his mother said firmly, "I told you we shouldn't come over here." Bobby said nothing, but he felt guilty for feeling so glad that they were leaving.

When they left the cabana, only Bobby and his father glanced toward the sliding glass doors, where there was still no sign of Jack or Rhonda. Fortunately, there was a side gate in the redwood fence, so that they could leave quietly that way and get down to the street and their car without having to encounter anyone. Bobby's father muttered something about "popping inside to say goodbye" but there was no conviction in his voice, and like Bobby he simply followed Bobby's mother out to the car. It would be a long time, surely, before Bobby would see his aunt and uncle and cousins again, which was perfectly all right with him. Bobby's mother insisted on driving the car—"You're drunk," she snapped at her husband—and Bobby sat in the backseat, as usual. His father said nothing, abashed in the passenger seat, and all three of them were silent during the long drive home.

All this happened a long time ago—in the late 1980s. Bobby grew up and went away to college and eventually took a job in another city, far from Atlanta. Still he often thought back, unwillingly, to that July afternoon of his parents' humiliation, and to the beginning of a new sensation for him—first as an adolescent, then as a young adult. It would happen at odd, unexpected times. He would be in a meeting with his boss, or sitting at dinner with some young woman or other, or simply driving alone in his car, listening to music, when out of nowhere that long-ago afternoon would come back to him and all at once a sense of humiliation would sweep over him, too, and no matter how well he was dressed, or how sane and accountable he might appear, still he would feel himself exposed and vulnerable, and utterly naked inside his clothes.